PRAISE FOR

THE LOST RECIPE FOR HAPPINESS

"A delectable banquet for the reader, celebrating the things that matter most—family, friendship, food, and the healing power of love." —Susan Wiggs, *New York Times* bestselling author

"As dark and deep and sweet as chocolate . . . I wanted to live in this book."

—Sarah Addison Allen, *New York Times* bestselling author

"Beautiful writing, good storytelling and an endearing heroine set against the backdrop of Aspen, Colorado, are highlights of O'Neal's novel. A tale that intertwines food, friendship, passion, and love in such a delectable mix is one to truly savor until the very last page." —*Romantic Times*

The Secret
of Everything

ALSO BY BARBARA O'NEAL

The Lost Recipe for Happiness

The Secret of Everything

A Novel

BARBARA O'NEAL

Bantam Books Trade Paperbacks
New York

A Bantam Books Trade Paperback Original

Copyright © 2009 by Barbara Samuel

Published in the United States by Bantam Books, an imprint of The Random House Publishing Group, a division of Random House, Inc., New York.

BANTAM BOOKS is a registered trademark of Random House, Inc., and the colophon is a trademark of Random House, Inc.

Library of Congress Cataloging-in-Publicaton Data

O'Neal, Barbara
The secret to everything : a novel / Barbara O'Neal.
p.   cm.
ISBN 978-0-553-38552-6
eBook ISBN 978-0-553-90739-1
1. Tour guides (Persons)—Fiction.   2. Family secrets—Fiction.
3. Families—Fiction.   4. Homecoming—Fiction.
5. New Mexico—Fiction.   I. Title
PS3573.I485S43 2010
813'.54—dc22
2009036613

Printed in the United States of America

www.bantamdell.com

2   4   6   8   9   7   5   3

FOR JIM HAIR.

*Because if all the fathers in the world were like mine,
there would be a lot fewer broken women in the world.
Thanks, Dad.*

ACKNOWLEDGMENTS

It would be impossible to get books out into the world without a solid network of help and support. My circle is rich, and they deserve the small moments of attention here.

I could never do this without Neal Barlow, my beloved Christopher Robin, who is cheerful and unflappable and laughingly reminds me of all the things I say at the end of every rough draft. I'm also grateful for that fortuitous and terrible spider bite you picked up whilst orienteering. Your pain and suffering were not for naught.

Thanks also go to Christie Ridgway, my lifeline on the end of the phone, for her infamous and incredible box plotting plan, which helped keep me on track with this complicated storyline; and to Teresa Hill for reading messy, messy drafts without freaking out.

I could never get anywhere without the brilliant team at the Jane Rotrosen Agency, primarily my agent Meg Ruley, and Christina Hogrebe; and with deepest thanks to my editor Shauna Summers, for helping me find my best work, over and over again, and challenging me to be better than I think I can be.

Special thanks to my aunt, Lisa Putman, a brilliant cook,

who helped poke holes in the recipes and helped me find the best ingredients and ideas. (All mistakes are my own.) You were a great help, Auntie, thanks so much! Baked French Toast is her own Christmas morning recipe.

Also, thanks to my mother, who reads cookbooks for fun, and turned me into a foodie a long time ago; to my sisters who sang the song in this book in rounds with me; and my brother who has more CDs than anyone I have ever met.

And last on the page, but not in my heart, thanks to my readers. The circle is not complete without you, so thank you from the bottom of my heart. I *love* hearing from you and hearing your stories and getting your recipes. Find me online at www.barbaraoneal.com or send me an email at barbara@barbaraoneal.com.

The Secret
of Everything

ONE

On a foggy August morning, Tessa Harlow had finally tired of her long wallow on the Santa Cruz beaches. Leaving her father's tidy little bungalow as she did every morning, she carried her breakfast down to the surf: a mango fresh from the local grocer, a hunk of sourdough bread, and a hefty cup of tea she bought from the stand on the corner.

Settling on the sand, she skimmed the thick outer skin from the mango and bit into the buttery flesh, mopping the juice from her chin with a bandana. The tea was hot and milky, sweet with real sugar, and the bread—while not quite as tangy as San Francisco sourdough—complemented the mango perfectly.

A woman walked purposefully along the water's edge, her calves showing ropy muscle. Gulls wheeled overhead. For the first time in months, Tessa wished for her camera. She would shoot the isolated piles of homeless men sleeping on the buffalo grass, and the boats bobbing in the distance, and maybe even the stack of mango skins on the sand.

It was time to get back to her life. She walked to the edge of the waves, dipped her right hand in the water, and washed her face and the fingers sticking out of the turquoise cast on her left arm. Letting her skin dry in the air, she sat back down with her cell phone and a sheaf of papers she'd printed out yesterday at the Internet café near her father's house. Luddite that he was, he didn't have a computer of his own, and Tessa had lost hers in a river three months ago.

Three months. The weeks had gone by in a wash of aqua and pale gray, deep-blue afternoons that she spent reading whatever she found at the laundromat or the local youth hostel—battered thrillers, dog-eared romances, ancient sagas. Whatever.

Three months. For want of a nail, the kingdom was lost. In Tessa's case, the nail was a spider that had crawled into her bed in the Rocky Mountains and bitten the sole of her left foot. Not such a big thing, ordinarily. It wouldn't have been this time, if she had paid attention to it right away.

Or if the rain had not been quite so persistent, so unexpected.

Or if the deluge had not softened the earth so completely that a tree fell sideways, taking the trail and her entire tour group down the mountain.

Or if the river had not been quite so high.

Or if . . .

Oh, so many details. For want of a nail, the kingdom was lost, and Tessa washed up on the beach here in her father's land.

Lately it had begun to creep into her mind that she couldn't exactly *live* this way. Her wounds, if not healed, were at least pretty well scabbed over. Mostly she could sleep again. Mostly she'd stopped having panic attacks and flashbacks. She had not purchased a new camera, but she would. Much as Sam, her surfer father, would love to have Tessa join him in his aimless drift, sooner or later she needed to explore the memories that had surfaced when she nearly drowned in Montana. Yesterday she'd spent a couple of hours online exploring the town she wanted to visit and had assembled a pitch for her boss.

Flipping open her cell phone, she dialed his number. "Hey, Mick," she said when he answered. "It's Tessa. How are you?"

"Well, hello to you, gorgeous," her boss said. "It's so good to hear from you. How are *you*?"

"Definitely getting there." She traced a long mark on her foot. "They gave me a new cast last week, this one only up to the elbow, and my foot should be a hundred percent before too much longer."

"I'm glad. How long do you wear this cast?"

"Only another four weeks or so."

"That's terrific. Is it tacky to ask when you might be coming back to work?"

"I'm not up to a tour yet." Maybe she wouldn't be again. "But we have been talking about the economy and the fact that overseas travel has been so expensive that we need to set up some food and hiking tours in the U.S., right?"

"True, true. You have something in mind?"

"I do." Tessa shook hair out of her eyes. Too long. She hadn't cut it in nearly a year, and the humid salt air made it curl. "Have you ever heard of Los Ladrones?"

"New Mexico?" She heard his skepticism. "Pretty rustic for a foodie tour, isn't it?"

"Some of it. But Los Ladrones is a very chichi spot these days, lots of Hollywood types drifting north from Santa Fe and Taos." She leafed through the pages in her lap. "A lot of really good restaurants—like, more than a *dozen* high-end places—

and a big organic farm with a vegetarian cooking school, kind of new, small, but getting some attention."

"Huh. Sounds intriguing. What else?"

"On the weekends there's a big market in the plaza, with local artisans and all that, and there's a café that's been written up a couple of times, in *Food and Wine* and—" She scowled, flipping through her notes. "Can't find the other one. Anyway, it's on the plaza, called The 100 Breakfasts Café."

Mick was silent, and she gave him space to digest. In her imagination, she could see him sitting at his desk in Santa Monica, drawing cartoon faces down the margins of a yellow legal tablet. "All good stuff, Tessa. What else can we do with it? Hiking? Rafting? There's gotta be some outdoorsy stuff in the mountains of New Mexico."

"Yeah, yeah, absolutely. There are hot springs, and a pilgrimage trek that goes to a famous shrine on the mountain, and a river, and a big lake up in the trees. It's also one of the oldest towns in the area, which means really old, like 1630 or something. A lot of history." She shrugged. "I can send you all the notes in email. You can give it some thought."

"Tell you what—send me the notes, but I'm onboard if you want to do the research. It's worth a week. Look around, see if you think it might actually work for our demographic."

She nodded, drawing a big heart in the sand beside her. "Excellent. I'll get out of here tomorrow if you want."

He chuckled. "Little stir-crazy, sweetheart?"

"Mmmm. Could be. I mean, how long can a person just lie around on the sand?"

"I'm glad. If this is viable, maybe we can get it on the schedule for next year. We have the new catalogs going out in late November."

As clearly as she could remember, today was August 25 or 26. "I'll email you the reservations and flight info this afternoon."

"Good. Welcome back, babe."

"Thanks." She hung up and sat with the phone in her palm, feeling both anxious and relieved. It was time. Time to get moving again. Time to open the Pandora's box of memories that had been haunting her since the Montana debacle.

Now to break the news to her dad. She gathered her flip-flops, her book, and her straw hat. Dressed in an embroidered Mexican peasant blouse and a pair of baggy capris that were so faded they no longer had a discernible pattern, she headed for the boardwalk.

Her father, surrounded by his three rescue dogs, was repainting the menu at his margarita shack in a careful, elegant hand. He'd studied calligraphy at some point and took pride in his lettering. She loved getting cards in the mail from him. "Hey, kiddo," he said. His voice was as gravelly as a gizzard. "You're back awfully early."

When Tessa was a child, Sam had been everybody's favorite dad. She felt sorry for other kids, who had to go home to somebody normal or—this being coastal California, after all—a pothead who couldn't keep his sentences straight. Sam was neither. He'd made his living as a magician, so he could do a billion tricks, and his vagabond life meant he had a store of adventure stories he told at random, and he could make a grilled cheese sandwich *exactly* right, with the bread turned just barely crispy, light golden brown. In his pockets, he carried Tootsie Roll Pops, which he gave away when you skinned your knee or got in a fight or fell for some whopper of a fish story he told.

This little margarita shack had been his dream for a long, long time. Tessa had helped him buy it seven years ago out of money she'd saved over a ten-year period. "Like Elvis," he said with his sideways grin. "Buying a house for his mama."

Sam surfed most mornings, talked all afternoon and evening with whoever stopped by Margaritaville. He wasn't much of a drinker himself, a help if you owned a bar.

This morning he wore long shorts and bare feet and a loose, ancient Hawaiian shirt. His skin was tanned even darker than Tessa's. He'd recently shorn his steel-gray hair into a crew cut, making him look younger than his sixty-two years, and it was a rare woman who could remain immune to the twinkle in his eye.

"I have something to tell you." She sat down on one of the stools in front of the bar. "I got a phone call. A job offer."

"You ready for that?"

"I won't be leading anything. Just doing some preliminary research for some possible food tours in New Mexico."

"New Mexico?" He dipped his brush into shamrock-green paint. "Whereabouts?"

"Los Ladrones."

He put the brush down, but not before she saw a faint tremor pass through his strong brown hands. "That's a bad place."

Tessa raised her eyebrows. He believed that your animals reincarnated, that the Great Spirit sent messages via feathers, and that there was magic in drums.

She believed in none of those things. "C'mon, Dad."

"I'm serious," he said in his drawl. "There are bad spirits there."

"Dad. Bad spirits?"

His lips twitched beneath a thick, glossy mustache that he

wore without the faintest self-consciousness. "That's where you fell in the river when you were little."

"I know where it is—that's the reason I'm going." She drew an *X* across her chest. "Promise I won't fall in the river again."

"Go ahead, make fun of me. But I don't have to like it. You damned near got yourself killed in the Rockies, so I'm allowed to worry."

"I'm sorry," Tessa said. "You're right. You don't have to like it, but I am going. My boss is pretty excited about it, honestly."

"Can't imagine why. There's nothing there."

"*Wasn't* much there," she corrected, tugging a thin blue bar straw out of the glass on the bar. "Evidently it's a fashionable resort town these days." Chewing on the end of the straw, she added, "Maybe all the rich people drove out the bad air."

"There you go, laughing at your old dad again."

"Gotcha." She pointed at him with the straw. "Did we live in town?"

"Nah. That was the commune days." He shook his head. "Bunch of crazies."

"Huh. Imagine that! Commune, crazies."

"Not the commune. The town, the place. There are old things afoot there."

"C'mon, Dad, admit it. You just want me to stay here."

"Maybe. Is that so bad?"

"No. It's sweet, and I do appreciate how much you've done for me, letting me crash at your house for so long." She reached out and touched his arm. "But I really am feeling better, and you know as well as I do that I've got to get back to work, back into my life. You can't run away from yourself."

He nodded. But he put his focus on painting a perfectly elegant *G*, and she had the feeling he was a lot more upset than he let on. "You're right. You've gotta do what you've gotta do."

. . .

It was Sam's habit to head out in the early morning to surf before the world arrived. This morning, he dutifully carried his board down to the deserted beach, but once he got there, he had to admit there wasn't much point. The ocean was gray and dark, restless in a petulant way that might prove dangerous. The thought pricked him like a red ant. His younger self would have scoffed at these conditions—what the hell was wrong with him these days?

Old, that was the trouble. He was getting old.

For long moments he stood there, dressed in a wet suit, his board by his feet, his narrowed eyes trained on the water. Thick fog obscured most everything, leaving him in a pocket of silence broken only by the sibilance of the waves ruffling against the beach. Not far out was a boat, rocking hard, back and forth, back and forth, at anchor. He wouldn't want to be asleep on that baby, that much was sure.

Damn.

He sat down, waiting for the dogs to tucker themselves out. No reason they couldn't have their romp. Wolfenstein, a giant yellow Lab, and Loki, a black springer mix, raced down the waterline, their paws making a braid in the wet sand. Loki found a stick and raced gleefully back toward Sam with it. Peaches, a raggedy old poodle mix who was defying records at age twenty-three, was asleep back at the house, snuggled on Tessa's legs. Peaches would miss Tessa as much as Sam would.

She was headed out this morning to Los Ladrones. Just the name made him feel sick to his stomach, a combination of memory and dread, worry and knowledge and superstition.

Before Tessa took off, he had to make some decisions. There were a couple of pieces of her childhood he'd kept from her, things it would only have hurt her to know, things he'd pretty much made up his mind long ago that she would *never* know. The life they'd lived might have been a little eccentric, but it was better than she would have had back there in that pissant little town.

Which really was riddled with all kinds of bad spirits. Maybe it was old missionaries slaughtered by the Indians, or maybe it was the Indians slaughtered by the conquistadores, or the seven women who had been carried off in 1826 by the Comanches— or maybe by a campful of miners. No one really knew. Lot of blood spilled in that little valley. Lot of people murdered for land, for money, for women. Sometimes, in the dark of a new moon, the screams of those ghosts echoed down the river with a terrible noise. Some people said it was a trick of the rocks lining the canyon; some said it was La Llorona, the weeping woman of the rivers.

Drawing his knees up to his chest, he took in a deep breath. For all that Tessa insisted she was fine, she hadn't fully recovered from her ordeal. She was a lot better, and God knew she looked a hell of a lot further along than when he'd finally got her home, rail-thin and hollow-eyed.

Still. She was the very center of his life, the one thing he'd done right over a life mostly wasted, and he didn't want her pushing too hard, too fast. He'd done some time in Vietnam. He knew how deep things could go. You couldn't unsee a thing once it was seen, unknow it once it was known.

Given how much she had yet to make peace with, Sam decided on the gamble of keeping what he knew about her childhood to himself for now. She might get to Los Ladrones, poke around a little, get tired of it, and come back to California without discovering a single thing.

He would protect her as best he could, as he had always done. When—if—that seemed like it oughta change, he could always tell the truth later.

For now, he'd let it be.

TWO

The flight from San Francisco to Albuquerque was only a couple of hours, and Tessa arrived at midday. The air was clear and dry, the forecast predicting much of the same for the rest of the week, with a peppering of afternoon thunderstorms.

She rented a decent-size passenger car and drove up through the heavy traffic on I-25 toward Santa Fe and, eventually, through the mountains toward Los Ladrones.

It took a little getting used to, driving with a cast, but it was good to be on her own again. Good to be *doing* something. She fixed her iPod to the dock and turned it to her "happy track," a playlist filled with every upbeat, sing-alongable song she could find—Kirsty MacColl and Cat Stevens and the Beatles and a lot of Top 40 hits from many decades, much to her father's despair. But hipness, in her opinion, seemed to always be at the opposite end of the spectrum from cheeriness. Who wore pink to look hip, for example? And nobody went to see a happy love story at the movies to be cool. She found comfort in pop songs and pink T-shirts and romantic comedies.

On the seat beside her was her camera bag, the camera within it a brand-new digital beauty she'd purchased yesterday.

Hard to believe she had not shot a single photo in more than three months, but she had not. This morning she'd nearly taken a picture of her father, glowering in pirate dourness, but he said, "You've got a million photos of me. Why don't you wait until you have something that excites your eye?"

Already there was so much. *So* much! How had she managed to skip New Mexico in all of her travels? She'd been in Colorado and Arizona and Utah, but somehow never here. Not since youngest childhood, anyway.

It was a visual feast. Once she left the slight haze hanging over the Albuquerque Valley, it seemed every object was alive with color—a pine tree pointing a dark arrow into a rubbery blue sky; an old man leaning in sleep against a stucco wall, his hat tipped down on his face; a roadside stand with piles of red and yellow apples spread over a Mexican blanket; and a white dog snapping at flies, his fur pristine against the red earth. She stopped for the dog, who let her fire off a dozen shots, posing as perfectly as a boy on a runway with his paws crossed neatly in front of him. Her dad would like that it was her first shot. She'd send it tonight from her room and her new laptop—another bit of equipment she carried with her, a new generation beauty that weighed less than a hardcover book.

She stopped in a village—not much more than a gas station and a café—for lunch, then headed up through the high mountains. It was uninhabited land for the most part, a two-lane road broken every now and then by a small village or a couple of houses crouched at the side of the road.

The views were spectacular—high blue mountains, craggy and empty. A deer dashed across the road, and when she pulled into a rest stop, a pair of raccoons sat on top of a picnic table, snacking on apple cores. Unalarmed, they let her shoot a couple of photos, then trundled off, as fat and sassy as house pets.

When she emerged from the latrine, however, she saw that there were clouds building in the west. Deep-purply clouds, heavy with rain. A skitter of fear ran over her ribs, the first, tingling warning of a panic attack, and she willed herself to take a long, slow deep breath. And another. Rain would not hurt her. It was never rain that had caused her troubles. Her throat felt tight and the edges of her ears prickled, and she bent over, bracing her cold cast against her knee.

Breathe.

After a few minutes, she felt the panic ebb and headed back to the car. Still, she consulted the map and checked the distance to Los Ladrones. Not as far as she thought—just under thirty miles. No problem. She'd be there in a half hour, check into her hotel, and find some supper.

A sense of accomplishment filled her at the thought. This was the first day she'd actually lived her life since she landed in Santa Cruz, wrecked and exhausted, on June 4, two weeks after the accident. To commemorate the moment, she found Kool & the Gang's "Celebration" on the iPod and sang along. Loudly.

An hour later, she was creeping along the high mountain road, hands clenched so tight around the wheel that her palms sweated and the knuckles stuck up in rigid white mountains. The clouds had moved in fast, and just as fast they split open so violently it was as if someone had knifed a hole in a canvas. It was monsoonal. Rain so heavy she could barely see even with the windshield wipers at full blast.

But she couldn't pull over, either, since there was precious little shoulder. Every time a car came in the opposite direction, it sent hers rocking. Aloud she chanted, "Be cool, be cool, be cool."

Finally she spied a road sign that said, LOS LADRONES, 4 MILES.

Four miles. She could drive four more miles. Even with shoulders cramped as tight as winches. It didn't take long to get to the outskirts of town, and, as if to welcome her, the rain began to ease. Her shoulders relaxed—

Until she spied a big blue truck coming toward her, with water sluicing from the tires in a ten-foot wave. She hit the wipers to supercrank and slowed down, bracing herself.

Which was how she managed to miss hitting an enormous rabbit that leapt out of the forest from the left. It dashed across the path of the truck, in front of her own car, and disappeared into the forest. She slammed the brakes. Hard.

Thank God. Because behind the rabbit came a big dog, running in exuberant pursuit, tongue lolling, ears flopping. The scene unfolded in excruciating, elaborate, horrific detail—the truck hit the dog and sent him flying into the grass at the side of the road.

The truck roared by, oblivious or evil. Tessa slammed to a stop, flung the car into park, and ran into the pouring rain.

"Oh, no, oh, no!" she panted, kneeling beside the big dog. He was fluffy white with caramel patches and black-tipped ears. Blue eyes trained on her wildly. Alive, anyway. He had a little gash on his hip, and she murmured softly, holding out one hand for the dog to smell, the other stretching out to the cut before she even knew she would. "It's okay, honey," she said.

He was too big to pick up. She began to sing some old song that surfaced, a ballad with low minor notes that would help calm him, and although he was panting hard, he rested his head in a pile of wet leaves while Tessa put her hand over the wound, gauging the depth. Rain poured down, soaking her hair and the shoulders of her blouse, the creamy softness of the dog's thick fur. What kind of dog could he be? Akita maybe, mixed with shepherd or maybe husky. His paws had black spats.

She sang:

> *"There are suitors at my door,*
>   *o le le o bahia*
> *Six or eight or maybe more,*
>   *o le le o bahia*
> *And my father wants me wed,*
>   *o le le o bahia*
> *Or at least that's what he said, o le le o bahia."*

She kept singing, running her hands over his ribs, his legs. His legs did not look good. She touched them lightly, and the dog whined. Her cell phone was in the car, but she was loath to leave him long enough to get it. If someone else stopped in a minute or two, she would ask them to call a vet.

The bleeding slowed, and the dog lifted his head and licked her wrist. A moment after that, he leapt to his feet suddenly, stared at Tessa for the space of a few seconds, and then ran, apparently unhurt, into the woods.

Tessa sank back onto her heels, shaking. Rain poured down on her, but she barely noticed. Her lungs felt squashed, and her hands ached, and from behind she heard a car swish by on the wet road. It did not stop. She must make an odd picture, kneeling in the mud, getting drenched.

After a long moment, she rose on shaky legs and walked back to the car.

Hotel. She needed her hotel. Shaken, exhausted, she headed into town.

The main part of town was arranged around a central plaza. Tessa's notes said that it had been built that way to defend against the Comanches who bedeviled the early Spaniards. Because she was shivering with cold, Tessa noted only that it was a much larger area than she would have imagined the word "plaza" would indicate. It was as large as a small park, surrounded by buildings on all four sides. Some were two stories, all were adobe. She was grateful for the deep porch that ran all the way around, its roof sheltering her from the rain.

The hotel opened off the plaza, too. It was an elegantly old Spanish colonial within, with heavy carved wood and vigas, but by the time she made it to the check-in desk, all Tessa cared about was a warm bath and a bed. The girl behind the desk, tidy in a black suit jacket, her long eyes sharpened with dark eyeliner, said, "We'll send up some tea, ma'am, in just a few minutes. Or would you prefer coffee?"

"Tea is great, if the water is good and hot."

The girl smiled. "Of course. Would you like some soup? I believe it is chicken tortilla today."

"Oh, yes, please." Tessa wanted to weep with happiness. She had not expected this level of service out here, in—the phrase came from the back of her brain—the wilds of New Mexico. But Mick had said the basic rooms were more than $200 a night. For that money, the service damned well better be at least decent.

She didn't have a lot with her, but the bellman brought up the small rolling case and her backpack. As always, she carried her camera bag herself.

Dropping everything on the floor, she stripped off her wet shoes and socks, wrapped her cast in a plastic bag, and ran a tubful of steaming water. After the tea and soup arrived, she sank into the bath with her hot, milky cup. The creeping unease in her limbs faded away, and Tessa relaxed. It would be okay this time. She would have a nap, then wander out and get some supper.

At the age of four, Tessa had nearly drowned, a story she'd heard so often she thought she remembered it. In fact, she didn't remember anything except the cold and a sense of panic. Nothing else, really, except weeping and weeping when Sam dragged her out of the river, screaming and fighting. She'd lost something in those waters.

But the nearly fatal drowning had reset something in her brain. It was as if all the drawers of her memory had been yanked out and the contents flung onto the floor. Her memory wasn't exactly *erased*, but the images were so mixed up they never made much sense. She remembered songs. She remembered a black-and-white dog sleeping on her bed. She remembered playing jacks with another child in a room that had windows all around.

The songs, though, the songs just bobbed up like golf balls from the shattered section of her brain, whole and complete. Old songs. Songs she sang in her strange husky voice, without even thinking. It wasn't only the old ones, of course. She always had a song playing in her head, and a slightly irritating habit of humming under her breath nearly all the time.

If she stopped and listened to the song of the moment, it was also running commentary on her life. A soundtrack that could actually be pretty corny, sometimes funny, sometimes piercing.

When she woke up from her nap after arriving in Los Ladrones, the song in her mind was an old song about a cat, *"El Don Gato,"* who sat on a high red roof reading letters. It was funny because she was lying in a pool of sunshine with her belly turned up to the light like a fat tabby. The storm had passed. The light poured through the French doors that led to a balcony, and Tessa stretched, put on some dry jeans, and opened the doors.

The world swirled in. A woman laughing and a dog barking and a swarm of chatter coming from a café or bar or something close by. Long, deep-gold bars of sunlight slanted through the clattery leaves of a massive cottonwood that stood sentry over the plaza. Once it would have been a hanging tree.

The air smelled of heat and dust and something elusive and familiar she could taste on the roof of her mouth. A wash of hungry, eager happiness poured through her, filling her lungs, her belly. She pressed her hands to her heart, one atop the other like a yogi, to bring the pale green feeling closer to herself, and tipped her face up to the light.

Here I am, she breathed into the sky, and for once it didn't matter that she had no idea who she was talking to.

Then the softly mystical moment passed, and she leaned over the balcony to see where the voices were coming from. Along the front lower level of the hotel was a roped-off area, where an elegantly dressed crowd milled about. White-coated waiters carrying glasses of wine and trays of hors d'oeuvres circled among them unobtrusively. A woman laughed, and there was something in the cast of her head that made Tessa realize she was a well-known character actress.

Huh. Tessa had been based in LA for the past couple of years, so celebrity sightings were nothing new. It did serve to underscore the point that the town was a lot glitzier than one might expect. She made a mental note to tell Mick.

She grabbed her camera, a pair of big dark sunglasses, and

stuck her thin wallet in the pocket of her jeans. Downstairs at the desk, she stopped to get a stylized hand-drawn map of the plaza, with red feet marching around it to various attractions. The tree. The old jail. The church where Indians once kept their sheep. A trail with an arrow pointing to the pilgrim route up the mountain.

Later she would explore all of it. For now she just needed to get her bearings.

In the center of the plaza was the ancient tree. Judging by the circumference of the trunk, it was at least a couple of hundred years old. Roots traveled beneath the pavers of the square, making hills and valleys that could trip the unwary. A pair of young lovers curled up against the trunk, a breeze riffling through the girl's long hair. A trio of old men, white and Latino, in tidy button-up shirts and cowboy hats, sat on a bench, watching the world go by. An obviously annoyed woman in a red dress and bug sunglasses paced back and forth, talking into a cell phone. Her stilettos clicked on the adobe bricks. Dangerous footwear around here, Tessa thought. Good way to break an ankle.

But then, her shoe passions ran toward high-end hiking boots and the battered, beloved walking sandals she wore now. Her feet were permanently tanned in a little box across the arch.

She stood with the map in her hand and faced north to get acclimated. The hotel pinned down the east side of the plaza, with shops and a restaurant on the lower level, two stories of rooms above. On the north end were more shops: a kitchen store and art gallery and an ice cream shop. An old-style movie theater had an Indian head in a feathered bonnet with neon letters lined up vertically to spell *CHIEF*. It triggered a waft of something, a slight memory, but of course Sam had always been a movie fiend. Surely they had gone to the movies even then.

On the west was the café that had become so famous in recent years: The 100 Breakfasts Café. It looked unassuming from the outside, made of the same adobe as the rest of the buildings—she thought it was a law here, as in Taos and Santa Fe—with a good sign and tables outside in front. Just now the chairs were stacked up inside the door, and when Tessa peered in the windows, she saw someone working in the back, with a light on.

From somewhere farther along came classic ranchero music, kindling a powerful, bittersweet burst of yearning. It was corny and old-fashioned, but it didn't matter—whenever she heard the guitars, the mournful Spanish, it made her ache. Tonight, it hooked her mid-chest and drew her out of the plaza and around the corner into a medieval little warren of alleys. The shops—a bookstore with a Siamese cat in the window, boutiques with clothing and jewelry, and a tiny shop called Le Fleur de Mer, which appeared to be stocked entirely with salt—were closed for the day, but the bars were hopping on a Friday night, each one featuring a different clientele. A spill of young men and women smoking cigarettes and drinking martinis stood outside The Bull Ring; at Las Golindrinas, old hippies in skirts and long hair listened to the blues and drank beers. Tessa lingered a moment. Maybe some of them had been Sam's friends, once upon a time.

A woman in a long purple India cotton skirt leaned on the wall, smoking. Her long blond hair was tangled, as if she had not combed it at all, and she eyed Tessa with faint hostility, drawing in on her cigarette, blowing it out. Her eyes looked hollow. A tongue of cold lapped at Tessa's throat, and she thought of what her father said about evil spirits walking in Los Ladrones. She hurried on, glancing back over her shoulder. The woman had gone inside.

The ranchero tunes were coming from a covered patio at the end of the lane. The band was arranged at one side, dressed in crisp white shirts and black slacks and cowboy boots. The woman singing had long red hair and abundant cleavage displayed in a sweetheart neckline. In front of them, couples of all ages danced a lively two-step. Little girls danced on their brothers' feet, grandmothers were whirled around by grandsons, and young couples showed off their skill. Tessa, snared, watched them and felt a soft breathless sense of expectation.

Here I am, said that little voice inside her again.

Tessa sat at a table near the wall and took out her camera. She shot the dancers lit from the west by rosy light, and the ropes of plastic flowers looping around the posts holding up the roof, and a little girl with an aqua dress swinging her feet as she drank a cola.

Everything in Tessa's body relaxed, as if she'd come home to her own living room. When a bosomy waitress stopped by the table, she ordered a cheeseburger. "What kind of beer do you have?"

The woman reeled off a long list. Tessa stopped her. "How about Tecate? With lime."

"I can do that."

A man dressed in jeans and a dark-blue T-shirt leaned on the wall nearby. Behind him, a dog as thin as a shadow slunk into the patio area, head down, and slipped under Tessa's legs. The waitress brought Tessa's beer, along with a glass rimmed with kosher salt. "Gorgeous," she said happily, squeezed the lime and poured the beer carefully, then took a long swallow. Cold, golden, thirst quenching. Fantastic.

The dog leaned against her ankle. "Hey, sweetie," she said. Beneath the table, she knocked off her sandal and put a foot against his skinny ribs. Poor baby. He was shivering a little, even though it was a warm night. Her toes skidded over burrs. When her burger came, she fed him meat and cheese and a little bread, and most of her fries. He was surprisingly polite, and Tessa figured this wasn't his first begging gig.

She watched the man by the wall with apprehension. Rage radiated from him in red waves, heating the space around him until it was faintly uncomfortable against Tessa's left arm. He smoked, exhaling blue clouds into the night with hard blows, his attention utterly focused on someone in the middle of the dancing, though it wasn't clear who was the object of his fury.

Out of the corner of her eye, Tessa could make out a few details—his hair was thick and black, long, tied back from hard cheekbones and a mouth that turned down at the corners. Fiercely handsome, like a coyote, but Tessa felt only repulsed. That radiating hatred began to make her feel faintly ill, and she was looking for the waitress when he abruptly straightened, tossed down his cigarette and ground it beneath his heel, then left, boot heels clicking on the stones of the alleyway. The eggplant softness of the gloaming swallowed him suddenly.

"Creepy," she said aloud. A shudder moved through the dog and into her foot. "One of the bad spirits, huh?" she said quietly to him. "You're okay now. He's gone."

"Sorry?" said a voice at her elbow.

Startled, Tessa looked up at a different man, who had come over to her table, two beers in hand. "Um. Talking to myself."

"Sign of intelligence, they say." He was a big man, with a rumbling voice. If the scary guy was a coyote, this one was an elk—tall, with muscular shoulders and thick dark hair. Not her type, but those thighs were something else. Solid. Enormous.

Probably a mountain biker, she thought, bane of hiking trails the world over. Inwardly, she scowled.

"I brought you this," he said, offering her another Tecate with a lime wedge balanced on the top. "If it's all right with your dog."

"My—? oh. Right. He's not mine."

"Is that so." His smile was very, very faint. And very, very sexy. As if the dog were a plant, he licked her foot.

Tessa gestured toward the empty seat on the other side of the little table. "Please. Have a seat."

"Thanks." He put one beer down in front of her, then wiped condensation off his fingers and held out his hand. "Vince Grasso."

"Tessa," she said, but didn't give her last name. "Are you a local?"

"Born and raised," he said, with slight sigh. "I left for a couple of decades, but here I am, back again. Where are you from?"

"All over. My dad was a magician for Renaissance festivals, so we traveled."

He inclined his head, and his hair caught the light and shone, glossy as a pelt. "Now, that's a new one. Did you like it?"

"Sometimes," she said. "I liked the clothes, and the people were generally really great—smart and eccentric. But it got old, traveling around. Eventually, we settled in Santa Cruz."

"And now?"

She took a sip of beer. It was a reasonable question, but she didn't have an answer. "Now I lead tours for a small outdoor-travel company."

"Like bungee jumping and white-water adventures?"

"No, not that adventurous. Mostly hiking, some rafting occasionally, and good food at the end of the day."

"Is there a tour here?"

"There might be in the future. I'm exploring the possibilities."

He lifted his chin at her turquoise cast, resting on the table. "Is that how you broke your arm, on a tour?"

She looked down at it. Thought of Lisa. "Yeah."

He took a sip of his own beer, as if waiting for her to add more. When she didn't, he nodded. "Do you get lonely? Traveling all the time?" He held up a hand. "Sorry, that sounds like a bad line, but I meant it at face value. I'm not looking to take anybody home."

"That's pretty forthright."

"Curse of the West, to say what you're thinking."

Tessa raised her beer in a toast. "To straightforwardness."

He lifted his beer, too, and Tessa saw that he thought she was beautiful, and it felt good on so many, many levels.

"So is it?" he asked. "Lonely?"

"Yes," she said. "Sometimes it is. Sometimes it's exciting. It's like anything else—a mixed bag." A ripple of memory—her bleeding foot, the deep water of the river—made her left eye twitch once, hard. "I'm not really sure I'm going to keep up with it, honestly."

A cell phone rang on his belt, and he made a face. "Sorry, I'm search and rescue. I've gotta answer."

She waved her hand. He stood up and barked hello into the phone. Tessa wanted to shoot his photo, the red light from the stage touching the edge of his jaw, his arm rivered with veins. His hands were enormous, graceful, beautiful, and she wanted to look at them more closely, shoot the fingernails, the scars, see the lines on his palms. She lifted her camera and looked through the viewfinder, captured a quick series.

So she saw the moment he closed the phone and spied her

looking at him through the camera. She zoomed in on his eyes, very brown, with the heavy black lashes of a buck. He stared directly at the camera and she clicked the shutter.

"Do you mind?" she asked, lowering it.

"No." He tucked the phone into his pocket. "Unfortunately, I've gotta go to work." He held out his hand. "Maybe I'll see you around."

She reached for his hand, taking a mental snapshot of the taut, wide palm, and shook it, surprised to discover she was disappointed. "Maybe so."

"Are you—" He smiled regretfully. "Never mind. Enjoy your stay." He lifted a hand and disappeared into the crowd.

Tessa finished her beer, listening to the music. The dog slept on her foot. Yes, she thought, eyeing the nearly untouched beer the man had left behind. Sometimes hers was a lonely life.

Eventually the dog got up, licked her hand in gratitude, and slipped out. She could see now that he was a pup, not much more than five or six months, ragged and dirty, maybe a border collie mix of some kind. From somewhere came a blessing for dogs, a prayer to St. Francis. "Bless that little dog," she whispered. *Take care, little one.*

She took her cue and headed back to the hotel. It was almost entirely dark, and as she moved through the plaza, she heard a woman weeping and weeping.

Although she was not superstitious, she couldn't help hurrying a little, as something rushed up the back of her neck. She was glad to get to her room and lock the door.

100 BREAKFASTS CAFÉ MENU
Breakfast #3

Hearty Oatmeal: Whole-grain oats cooked just for you, the slow way, served with cream and our own thick-sliced raisin bread slathered with butter. Additions available: raisins, dates, pecans, walnuts, berries (in season only). Try it with milk and a pot of hot tea.

HEARTY OATMEAL

1 cup water
¼ cup raisins
Dash of kosher salt
½ cup old-fashioned oats
    (never, never, never use the quick-cooking kind!)
Cream, honey or brown sugar, and butter for serving
2 slices of thick-sliced bread of your choice

Put the water, raisins, and salt in a small heavyweight saucepan and bring to a strong boil. Add oats, stir, and turn heat down to medium. Cook for 4–5 minutes, stirring regularly. Remove from heat, cover, and put the bread in to toast. Serve with whole cream, butter, and honey or brown sugar.

THREE

Tessa awakened very early. For a long moment she hung between worlds, wondering where she was. One of the side effects of traveling for a living.

Birds chirped somewhere. The air was light and dry. She opened one eye and saw the kiva fireplace in the corner, the elegant, worm-marked vigas in the ceiling. Oh, yes, New Mexico.

Wrapped in a sweater to stave off the sharp morning air, she used the coffeemaker to boil water and carried a cup of tea out to the balcony overlooking the plaza. Again that soft sweetness rushed through her—*here I am!*—and she sipped the sweet, milky brew until her brain woke up. It never took very long—she was very much a morning person, just like her father. Even as a teenager, she had awakened automatically by six and fallen dead asleep by ten over homework or—more likely—a novel. Healthy, wealthy, and wise, as good old Ben Franklin said.

She fired up her laptop and read over the notes she'd compiled for the town, mulling over her plans for the day. The farmers' market would take place in the plaza, and there were already a few early arrivals trailing into the area, carrying tents and tables. Of course she'd spend some time exploring that, shooting some photos, offering it to her boss as a possible feature of the tour.

She also wanted to find the church, which was a little to the north of the plaza itself. It was the first thing that had been built here, erected in 1632 by Spanish missionaries. They had been slaughtered in an Indian uprising a decade later, and the Spanish left it alone for twenty years or more. The Indians used the church to house animals, mainly the merino sheep the missionaries had brought with them, and learned to weave the long, elegant wool.

When the Spanish returned, they quelled the Indians and built the plaza around the tree—as Tessa had suspected. It couldn't possibly be the same tree, could it? Did a cottonwood live to be almost four hundred years old? She put her notes down and admired it once again. In the early quiet, its leaves clattered lightly in a soft breeze, and the deeply patterned bark caught only the gray notes of dawn, like a rubbing with a very hard pencil.

In sudden decision, she gulped the last of her tea, scrambled into some jeans and a T-shirt, and headed down to shoot the sunrise as it crept into the plaza.

Just as she emerged from the hotel, the first fingers of sunlight tipped over the roofs at the eastern edge of the plaza. The light was a delicate pale butter, washing the ruddy color of the adobe to soft peach, hazing the edges of the vigas, and catching on the point of a tent going up. The very top leaves of the tree were illuminated, waking up the inhabitants in its branches. Birds whirred and whistled. A pair of squirrels ran in circles around the mountainous terrain of the roots.

She looked at it all through the square eye of her viewfinder. It had been so long since she'd lost herself in the joy of seeing the world this way! Giddy, she shot frame after frame, each one a split second of truth. A few shopkeepers began to appear, bringing out freshly chalked signs, tables for their customers, mannequins, racks of T-shirts, and even a cigar-store Indian. Locals greeted one another, stopped to chat in a mingling of Spanish and English. For a moment she closed her eyes, letting the harmonious sound of the two mingled languages fill her. The best sound, she thought. Friendly.

The air held the crispness of mountain-born water and autumn lurking in the shadows creeping down the mountains. She smelled, faintly, burning leaves.

And suddenly she remembered standing in this very spot.

The memory slammed her like a gust of wind. A pair of red cowboy boots on her feet, a woman with long blond hair, angry. Another child nearby. A brother? A sister? A hand her own size squeezed Tessa's tightly.

"You are so stupid!" the woman said. The children were afraid of her.

That was it. Tessa opened her eyes and blinked once, feeling the slight disorientation of seeing things as they were in this day and time, though she couldn't have said what was so different.

Her stomach growled and she put the camera away in its bag, awkwardly tipping it in with her stiff left arm. She would check out The 100 Breakfasts Café this morning, get a feel for the vibe before she made arrangements to interview the owner.

By the time Vince half-staggered, half-crawled into Vita's, it wasn't quite seven. He'd been up all night and smelled of soot and cave dust, and ought to go shower, but all they'd had to eat were Clif Bars and Gatorade. He needed real food. Vita's food. Breakfast.

The well-lit quiet smelled of freshly brewing coffee and ham. Only a small handful of customers had straggled in so early in the morning. An older couple, likely marooned in town by the gully-washer yesterday, read the newspaper and drank coffee peaceably in a booth. Derek Trueblood, who drove a wrecker for the state of New Mexico, propped his Popeye forearms on the counter and glowered at somebody in the kitchen. A pair of uniformed state patrolmen waved at Vince as he sat heavily on a stool at the counter and stripped off his jacket.

A few stools down sat the woman from the cantina last night. It was her turquoise cast, painted with a scene of mountains and trees, that caught his eye first. She was bent over a thick sheaf of notes, her hair pulled back haphazardly in a scrunchie. The sight of her nape, delicate and vulnerable, caught him right in the midsection.

Bizarre. He rubbed a hand over his face.

She glanced up. "Hey. You're the guy from last night."

"So I am."

"How did it go?"

"Badly." They'd been too late to save a climber who'd fallen more than a hundred feet down a ravine. "Badly," he said again.

"I'm sorry," she said.

He nodded. Last night he kept thinking there was something familiar about her, and again he tried to place what it was. *Who* she was. It slipped away, elusive. Maybe she was an actress or something. They'd all learned not to ask around here these days. Learned to give famous faces the space of a dinner conversation or a stroll in the plaza uninterrupted by requests for autographs or staring fans.

No, not an actress. He remembered she was a tour guide.

Vita herself came out of the kitchen, bearing a full pot of coffee. A sixty-something woman with the ropy physique of a marathon runner and severely cropped silver hair, she asked, "How you doing there, soldier?" Even as she spoke, she pulled a heavy ceramic mug from the stack by the machine, set it down in front of him, and poured coffee into it. She also poured him a big glass of ice water. Vince picked it up and drank deeply.

"Bad news?"

He nodded. Took another gulp of cold water and ordered the French toast. And scrambled eggs with chiles and potatoes. And bacon. The room seemed surreal and echoey because he was so exhausted.

Vita brought him a glass of orange juice. "It'll bring your blood sugar up a little bit. You're white around the mouth, sweetheart."

"Thanks." He went to the bathroom to wash his hands and face. When he came back, the woman on the other stool gave him a small smile. She was deeply tanned, with a thick tumble of streaky hair falling down her back. Too young for him, but great eyes, big and fish-shaped, like a girl in an anime film.

Familiar, he thought again. Somebody's granddaughter or cousin up from Albuquerque. "You in town for a while?"

"A little while." Her voice was low. Rich. He thought of hot chocolate laced with cream. It almost felt as if it touched him, his neck, his brow. "Listen, I can see you're totally wiped out," she said. "You don't have to talk. Just eat your breakfast." She pulled a card out of her pocket and wrote something on it. "Call me when you feel better."

He took the card. Tucked it in his pocket.

A knot of mountain bikers in gear came in. Vigorous and eager, filling the room with a scent of testosterone, they made him feel in the area of twelve thousand years old. He watched them jostling one another, feeling his achy knees, his lower back. It had been more than a decade, but he still missed it.

He'd made his fortune in endorsements earned through the sport, until a final wreck demolished his left knee and ended his career for good.

"Don't tell me," the woman said. "You're a mountain biker, too, aren't you?"

"Was." He eyed her. Lean arms and legs, but too much chest for a serious runner or cyclist. "You don't approve?"

"Hiker." She pointed a thumb back toward her chest. "We're natural enemies, right?"

"Don't have to be, if everybody is willing to be thoughtful."

"In my experience, that usually means the hiker has to listen carefully and get the hell out of the biker's way."

There was enough truth in the statement that he didn't argue. Not today. "Is that all you're having? Coffee?"

She looked at the cup as if it had the answer. "It's tea. But yes, so far."

"No, no, no. Not here. This place is famous for the breakfast. You have to try something." From the small steel clip on the edge of the counter, he tugged a menu and folded it open in front of her. "Just take a peek. There's gotta be something you'd like." Was he flirting with her again? Like there wasn't enough going on in his world. "I wouldn't push it so much, but, seriously, Vita is famous. World famous."

Her mouth turned a tiny bit upward. "Ah! *World* famous." Her fingers touched the print.

"I'm betting you're a pancakes kind of woman."

"Not so much, honestly."

"Don't tell me you're a yogurt head."

She laughed. It made her eyes crinkle, and he realized she was older than he originally thought. "And what would be wrong with that?"

"Eat yogurt somewhere else. Here, the beauty is in the big

breakfast." His food came, and he gestured to the steaming, fragrant mass. "Look at this. Homemade raisin bread French toast with orange. Who wouldn't like that?"

The woman—he could *not* remember her name—looked at Vita dispensing coffee, carrying plates, hustling around the kitchen, visible through the pass-out bar. "That's Vita?"

He nodded. "She's had this place since the late seventies, I reckon." He picked up his fork and gave a moment of reverence to the food, then took a bite. Let it explode. "Jesus, that's good."

"All right," she said, and looked up as Vita came over to refill his cup. "I'll have the oatmeal, please. Plain."

Vita grinned. "Whole-wheat toast?"

"Absolutely. And plenty of butter on the side, please."

"You got it, sweetheart."

."Oatmeal," Vince said. "All those beautiful things and you pick oatmeal?"

"Now, you don't get to do that. You badgered me into eating. I'm eating. Maybe *you* don't love oatmeal, but my dad made it for me every morning."

"Fair enough. Next time, though, you've gotta try the French toast."

For a minute, she looked at him. "Next time."

"You in town long enough for a next time?"

"Maybe. I wish I'd brought a dog, though. All this outdoor living."

He nearly nodded off, right into his plate. "I have dogs," he said, to keep himself awake. "A big mutt who's a pain in the ass, and a scavenger terrier who lives for whatever scraps might fall into her mouth. Or whatever trash might be left unattended."

She grinned with one side of her mouth, and it gave her an impish look. Elfin. Familiarity tickled his brain again. "A little spoiled, are they?"

"Uh, yeah, slightly. Sasha is the terrier. She's fifteen and getting pretty deaf."

"And the other one?"

"Pedro doesn't mean to be bad. He's just a wild man—an escape artist and rodent killer and garden destroyer and crotch sniffer." He winced. "Sorry."

"Sounds like a character."

"That's one word for it." He took another bite. Hot orange and vanilla, syrup and raisins and cinnamon filled his mouth, his throat. "You like dogs?"

"Love 'em. Just can't have one with my lifestyle. I visit my dad's. He has three. He believes they are the same three dogs he's had his whole life."

"Come again?"

She laughed. "Exactly—he thinks they reincarnate, over and over. That dogs are sent by God to be our companions."

"Like angels?"

"I suppose so." She sipped her tea. "Speaking of characters, that would be my dad, too."

"Sounds like it. Renaissance festivals and reincarnated dogs."

"He's also a surfer and runs a drinks shack on the beach that's called Margaritaville."

Her voice really was peaceful, he thought in his sleepy way. Not hot chocolate now but something soft and silvery, like a rain cloud. He wanted to lie down in it, let it carry him away. He jerked awake again. "Damn. No reflection on your conversation, but I don't think I'm gonna make it. Gotta get home and get some sleep."

"No offense taken."

"You're not driving like that, are you?" Vita said, and looked around the room. "Alex!" she called to one of the mountain bikers. "I need you to drive our firefighter home."

"Absolutely," the youth said, jumping up. He slapped Vince on the back. "C'mon, man."

Vince looked at the woman. "I can't remember your name," he said gruffly.

"It's Tessa," she said, holding out her hand.

He took it, fine-boned and brown, in his giant paw. "I'm Vince."

"*I* remembered." She smiled and it reached her eyes, and he *knew* that face. Knew it in his bones. It was not a usual sort of face, with those big tilted eyes and high-bridged nose. Cherokee nose, he thought, and didn't know why. Not pretty, exactly. Something else.

Vita pushed his boxed food over the counter. "Nice to meet you," he said, and stumbled out. Alex drove him to the ranch, and he collapsed.

When her oatmeal came, Tessa gave a happy sigh. It was fresh and not at all porridge-y or gray, which would have completely ruined it. This was hearty oatmeal, grainy, chewy, robust. Carefully, she slivered the butter into very, very fine layers and covered the top of the cereal, then salted the whole lightly. She took a bite and marched right back to childhood, to her father cooking every morning so they could have a hot breakfast together. Butter melted on her tongue like love, and halfway through she added another fine layer. A little bit more salt. Perfect.

She took her time, focusing entirely on the food. Business grew brisk around her, and she nursed her tea, reading the book she'd brought in with her, a memoir about Kashmir that she'd found in the hotel lobby. When a waitress came by to refill her steel teapot, she asked, "Is this okay? Me sitting here so long?"

"You sit as long as you like, sweetie."

So she read and sipped tea and watched the flow of people and service all around. It wasn't a particularly large café. Booths lined the long windows in front, and the dining room drove toward the back with four-tops and two-tops along the wall. The counter was the best part, however—a horseshoe facing the pass-out bar, with a view of the kitchen over a stainless-steel counter. Watching the kitchen staff was like watching a waltz—they moved instinctively around one another, Vita in the middle, on the side, out in front, carrying plates, taking orders, cooking, making fresh pots of coffee. Whatever. She was the puppetmaster, making sure the waltz went smoothly.

When the restaurant hit a bit of a lull, Tessa pulled out another of her business cards. "Excuse me," she said to Vita. "May I speak with you for a minute?"

Vita looked suspicious as she came forward. "Yes?"

"I'm Tessa Harlow," she said. "I'm with a travel company, and I'd like to talk to you about some possibilities if I can."

"Possibilities?"

"We're thinking of active tours—some hiking, some food, some history, that kind of thing. I'd like to talk to you about your café but also about the area, get your reading on it."

"I'd be open to that." Over her shoulder, Vita spied something in the kitchen. She held up one finger toward Tessa and went to the pass-out bar. "Donald, wash that by hand, kiddo. It won't fit in the dishwasher." She shook her head on her way back. "Weekends are bad, but how about early next week?"

"Great." Tessa could see a woman waving at Vita from the kitchen. "I'll let you go. See you soon."

Noticing the slight congestion beginning at the door, Tessa reluctantly gathered her things and settled her bill, tucking a dollar down the back of her cast for the moment.

The minute she stepped outside, she smelled roasting chiles and stopped dead to suck the aroma drunkenly into her lungs. Deep. It was a smoky scent, thick and hot and spicy, as powerful in its way as coffee brewing. She was convinced it had healing properties, that, even as she breathed, her arm was knitting together more quickly, her fingernails grew faster, and all the shredded places on her heart were smoothed.

At least a little bit.

While she'd been lazing through her breakfast, the market had sprung to life. White tents poked up like little mountain ranges in rows throughout the plaza, the monstrous arms of the cottonwood tree offering shade to everything below it. It was barely eight-thirty, but already the aisles milled with shoppers.

Everywhere around the world there were open-air markets like this. In Morocco and London and Asia and Tasmania. Everywhere she shot them. Everywhere she loved them.

Here on this August Saturday, Tessa waded in, shooting everything—tomatoes as big as her fist stacked in juicy rows, red and yellow, striped and black and mottled green; piles of melons and corn; and acres of peaches, one of the crops the Spanish had brought that had then thrived in the high valley. She bought a yellow tomato, three peaches nearly the size of her head, and wandered on.

Despite the slight awkwardness of her cast, she photographed everything, in an artistic binge. She captured the wrinkled, weathered faces of old Latino farmers, and their gnarled hands and scuffed boots; spent a long time shooting a Native American woman of an age impossible to determine, blackest hair streaked with silver caught in two braids that fell over her breasts. Strings of turquoise looped around her neck, looking too heavy for her fragile upper torso.

There were plenty of Anglos, too—ranchers and farmers alike, with outback and cowboy hats shading eyes that had squinted a long time into the sun, and women with leathered skin. There were well-tended matrons in expensive jeans and the odd purse dog poking a curious nose out of a bag; masters of the universe masquerading as the little people, their exquisitely expensive sunglasses and watches giving them away. Tessa shot them, too, discreetly.

She finally found the Green Gate Organic Farms booth at the far end of the market, taking up four lengths of tent. Here was a mix of nations, ages, colors, sexes. A young African American man with a big Afro weighed beans. Hippie twenty-somethings in blond and red dreadlocks kept an eye on the chile roaster. And, of course, there were the older ones, people who had probably been with the farm since it had been a commune, settled in the late sixties by a bunch of California hippies fleeing the scene on the coast. Including Sam, of course.

As Tessa walked slowly among the overflowing tables of tomatoes and chiles, corn and radishes, onions and potatoes and beans, she glanced at the people manning the stand. Aside from the young ones, no one here really looked particularly counterculture, although one man had long gray hair he'd tied back from his lean, handsome face, and a couple of women wore a lot of bracelets and long earrings.

But then, Tessa wore a lot of bracelets herself. Right this minute, she had a silver cuff she'd bought in Tasmania, at a market very like this one. The memory brought Glenn's face to her, and she pushed it away. She had enough to think about without adding a big wallow over the Aussie who'd broken her heart. It had been almost two years, after all.

And yet she had to admit that a part of her still wished for his company, wished he was here with her now, running his acerbic commentary on everything from the heartiness of beans to the tarot readers turning cards for patrons. She remembered reading once that a person had to grieve for half the length of the relationship itself. She'd lived with Glenn for nearly four years. Surely she must be close to finished by now.

Enough. Deliberately, she shifted her attention to the bounty in front of her, gathering another breath of chile-scented air. There, in the back of the booth, was the woman with long blond hair that she'd seen last night at Las Golindrinas, the hostile woman who still wore the same floaty purple skirt. And still hadn't brushed her hair.

Tessa had expected more people like her. Instead, most of them had the look of the prosperous lazing around for the day, good haircuts and clean jaws and tidy jeans.

It was odd to imagine that some of them might have known her father. And her mother, whom she couldn't remember except in the barest fragments. What would they say if she introduced herself, made conversation about her father living at the commune?

Weirdly, she found herself feeling a lot of anxiety over that thought. Was it possible she wanted to let sleeping dogs lie?

Maybe.

She wandered down the tables, smelling a cantaloupe, thumping a watermelon. A woman with her hair hidden beneath a big scarf said, "What can I tempt you with?"

A frisson of memory skated over Tessa's nerves. Startling. The voice was familiar, she thought, though the face didn't seem to trigger anything.

Or maybe—more likely—she was *expecting* to recognize someone here. "I'm not sure," she said, peering into the woman's face for a possible clue. She had no eyebrows, and

Tessa realized she must be a chemo patient. "I'm really only in town for a couple of days. Can't cook anything."

"Fresh food, then. Peaches? Cantaloupe?"

Tessa raised her blue arm, with the bag slung over her casted wrist. "Peaches were already irresistible. But, yes, cantaloupe should be easy enough."

"And it's very, very good for you. Lots of antioxidants."

Tessa nodded. "Do you have any literature or background on the farm?"

"We ran out this morning, actually," she said, "but if you come over to the farm during the week, we have a little cottage devoted to all that stuff." She gave Tessa the enormous cantaloupe she'd picked out for her and picked up a card from the table. "It's all right there. You can find us on the Web."

"Thanks." Tessa tucked the card away.

Now the aisles were growing very crowded. People attired in costly casual clothes and sleek coifs and the fragrance of big money joined the housewives and young families and teenagers huddling around the edges, trading giggles or gossip, depending. Tessa saw an LA type, a woman who had to be well over forty with hips no larger than the young teens nearby. It always startled her, that perfection. What did it take? A glass of chardonnay and a vitamin every day, hold the food? What kind of life could that possibly be?

Then again, she wasn't married to a billionaire. Maybe it would be worth it.

Shaking her head, she stepped out of the flow nearby the retaining wall around the tree, pushing her sunglasses up so she could check some of the photos she'd captured thus far.

Something slammed into her legs, and Tessa staggered sideways. "Hey!"

A big white dog twirled in that particularly endearing circle of happiness, head down, tail swirling with him, mouth and tongue smiling all the way to his black-tipped ears. He wiggled up to her legs, and Tessa realized that it was the dog who'd been hit by the truck yesterday.

"Oh, baby!" she cried, kneeling. She put her camera in the bag for safety and reached for the mutt. He danced, wiggling all over. "Hi, honey! I'm so glad to see you. How are you?" She rubbed her hands over his fluffy neck, his shoulders. He half-moaned, half-yelped in ecstasy and licked her face with no apology whatsoever. "Yes, thank you. I'm glad to see you, too. You look good."

"That's *our* dog, you know."

The little girl was maybe seven or eight, a bit plump. Fine blond hair was barely captured in a ponytail high on the back of her head. Wisps and locks escaped all around her face. She wore blue glasses. "He's beautiful," Tessa said.

"He's an Akita. They're very smart."

"I've heard that." The dog leaned hard against Tessa and she couldn't help giving him a hug. "Is he—"

Another girl, maybe a little younger, as tidy as her sister was unkempt, approached, "He isn't a *purebred* Akita, Natalie," she said with superiority. "He's only half. We don't know what the rest is." To Tessa, she said, "He gets in a lot of trouble."

"He's still *our* dog," said Natalie.

"I was just petting him," Tessa said, chuckling. "I would never steal him or anything."

"Girls!" a tall, sturdy-looking woman called. She held a blond moppet in her arms, all big eyes and soft red mouth. "Get the damned dog and come on, will you? I've gotta get you home and go to work."

"Grandma! You swore!" the first girl said, but she grabbed the dog's leash and yanked. He got up willingly enough and trotted after her, looking over his shoulder as if to wink at Tessa. She grinned.

"Goodbye," said the second little girl.

"Bye. Thanks for letting me pet your dog."

Natalie had a quarter in her pocket. She could actually feel it against her thigh, a round hot spot she needed to get rid of. When Grandma wanted to stop at the grocery story on the way home, Natalie was so relieved she almost cried. They left Pedro in the car with his head sticking out, and all trooped into the Safeway. Jade danced ahead, as usual, and grabbed the shopping cart. "I'll push it," she said with a sidelong look at Natalie.

It was Natalie's turn and Jade knew it, but that coin was burning her, so Natalie let it go. They went to the produce section first, where the apples were coming in now in giant piles. On the Food Network, a chef said to look for all different kinds of apples and try something new, like a Pink Lady, and Natalie thought it sounded so enchanting, like an apple in a fairy tale, that she was dying to try one.

Not *really* dying, like Snow White and her poisoned apple, but, anyway . . .

Carefully, she read the names of the apples. Delicious and Fuji, green Granny Smiths, and Braeburn. A pile of small yellow and pink apples caught her eye. "Pink Ladies!" she cried, pointing. "Grandma, can I have one?"

"No, not today." She briskly piled onions in a bag.

"Please? Just one. It's a Pink Lady. I heard about Pink—"

"I said no, Natalie."

"I have a—"

"No."

Crushed, Natalie turned away. The apples, softly streaked with palest green and threads of yellow, as round as cherries, seemed almost to be laughing. Not at her, of course, but just laughing, happy. Bright and pretty, like a Pink Lady.

"I have a quarter," she said. "I'm going to the tattoos."

"No candy," Grandma said. "You've had plenty to eat this morning."

"A *tattoo*."

"That's fine. I'm just going to get a few things to take to your daddy, so stay right there and don't go wandering all over the store."

"I can find you," Natalie said with a scowl. There were only seven aisles in the whole store, for heaven's sake. Not like Denver, where they used to live. Before. The stores there had so many aisles a person really could get lost.

"I said stay by the machines, Nat. Or come with us now."

Jade, swinging her body back and forth on one foot so that her hair swirled out around her like a shiny cape, smirked. Natalie resisted the urge to pinch her and headed for the machines.

She took her time deciding. There were two rows of machines up against the wall next to the machine horse. Gumballs and jawbreakers and the fruit-shaped sweets Nat loved, cherry hearts and yellow bananas and tiny green limes with hard candy outsides and melting sugar insides. Who would know? She glanced over her shoulder, but Grandma was long gone. She could eat them before anybody got back.

The quarter burned her fingers even at the thought. No. Bad enough that she'd stolen the coin right out of her grandmother's wallet, from the little envelope that held nickels and dimes and plenty of quarters. She never took one if it might be noticed.

Next to the fruit candies were the tattoos. Before she could add the sin of lying to stealing and the list of other bad things she would have to ask forgiveness for in her prayers tonight, she plunked the quarter in the slot and turned it. A plastic ball fell into the mouth and Nat took it out, pulling the container apart to see which tattoo she had.

MOM, it said, in little sparkly letters with hearts and flowers, and Nat felt so guilty she dropped the stupid tattoo right on the floor and ran through the store, feeling the breath of her mother's censure rushing up her neck.

When she got home, she would go right to the altar in her bedroom and say as many Hail Marys as she could count, and she would never, ever, ever steal anything again.

This time, she really meant it.

Breakfast #14

Sopa De La Mañana: Our fresh fruit soup of the day, made from locally grown peaches, cantaloupes, apples, and strawberries, mixed with fresh, lightly spiced ricotta cheese and topped with chunks of our special, secret granola. Served with sourdough toast and butter. Ask your server for today's variety.

SOPA DE LA MAÑANA

6 cups peaches, peeled and sliced
1 cup ricotta cheese
1 cup plain yogurt
1 T honey
1 tsp orange zest

$^1/_2$ *tsp vanilla*
$^1/_2$ *tsp nutmeg*
$^1/_4$ *tsp ground cloves*

Puree fruit in a blender or food processor, add cheese and yogurt, blend. Add honey, zest, vanilla, and spices. Chill for at least two hours. Top with granola or sour cream.

VARIATIONS: Berries, cantaloupe, and apples are all great, too. Try it with buttermilk instead of yogurt, and omit the nutmeg and cloves.

FOUR

Vita Solano had three passions. The first was for food and, by extension, the café she had opened thirty years ago, a café that had become an icon in the mountain town of Los Ladrones.

The second was for running, which had saved her life after a man tried to steal it away from her.

The third was for extending the possibility of hope to women who had, usually because of a man, ended up in prison. In her café, she taught them to cook, and sometimes in the cooking, in the sweetness of tending those small things, they learned how to live.

After the restaurant closed for lunch this afternoon, she finally had time to work a little more with the new parolee in her kitchen, Annie Veracruz. The woman was a waif, too thin, hands too big at the end of skinny wrists. There were scars on her face and arms, some burned, some cut, probably self-inflicted. There were others, not self-inflicted at all. A long-healed scar through the eyebrow, the crookedness of a broken nose. Tattoos circled her wrists, decorated her back, her ankles. But she was only in her mid-thirties or so. Plenty of time to make a fresh start.

Right this minute, she was so nervous that she looked like she might nibble right through her mouth. She stepped forward with an expression of extreme concentration and took the pancake turner from Vita's outstretched hand.

"The trick to a perfectly cooked pancake," Vita said, "is to let the back get full of these little holes. See?" Air bubbles rose and gently exploded on the pancakes, leaving holes for steam. "You can see that the edge is getting a little bit done. Go ahead, turn it."

Annie slid the big spatula beneath the pancake and turned it as carefully as if it were gossamer. The edge caught on the way down and the pancake folded over, half cooked and half splayed. "Shit."

"That's all right," Vita said. "Just takes a little practice. Try again."

Anxiously humming an unrecognizable tune under her breath, Annie flipped the next one without incident. The baked side showed a beautiful toasted brown, exactly perfect. "Beautiful," Vita said. "Did anyone ever make pancakes for you?"

"Not really," she said, touching the edge of the next pancake with the very corner of the spatula. "I ate at the IHOP sometimes, though. I liked the pancakes there."

"How much have you cooked on your own?"

Annie shot her a wary look.

"There's no right answer. You're safe in the job as long as it's working for both of us. Most of the women who come here from the penal system haven't done much cooking. The idea is to equip you with a marketable skill."

"Right. Um. Not much." Her smile, lifting on just one side, was unexpectedly winning, with straight teeth and a whimsical aspect. "I can make mac and cheese out of a box."

"Good for you," Vita said with a smile. "It's a start. Slide those babies on the plate and we'll work with eggs. What's your favorite?"

"Fried, over easy," she said. "Just that edge of crispy white, you know what I mean?"

"Absolutely. To get that, you need a little more fat on the grill . . ." She dipped a brush into the square steel dish of butter at the back of the grill and slapped the bristles generously over the hot grill. "Eggs are particular," she said. "Make sure the grill is good and hot, and let the butter start to bubble a bit. Now crack the eggs on the counter, and gently empty the shells into the fat so the whites start to cook right away. See?"

Annie nodded.

Vita gave her an egg. "Try it. Right next to the first one."

Her fingernails were bitten clear down to the quick, Vita noticed. Annie cracked the egg smartly and eased the insides onto the grill.

"Perfect." Vita illustrated the moment to turn for an over-easy egg, when the whites still had the slightest bit of clear to them. "Make sure your spatula doesn't have anything clinging to it," Vita said, scraping it clean on the edge of the grill, "then slide it under the whole egg and turn it gently. Voilà!"

When the eggs were finished and plated, Vita fixed a slice of orange at the top of the dish, a ball of butter atop the pancakes, and said, "Go eat, babe."

"Really?"

"It's one of the fringe benefits of restaurant work." She patted the girl on the shoulder and headed into the office to do the book work. "Call me when you're done and we'll go over a couple of other things before you leave."

"Cool," said the woman, already forking the eggs into her mouth as if they might be stolen away.

Oh, baby, Vita thought. *Has anyone ever been good to you your whole life?*

At least she'd landed here. She would be here for a hundred days, as per the parole order. By then, maybe Vita could feed her enough love that she could make it out there in the world on her own, without trying to find another man who would abuse her.

It was worth a try.

After sleeping a few hours, Vince was a new man. The minute he got up, he called his mother to bring the girls home, and he was sitting on the front porch when she drove up in her sturdy, ancient Bronco. Sasha raced out of the yard, where she liked to sleep beneath an elm tree, and rushed into the curve of the drive, barking in frenzied greeting. Pedro stuck his head out of the window of the Bronco, telling his own stories.

The girls tumbled out of the truck like little blond lemurs, making so much more noise than it seemed possible for three small beings to make. They waded through the dogs and headed for the porch with some news, two of them looking like they'd rolled in something, the other as pristine as fresh laundry.

"Daddy! You're back! We got to—"

"*I* want to tell him!"

"Daddy, guess what?"

They raced to the porch and filled up his lap and arms with their sky-smelling hair and slight sleep-sweatiness and bony knees. "So what's the news?"

Natalie was the oldest, just turned eight, round and owlish in her little spectacles. She said, "Grandma got a kitten. He's—"

"I want to tell some of it, too!" Jade was the middle child, age six, with perfect long blond hair to her bottom.

The baby was Hannah, age three, still soft and cuddly and his alone. She crawled up in his lap, dragging her blanket and sucking her thumb. Her eyes were still swollen with sleep, and he kissed her head. "Okay, Jade, you tell something now."

She elbowed her sister, and Natalie shoved her back. They were way too close in age—seventeen months—and lived their lives in eternal, deadly competition. "His name is Leo, and he's six months old."

"He's black and white, with super-supersoft fur."

"And he has these little black mittens on his feet."

"He sounds really cute." Vince bumped his shoulder against Hannah's head. She grinned around her thumb and banged back against it. "How 'bout you, Little Bit, do you have anything to add to this tale of the cat?"

"He purrs. Like this—" She made a motor sound with her throat.

As if he'd heard, Pedro trotted up the stairs and shoved his fluffy big head under Hannah's hand. She laughed.

Vince's mother came up the steps carrying a duffel and two canvas bags that looked heavy.

"I would have carried those in if you'd said something."

Judy, more than six feet tall, with broad shoulders and a Katharine Hepburn sort of handsomeness, pished in dismissal. "I brought your chaos back to you."

"Happy chaos," he agreed.

"I washed all their clothes." She indicated the duffel. "And there's a lasagna and a bag of groceries here. I didn't think you'd have had time yet."

"I couldn't do it without you," Vince said. "Thanks."

"Grandma wouldn't buy me an apple," Natalie complained.

"That's because she had plenty to eat earlier, although she did refuse to eat any fish sticks last night."

"It's box food! You're not supposed to eat food like that!"

"Who says?"

"I watch food television," Natalie said haughtily.

Vince chuckled at his mother's sigh of exasperation.

"Oh, I forgot," Judy said drily. "That explains it all. Gimme kisses, girls. I've gotta get to town and take over for my hired help."

"Bye, Grandma!" They all waved, and when she was headed up the road, Vince said, "Did you guys have lunch yet?"

"We want peanut butter!" Jade cried.

"Peanut butter!" Little Bit said around her thumb.

Natalie groaned. "Why do we always have to eat little kid food?"

"You're a kid, stupe," Jade said.

"No name-calling," Vince cautioned.

"I don't have to eat idiotic things like you!"

"Maybe you should try eating like a kid and then you wouldn't be such an oinker!"

Before he could stop her, Natalie howled, "I hate you!" and shoved her sister off the porch. Jade fell in the dirt and leapt up with a screech, her perfect outfit marred by the heavy red dust of the New Mexico mountains. "Dad-*dy!*"

"That's enough, both of you." He stood up with the baby on his hip and nudged Nat toward the house. "Go to your room, Natalie."

"Me? She called me a pig!"

"Oinker," Jade corrected.

If Vince hadn't held fast to her arm, Natalie would have been on her sister again and likely would have drawn blood. "Go. To. Your. Room," he said to Natalie. "Jade, you're going to clean the bathrooms."

"But she—"

"Not another word. Go."

Crying, both sisters stomped into the house. Hannah patted his arm, silently sucking her thumb. Pedro had slid beneath the porch and now crawled out, covered with red dirt himself. He wagged his tail slowly as he looked to Vince for reassurance.

"You're a dog," Vince said. "A *big* dog. You're not supposed to be scared when little girls are having a fight."

Pedro, who stood as tall as the middle of Vince's thigh, came over and leaned on him. Absently, Vince rubbed his head, looking back toward the house. Did all sisters fight like this? It seemed unnatural, evil—though his mother said not to worry about it, they would outgrow it. They'd better, or he would end up wringing their necks.

"Peanut butter," Hannah said.

"You're right. Come on."

Beneath her pajamas in her bottom drawer, Natalie kept a cigar box. It was made of smooth reddish wood, varnished, with a metal clasp and carved words that were painted red and said, *Royal Butera vintage Premium Blended Cigars*. It wasn't very deep. She only had room for a few things. A plain black comb with a few long blond hairs clinging to it. A pair of turquoise earrings she would wear someday when she was allowed to get her ears pierced. A tarot card showing a castle tower on fire. A photo of her mother at age twelve, dressed up in a very short dress and poofy bangs. An embroidered bag that had herbs and a crystal inside. There was also a tiny crystal dish with fluted sides. It sat on a tiny metal plate and had a tiny silver spoon, carved with teensy swirls, to go with it. A salt cellar. Natalie loved it.

They all had belonged to her mother. Natalie took them out now, lining everything up in a row on her desk, which looked out over the meadow to the mountains. Once she'd seen a bear walking through the grass, looking so ordinary she didn't even think to be afraid until after he was gone, and then she'd been so scared she almost peed her pants.

Everyone thought she was forgetting about her mother, just like Jade, who didn't remember her because she was only three when Mommy died, or Hannah, who wasn't even three months old. Natalie had been five, and it was her job to make sure Mommy never got forgotten, so every week—she used to try to do it every day, but it was hard and she sometimes had to do homework—she brought out all these things and went through her list.

The comb made her think of Mommy's long blond hair, which she let Natalie brush sometimes when she wasn't too tired, and how it smelled of bacon sometimes after she finished making breakfast for everybody, or like soap after a shower, or sometimes perfume when she had gone out to dinner with Daddy. When she looked at the picture, Natalie could remember how Mommy's mouth looked when she smiled. Natalie had stolen the tarot card off the table when her grandma Leanne— who lived in Denver, where they used to live—came in and swept all of them on the floor the day Mommy died.

The salt cellar was the most precious of all. Her mother had it for years and years before she even met Natalie's dad. She bought it at an antiques store in England, which was far across the ocean. Mommy thought the salt cellar was so adorable, she just had to have it, even though it meant carrying it around all over Europe in her backpack. She carried it home and kept it forever.

Natalie would keep it forever, too. Today, with her heart stinging over getting in trouble and the hatefulness of school starting, Natalie felt empty and cold, looking at the things on her desk. It was getting hard to remember things sometimes, like exactly how Mommy sounded when she talked. She could remember the singing, because she had a tape with Mommy singing songs to help her fall asleep, but the talking voice seemed far away, and that scared her. What if she *forgot*?

She was supposed to stay in her room, but she had to talk to her dad about this right now. She rushed down the stairs and found him in the kitchen, making a sandwich for Hannah, who didn't get in trouble ever because she was the baby.

"Dad," Natalie said, "what did Mom's voice sound like?"

It was a fact that her dad was the most handsomest dad in the whole town. Even Emma Richardson, the richest girl in her class, who had a *planetarium* in her house, had to admit it. And right now, when Daddy's dark brown eyes got all soft and he made an exaggerated frown to make her feel better, putting Hannah down so he could put Natalie on his lap, he was even handsomer. "You missing your mom?"

"I just can't remember things sometimes. You remember, don't you?"

He rubbed her back. "Of course I do. She had a nice soft voice, remember? Kind of like your auntie Cheryl, but a little bit higher."

Natalie closed her eyes. It helped. Her neck didn't feel like it had turned into a rock anymore. "I do remember," she said.

"Hey!" Jade cried, coming out of the bathroom with stupid

yellow gloves on her hands. "She's supposed to be in her room!"

Her dad patted Natalie's arm. "It's true. Why don't you go back to your room and we'll talk later, okay?"

She shrugged off his hand. "Whatever." In front of Jade, she bent over and whispered, "I hate you!"

In the late afternoon, Tessa carried her laptop down to the courtyard of the old hotel and ordered an ale from the extensive menu. Geraniums and marigolds bloomed in pots around a chuckling fountain. Small knots of people, twos and threes, grazed on chips and salsa and drank glasses of white wine. They were a tanned, gleaming set, with men in dark sunglasses and women who had perfect blond streaks. Not Tessa's usual scene, but Mick always liked to choose a high-end hotel as a starting point.

At least here she could see some others in her general tribe: hikers with hundred-dollar hydration packs on the chair beside them; runners who probably had six different pairs of trail shoes; women in sports tanks and hiking pants. They had the satisfied look of having bagged a good hike, and it made her anxious to get out on the trails. Her foot still got sore very easily, but she was anxious to find some trails and put it to the test, just to get a feeling for the landscape and area.

The beer came, a rich amber, and Tessa took a long swallow. Beer was one of the great inventions of the universe. She loved all of them—stouts and lagers and ales—and with the explosion of microbreweries around the country, she could nearly always get something terrific. This was a hoppy, malty ale, dense and rich. Perfect for a hot late-summer afternoon.

Feeling mellow, she turned on the computer to edit the photos she'd uploaded before coming downstairs. The raccoons made her laugh, looking straight into the camera with an expression of *What? You never saw anybody eat before?* She sent the picture to her father, along with the shots of the white dog in the red dust. One of them was particularly good—the dog's white fur contrasting with the turquoise sky and brick-red earth, and she uploaded it to her Flickr account, which she'd been keeping for years now. Several times she'd taken a photo that showed up on the *Most Interesting List,* and her photos routinely garnered dozens of stars and favorites and invitations to post to groups.

She titled the photo *A variation on red white and blue. This is America, too.*

It was the first time she'd been lost in her photo world for ages, and it was remarkably peaceful, a pursuit without much thought, playing with color, with shadow and light, with composition and balance, with the exact mix to bring focus on what the eye should see. The shots of the old farmers at the market this morning were fantastic. She loved their hands, their crisp shirts, the sharp line of hair above their collars.

There were more. A few other shots of the farmers' market that burst with color and shape and vibrancy; a shot of the ancient cottonwood; one of the lane last night, narrow and ending in the cantina.

As a teenager, Tessa had written an essay declaring the goals for her life. There were three: She wanted to see the world, buy her dad a house, and have a photo published in *National Geographic.* On the first one, she'd made fairly decent progress—she'd been to thirty-seven countries and actually lived in four. The second had been achieved when she helped her father buy the little bungalow in Santa Cruz seven years ago. She'd given up the idea of getting a photo published in *National Geographic,* but she still loved photography as part of her job— really, her avocation.

By the time she'd edited the photos she'd uploaded since arriving in Los Ladrones, she was starving and ordered a casual supper of soup and bread. While she waited, she surreptitiously watched a pair of lovers—she a vision of cascading hair, he much older and smitten and wealthy.

On the table, her phone flashed and spun around in a vibration dance. Tessa picked it up. "Hi, Dad," she answered, turning away from the other diners and lowering her voice to be polite. "I just sent you a picture you will love."

"In the mail?"

"No," she said with the exaggerated patience she used for his computer allergy. "To your email address. It's totally free."

"It won't be free when I have to pay the guy at the Internet café."

"You know the answer. A computer of your very own!"

He made a dismissive noise. Honestly, she thought with a smile, it seemed like the most computer-resistant population was in Sam's demographic: ex-hippies and Vietnam vets suspicious of "the man." "You having a good time?"

"Ran into some rain on the way in, which was freaky, but other than that, it's great. Did we go to movies at the Chief Theater?"

"Probably. I don't remember. Look familiar?"

"Yes."

"Learning anything?"

She drank a long swallow of beer. "Not really, not yet. I'm in the main hotel, on the plaza, and I went to the farmers' market this morning and ate at the famous café, where," she said, smiling, "I had the *best* oatmeal. In your honor."

"That's sweet." He told her about his surfing on great waves stirred up by a front, and hearing his voice made her miss him a little. There was no one like Sam.

What, she wondered, had he been like when he first arrived in Los Ladrones? He'd gone to Vietnam and come back furious, dropped out, and traveled the country on a motorcycle. More than one of his endless store of adventures involved brushes with the police and not a few actual arrests for petty trespasses—fighting, drinking, the usual.

That had all stopped when Tessa was born, and although he'd still pursued an unconventional career, he'd been sober and straightforward and never in trouble.

"Do you have any pictures of yourself when you were at the commune, Dad?"

"Maybe, somewhere. Why do you want them?"

"Just curious, really. I'm thinking about the past, thinking about you, what you looked like then."

"Handsome," he said.

"Of course."

"You know, Tessa, there are times in a person's life that aren't worth remembering. I've tried to forget about the commune days. I understand why you're there, but it wasn't the best time in my life, you know?"

"Right. Sorry."

"No apology necessary, kiddo. I'm just not all that crazy about revisiting the whole thing myself."

"Understood." The waiter brought her soup, and Tessa straightened. "My supper just got here. I'm going to let you go, all right? Kiss Peaches for me."

"Will do. Give yourself a hug from your dad."

"Go look at the pictures I sent!"

"I will."

Tessa clipped the phone closed and buttered her bread, wondering why the conversation had left her feeling so uneasy.

FIVE

When she was released from prison, Annie Vera-cruz had rented an efficiency apartment above the drugstore, right on the plaza. It was small and, to be honest, slightly grimy. The couch was brown with itchy specks in it, and there was a recliner that listed to the left and would only actually recline if you reached down and pulled on the foot part. An old-school television that had a good strong picture and a box to bring in basic cable was shoved against the wall. The kitchen was just a fridge, a sink, a skinny battered old stove, and six inches of counter, but there was a big window that looked over the mountains and a red table with red vinyl chairs.

She loved that table. Yesterday, she'd gone out specifically to collect yellow flowers to put in a water glass with blue and yellow stripes. Now, as she walked into the room to get ready for work, there they were, glowing, mostly sunflowers but a few other wildflowers she didn't know how to name. It was beautiful. The whole time she was making her breakfast—pouring Cheerios into a bowl and slicing a banana into it, and smelling the tea in the air—she was sliding glances toward that glassful of yellow against the red table and plain wall. Sunshine started to edge into the room from the east, and in a few minutes it would all blaze. Annie was ready.

And when it happened, she was sitting at her table with a bowl of her favorite cereal, Honey Nut Cheerios—not just the plain ones, which sometimes they did give you in jail, and the perfect arrangement of bananas, just like on the box, and a cup of milky tea. Then the music of the light moved right over the petals of the flowers, setting them afire, and Annie took a bite of cereal, her own heart blazing with joy.

Free. She was free. There was a thick bracelet around her ankle that she'd have to wear for a year, but the jail time was done, and, even better, her time with Tommy was done.

Free. And she didn't intend to waste a single second of it. She celebrated with yellow flowers and Cheerios and tea made just as she liked it.

Free.

Church bells rang exuberantly, welcoming the faithful to Mass. They clanged Tessa awake on Sunday morning. Turning over, she tossed the wilted covers off her body—and slammed right into the black hole that had been living in the middle of her chest for three months.

She did not believe in wallowing and lacked patience for navel-gazing dramas. And yet here she was, stuck in this airlessness, struggling to breathe while the black hole sucked her down.

It was a dark place, created equally from genuine sorrow, searing regret, and bitter self-recrimination. Because Tessa had not done her job, a woman was dead. How, exactly, did you ever make that right?

She was as good as a man at compartmentalizing her life—

putting everything into its own box and dealing with only what was right in front of her. To some degree, that still worked with the disaster in Montana. Aside from panic attacks, the odd nightmare, and these unguarded moments when it all showed up to crush her.

I'm fine, she thought, turning over. *Why do you ask? Ha-ha.*

A psychologist in the hospital had told her that if she didn't deal with all the emotion attached to the doomed trip, she could expect to continue to be ambushed by panic attacks.

Mostly, she could avoid thinking about it. Mostly, she simply pushed it away. But then she would notice the still-shiny scar tissue on her foot, and suddenly she'd be back on the morning of that last day in Montana. She had thought, clearly, that she should not go out, that the spider bite was too infected.

But she powered through, because that's what she did—she was strong, she was the leader. When the mountain came down in an avalanche of mud, dumping Lisa and her into the river, Tessa was so addled from the infection that she'd made huge mistakes.

There was the black hole. Nothing she could say, nothing she could do would ever justify it or make it right. Lisa had died directly because she had entrusted herself to Tessa's care. Lisa headed out to save them because Tessa told her to, and she died.

Lying very still in the center of the bed, with the bells ringing and ringing, Tessa let the weight press her down, smother her. It was so unfair that she was still on the planet, walking around, while Lisa's mother was probably breaking down over a kitchen sink somewhere, her hands in rubber gloves, the forks falling back into the water as she bent over, crying.

So unfair.

Lisa was gone for good. Forever. Because, plain and simple, Tessa did not do what she should have done. How did a person ever make that okay?

She didn't know. Wallowing would be too easy and would only add to her sins, trying to get sympathy for the crime of hubris.

"Enough," she said aloud, and pulled herself out of bed.

Slightly sweaty even in the skinny cotton tank and gray shorts she slept in, Tessa washed her face, brushed her tangled hair and pulled it into a scrunchie, and made some hot water for tea. While the water heated, she opened the French doors to the plaza to let a breeze in, thinning the stale overnight air in her room. It smelled of spruce and possibility, and she breathed in gratefully.

Here I am.

A waft of a dream came to her as she stood in the doorway, arms crossed loosely. Tasmania. She'd been dreaming of Tasmania, where she had lived for six happy years, four of them with the man she had believed she would marry. The happiest she had ever been in her life. Something about the air here, halfway around the world, made her think of Glenn and the town of Hobart, where they had lived between a towering mountain and the sea. It must have been the market yesterday, reminding her of the Salamanca Market on Saturdays in Hobart.

It was in Tasmania, while living with Glenn, that she had become accustomed to drinking strong Australian-style tea, made the English way with milk and sugar. She carried English tea bags with her whenever she traveled in America.

While her cup brewed this morning, she checked email and

then started working with her photos again. She selected a few to send to her boss and then pulled up the little girl watching the dancers at the cantina the other night. Idly, one foot tucked under her knee, tea steaming at her elbow, Tessa cropped it, bringing the focus to the chubby little fingers, the falling-down sock.

The photos of Vince were there, too. *Mama mia.* He was freaking gorgeous. A soft wash of red light illuminated his throat, caught in his hair, along the curve of his lip. His chest, one sturdy thigh.

A quiver of lust moved through her. She wasn't usually attracted to such big men, but something about his giant legs and giant hands was working on her libido.

Search and rescue, she thought. How appropriate.

She heard herself humming "Rescue Me" under her breath, and snorted. It broke a little of her dark mood, and she took a sip of tea, laughing at herself.

Maybe she was just horny. It had been a fairly long time since she'd had a man in her bed. Only a couple of times since she broke up with Glenn, which was probably a good thing. She really had not wanted some big rebound thing. Too much drama.

She clicked forward, found the picture of Vince looking into the camera, long lashes and direct gaze, and a distinct zing worked its way through her belly.

Anyway. She clicked the photo closed.

A plan for today.

There was no big hurry—she had decided last night that she wanted to spend more than a week here. She'd find a cheaper room in a few days, allow herself the time and pleasure of exploring the town that so charmed her, follow whatever links might come up to help her piece together her shattered memory.

She did need to get organized, however. She wanted to meet with the woman who ran 100 Breakfasts and visit other restaurants in town, map out some possible hikes and outdoor activities. On the table was a thick glossy book of trails in northern New Mexico, and she flipped through the chapters on the area around Los Ladrones with keen hunger. She was dying to get out on the trails again! She absolutely respected the healing process, but it had been way too long since she'd been able to take a good long walk.

Easy does it. She'd have to pace herself. Start small and gauge her progress carefully.

In between, there were plenty of other things to do. She would definitely explore the church and the pilgrimage route to the shrine, and discover any attractive legends and stories they could use in the brochure. She also needed to visit Green Gate Farms. And, for herself, she needed to go down to the river.

A coppery cold moved along her spine at the thought. It could wait.

This morning, she'd head down to the hotel restaurant and check out their brunch. Much as she'd love to just go back to 100 Breakfasts, she should sample more than one meal at the hotel. And there might be some celebrity-sightings, too. Always fun.

The heat surprised her when she left the hotel in late morning. It murmured around her as she walked down the portico in the deep shade, but when she stepped out of the shadows, the sun fell on her skin like a skillet, heavy and hot. She paused for a moment, closing her eyes, letting it sink deep into her bones. Sunlight at such a high altitude had ferocity to it, texture, weight.

"Don't forget your sunscreen, young lady," said a man passing by.

Tessa opened her eyes. He was thin and stooped, maybe eighty or a little more, and she'd seen him doing his loops around the plaza yesterday. She smiled. "It feels good, doesn't it?"

"I like the snow myself, but we're not long off for that, so it's all right I reckon." He waved twisted fingers her way and marched onward.

Earlier, the church bells had been ringing loud and long. Tessa had looked up the history of the ancient church on the Internet as she ate her breakfast on the patio, covertly watching a pair of actors feed each other cubed cantaloupe.

Her father had told her there were ghosts attached to the church, and the history of the place certainly lent itself to that idea. Maybe the missionaries slaughtered by the Indians, or the Indians the Spanish slaughtered when they returned. There had also been a raid by the Comanche, who stole seven women from a wedding feast.

Standing now in the high, hot sun, Tessa shaded her eyes to look at it. It was the kind of church painters could not resist, with adobe covering its curved bones like peachy flesh, exaggerated by the sharp shadow cast by that fierce sun. Over the whole stretched the plastic blue sky. Constructed simply, it had two bell towers, with a heavy pine doorway between them. A wall created a protected garden in front. A bus with its motor still running was parked in the narrow street in the rear, and milling tourists shot it from several angles.

Tessa resisted shooting it now, when there were so many people about. Not only the cluster of tourists from the bus but another knot of people had gathered outside the wall, at the base of what looked to be a trail. Most of them were barefoot, and as she watched, they took off their hats and gave water bottles to a young man collecting them in a box.

She asked a man nearby, "Do you know what they're doing?"

"Pilgrims," he said. "They walk to the top of the mountain to visit a shrine."

"Ah, I read about that."

Through her viewfinder she focused on a woman who looked to be in her sixties, with curly salt-and-pepper hair and knobby knees. A rosary looped around her left wrist, green beads glittering. For a minute, Tessa was lost in the repetitive shapes—curls and kneecaps and beads. Joy, the soft white of clouds, moved in her. She was shooting everything in her drunken rediscovery and would be lucky to get even a handful of great shots, but it didn't matter. The colors and shapes, the quietness of seeing the world only in a single frame at a time was filling some empty chamber of her heart.

She made a mental note to check the length of the pilgrimage route and its difficulty. It was the kind of walk she always did in any locale—whatever was notable or interesting. Maybe, before she left, she'd be able to hike it.

For now she would explore the church. Entering through the wooden gates set into the adobe wall, Tessa found herself in a splendiferous garden. Trumpet vines, blooming orange in defiance of the heat, covered the internal walls, mixed with wilted morning glories. Corn with silky new tassels grew in tidy rows, along with the elephant-ear leaves of squashes and tomatoes staked within wire supports.

A young priest with dark-framed glasses and a black shirt with short sleeves filled a basket with zucchini and crooknecks. When he spied Tessa, he nodded. "Good morning."

"Weren't these courtyards usually given to graves?" she asked him.

"They were. Very good." He straightened, brushing off his knees. "It was so dangerous here at St. Nicholas that the garden was created inside the walls and the bodies buried behind the church. Even so, the first missionaries were killed."

Tessa held back a slight smile. "That's what you get for 'nailing lifts to the natives' feet.'"

His dark eyes held a bright twinkle. "George Carlin."

"Very good."

"We do get out now and then to hear something of the world."

"Touché." She gestured to the healthy plants. "It looks very fertile."

"Well, we have animals in the pasture. Once, they kept the animals inside the walls, too, but that's not such a problem for us nowadays." He slapped his gloves together.

"Do you sell what you grow at the farmers' market?"

"Oh, no, my dear. All of this produce goes to the poor. We feed many every year."

"Now, that's a church program that makes sense. Do you do all the work yourself?"

"Afraid not. I mainly putter. There's a garden committee that plans and tends it for us. One of our parishioners runs the kitchens at Green Gate Farms, and she's been gardening organically for twenty years. She's helped us set up a system that works very well."

Tessa watched a fat bumblebee, heavy with nectar, launch himself lazily from the wide trumpet of a squash blossom.

Pumpkins ripened near the wall, and she could make out peppers, garlic, onions, and what might be potatoes. "So is this all organic, too?"

"It is," he said proudly.

The sound of the bus trundling up the hill, away from the church, barely disturbed the depth of silence. "Why St. Nicholas? Isn't he Santa Claus?"

"He's the patron saint of thieves—*los ladrones.*"

"Ah! Of course." She grinned. "Is the pilgrimage to St. Nicholas, too?"

"No, it's a shrine to the Blessed Mother."

She nodded. "Do you get a lot of tourists here?"

"A few. The pilgrims—did you see them leaving?—come once or twice a month. It's usually a church group or something like that. Once," he said with a grin, "we had a Red Hat Society make the trek."

Tessa chuckled.

"Mostly, it's just a bus that stops on its way to see something else. The church is not that important or particularly unusual." He stabbed at a weed with his toe. "The tourists come for the town."

"How long has the foodie thing been going on?"

"Oh, that." He waved a hand.

"You don't like it?"

He smiled gently. "It's very indulgent, isn't it? Greed and gluttony mixed together with a big helping of lust."

Startled by the acuity of his observation, Tessa laughed. "True. But it's also beauty and nurturance and creation, right?"

"Absolutely. All things in balance." His smile broadened. He couldn't be thirty, and yet an old soul gazed at her through dark brown eyes. Stepping forward, he offered his hand. "I'm Father Timothy," he said.

"Tessa Harlow." His grip was strong and solid. "How far is it to the top of the mountain?"

"Four miles and a bit, and nearly twenty-five hundred feet in altitude."

She raised her eyebrows. "Wow. Steep!"

"Well," he said gently, "a pilgrimage is meant to be trying."

"I see."

"If you'd like a less challenging walk, the lake is only a mile and a half."

She wanted to protest, to present her credentials, like a badge of fitness—she had led adventure tours all over the world! She had sometimes hiked more than twenty miles a day in rugged terrain!—but it would all be a smoke screen. Four miles—eight by the time she returned—would be far more than she could do on her still-healing foot. Even a mile and a half might be pushing it, but she was going to give it a try. "Thanks."

"The views are magnificent."

A woman with the cropped hair and round shape of a life-long nun appeared at the door of the rectory. "Father? There's a call for you."

"Excuse me." He bowed. "Good to meet you."

Before Natalie's dad had to work on Saturday morning, rescuing somebody who wasn't supposed to be climbing the rocks anyway, they were all supposed to go on a picnic. Instead, they got stuck at Grandma's, and now they were going on a picnic today and it was hot, hot, hot.

Natalie sat in the shade beneath the tree in the plaza, holding her sister Hannah's hand, waiting for her dad to come out of the drugstore with sunscreen. They had to *walk* to the lake, naturally, because nobody could ever just drive anywhere around here. Already her skin was prickly down her back. Her grandma said she should wear a hat, but Natalie just did not see how that would make a person cooler.

She would rather stay right here in the shade all day and read a book. Climb up into the tree, maybe, and then come down later and go into Le Fleur de Mer and look at salts from the Dead Sea, which she imagined was probably a desert, all glittery in the sunshine like diamonds even though it was big crystals of gray salt. The lady in there didn't like Natalie to come in by herself; she said it was nothing that would interest a child, but she didn't know Natalie. Or that she had her own salt cellar and was just waiting to find the right salt to put in it.

She swung her feet, banging her heels against the wall, and slapped a fly away from her neck. He was drinking the sweat, she thought. Disgusting.

After she visited the salt store, she would go into the drugstore for a cherry phosphate, made with cherry syrup and lime juice and plain soda water right out of the fountain. The man took a maraschino cherry and a triangle of lime, stuck them on a tiny plastic sword, and propped it on the top of the ice. It came in a shapely glass in a silver holder, with a fat paper straw, not plastic. She would sit at the counter on one of the turquoise chairs that swung back and forth and look at magazines, maybe the one with Rachael Ray on it, because she always seemed really really nice, or one of the ones that had beautiful pictures of cakes on the front. It didn't matter. When she opened those magazines, it seemed like a whole world whispered out at her, inviting her inside their glossy pages to share a secret.

If she closed her eyes, she could imagine the counter inside the drugstore, the fan swirling air over her head, the pages of her magazine riffling a little. She would take tiny, tiny sips of the phosphate to make it last an hour, and only then would she eat the cherry.

"Don't nod off on me, sleepyhead," her dad said, all cheery, like she wanted to walk to some stupid lake and eat stupid mushy bananas and stupid lunchmeat sandwiches.

"I'm not," she said crossly. "Do we have to go on a picnic? Can't we just have a picnic here?"

"No!" Jade roared. "I want to swim!" She had a red-and-white polka-dot bathing suit under her shorts, and her hair was braided tightly in one long white horsetail down her back.

"Me, too! Swim!" said Hannah, who still talked like a baby, even though she was three. Grandma said it was because everybody talked for her.

Daddy sat down next to Natalie. "You don't want to go swimming? It'll feel pretty good up there. And I got you a surprise for lunch."

"What surprise?" she asked without excitement. "A candy bar?"

"Nope. Something good. Something only you would think to ask for."

A kindling of hope sparked in her chest. "Really?"

Sometimes, not often, he actually got it right. She wasn't holding her breath or anything, but she stood up and put her backpack on. "Okay." Pedro scrambled to his feet and she took his leash. "Let's go."

Breakfast #59

Baked French Toast with Fruit: Our special-recipe French toast, made with fresh raisin bread, honey collected from local bees, and spices, served with fresh strawberries or peaches, and bananas, fresh whipped cream, and organic butter. Served with organic or soy sausage, coffee, tea, or milk.

BAKED FRENCH TOAST

8 thick slices raisin bread*
6 eggs
³/₄ cup milk
¹/₄ tsp baking powder
1 T vanilla

FOR FRUIT LAYER
10 oz. frozen or 2 cups fresh strawberries, sliced
4 bananas, thickly sliced
¹/₃ cup honey
1 tsp cinnamon
¹/₄ tsp nutmeg
¹/₄ tsp allspice
Pinch of cardamom
Cinnamon sugar

Place bread slices close together in a flat pan with high sides. Combine all other ingredients and pour the mixture over bread, cover, and refrigerate overnight.

* See recipe for fresh Raisin Bread on page 229.

In the morning:

Layer strawberries and bananas in a glass casserole dish.
Pour honey over them, then sprinkle with spices. Carefully
place slices of egg-soaked bread on top. If any egg mixture
remains in the pan, simply pour over the top. Sprinkle with
cinnamon sugar.

Bake at 450 degrees for 20–25 minutes.

SIX

After the priest went inside, Tessa wandered around the garden at the church, making notes. The harsh early-afternoon sun didn't lend itself to photos, but she'd come back another time. She had planned to also explore the interior of the church, but when she peeked in, a handful of people were gathered in a circle, praying, and she didn't want to intrude.

Exiting the garden, she wandered around the outside of the walls, half expecting to remember something. Although there was something intimately familiar about the hot sun and the smell of the earth, the church itself gave her nothing. Her mother had been a hippie, after all. Why would she have come into town to go to Mass?

In the distance, she spied a man with long dark hair, walking fiercely toward the back of the church. Reminded of the man—"the Coyote Man"—who had radiated such fury at the cantina, she followed him, curious. The smell of his cigarette fouled the air as she came around the corner.

Behind the church, nestled beneath the shade of elm trees that had shed a shower of twigs over the buffalo grass, was a small graveyard. The man was gone, maybe up the path to the pilgrim site or on a path down toward the river.

She shrugged him off and shot a quick series of the shaded churchyard—very old, judging by the tilt of the headstones. Its picturesque light would appeal to her boss. It would look beautiful in the brochure.

Across the yard, on a park bench next to a chuckling little fountain, was a dark-haired woman and a white cat. Both were skinny, cat and woman, and the angles of the woman's cheekbones were echoed in the sharpness of the cat's triangular face. There was grace in their movements, something feline in the angle of the woman's head, something female and hungrily human in the cat's acceptance of the long strokes down her back. Around the woman's wrists were tattoos, and her collarbones stuck out in sharp relief. Tessa took out her camera and focused her lens on the pair.

A press of sorrow sliced through her, and Tessa jerked involuntarily. She lowered the camera, pressed a hand to her heart. Maybe there *were* ghosts around here.

Maybe she didn't want to bother these two. Or be here right now. She slipped away, around the tree, leaving them alone. She put the camera away in her pack, retied her left tennis shoe, and took out a bottle of water and an open weave hat she adored. Putting it on made her feel more in control, as if she was a tour leader who knew her stuff after all.

From the other direction came a ragged black-and-white dog. She glanced at him, then glanced back, suddenly recognizing him. It was her friend from the restaurant the other night.

"Hey, you," she said, kneeling. She held out a hand, palm up. He glanced over his shoulder with a worried expression, then came over to her, head down apprehensively, and sniffed her fingers. Tessa murmured to him, running her hands over his head, down his spine. Each bone was as big as a knuckle. She searched in her pack for food and gave him half of a protein bar. It took him a long time to chew it, but he didn't give up.

"I have to go now, honey," she said, and tossed a roll into the forest for him. Maybe that was the wrong thing to do, feed him. But how could she not? He dashed after the roll, white socks flashing. Turning her back, Tessa headed toward the lake. When she looked back after a minute, the dog was gone.

The trail headed up the mountain beneath stands of mixed pine, ponderosa with their long needles and spicy bark, paler spruce, and ordinary red pine. As she walked, Tessa made mental notes about the trail itself—well traveled and tamped down, with exposed rocks and roots in places. It would be a mess after a rain, the earth a deep clay red that would stain everything it touched, but in the worst spots the park service had laid railroad ties. The flora was standard Rocky Mountains at eight thousand feet—mixed in with the pines were yucca and prickly pear, scrub oak and wild raspberries. Another thousand feet of altitude and there would be aspens, but the trail toward the lake split off before it climbed that high.

The air smelled of sunbaked pine needles and freshness. She was alone, in her body, walking. Finally. Her foot was sore, and she made a conscious effort not to limp, but it wasn't bad. Unused muscle came to life in her thighs and shoulders and glutes, and light sweat broke down her neck and over her chest. The altitude made her breathe a little harder than normal, and the climb got her blood pumping. Suddenly she felt little explosions of endorphins that flooded her with a happiness so fierce she almost wanted to weep.

This was her world. God, she was missing it!

Although Tessa and her father had always spent a fair

amount of time outside, sometimes camping, they'd never done any hiking. Sam preferred the water. And while Tessa had reluctantly learned to swim finally—at a pool, inside, at the YMCA—she had never found any love for the ocean or rivers or lakes. She wasn't phobic; she just didn't enjoy swimming that much.

So she'd tended to think of herself as a person without athletic inclinations. She loved reading. She loved movies and television and friends and music and dogs.

In college, she'd fallen for a guy who was an avid hiker and camper, and to spend more time with him, she tagged along, to Lake Tahoe and on trails overlooking the ocean and into the mountains. To her amazement, she found joy in the soft buzz in her legs and hips at the end of a long day of walking, the genial company on the trails, with the boots and packs and the reward of drinking beers with like-minded souls afterward.

Mostly she loved the feeling of being alive under the sky, touching the earth, being wholly herself. Sweating. Walking. Thinking. Admiring. On the trail, she didn't bring her troubles. There was only room for wind and sky and sun and rain and humming under her breath.

As she did now, on the trail toward the lake above Los Ladrones. A breathy tune. She paused to listen: "Climb Every Mountain." She laughed. *The Sound of Music* was in the regular rotation, but it was usually the title song.

"Corny, Tessa. Very corny."

She made it to the lake in just under forty minutes, not a bad time for the distance and climb. It would be quite accessible for nearly anyone in her groups—even those who had not hiked a great deal before. The walk could take an hour up and an hour back down, and they could eat on the sandy shore of the small blue lake.

Nice.

She had expected that there would be more people, but on this side it was deserted. In the distance, on the other shore of the lake, were fishermen and picnickers, who must have driven up from the north end of the mountain. A trail ran around the water, maybe a couple of miles. Tumbles of boulders provided perches for sunning; the beach was flat and clean.

Beautiful. Tessa stood with her hands on her hips, sweating lightly, surveying the scene. Perfect! She could lead the group up the hill, around the lake, stop for a lunch, and walk back down. Most of their tours were more vigorous than that—with hikes of up to fifteen miles in a day, several days in a row—but there were always easy and/or optional days of mellower walks thrown in.

She sat down on a rock right at the waterline and took a long swallow of water from the bottle she carried. As the priest had promised, the views were stunning, postcard cutouts of mountains layering one against the next into the distance, with a long valley between. A river snaked through the valley floor, silvery in the bright afternoon. It must be the Ladrones River, she thought, orienting herself. And there, like a toy village, was the town of Los Ladrones.

Something about it—the colors or the angle, or the mountains, or maybe her dream from the night before—made her think, suddenly and with a piercing longing, of Tasmania. The island lay south of mainland Australia, an underpopulated landscape of mountains and water—equal parts Scotland and Australia and American West—that had captured her imagination completely.

Or, more truthfully, it had been Glenn who captured her. Tasmania was simply the landscape that had spawned him.

How could it sting so much, after two years? How could she,

who had made an art form of footloose, easy connections, have allowed herself to fall so madly, passionately, *blindly* in love? It was embarrassing how much she had loved him, how snivelingly devastated she'd been when he fell in love with a fellow scientist and cleanly, matter-of-factly broke Tessa's heart in two.

Humiliating how much she *still* sometimes missed him, or at least the life they had created together. Missed Tasmania and a sense of having roots in a place.

"Don't start, Harlow," she said aloud, and irritably stripped off her shoes and socks. The scar where they'd had to clean out the infected spider bite was still angry and dark, nearly two solid inches across, in the shape of Texas. She poked the flesh, feeling the tenderness deep within. Not healed yet. After the long walk, it was sore, and tonight she would probably have to soak it before she went to sleep. She thought about sticking it in the lake, but maybe it would be better to avoid that for a while longer.

Time. Things took time to heal.

Taking a towel out of her pack, she stripped off her shirt and lay back on the beach in her sports bra, letting the hot sun sear her eyelids and belly and knees. The buzz of exercise moved in her limbs, and her brain was happily tired, too.

She must have dozed off, because she came awake sometime later to the breath of an animal in her ear. She sat upright, startled. A dog barked a greeting.

Her friend from the first day, the Akita mix, white and fluffy with black-tipped ears.

Again.

"What are you doing here, buddy?" she asked, reaching up to bury her hands in the fur around his neck. "How do you keep finding me? Are you my soul mate?"

He grinned at her, bowing happily before giving a cheery little bark–growl, like Scooby-Doo, then looked back toward the trail. Behind him trooped the three little girls he'd been with yesterday, the older girl looking hot and sweaty and annoyed. Bringing up the rear was a man, obviously their father.

He carried a midsize dog over his shoulder, and he wore no shirt, only a pair of jeans and hiking boots. A blue T-shirt was tucked into his back pocket, swaying like a tail. As he reached the beach, he bent down and tenderly put the old dog on the ground so she could make her pigeon-toed way toward the shade, panting hard but happy.

Tessa noticed that his biceps were ringed with tattoos and a star adorned his inner left wrist. It was only when he raised his head that she realized who it was. Vince. The guy from the restaurant.

Again she was captured by his hair, thick and dark and glossy, and the powerful cage of his ribs. His belly was faintly soft, pale, as if he didn't go without his shirt very often. "Girls, slow down!" he roared.

Sitting there with the sun pouring down hard on her head, Tessa's hands got sweaty and her starved libido sat up straight and said, *Okay, he'll do.* Hot. Very hot.

Of course he had three little girls, and of course *this* dog was the crotch sniffer, and of course the owlish little creature who'd been so hostile in the plaza now glared at her again.

"He's *my* dog," the girl said, tugging on his collar. "Come on, Pedro."

"Is it okay if I just pet him?" Tessa asked. "I think he likes me."

"Natalie," said her father. "Let him go. He's fine."

Pedro leaned heavily against Tessa, and she instinctively put an arm around him. His lungs moved against her side, panting. "You must be his favorite," Tessa said to appease the little girl.

"No," she said with a very adult understanding. "He's *my* favorite." She wore an unfortunate combination of clothes— a shirt in horizontal stripes that was too small and showed a slice of smooth, plump tummy and a pair of shorts that rode up between her thighs. Her cheeks were flushed. "Our other dog just wants food."

Tessa nodded. "My dad has three dogs, and one of his is like that. Lives to eat."

"Three dogs?" Behind her glasses, the little girl's eyes were the color of blue raspberry syrup. "That's a lot."

"It is," Tessa agreed. "And one of them? Guess how old she is?"

The girl looked at the old dog panting in the shade. "Sasha is fifteen. Older than that?"

Tessa nodded and pointed her thumb at the sky.

"Eighteen?"

"Twenty-three," Tessa said.

"No way."

"True story." Tessa raised her right hand to swear it.

The girl narrowed her eyes. "That's impossible."

Vince came up beside his daughter. "Get into your swimsuit, kiddo." He held out a red one-piece and tilted his head toward the trees. "Nobody will see you over there."

"I don't want to go swimming."

"Nonnegotiable. You want your surprise, don't you?"

She glared at him from under her eyelashes. "It better be good." She grabbed the suit and stomped off.

"Hello," Tessa said, shading her eyes to look up at him. "We've got to stop meeting like this."

"Tessa, right?" He sat down beside her, arms resting on his knees. The tattoo on the right was an elaborate tribal, woven with color.

"That's right."

"I'm Vince."

"*I* remembered." She scrubbed the dog's chest. "And this is your crotch sniffer, I guess."

"Yep. Pedro the wild man."

"And the girls, all yours?"

He nodded. "Guilty." Looking in the direction of the trees, he said, "She's not always a brat. Eight has not been the best year so far."

"She's not bratty. Just forthright."

"Yeah. Just wait."

He wore no wedding ring, but Tessa asked, "And where is their mother?"

"She's dead. Three years."

"Oh." She hadn't been expecting that. "I'm sorry."

He nodded, scratching the dog's head. "What'd you do to my dog? Give him a love potion? He's not usually all that friendly."

"I met him before I met you, actually," she said, and traced the line of black on the tip of his ears. His eyes were half closed, and he suddenly fell over on his back and turned his belly up to her. She rubbed the silky tummy as she weighed how much to say. "He was chasing a rabbit, just outside of town."

"Jeez, I've never seen him act like this."

Tessa met the dog's blue eyes. Kept his secret. "Dogs like me."

"We want to go swimming, Daddy!" said the middle girl, a slim brown pencil with a white-blond braid that swept her butt.

"Hold your horses, babe. Let your sister change her clothes."

"Can we just wade right there at the edge?"

"To your ankles, that's all. Hold Hannah's hand." He dropped a pack and yanked a zipper open. From within, he grabbed a bottle of sunscreen and stood up. To Tessa he said, "Don't run off, huh?"

"The dog and I will hold down the fort."

"Pedro is his name," Vince said.

Tessa met the dog's eyes. "Pedro and I will hold down the fort."

The other dog, who had a terrier face, hauled herself to her feet to take an endless drink from the lake, then wobbled back to the shade and collapsed not far from where Tessa sat. The girls stood with their feet in the water, knees like cypress trees reflecting back on the surface, holding their arms out and tilting up faces for sunscreen, rotating by degrees to let their father rub lotion from strap to strap. He was very thorough. The baby was very fair, and Vince dabbed lotion under her eyes, along her scalp, and rubbed a second helping over her tiny shoulders. She giggled and danced away. He hauled her back, patted her bottom. "Scamp."

Impossible not to like a man who could be that tender. Genuine.

She hummed "Rescue Me" under her breath and stopped the instant she heard what it was, her cheeks flushing.

Out of the trees came the oldest girl, poured into a red one-piece. Her tummy jutted out in a little Buddha shape. She dropped her shirt and shorts in a pile next to Pedro and paused, looking at the clear blue lake shining like a mirror in the bright, hot afternoon. She sighed.

Tessa asked, "Don't you like to swim?"

"Have you ever *been* in that lake?"

"No, I don't live here."

"It's cold," she said, and rubbed her arms.

"Really? Like how cold?"

"Like filling-up-a-bathtub-and-pouring-ice-cubes-in cold."

"Oooh, that's pretty bad. Maybe it would help if you got really, really hot first? Lie in the sun with me for a minute, and then when we can't stand it, I'll dive in with you."

The girl blinked. "I don't even know you." She primly walked barefoot across the sand to join the other two girls.

Tessa leaned into Pedro. "She told me, huh?"

He licked her nose, his blue eyes direct and adoring.

"Wow," she said, "you are some dog. I'm glad to meet you."

He stuck by her side while the girls splashed and played for a half hour. Vince hovered nearby, but none of them wanted to actually swim, just dance along the shallow water, and after a few minutes he sat down with Tessa. He smelled of sunscreen and sun-dried laundry and a note that was entirely his own, a watermelon scent of freshly cut grass. His bare arm was only inches away from her own, and she fancied she could feel the heat of it.

"Tell me their names," she said.

"Natalie, the oldest. Jade, the middle one, and Hannah is the baby." They were splashing one another, and Natalie, despite her protestations, was as splashy and playful as the other two once she let down her guard. "Do you have sisters?" he asked.

"No, I'm an only child."

"Me, too, and I think it's a disadvantage as a parent. These guys fight like the Crow—counting coup if they can't draw blood. It's crazy."

"I think kids just do that."

"So my mother says." He looked at her. "No kids?"

"Nope. Never been married."

He inclined his head, smiled lightly. "You're just a lone wolf, aren't you?"

"I guess I am," she said, shrugging one shoulder. "It suits me."

"No pack anywhere?"

Tessa thought about it. "My dad is my pack. Him and his dogs."

"How about your mother?"

"She died when I was four. I don't remember her at all."

"Probably a blessing." He paused, looking at his children. "Jade doesn't remember, or Hannah. Natalie does."

She looked at him, at the hard slant of cheekbone, his jaw. She wanted to ask, *And you?* But she didn't.

They sat side by side in the quiet, watching the girls. The views of trees and sky and water eased into some of the little cracks and sore spots in her spirit, mending them. The undiluted sunshine was good on her arms, and his company was especially pleasant. She liked that he was the kind of man who could sit and not fill every second with chatter.

After a while, the girls started to shiver so much that their father insisted they come out of the water and dry off.

"Are you hungry?" Vince asked, spreading a feast out on the blanket. The girls, wrapped in beach towels, pinned the edges, with the dogs banished to the outer perimeter.

"I don't want to interrupt your family picnic," Tessa said. "I can leave you guys to it."

"You were here first," the middle sister—Jade?—said.

Vince took a peach, pink and orange and curvy, from his pack and held it out in the palm of his hand. "Please stay."

"Okay." She plucked the fruit from his hand without touching him. It was warm from the sun, like skin. "Thank you."

"We have peanut butter and jelly sandwiches on whole-wheat bread, crusts removed," he said, arranging them on a paper plate. "Smoked turkey on sourdough, chips and salsa, Fig Newtons because they're my favorite, bananas, and root beer."

"What's *my* surprise, Dad?" Natalie asked. She tugged her shirt over her head and pushed her glasses back on her nose.

Vince held up one finger. "You have been such a trooper, Miss Scarlett, that I have three things."

"Three?" her sister protested. "Why is she so spoiled?"

"We came to the lake to swim because you like it, Jade." Vince produced a sandwich. "First, a peanut butter and Dijon mustard sandwich on whole-grain bread."

Natalie grinned. "Perfect."

"Next, one perfect Haas avocado, whole." He put it down in front of her. "And last"—he took out a tiny envelope—"Hawaiian Alaea red sea salt."

Watching curiously, Tessa was touched to see the suspicious shine of tears in Natalie's eyes. "Oh, Daddy! The red salt?"

"Yep. Only the best for my girl."

Natalie jumped up and kissed him. "Thank you."

"No problem." He picked up the avocado, neatly cut it open, and sliced the fruit within. "There you go."

With reverence, Natalie pinched out a measure of salt and sprinkled it over the sliced avocado. "Ooooh," she said. "Look at how pretty that looks!"

"Gross," Jade said. "That doesn't even go together. You're just weird, Nat."

"Leave her alone."

With ceremony, Natalie took a bite and closed her eyes. "Good," she pronounced.

Vince winked at Tessa over Natalie's head. "Peanut butter and mustard?"

"I'll stick with my peach, thanks." But as Natalie focused so intently, Tessa put down her peach and took out her camera. "Can I take a picture of that, the avocado and the salt?"

"You really want to?"

Tessa nodded. "Please."

Natalie held out the slice of avocado sprinkled with coarse red salt, and Tessa grinned as she shot the little fingers with chipped polish on short, squat nails. She took several photos, then asked Natalie to pour some salt in her hand and hold it out.

"Hold this, Daddy," Natalie said, giving him the avocado slice so she could pour salt into her palm. "Are you a food photographer?" she asked Tessa.

"No, I just play around with my camera for fun mostly." She zoomed in on the little-girl palm curling up around the salt, shot a series, *click click click*. "But I do work for a travel company, and they might like these pictures for a brochure, if you don't mind."

"Will she get money for being a model?" the next younger sister asked. She had a smear of peanut butter on her cheek, and her hair was mussed from the water.

"Probably not. My boss is pretty cheap."

Jade laughed. Tessa snapped her picture, too, the long braid and peanut butter and great bones. She was pretty and she knew it.

"Get out of here!" Natalie said. "She's taking pictures of my salt!"

"Nat, settle down," Vince said. "It's not a contest."

"*Everything* is a contest," she said, and huffed away, her hand closed tighter around her salt.

Tessa took her picture anyway, shot the rigid heat in her spine, the fingers clenched on the salt. "Hey, Natalie, if you keep your fist tight, the salt will dissolve," she called.

Natalie opened her hand right away, stared down at her palm, and burst into tears. "I ruined it!"

Vince leapt to his feet and went to her. And Tessa, sap that she was, took pictures of that, too. Elk dad and elk daughter and the little dragonfly princess calmly watching.

Tessa said to Jade the dragonfly, "Did you know she would do that?"

The girl hunched her shoulders, giggling, and covered her mouth. "Yes. Mean, huh?"

Tessa nodded. "Pretty mean. If I had a sister, I'd want to be really nice to her."

"You only think that because you don't have a sister," Jade said with full superior knowledge.

Vince calmed Natalie down and led her back to the group. "Look," he said, "there's plenty of salt left."

Over the top of the girl's head, Vince met Tessa's eyes, and she caught an expression of weariness and sadness and hopelessness. Then he smiled ruefully and it was gone.

He sat back down. "All right, everybody, let's eat lunch without a war, all right? Can we do that?"

After lunch, the girls sat by the lapping water in the shade, digging with plastic shovels. The dogs sprawled by the blanket, snoring. Tessa suddenly felt panic over the way she was tucked into the scene almost without noticing. "I guess maybe I should go," she said.

"Why? What else are you doing on a Sunday afternoon?"

"I'm supposed to be working, checking out the town."

"So, nothing?"

She smiled. "Right."

Hannah squatted next to Vince and reached out to touch Tessa's foot, the blot that looked as if she had been burned. "What'd you do?"

Tessa nearly answered truthfully, then realized how terrifying "spider bite" would sound to a trio of little girls. "I hurt it on a hiking trip."

"How?" the little one persisted. She tucked her hands close to her chest. Her eyes were serious, searching Tessa's face.

"That's a personal question, Hannah," Vince said. "Don't be rude."

"I bet it's something really gross," Jade said, tossing her braid over her shoulder. "And you don't want to tell us."

Tessa inclined her head. "Well, if it was something like that, I would be trying to protect you, right?"

"We're not afraid of things," Natalie said fiercely. "Why don't you just tell us what happened?"

"Natalie, watch your tone."

Tessa met her eyes. "No, I don't think so."

"Why not?"

"Nat!" Vince said sharply.

"Because," Tessa said, not breaking eye contact, "it is personal and I'd rather not."

Natalie opened her mouth, prepared to battle, but her father cut her off. "Go play," Vince said. "Mind your own business and do something constructive."

They obeyed. Vince watched them go with a faint flush on his cheekbones. "Sorry."

Tessa shrugged. "No big deal. I just couldn't come up with a good lie so fast."

He laughed. "It must have—never mind. Now I'm being rude."

"It was a brown recluse spider bite, and I didn't get treatment for four days, so by the time they got to it, it was a raging infection. I couldn't walk for about three weeks."

"A brown recluse?" He peered at her foot. "Really. I've never seen a bite before."

"Lucky you."

"I had the impression it was a painful bite."

"It wasn't, to tell you the truth. Not until it got infected, and by then—" The black hole punched through her ribs. "I was an idiot, basically."

"Yeah, well, been there." He tugged up the cuff of his jeans to show a knee crisscrossed with scar tissue. "I was a"—he paused with a glitter in his dark eyes—"*professional* mountain biker."

Tessa found herself laughing. "Ah, a professional!" She made a face. "'Were'? You don't do it anymore?"

"Ah, hell, even if my knees weren't shot, I'm way too old."

"What, thirty-five?"

He grinned sideways. "Flattery will get you everywhere."

Sun bore down on the top of her head, singed the bridge of her nose, and she just looked at him; his brown eyes moved over her face, touched shoulder, breasts, legs, then back to her mouth. A heat shimmer rose between them, bending the light, gilding the circle around them, and Tessa had a sudden, hot vision of his naked thighs in her bed for a day or two.

Abruptly, she reared away. "I have to get back before I turn into a lobster," she said, standing to brush off her butt.

"Will you still be in town for a day or two?" he asked.

"I'm staying for a couple of weeks, I think."

"Let's have a beer or something, huh?"

Tessa nodded. "You still have my card?"

"I do."

"Good." She paused for a moment, torn, looking at the crown of his head, the woven circle around his arm. "See ya."

SEVEN

It wasn't until she reached the bottom of the trail at the church that Tessa remembered she had planned to go to the river today. Too late now. Her foot was fiery. She'd picked up a good strong pine bough to use as a walking stick, but she was still hobbling as she came around the graveyard and spied the black-and-white pup. He lurked behind a tree, his head low, and Tessa stopped.

"Hey, sweetie," she called. He started to move toward her, but a door slamming nearby sent him skittering back into the trees.

It was the doggiest town she'd been to in a long time. There were more dogs than people. Maybe, she thought, she should see about taking the pup to the animal shelter. If she saw him again, she would do that.

Back at the hotel, she took a shower and called down to room service for a glass of wine. Then she filled a bowl with ice and water and rested her foot in the ice for ten minutes at a time.

While she sipped wine and cooled the foot, she looked up Green Gate Farms on the Internet and sketched out her plans for visiting. She wanted to speak to whoever was in charge of the farm itself and also meet with the manager of the cooking school to see if there was any chance of setting up short-term small-group offerings. A vegetarian cooking school was still avant garde enough to be pleasing, especially in the Bourdain-influenced world of meat-heavy French cooking that was all the rage. She liked the angle of gourmet vegetarian and the Alice Waters-ish emphasis on whole and organic. She made a couple of phone calls, set up a tour and interviews for the following Thursday, and then sat back and enjoyed her wine.

Long gold light spilled into the plaza, illuminating dust in the air. The scent of sizzling meat and garlic swirled in fragrant clouds, and somewhere a guitar played melancholy Spanish music for diners dressed in casual chic as they sipped their twelve-dollar margaritas. A trio of pigeon-breasted Anglos in pastel fishing hats crossed the cobblestones, obviously tourists on their way to supper. A man politely tipped a black hat at them, and something cracked in Tessa's memory.

She stood at the window of a bedroom, petting a cat. A big cat, black and white, with yellow eyes and little spats on his paws. Behind her, someone sang in a breathy voice:

> *"El Señor Don Gato was a cat*
> *On a high red roof Don Gato sat*
> *He went there to read a letter, meow meow meow*
> *Where the reading light was better, meow meow meow."*

Tessa sang the chorus, her hand moving and moving on the cat's head.

And then, just as quickly as it had opened, the shutter slid closed. *Click.* Although she stayed very still, peering into the dusty gold light, nothing more surfaced.

The song, however, lodged itself in her head. She hummed it under her breath.

Over the years, she'd often tried to remember—or rather, re-order—her memories, sweeping them all into a pile that she then tried to smooth into something that made a picture, but there were too many things that didn't fit. Angled shards with chunks missing, like a broken mirror.

As she sat here now, she wondered if her approach had been wrong. Maybe she'd been looking too much for the missing parts, feeling around for something that slipped out of sight, rather than focusing on what she did remember.

Pulling the white tablet over to her, she picked up a pen and started scribbling a list.

Songs. Whole folk songs. Lots of them.
A blond woman who seems mean (probably my mother?).
A black-and-white dog sleeping with me (Brenna).
A sidewalk covered with colored chalk.
Playing jacks with another girl (boy?).
A forest fire.
Playing hide-and-seek in really high grass or something. A big
    field.
Getting scared and lost.

Something clattered below her balcony, and Tessa was jolted abruptly from the trance of memory. She startled so hard that she dropped her pen, and she suddenly felt a clammy sense of terror that was utterly out of proportion to the prosaic list of memories.

Maybe things were buried for a reason. Maybe she didn't really want to know what lay back there in the darkness. Sometimes a broken memory hid a trauma.

Well, but she knew what her trauma was: She had nearly drowned. She'd always known it but never remembered anything about it until the ordeal in Montana, when she'd nearly drowned again. Climbing out of the Snake River with an arm broken in two places, she had remembered being hauled from the river when she was four. It had unnerved her so badly that she'd had panic attacks for weeks afterward.

Which was when she decided it was time for her to stop ignoring the dimly lit memories and try to put them to rest. But at this moment, rubbing her hands on her thighs, feeling a shaky sense of dread, she couldn't really remember why she had decided it would be such a great idea to come out here and try to sort it out. How would that help the current problem, which had nothing to do with her past and everything to do with making peace with the fact that her bad judgment had led directly to the death of a young woman who had trusted Tessa implicitly?

It wouldn't. And it was making her father nervous, and she really had no idea what she might discover. There were oddities, like the fact that she didn't remember her mother. Sam told Tessa that her mother had been at the commune, a hippie, but Tessa didn't remember anything about her.

Weird.

Her pulse grew suddenly thready, unsteady, and panic began to stir in her limbs. In the plaza below, a man laughed, and it sounded so much like Sam that she picked up her cell and punched in the number. "Hey, baby girl," he said, answering on the second ring. "How's it going out there in Thieves Land?"

"Good," she said, pleased that her voice sounded calm. "I walked up to the lake this afternoon and talked to the priest at the church. It's all so beautiful I can't believe it."

"I remember," he said in his deep voice. "No place on earth like Los Ladrones River Valley."

"I think we're going to get some great tour possibilities out of it. It's really too bad you're not here with me."

"Yeah, well, some of us have to work, you know."

Tessa smiled. The sound of his voice calmed her racing heart. "You poor thing." She sipped the last of her wine, crisp and white and dry. "I've met some great dogs here, too. An Akita mix who nearly got himself killed the first afternoon, and the sweetest little border collie stray who keeps showing up."

"A border collie? Could it be——"

"Don't say it!"

"Brenna!" he said, and laughed. The familiar charm of it made Tessa miss him acutely. "Sounds like you're having a good time."

"So far so good I'm headed over to Green Gate Farms later this week, do some interviews."

"Is that right?" His voice was suddenly bloodless. "Who are you talking to? Maybe I know some of them."

Tessa slid her thumb over the mouse square on her keyboard. The screen came up and she read a couple of names. "Sound familiar?"

"Nope."

"Well, it was a long time ago."

"It was."

"You sound kind of funny, Dad. You all right?"

"Me? I'm great. Getting ready for the rush."

"I guess I'll let you go, then."

"Keep in touch," he said.

"You can call me, too, you know."

"I don't like to bug you, you know that."

She shook her head. "Bug me, Dad. Please? It's better than you sitting out there worrying about me."

"All right, kiddo, I will."

"Love you."

"Love you, too."

As she hung up the phone, Tessa pursed her lips, staring at the dusty sunlight burning a ribbon along a craggy blue mountain range. He was really not happy about this, and considering how laid-back he was about everything on the planet, maybe Tessa should pay attention. Maybe sleeping dogs should stay asleep. Instead of poking around in her past, maybe she ought to finish up her research and get back to her regular life.

Or not.

The truth was she needed to make peace with the distant past in order to know who she was and maybe make peace with the recent past. A healthy person faced things. As long as that black hole of regret lived inside her, waiting for her to lower her guard, she wouldn't be whole and healthy. She'd written a letter of apology to Lisa's parents. She'd made a confession to her father. She'd written out a long journal. None of it really touched her guilt.

Since the direct route wasn't working, the next best thing was to work on the other black hole—that jigsaw puzzle of a mixed-up memory. That, too, was a step toward wholeness.

With a sigh, she shoved the subject away. Right now she could live in this moment. Live *here*, on a late Sunday afternoon in August, in Los Ladrones, New Mexico. She fetched the camera from the bed and, sitting with one foot in ice, the other propped on the railing, she shot the ribbons of molten gold over the mountains, and the vast tree in the plaza, and even her toes, plain and unpainted, sticking up into the sky.

Sometimes, the moment was enough. A moment was a place you could live.

Vince got the girls—sunburned, cranky with sunshine and exhaustion and food—into bed by eight-thirty. Not even Natalie complained. He wandered back into the living room, kicked the dogs off the couch, and picked up the remote but didn't push any buttons. He just didn't want the noise.

Old, he told himself. *You're old now.*

Once upon a time, he'd been a metal fanatic. Iron Maiden, Pantera, Slayer, and later, System of a Down, had blasted in his ears twenty hours a day—on the radio, in his car, on his Walkman, on the stereo. He'd burned out on noise before getting an iPod, or he would have listened to it on that, too.

Now the silence, mountain silence, broken only by the faintest of crickets somewhere out in the fields, fell on him like a quilt. It had texture and depth, a velvety weight to ease his jangled nerves, his weary brain.

Natalie and Jade had gone at it again on the way home from the lake, kicking and screaming and biting, pulling each other's hair, calling each other awful names. He roared over the seat back for them to stop, but they ignored him, locked in what seemed to him to be mortal combat. Hannah, terrified, started to cry. The dogs, safe behind a grid in the very back, had started barking and howling, until it seemed the vehicle would split from the noise. Vince had slammed on the brakes, pulled the car over, yanked open the back door, and bodily separated his two fighting hellions, then spanked them both. Firmly.

It shocked them both enough that they burst into tears, flung themselves against him, and wept out their apologies.

Natalie had long scratches down her forearms, beading blood. Jade had teeth marks on her upper arm.

He had no idea what to do with them or why this war had suddenly broken out. As far as he could tell, it had exploded about a month ago, when he'd taken them to Albuquerque to go shopping for school clothes. Natalie was surly and hateful all the way, and Jade needled her about her size, and it got out of control. He'd come back home without buying anything; in fact, his mother was taking them to her sister's in Pueblo to shop next week. Before they left, he needed to have a talk with them, each one of them, and see what he could find out about what was going on. Maybe he needed to spend more time with them, one on one. Maybe Natalie was still having problems with her mother's death.

Maybe it was all just normal.

Times like this his anger at Carrie could consume him. How could she have checked out like that, leaving him to manage so much on his own? Rationally, he knew she had been troubled, that suicide wasn't exactly a choice. Rationally, he knew she'd been depressed for a long time—and that, too, had been a burden, much as it shamed him to admit it.

On another level, an emotional level, he was flat-out furious with her. How could she have deserted her children? Who did that?

All he knew was that he was exhausted. Lonely. Tired of doing everything himself.

No, not by himself. His mother was a huge help, bringing casseroles to supplement his wretched cooking—not that her cooking was that much better. She took the girls overnight on a regular basis, intervening with parenting advice and insights when he asked.

But it wasn't the same as having a partner. Sprawled on the

couch, too tired to even turn on the television, he surveyed the disaster of the living room. Clothes, toys, dishes, blankets, dog toys, pens, newspapers, kids' books, shoes, and dust and dog hair littered everything. He tried to give it a cleaning once a week or so, but sometimes it didn't even get done that much. Between work, kids, the modicum of cooking he could do, the general hygiene of the girls, and care for their clothes, he barely had time for a shower, much less vacuuming the living room.

Pedro shoved his head beneath Vince's hand, and even in his current state, Vince had to chuckle. "If it's just sitting there, it might as well be doing you some good, huh, dog?" he rasped aloud, rubbing the dog's ears.

It made him think of Tessa, lean and tan, on the sand this afternoon. A very intriguing woman. She wore an air of aloof mystery like a cloud of perfume, with exotic notes of foreign travel and that strange childhood. He could listen to her smoky voice for ten thousand years and never get tired of it.

He closed his eyes and thought of her lying there on the beach this afternoon, her belly flat and brown, her hair swept away from her neck. Her breasts were constrained in a sports bra, which covered more than a bikini top but not in the same way. He'd seen the outline of her breasts very clearly, the slight pear shape, the outline of her nipples. He'd been careful not to stare.

She had the loose, comfortable body language of a woman who liked herself, and it wasn't hard to forget about all the shit in his life and imagine her lying flat on that sand, minus the sports bra. He decided she was asleep, her breasts white and tipped with dark-brown nipples. No, maybe not dark. She was blond. Pink nipples, then. Soft in the hot, hot sun.

In his imagination, he arrived at the lake without any children in tow. Just him, discovering her there on the beach, topless, a treat for him only. He stopped beside her and he bent to put his palm flat on that belly, the skin so hot it practically blistered his palm, but she didn't wake up, not until he flicked his tongue over the pink nipples and made them hard, sucking them into his mouth. She woke up, pleased, and reached a hand out to stroke him.

Yeah.

In the darkness of his living room, all alone, Vince gave himself some comfort, thinking of Tessa's tits, then hauled his ass up and went to bed, too damned tired to care when the dogs leapt into bed with him.

Vita's day began at three a.m. It made people wince for her, but she loved it. Loved rising in the dark while the world slept and putting on her clothes and going downstairs to the café to make a pot of coffee. The kitchen was starkly clean, its tile floor swabbed with bleach water by the dishwasher the night before, all the stainless counters polished and empty, utensils neatly in their drawers and on hooks—whisks and spatulas in a dozen sizes, ladles and spoons and knives. The pots, battered and sturdy, in every imaginable variety—stockpots to sheet pans to skillets to tiny saucepans—were stacked below the counters and on the shelves around the room. The grill had been scrubbed clean with a brick after the last meal was served and now waited for the new day, when it would give its heat to nourish the humans who would pass through on her watch today.

Wednesday's special was an egg casserole that never failed to sell out completely, usually before eight-thirty. Which was fine. Letting it run out rather than making more gave it a special cachet.

She poured a cup of coffee, stirred in heavy cream and two

teaspoons of sugar, and took her first sip of the day. Coffee was her constant companion, coffee made just like this—from freshly ground, excellent-quality beans, brewed strong enough to put hair on your chest, so that it *needed* heavy cream and some sugar to thin it out. No lattes for Vita. No extra whip mocha bravo whatevers. She loved good, plain coffee as much as anything in the world, and she drank a lot of it. It was a great smug pleasure to hear science upholding her claim that it was a health drink—nothing that smelled that fantastic could possibly be bad for you.

On a shelf above the main work counter was a small stereo. She used to go through radios at a pace of about one every six months; now she used an iPod deck with an iPod encased in a vinyl sleeve. The first had lasted almost a year. This one was well past the year and going strong. She didn't allow individual players for the staff, even when they were working alone—it was too dangerous to be unable to hear what was going on around you, especially in an environment riddled with fire and sharp knives—but she did allow people to bring in their own mixes and play them. Sometimes. She had a preference for Bob Dylan and the Stones, Canned Heat and It's a Beautiful Day, the soundtrack of her youth, when she'd drifted west from Ohio on a cloud of patchouli and pot, riding in a van with a cluster of college friends. They landed in Boulder, sharing a ramshackle Victorian house that was freezing all winter and had plumbing problems year-round. Still, there were plenty of bedrooms, a wide porch that looped around the downstairs, and a kitchen that could seat twenty along a wall of windows overlooking the mountains.

It was in that kitchen that Vita first learned to love cooking, love the pleasure of nourishing and feeding other people but also the pleasure of handling food, preparing it, enjoying its beauty. A good number of her recipes came directly from those gilded days, when she was young and listening to rock that wasn't yet classic but was fresh and passionate and capturing everything about the world that they wanted to say and couldn't. Some of the happiest days of her life, those years in Boulder in the late sixties.

This morning, as she hummed along with the raw, hungry voice of Janis singing "Turtle Blues," Vita broke eggs and sliced organic naturally smoked ham into thin, elegant slivers and let the spirit of those lost days waft over her. All that youth and happiness. The memory of them could give her a sense of wistfulness that could still rip her heart out.

Funny how you didn't know when you were happy.

She was happy now, too, of course, but not with that same sense of gilded . . . what? Expectation. The sense of possibility and wonder. Anything could happen. Life could carry you anywhere. When you were young, you didn't realize that the "anywhere" could be a place you didn't want to go.

The man who tried to steal Vita's life had drifted into that joyful Boulder house with another man, the boyfriend of one of the other girls. Vita was sleeping with a philosophy student at CU, but one look at Jesse and she was lost, lost in his unholy, unwholesome beauty—eyes dark as a midnight dive, lips like slices of overripe melon, hands as lean and graceful as a musician's to pluck the strings of a woman's body.

And God knew he could play. He could make love for hours, days, twining his spell tighter and tighter around her, until she could not move unless he pulled the strings. He followed work to Texas, then to Arizona, and Vita followed him, tugged along in his wake like a leashed dog.

She lost herself so slowly, she was shocked to realize one

morning that she had become a shell, something empty and echoey, filled only with reflections of Jesse and his cruelty. That, too, had begun so slowly she barely recognized it. A nip or a pinch, a sharp nudge, a criticism that stung and then was smoothed away by those sweet melon lips.

People never understood how an abuser worked. It wasn't all abuse, because who would ever put up with that?

No, Jesse was masterful, alternating terrible cruelty with grand gestures, genuine remorse, and that mind-blowing sex. She always knew she was safe if he was making love to her.

By the time she got away from him, she'd lost that woman who cooked so joyfully in a house in Boulder. She weighed less than one hundred pounds and had the marks of him all over her, in bones that had been broken, in scars where he'd broken the skin, in a thousand broken things in her psyche. She ran away from him after he killed her bird, and she had never quite forgiven herself for putting a helpless creature at risk. She ran under cover of night and didn't stop driving until she came to Los Ladrones. She'd never heard of it and trusted that Jesse never had, either. The commune took her in.

She'd started cooking again and running for simple, easy hours along the banks of the river. Slowly, she came back to herself. An egg and a smile, a hearty burp and the sizzle of onions in a pan, a gleaming sink and baking bread. It fixed her. Even after everything fell apart at the commune, she didn't lose herself again. Vita came into town to cook for the hotel first, then to open 100 Breakfasts.

Because breakfast was the secret to everything.

And here, making breakfast, she could offer healing to other women.

By five a.m., when her crew began to trickle in, she'd long

since had her own breakfast—a hard-boiled egg and toast with butter and jam—and had baked casseroles, fresh and steaming, to serve to the customers who would file in the doors the minute she opened them at five-thirty sharp. Together, she and the line cooks and dishwashers and waitresses bustled around, starting pots of coffee, setting up stations for the cooks, measuring out pancake mix, and heating up waffle irons. Annie, the new girl, had her badly dyed hair pulled tightly away from her face, and Vita thought again that a little weight would do the woman a world of good. She was so thin you could see the bones in her arms, the ribs across the top of her chest.

"Good morning," Vita said. "Are you ready to handle the waffle station this morning?"

"I guess. Am I ready?"

Nancy, a sturdy woman in her fifties with the red-tipped nose of a long-term drinker, rasped, "Piece of cake, honey. Come on over here and stand by me and we'll get you going. You can do the bacon, too."

Vita touched Nancy's shoulder, quietly thanking her, and moved into the dining room to open the blinds, run a check to make sure it all looked clean and tidy. When she was satisfied, she headed for the front door. "Ready, gang?" she called.

"All systems go," someone called, and Vita turned the *Closed* sign to *Open*.

Wednesday Breakfast Special

*Ham and Egg Casserole: This one sells out early,
so don't lollygag.*

VITA'S HAM AND EGG CASSEROLE

3 T butter
1/2 cup diced red onions
4 cups shredded potatoes
1 1/2 cups slivered organic ham
*1 1/2 cups mixed shredded cheese, equal parts
    sharp cheddar, Jack, and Colby*
*1 cup finely diced mild green chiles, roasted,
    skinned, and seeded*
8 eggs, beaten
1 1/2 cups heavy cream
1/2 tsp freshly ground pepper

Melt the butter in a heavy skillet and cook onions until
tender. In a large bowl, mix cooked onions, potatoes, ham,
chiles, and cheese together, and spread in a 13x9-inch
buttered baking dish. Beat together eggs, cream, and pepper,
and pour over the potato mix. Bake for 45–50 minutes, or
until a knife in the middle comes out clean. Serve with sliced
tomatoes.

EIGHT

Tessa made it over to Green Gate Farms on Thursday morning. After the hike to the lake, her foot needed some coddling, and she gave it without question, lazing around the pool, reading, and watching a movie in the cool depths of the Chief Theater, which was hung with old velvet drapes, the walls painted with murals of the Old West.

According to Google, Green Gate Farms was just on the other side of the river, but the bridge was nearly five miles north of town. It was a cloudy morning, for which Tessa was grateful, since she had managed to get sunburned reading a ghost story she picked up poolside yesterday. High-altitude sunlight was nothing to mess with.

Right after she crossed the bridge there was a sign, with the main portion carved in exuberant, colorful script:

Green Gate Organic Farms
Fresh produce
Café
Retreats and cabins
Green Gate Vegetarian Cooking School

Vegetables and flowers were painted on the sign. Her father's elegant hand could have provided the pattern for the carved lettering, and she definitely felt his spirit here. Following the road beneath a stand of thick pines, she noticed that the landscape rose steeply to her right. The road curved and then opened into a wide green clearing that overlooked the river, the valley with the town of Los Ladrones lined up in rows and, farther north, the San Juan Mountains. It looked like something that could be drawn on a label for luscious, healthy food, for sure. Breathtaking.

She heard herself humming and took a moment to listen. Crosby, Stills & Nash, "Guinnevere." She frowned. Odd choice for her brain to make. Maybe she'd heard it without realizing it.

A cluster of modern buildings sat beside a gravel parking lot, with wooden signs on a post pointing visitors toward the cabins, the produce stands, the farms, the cooking school, and the main building. Vegetable plants and herbs grew in all the whiskey barrels and vined around signposts. As she stepped out of the car, Tessa smelled thyme.

Pushing her sunglasses on top of her head, she gathered a few long shots of the river running silver through the middle of fertile fields, the rustic-looking buildings, the trees and mountains.

None of it looked familiar. Nothing made all the jumbled pieces of memory suddenly align themselves. Which she supposed she had been expecting.

"Hello," said a young woman in a pair of loose, vibrantly printed trousers and a simple white T-shirt. Her dark hair was cropped close, and a pair of delicate silver earrings hung in her lobes. "Can I help you find something?"

"I was just admiring the view," she said.

"Are you the one who's here from Rambling Tours?"

"Yes, actually." She stuck out her hand. "Tessa Harlow."

"Jessica Cunningham. I'm interning here. They sent me down to meet you. Some crisis in the greenhouse this morning." She gestured toward the café. "Let's get a cup of tea and you can ask me some questions while we wait for Cherry."

"Sounds good." She wanted to continue shooting the area, but that would wait. From the big shoulder bag she carried, she pulled out a stenographer's pad and a pen instead. "What kind of intern are you?"

"I'm on the farm side." They stepped onto a deep porch furnished with rocking chairs overlooking the view, and Jessica pulled open the wooden screen door. "Organic systems. I'm taking a degree at Colorado State University."

Tessa ducked inside the café. A blast of exotic scents hit her—ginseng and cinnamon and something else. "Is that tea? Smells fantastic."

"Our own secret recipe. You can buy it in bulk, of course." She pointed to small bags lined up along the counter, each with a stylized, beautiful label bearing the name *Green Gate Farms*. "Would you like to try it?"

"Absolutely." Eyeing the bakery offerings in the case, she asked, "What else should I try? What's your favorite?"

"The carrot muffins, hands down." She pointed to caramel-orange-colored muffins studded with pineapple. "Give us a big pot of tea and a couple of muffins, will you, Andrew?"

They carried a tray to a table by a window that overlooked the fields. Tessa made notes—the café was small, wouldn't serve more than ten at a time, but it had a cozy feeling, like headquarters for a summer camp. The wood was rough-hewn, the tables made by hand, each individually wrought of twigs and planks and knotty pine. She rubbed her hand over the tabletop. "Beautiful."

Jessica poured tea from a utilitarian steel pot, releasing the fresh fragrance into the air immediately above the table. Tessa leaned in and breathed it, a tickle of memory moving over her brain, then slipping away. She broke apart one of the muffins to examine the crumb. "I noticed that The 100 Breakfasts Café uses a lot of baked goods from Green Gate. Is this the bakery, here?"

She shook her head. "It used to be. We've moved everything to the cooking-school building. It's brand-new, state-of-the-art everything."

"And everything is organic and vegetarian?"

"It is—and we go with as much local food as we can. Obviously we can't grow everything—wheat doesn't do well in this location, for example—but the honey is from our hives, the carrots from our gardens, and the eggs from our coops."

"I'm not always a fan of the granola-groovy world," Tessa said, "but the grain in this muffin is gorgeous." Pinching a chunk out of the middle, she found it moist to the touch, tender and sweet in her mouth. She widened her eyes in approval. "Mmm!"

"I think you'll find the food here is all that good."

"So can I get some background from you while we're waiting?"

"Yep. That's why I'm here."

Tessa asked a lot of questions she pretty much knew the answers to: the basics of the farm, the numbers of people who lived here year-round, the kind of tourism they were already hosting.

"Not a lot," Jessica said. "The cooking school is the brain-child of Cherry's mother, Paula, who did the research and organized staff and brought in the whole team. She was one of the original members of the commune here—the tea is her invention." She pointed at Tessa's cup, which Tessa had not yet tasted.

Tessa held up a finger to pause the conversation and picked up her mug in both hands. The scent rushed into her sinuses, and the tea struck her mouth—swirled over her tongue and her palate and hit the back of her throat, and she tasted sunshine hot on high grasses and bees buzzing in the distance and—

—*she closed her eyes, seeing a field and herself running through grass well above her head. She was laughing, being tickled, splashing somebody in a baby pool, completely naked. She saw herself tucking a doll into a shoe-box bed—*

Jolted by the sudden blast of memories, Tessa put the cup down and shook her head slightly, as if the tea was the source of her reaction. "Wow," she said.

"Amazing, isn't it?"

Tessa nodded. "Tell me a little more history. It started as a commune, right?"

Jessica reiterated what Tessa knew from both her research and her own father. The commune was started in 1969 by a handful of serious counterculturists dropping out and turning on. "They grew a lot of pot, and some of them lived in tepees, the whole nine yards," Jessica said. "There was an old Victorian house, but it was in pretty bad shape."

"Is it still there?"

"Yes, and it's been updated. They use it for retreats and things like that. Kind of big and drafty, hard to heat, so it's closed through the winter."

A quickening told her that she wanted to see the house if she could get a look at it. In the meantime, her boss would want some facts and figures, a way to sell the farm to his customers, who wouldn't be impressed by the ancient hippie-commune angle. Erecting a wall between herself and the past, she donned a business hat and gathered facts, figures, and possibilities, like the professional she was.

After they drank their tea at Green Gate Café, Jessica gave Tessa a tour of the grounds and main buildings. "How many of the original commune members are still here?" Tessa asked as they walked along a field that had just been turned under.

"Not many, I don't think. Paula, who invented the tea, is one of them. Her daughter was raised here." Jessica smiled. "Can you imagine what a great life that would have been?"

Tessa raised an eyebrow noncommittally. "Anyone besides Paula?"

"Sure. The guys who run the fields, Jonathan and Robert, are brothers and they were raised on a farm in the central valley in California—and the midwife, Anna. They're all old now, like in their sixties. Some of them have grandchildren working here. It's mostly the middle group, the kids, who've managed to get the systems working—getting the produce to market, establishing the retreat center, making the website." She stopped at the greenhouse. "A lot of the original members of the commune are Luddites. They really don't want anything to do with computers."

"Or iPods or capitalism," said a woman with dark hair cut into a crisp and shimmering bob to her jawline. "Or even electricity, some of them," she added with a grin.

"I know a guy like that," Tessa said.

"You must be Tessa." The woman, around Tessa's age, stuck out her hand. "I'm Cherry. Sorry to keep you waiting. Had an emergency in the greenhouse."

"No problem."

Jessica said, "I've gotta get to the barns."

"Thanks for your help," Cherry said, and turned, gesturing for Tessa to come with her along a path cutting through an open field bounded on three sides by the rising mountain and forest. "This is the meadow. It was one of the original settlement sites. They had tepees and tents here before they fixed the house." She pointed as they rounded the edge of the trees.

Tessa halted, almost without realizing it, slammed by recognition. The house stood against the dark day, three stories of rambling Victorian, eccentrically decorated with gingerbread and a tower rising like a Russian dome above the pines surrounding it. A wide porch wrapped around the front and both sides, facing the river and the town on the other side and the ridge of the Sangre de Cristo Mountains behind Los Ladrones. It was painted the wrong colors, she thought, very clearly.

"Are you all right?" Cherry asked.

"Fine. I just—" She shrugged. "Déjà vu or something."

Cherry nodded. "We can't go in right now, because there's a conference going on. Psychologists, I think."

"So there are meeting rooms? Bedrooms? How does that work?"

"It can accommodate a small conference, maybe up to twenty. Otherwise, we use the cabins, which will hold up to a hundred fifty. They were built in the early seventies. It was a thriving commune at the time. More than two hundred people lived here for nearly a decade."

"Really? Two hundred? What happened?"

"Officially?" Cherry stopped, eyeing the house. "Officially it was a feud between two camps of the original followers. One group wanted to leave it natural—live without electricity and all that—-but the others wanted to start coming into the modern world."

"And unofficially?" Tessa asked.

"One of the leaders was killed. Shot to death. Details have never really become all that clear. There was a writer out here a few years ago trying to piece it all together, but nobody talked." She eyed the house. "They'll take the story to their graves."

"You lived here then?"

"Yeah, but I was only two. I don't remember anything about it." She rolled her eyes. "A lot of the students around here think it would have been so great to grow up here, but believe me it got old."

Tessa touched her chest ironically. "Hi, my name is Tessa, and my dad was a magician for Renaissance festivals until I was thirteen."

Cherry laughed, a robust sound. "So you get it."

"I get it. I adore my dad, don't get me wrong, I do. But I was really glad to go to a normal school and wear pink T-shirts and glitter fingernails."

"I would have *killed* for that." Her eyes showed raw longing. "Eventually I talked my mom into letting me go to normal high school, but by then I was already a weirdo kid from the commune and it wasn't that easy to break into the cliques."

"I'm sure."

Cherry waved a hand. "Let's keep walking. Where's your dad?"

"Santa Cruz. He's a surfer now. Runs a drinks shack on the beach." Looking briefly over her shoulder at the house, Tessa said, "You must like it here if you stayed all this time."

"Are you kidding? I got out of here the minute I turned

eighteen. I have to admit that the commune educated me brilliantly, so I landed a great scholarship to CU Boulder, mass comm. Never looked back." She raised a finger. "Until my mother got breast cancer last summer. I came back to make sure she had the help she needed through chemo."

Tessa thought of the woman with no eyebrows. "She works the farmers' market, right?"

"Yeah. She's doing great, actually, in complete remission, so she'll be fine." Cherry smiled fondly. "Funny, though, now I don't want to live away from her anymore. I grew up and noticed that she's this incredibly amazing person. I'm divorced, and newspapers are dying, so I'm doing the PR and Web marketing for the farms. Thanks to the demand for organic vegetables, the place is booming."

"I can see that."

"Let me show you one of my favorite things," Cherry said, leading the way into the forest.

The smell of minerals and forest floor—pine needles rotting and warming to release their spiciness, mixed with earth and rocks and water—swamped Tessa. Dizzy, she stopped and put a hand on a tree, suddenly seeing herself holding hands with another girl.

"Smell this one. It's vanilla."

Blinking, Tessa said, "Hot springs. There's hot springs, right?"

Cherry turned. "Yeah. Have you been here?"

Tessa wasn't ready to say she had lived here. "Maybe?" she hedged. "I don't really remember. We traveled through New Mexico when I was little. It looks very familiar."

"Wow. We probably knew each other. How old are you?"

"Thirty-seven."

"I'm thirty-five." She peered at Tessa's face, hard. "You have the look of the commune kids, actually. Do you remember when it was?"

Tessa peered into the middle distance, trying to puzzle out the year they would have left. She had been four, so—

A sharp pain arrowed over her left eyebrow. "I don't remember. My dad will. I'll ask him."

"Wouldn't that be funny, if we met before?" Cherry grinned impishly, and for one long second Tessa was reminded of him, of Sam. Suggestion? Or fact?

"You talked about your mom," Tessa said, "but not your dad. Does he not live here?"

She rolled her eyes. "I have no idea who my dad is. I'm sure my *mother* doesn't know. We were all just the children of the tribe," she said with exaggerated emphasis. "Everybody was my dad. And nobody."

Tessa squeezed her arm. "Sorry." But she found herself peering at Cherry's face to see if there really was a resemblance to Sam, and there was, in a way. The pale eyes. The high cheekbones and full lips.

In a way, she realized with a start, Cherry actually kind of looked like Tessa. The high-bridged nose, the same long-limbed body type, the elliptical fold at the eyelid.

The children of the tribe.

"I never really knew my mom," Tessa said. "She died when I was little and I don't remember her at all."

"Well, then, I'm sorry for you, too."

Tessa stopped. "Despite the hippie parents, we seem to have done pretty well, huh?"

Cherry smiled. "Yeah." She waved Tessa along the trail. "Come on, I'll show you another part of the unofficial reason the commune broke up." At an open, slightly marshy spot, she paused. "Ta da."

Tessa blinked. "I don't get it."

"These were the pot fields. It was the main source of income for the commune, and then someone came in and stole it all. They got away with kilos and kilos of weed."

Tessa laughed. "Wow."

"I get the feeling that was the beginning of the end." Cherry gazed over the open meadow. "The thieves stole the dream."

"Los Ladrones," Tessa said.

Cherry looked at her. "Right." Then, briskly, she turned toward the path. "Enough of the past. The present is much, much better. Come on. I'll take you down to the school and you can see what we're doing. It's just getting up and running, but maybe that would be something your demographic will enjoy. Cooking with organic and local food."

"Perfect," Tessa said, and glanced over her shoulder. She couldn't wait to call Sam tonight.

Green Gate Cooking School was housed in a long, low adobe building, built recently in the old Santa Fe style, complete with wooden window casings painted turquoise to keep out evil spirits, and corners like an old woman's shoulders, soft and round. Deep porticos ran around the entire outside of the rectangular building, furnished with benches, and pots of marigolds and herbs faced the fields and river and mountains.

Inside, the kitchens and classrooms opened onto an internal garden. Tessa stepped out of the foyer into the courtyard and stopped, this time halted by sheer delight. A fountain chuckled in the midst of a vast herb garden, and a series of traditional *hornos*—wood-burning outdoor ovens—graced one wall. A multicolored Siamese cat sunned himself on a bench, tail flicking. He had paws practically the size of baseball mitts, and Tessa couldn't resist stopping to scratch his head. His eyes were bright blue.

The air smelled of thyme and rosemary and basil, the oils heavy in the hot sun, mixing with the scent of wood smoke and roasting onions. A woman in a pale-green chef's coat trimmed basil from a hearty plant, and she looked up with a smile. "Hello." Her hair was pulled back beneath a purple-and-green bandana printed with Teenage Mutant Ninja Turtles. Tessa liked her immediately for the whimsy. "You must be Tessa. I'm Zelda."

"Zelda is our head teacher and executive chef at the school," Cherry said. "We were very lucky to lure her away from the West Coast, where she worked with some of the best organic chefs in the country."

"It was me who got lucky," Zelda said, straightening. She was quite tall, and her hair, spilling from beneath the bandana, was coppery. Very pretty, Tessa thought, always a bonus.

"Glad to meet you." Tessa shook her hand and was pleased by the chef's strong, confident grip. "I'm so excited about this whole idea. How long has the school been open?"

"We taught the first quarter last spring. Just starting the third quarter at the end of October. The students are required to put in time in the fields or the farm stands, too, so we have six-week breaks during the planting and the harvest periods, with a lighter schedule through the summer."

"Ah!" Tessa said, "Perfect. Because, as I said on the phone, I'm very interested in talking to you about the possibility of setting up some kind of shorter, camplike experiences for adult tours."

"I am *so* onboard for that," Zelda said. "A lot of people don't really understand how easy it is to cook with sustainable ingredients or how much better local food will taste. It's just a blast."

Tessa felt a rush of excitement, as if she'd been led right to this moment, to this woman, to this school, for some bigger purpose. She gestured toward the courtyard. "The garden is part of it?"

"Right. This is a very extensive herb garden, and because it's so protected in the courtyard, we can use a lot of it all year-round. We have plans for a greenhouse closer in next year, but for now we can always use the farm's."

"Which reminds me," Cherry said, lifting a finger. "I have to make a couple of calls and make sure that problem is addressed. Excuse me for a few minutes, will you?"

"Sure," Zelda said. "Let me show you the kitchens and tell you some ideas I had for possible short tours."

The courtyard was rectangular, and Zelda led Tessa into a door on one of the long ends. "This is the main teaching kitchen," she said. Banks of gas stoves and grills lined the back wall, with stations of stainless steel counters through the center and sinks and storage along the other long wall. At the back were the doors to walk-in fridges. "As you see, there's plenty of room here."

"So, could you teach a group of, say, twelve? That's the average size of one of our tours."

"Perfect." She folded her arms. "I was thinking that we could divide the basics into four or five days. We have the main kitchen here, and along the north end of the courtyard are the bakery and pastry kitchen, and opposite the kitchens here, on the other long arm of the rectangle, are living quarters." She grinned. "They're dorms, really, nothing fancy. Showers, bunks, lockers, in case there are housing issues. The students can rent a bunk very inexpensively—not always possible in Los Ladrones—or they can share cabins for a little more."

"And would it be possible to offer that kind of pricing to my tour members?"

"Absolutely. We can work out a rate for the group. And if they're in the cabins, they can take yoga or tai chi in the mornings."

"Or hike. One aspect of my tours is the hiking."

"Also fine."

Tessa nodded, looking around, imagining a group of women—it would almost certainly be nearly all women who booked this tour—gathering here. Windows looked out to the herb gardens, and a breeze fluttered in through the screens. She felt a strong desire to take the entire tour herself, always a good sign. "How would I pitch this to my boss, then, Zelda? What's my slug line?"

"My big quest is to show people how terrific vegetarian— even vegan—food can be. We've come a long way from the cardboard soy imitations of the seventies, and I'm not sure America knows enough about it yet." Zelda picked up a packet of papers. "I've printed out some ideas. I've not done this before for amateur cooks, so let me know if it seems too intense or not evolved enough."

Tessa took the packet and looked through it. "Okay."

"You can take that with you, but basically we'd start with the idea of sustainability, and why it matters, and then gather food either from the greenhouse or the fields, bring it back here, and cook something beautiful and simple, like soup and bread. Then move through the basics of good nutrition for vegetarians, address some of the big myths. I've included some recipes I thought might work."

Tessa continued to leaf through the packet. Her eye caught on a recipe for spinach tortellini soup. Again, a shiver rushed up her spine. "I'm really excited about this."

Zelda grinned. "Me, too."

"I do feel obliged to mention at this point that I'm not a vegetarian." She inclined her head. "In fact, I'm a total carnivore."

"That's all right," Zelda said, laughing, and flung an arm around Tessa's shoulders. "Carnivores are people, too. The idea is humane and sustainable eating."

"Humane and sustainable," Tessa said. "That's kind, isn't it?"

"Yes. Let me show you the dorms."

Breakfast #83

Vegetarian Delight: One organic egg, cooked to order, served with a moist and tender (really!) whole-wheat carrot muffin delivered fresh every morning directly from Green Gate Organic Farms, fresh butter or cream cheese, and coffee or tea. Try the Green Gate herbal tea blend for a rush of powerful flavor! You'll never know it's caffeine-free!

MOIST AND TENDER WHOLE-WHEAT CARROT AND PINEAPPLE MUFFINS

½ cup + 2 T whole-wheat flour
¾ cup all-purpose flour
2 tsp cinnamon
½ tsp nutmeg
½ tsp salt
1 tsp baking powder
½ tsp baking soda

1 cup walnuts,
     toasted and chopped
2 large eggs
2/3 cup honey
1/3 cup vegetable oil
1 tsp vanilla
2 cups grated carrots
1/2 cup pineapple, medium dice

Preheat oven to 400 degrees. Mix dry ingredients together, including walnuts. Beat the eggs and add the other wet ingredients, including carrots and pineapple, and mix well. Quickly mix wet and dry ingredients together, just until evenly moist. The trick to quick breads is to stir as little as possible.

Divide batter into muffin pans. Bake 20–30 minutes, until toothpick comes out clean. Makes 18 muffins.

NINE

Natalie liked to go to Pueblo, where her auntie Charmaine lived with her husband—who was a lot younger than her, though nobody seemed to care. Charmaine had a swing set, even though she didn't have any kids, and she had a pool set up in the backyard with a platform built all around it, so you could sit kinda high and soak your feet in the water and read and nobody cared. Charmaine's husband, Albert, would make grilled bratwursts and hamburgers and roasted vegetables on his grill, and it was really good food, which spared her having to eat Grandma's suppers or Charmaine's, either, because neither one of them believed in salt. Grandma also thought her lasagna was good, but she just put white cheese on top of noodles with canned tomato sauce. Not even spaghetti sauce, just plain old tomato sauce with no salt added.

In Pueblo, there was good food all over the place. Right in Charmaine's neighborhood was a tiny store that had salty black olives and pickles and salamis. On the corner down the street was a bar that kids could go to in the daytime and eat one of the best plates of spaghetti *ever*. Even in the Pueblo Mall, there was really good food—a Chinese restaurant that made hot grilled vegetables right in front of you, and a Mexican restaurant that made a pork-and-avocado burrito that was one of Natalie's favorite foods in all the world. She begged to eat the burritos at Los Tres every time they went to Pueblo.

And since they came up here to get school clothes, they were definitely going to the mall this time. So she was in a pretty good mood when they started out shopping. Not that she liked school, but you had to go anyway, so you might as well get some new clothes for it. Jade, of course, had to try on *everything* in JCPenney and Sears, and Grandma had to keep telling her things were too old for her, which put Jade in a bad mood. She said, "I'm going into second grade! I'm not a baby!"

Natalie didn't particularly care what she wore as long as it was comfortable, so she put on the jeans her grandma picked out, and she herself chose some really pretty red cords and a floaty white blouse. When she came out to show it to Grandma, Jade snorted. "You look like a red velvet cupcake!"

Nat turned to look at herself again, and she still liked it. Her tummy was kind of round, but it always was, so it might as well get a little poof over it. The shirt gathered around her chest and puffed out so it kinda looked like she might have breasts, and it had long fairy-tale sleeves. Lines of red and purple and yellow embroidery looped along the hems.

"That's not terribly flattering, Natalie. Sorry. Maybe not white, huh?"

"What's wrong with white?"

"Nothing. It just might make you look a little bigger than you are."

Jade snickered.

"I don't care." Natalie waved her hands like a flamenco dancer she'd seen on TV. The cuffs fell over her hands. "I want it anyway."

Grandma said, "I don't think so."

Nat spun. "Why? It's not too old for me. It doesn't look like a grown-up girl. I *like* it." She almost never found anything she really loved. She smoothed her hands over the sleeves. "Please, Grandma?"

"Let's think about it. Try on the other things first, and I want to check Dillard's before we finish."

They all trailed from store to store, until the only person who was enjoying any of it was Jade, still trying on everything she could get her hands on, flipping her stupid hair all over the place. Nat had a headache. She'd already picked out two pairs of pants and four shirts, which was more than enough, and she more or less let Grandma pick all of them so that she had more bargaining power when it came to the flamenco shirt and red pants.

Finally, they sat in the food court and had their lunch. Hannah ate pizza, so they got that first. Jade liked the pretzels with cheese, and Grandma ordered there, too, just because it was easy. She gave Natalie a ten-dollar bill so she could order her burrito. She felt proud and grown up, ordering at the counter. The woman didn't seem to notice that Nat was only eight. She probably thought she was way older, like ten.

Natalie carried the burrito carefully back to the table, but nearly everybody was already finished. Nat had been thinking about this burrito for two weeks, and she really didn't want to rush through it. Carefully, she cut a triangle of tortilla, revealing the chunks of meat and avocado and chile inside, and took a slow, thoughtful bite.

Salt and softness, tender meat and a chunk of tomato all exploded in her mouth. She chewed it very, very slowly, then took a small sip of water and ate another bite. She didn't talk. She didn't look around. She just ate her burrito.

Grandma chuckled. "You sure know how to eat, kiddo."

Natalie looked up, pleased at the compliment. "Do you want to try a bite?"

"No thanks, sweetie." She shifted Hannah on her lap. "Finish up so we can go home."

Natalie said, "What about my other clothes, the ones at Penney's?"

"Let me think about it. Eat your burrito."

But the moment was spoiled. Nat knew she wouldn't get them. If she were Jade, she would throw a big fat fit and cry and yell and not even care who looked at her. She put her fork down. "I'm done," she said, but to her horror, her eyes filled up with tears and she couldn't stop them. She folded her hands and tried really hard, but they fell out of her eyes anyway.

"Oh, sweetie," Grandma said. "If you want them that much, we can go get them."

Even Jade didn't say anything as Natalie nodded her head. "Yes," she said, and the word came out all sloppy because she had tears in her mouth.

They went back to Penney's and got the pants and blouse, and Natalie held them close to her chest, her heart singing and singing. She couldn't wait to get them home and try them on again.

As she drove back from the farm, Tessa had the radio on, and just as she pulled onto the main drag, a Crosby, Stills & Nash song came on—"Helplessly Hoping," with all its beautiful alliteration. Tessa reached for the sound control to turn it up, and when she touched the button, a memory bobbed up from the murk of her brain.

Dancing with another little girl in a room with windows all

around the top. The tower. The two of them held hands and
leaned back, each pulling against the weight of the other, spin-
ning, laughing, holding on very tightly. Music played loudly, and
they sang along.

She pulled into the parking lot and turned off the car, hoping something more would follow, but there was nothing except the lingering sense of yearning, that sense of nearly getting
a major piece before the window slammed shut again.

Damn it.

Rubbing at a slight headache at her temple, she got out and
locked the car, then slung her bag over her shoulder. Ambling
into the plaza, she sifted mentally through the visit at the farm,
letting it all—excitement and worry and foreboding—whirl
around.

Her distracted brain didn't notice that her feet had carried
her to The 100 Breakfasts Café until she was standing right in
front of it. Her stomach growled. She glanced at her watch. Only
one-thirty. It would be open for another half hour. Maybe she
would have to try one of the cinnamon rolls. And a cup of tea.

It was pretty quiet inside, with only a few customers lingering in the booths and dotting the counters. Tessa settled at the
counter with her bag, and pulled out a notebook and pen and
flipped back to the list of things she remembered.

Songs. Whole folk songs. Lots of them.
A blond woman who seems mean (probably my mother?).
A black-and-white dog sleeping with me (Brenna).
A sidewalk covered with colored chalk.
Playing jacks with another girl (boy?).
Playing hide-and-seek in really high grass or something.
  A big field.
Getting scared and lost.

Now she added:

A white cat.
A "tower" room.
Playing with a little girl in that tower.
The house painted the "wrong" colors.
Splashing somebody in a baby pool, completely naked.
A shoe-box doll bed.

She leaned her forehead into her palm and peered at the page, as if more would appear.

"Do you want to order something, hon?" asked a waitress.

Tessa straightened. "Oh! Yes. Do you have any cinnamon rolls left?"

"Sorry. Wanna look at a menu?"

"Sure." But she didn't. Her heart was set on a cinnamon roll. So set that, to her horror, she felt strongly as if she might *cry* about it. It was absurd, and she kept her head bent over the menu until the overwhelming emotion passed. "Um . . ."

"Today is the day for baked French toast," said another woman.

Tessa looked up to find Vita standing there, all ropy leanness and kind eyes. The first time she'd been here, Vince had tried to convince her to eat the French toast. "All right, I'm game."

Vita put the menu back in its holder. "Coming right up."

In the kitchen, Vita gave the order to her cook and went back to the task she'd left, which was clearing off the stainless-steel counter in the center of the room so that she could make cinnamon rolls for the week. They were a signature item at the café, and Vita had planned to give Annie a lesson in preparing the dough this afternoon. To that end, she'd prepared two batches of dough, an hour apart, and now pulled out the ingredients for the third. She didn't make fresh rolls every day—it would be too time consuming—but kneaded, rolled, and shaped the rolls to be frozen. They could then be pulled out, thawed, and allowed to rise a second time, and baked day by day.

Through the pass-out window, she could see the woman from the tour company. Tessa. She reminded Vita of someone, but try as she might, Vita couldn't bring it in. It was gestures as much as anything, the way she sighed just now and tapped her pen against the page between bursts of writing.

Pretty, with that crazy tumble of wavy blond hair, as shiny as a child's because she didn't put anything on it. Or wear much makeup. Her body was lean and long-limbed, but not at all delicate. She exuded confidence and strength, even arrogance.

And sadness. It quivered around the edges of her all the time, something a bit lost, hungry. Lonely, maybe.

When the plate of French toast was ready, Vita carried it out herself and put down a small glass bowl of powdered sugar with a spoon. "Do you want fruit? We have some peaches from Green Gate."

Tessa's head popped up. "Do they have *orchards* there, too?"

"The orchard is where it all started. The Spanish brought peach trees with them, and they flourished. When the Nathan brothers came here in the late sixties, they bought the orchard and all the ranch land around it."

"Well, then I really should have some peaches, shouldn't I?"

"Be right back." She headed into the kitchen, dished out some peaches, and popped them in the microwave for thirty seconds. While she waited for the bell to ding, she dismissed the dishwasher and the fry cook and told Annie to go smoke a cigarette before they got moving.

"I don't smoke," Annie said, offended.

"Good, then. Have a little break and stretch your legs. We'll start the rolls in about twenty minutes."

Annie saluted her. Vita watched the woman go, and it seemed that even in a week she was standing straighter. That was what cooking and kindness could do for a person. Carrying the dish of peaches out to Tessa, Vita had an idea. "Do you bake?"

"Not really," she said, dumping all the peaches over the bread. There were shadows under her eyes and Vita wanted to smooth her brow. "I'm on the road all the time, you know?"

"Want to help bake some cinnamon rolls this afternoon?"

"Really?" Tessa's eyes, a strange pale green like new spring shoots, lit up. "That would be a blast, actually. I'd love it."

Vita tapped the counter. "Good, then. Finish up and we'll get started."

Tessa felt shy walking into the kitchen, even though Vita was leading her. "Annie," Vita said, "this is Tessa, and she's also going to be making rolls with us. You can wash your hands at that sink over there, Tessa."

Annie gave her a nod, and Tessa recognized the feline-looking woman from the graveyard behind the church. "Hi."

Vita took an iPod out of a dock. "Any suggestions?"

Tessa waited to see if Annie would say anything, and when she shook her head, Tessa said, "Do you have any Crosby, Stills and Nash?"

"Why, yes," Vita said, raising an eyebrow. "I do."

"I just heard 'Helplessly Hoping' in the car." A wisp of the yearning wove through her chest. She felt very unsettled today, almost dizzy.

"I don't have that one, but let's see what we can do. I love it when somebody who isn't ancient knows my music."

"I grew up with it," Tessa said. "My dad's a surfer and hippie from way back."

"Is that so? Where's your dad?"

"California."

Vita nodded. She put the iPod in its dock and came over to the table. "All right, ladies, we're going to make cinnamon rolls here today. Since I knew I was going to show Annie here how to do it, I've already got one batch of bread dough rising, which we'll work with in a few minutes, and I'm going to start a fresh one so you see how to do it."

Tessa hummed along with the music, watching as Vita illustrated the first steps of the process. "I like to give the yeast a head start," she said, "by letting it dissolve in a little sugar water. The trick with yeast is that it's easily killed if the temperature is wrong, so imagine you need it to feel barely warm to your fingers." She pushed the bowl toward each of them. They took turns sticking their fingers into the water to test it, and both nodded.

Vita measured yeast out of a large dark jar and sprinkled it over the top of the water. It piled up, then skidded into the lake and started to dissolve. Almost immediately it started to grow.

"Cool," Annie said.

"It is cool," Vita agreed. "Bread is magical."

Tessa breathed in the smell with pleasure, surprised at how it eased the tension in her shoulders. They found a bag to put over her cast.

"Kneading bread is one of the most therapeutic things I know of," Vita said. She sprinkled flour over the entire surface of the counter and slapped down the dough she had ready to go, divided into three pieces, one for each of them. "It's going to be sticky to start with, but just keep kneading and it will get better. If it's too sticky, dust it with a little more flour."

"How do you know if it's too sticky?" Annie asked. Tessa was surprised by how beautiful her speaking voice was—low and mellifluous, almost hypnotic.

"You'll know," Vita said.

Annie shot Tessa a worried look, like, *Is this scary or what?* Tessa widened her eyes in agreement.

"You knead bread by folding it," Vita said, "and then pressing the heel of your hand into the fold, like this." She folded, pressed, folded, pressed. "Now you guys try it."

Both women pulled their dough toward them and followed Vita's lead. Tessa loved the way it felt, spongy and cold, and how it started to change under her palm as she kneaded it. "Cool," she said, and at almost the exact same moment, Annie said, "Awesome," and they both laughed.

Vita nodded. "I'm telling you, cooking is a very healing thing." Her lean arms showed muscle as she kneaded her own dough. "Keep it steady. We have to knead this particular dough for fifteen minutes."

Tessa could feel the action in her biceps and forearm. "This would be a good way to build up my arm when I get this cast off."

"How much longer do you have to wear it?" Annie asked.

"Three more weeks. It's been in a cast all summer. I broke it in two places." She punched the dough with extra force. "I'm pretty sick of it."

"I broke my right arm in two places," Annie said. "It was so itchy. That was what I hated."

"And it's so awkward." Tessa flung the arm around. "So heavy!"

"How long are you going to be in town, Tessa?" Vita asked. Her movements were smooth and rhythmic, like a Buddhist meditation, pull and turn, fold and press; pull and turn, fold and press.

"Not sure exactly, since it will depend on how fast I get all the research done, but I'm also having a good time here. I might hang around for a couple of weeks just to enjoy myself." She turned the dough, rolled the heel of her hand into it, turned, rolled. It felt clammy. "This morning I went to Green Gate Farms, and on Sunday I walked to the lake, but I still need to check out the other hiking trails around here and probably do the pilgrimage route to see what it's like."

"What kind of hikes?" Annie asked.

"That's what I need to find out, really. There are tons of trails, so I guess I need to find out which ones would suit my demographic." She stopped to pluck a glob of stuck dough from the back of her hand. "Do you know, Vita? Any suggestions?"

"I'm a runner more than a hiker, but I've run on hundreds of miles of trails around here. You two should go."

Annie shot Tessa a shy look. "I'm not very good. I'm also not sure how far I could go." She gave Vita a meaningful look. "If you know what I mean."

"Sure."

"I'm a little hobbled at the moment myself," Tessa said, sticking out her foot. "Still recovering from an accident. I'd love the company if you want to come along."

"Maybe," she said, in a thin little voice.

It plucked the cheerleader in Tessa's breast, and she thought painfully of Lisa looking up to her with clear pride on her young face. Maybe she ought to make peace with that before she dragged anyone else out on a hike.

Tessa watched as Annie kneaded her own ball of dough. She

had tattoos around both wrists, in delicate beautiful colors. "Those are beautiful tattoos," she said.

Annie seemed pleased. "Thanks," she said shyly. "I drew them myself."

"Really? Are you a tattoo artist?"

"No. I just like to draw."

Tessa bent in to look closely. The design was elaborate and stylized, sophisticated. "Impressive." She frowned. "I was noticing some guy's tattoos the other day. Maybe I should get one. I wear so many bracelets, it would be like having permanent jewelry."

Annie and Vita laughed. "Think about it before you leap in, sweetie," Vita said. "They don't go away."

"Do you have a tattoo?"

Vita paused and pulled aside her T-shirt, showing a name tattooed on her upper chest. *Jesse.* "He was an abuser and a bastard, and I keep it to remind me to never let a man take over my life that way again."

"Beautiful," Annie said. She held up her left hand. "I had the girls in jail give me a tattoo ring on my wedding-ring finger for the same reason. Never again."

Tessa looked at her own bare hands, thinking how badly she'd wanted a ring from Glenn, something to tattoo her, brand her to the world as his woman. Not a diamond or jewels, just a simple gold band.

Unity. Family.

Vita said quietly, "How about you, Tessa? If you had a tattoo to remind you of something, what would it be?"

She folded the bread, pressed it down, saw Lisa's terrified face as she went under the rushing water. "I don't know how I would symbolize it," she said finally, "but I'd put something to remind me of the sin of hubris."

"What's hubris?" Annie asked.

"Too much pride."

Vita met her eyes, a glitter deep in them. "A skull and cross-bones?"

Tessa thought of her dad, with his single earring and pirate ways. "Oh, that would be priceless, for so many reasons."

"Better to have too much pride," Annie said, "than not enough."

Tessa looked at her, seeing the scars, the piercings, her brittle thinness. Annie met her gaze evenly. Proudly.

"It's a lot harder to break someone who has a lot of pride," Vita said.

"That's true." Tessa poked a finger into the dough. "Where does that come from?"

"Good parents," Vita said.

"Someone to tell you that they think you're the greatest," Annie said.

"I definitely had that. Have it," Tessa said.

"Good parents?"

"No mom. Great dad."

"The surfer?" Vita asked.

"Yeah. And he is that person, you know, who always said that I was the best, the most beautiful, the smartest. Whatever. I am the apple of his eye, and I always have known it." The other two were looking at her with such longing that she said, "I guess I'm lucky, huh?"

"Yes," Vita said. "My mother was fine, but sort of ineffectual, you know? Really a prisoner of her times. My father just didn't register girls. He spent all his energy on my brother."

Annie punched her dough so hard that both women looked at her. "I lived in foster homes most of my whole life. In Albuquerque, mostly."

"That sucks," Tessa said.

"It did," Annie agreed. "It totally did." She took a breath. "But I'm looking forward in my life, not back."

"Bravo," Vita said. "It's really all we've got, isn't it?"

Tessa said, "But if you don't know where you've been, how can you know where you're going?"

"Oh, I know where I've been," Annie said.

Tessa felt suddenly ashamed to be poking around in her little identity angst when she'd had so much more than either of these two, when her problem was too much pride instead of not enough.

"Are you guys ready to add the cinnamon?" Vita said.

"Yes!"

Vita rolled the dough out very thinly on the floured surface of the steel work space. "We need to have a fairly even rectangle," she said, folding down a round edge and rolling her heavy marble rolling pin over it. Tessa and Annie, stationed at either end of the table, imitated her as best they could. "A little thinner, Tessa," she said. "Very good, Annie. Get that corner a little more square. It's not desperately important, but you're kind of a perfectionist, so you'll like getting it exactly right."

Annie smiled, a crooked half smile that made her look about twelve.

Vita dipped a pastry brush in melted butter and brushed it over the dough until it glistened. "Cover the whole thing," she said. "Then sprinkle the cinnamon mixture over it. It doesn't have to be perfectly even, Annie. It's kind of fun to have surprises."

Tessa found herself humming under her breath as she rolled the dough into a tight, long tube, and she stopped to listen to what it was.

"Come all ye rolling minstrels," she began to sing aloud, *"and together we will try to rouse the spirit of the earth . . ."*

"Those that dance will start to dance," sang Vita along with her.

And Annie, too, said, "Hey, I know that song!"

"It's on the folk-song loop," Vita said, nodding at her iPod dock. "Fairport Convention. It's good music for the rush."

"Ah, that's it."

Tessa smiled, pinching the edges of the loaf, and sang, *"Come all ye rolling minstrels,"* and the other two joined in, *"and together we will try to rouse the spirit of the earth . . ."*

When the cinnamon rolls were baked, they sat at the table in the back of the kitchen, muscles aching, and ate them freshly out of the oven, covered in fresh butter cut in thick pats and allowed to melt into the hot bread. It was, Tessa thought, one of the best foods she had eaten in her life.

Ever.

When she got back to her room, Tessa tried to make notes on all the information she'd collected today, but her brain refused to do one more task. Leaving the French doors open to the late-afternoon breezes, she sprawled on the bed, flat on her belly, arms flung upward, and fell instantly asleep. She dreamed in fragments. Music and a red bike and a fire and something about pie.

It was the wind that awakened her. It slammed with sudden and muscular strength into the day, bringing clouds that smelled of rain, gusting and bellowing, knocking over a chair on the balcony and swinging the wind chimes into a frenzy of clanging. A scatter of loose cottonwood leaves flew into the room through the open doors like giant confetti.

Tessa rolled over to her side and looked out to the darkening sky, feeling suddenly lonely. Why had she come here? Why did she still think she had to wander all over the universe instead of picking a place to settle in?

Partly because she didn't really have any other job to do. Tourism had been her career for nearly sixteen years.

She missed her father. He was the through line in her world, the one thing that stayed the same, year after year, move after move. She always missed him when she first left Santa Cruz on one of her long breaks. No one had ever "got" her like her dad, got her jokes, got it when she was cranky and tired and didn't want to talk, or listened endlessly when she was in a mood to talk and talk and talk. She missed the dogs. Missed Peaches curled up on her bed whenever she woke up. Missed Sam's eclectic music collection—all on CDs and vinyl, of course, since he wouldn't buy a computer, and an iPod required a computer.

She'd get over missing her dad again, but today the contrast of having had his easy companionship every day to being alone again made her life seem kind of pathetic. Maybe she was tired of traveling all the time. She'd be forty in three years. Maybe it was time for a change.

For now she tried again to focus on the information she'd collected today. Green Gate Farms and the beautiful cooking school there that made even Tessa—lifelong indifferent cook—want to buy knives and wear a pale-green coat with her name embroidered on it. Hmm. She should definitely find out if they could get a coat personalized for each person on the tour. Great souvenir and conversation piece.

She thought, too, of baking bread with Vita, who had told Annie and Tessa about her habit of running every evening for three to ten miles. She'd shown them the medals she saved from the marathons she'd run around the country. Every year she picked a different race in a new city—this year she had run the Chicago Marathon. It was a vacation for her. And she had said, quietly, that running made her strong after she'd escaped an abusive relationship. Annie had looked at her for a long time. "How did you get away from him?"

And Tessa noticed the crookedness of Annie's nose, the scar along her forehead, and wanted to cry. Cry for Vita and Annie and their scars. Cry for women who had not had anyone in their lives to make them fierce. Cry for Lisa, who had been learning fierceness when nature knocked her flat.

Before the black hole could open again in her chest, Tessa sat up and found her cell phone and called her dad.

"Hey, girl!" he said. "I'm so glad to see your number. How's it going?"

"Dad, I had such a good day. I went out to the commune, or what was the commune."

"Wow. Did it look familiar?"

"Maybe a little, and there was an old house I wanted to visit, but there was a conference going on there."

A little bubble of silence came down the line. "A conference?" he repeated, perplexed.

"Yes." She laughed. "I'd bet a fair sum of money that you'd never recognize it now. It's big business. The farms are still organic, and they raise bees for honey and have retreats and conferences there."

"Holy shit."

"It's really cool. And I'm pretty sure I recognized the tea they served in a little café."

"Is it like a cinnamon ginseng lemony thing?"

"That's it."

"Gawd, I love that tea!"

"It was fantastic," she agreed. "They have farm stands, and they bottle the honey and ship produce to cities all over New Mexico and Colorado, and they've just opened a vegetarian cooking school. It's amazing."

"A school! Huh." He laughed. "I'm having a little trouble wrapping my old brain around the whole thing."

"You should come on out here, check it out. You'd have fun."

"Nah. You're gonna be done in a couple of days, right?"

Tessa thought of the school, the hikes. "I might need to stay a little longer. There's a lot to explore."

"Sounds like it."

"You'd have a good time, Dad. Why don't you take a week and come look around?"

"No. Thanks. I'm not interested in digging around in the past. Look forward, never back."

"Mmm."

He said, "How are you doing with all your . . . stuff?"

"Fine. I'm fine." She led him back to her questions. "Did we live in the old house at the commune?"

"Yeah. It was a wreck, but it was better for you than a tent in the wintertime."

"I wish I remembered."

"You were pretty little."

She nodded. "I just keep getting the feeling . . ."

"What?"

"That there's something I should remember, something important that I forgot."

"Like what?"

Tessa narrowed her eyes, letting the sensation rise in her memory. "I don't know. I can't bring it in."

"Well, let me know if it shows up. And call me if you need me."

"I will. Thanks, Dad."

Her phone beeped, and she pulled it away from her ear to see who was calling. *Vince Grasso* showed on the screen. Something hot ran down her spine. "Hey, Dad. I've got a call coming in, okay? I'll call you tomorrow."

"Bye, kiddo. Take care."

Breakfast #6

Decadence: Vita's special homemade cinnamon rolls, hot and sweet, served with organic pork sausage, one egg, and coffee (we recommend you drink it black).

VITA'S CINNAMON ROLLS WITH ORANGE CREAM CHEESE FROSTING
〜 About 16 rolls

1 package yeast
½ cup water
1 tsp plus ½ cup raw sugar
1¼ cups of milk
½ cup butter
2 eggs, beaten
1 T vanilla extract
5 cups white flour
1 tsp salt
(Vita's secret spice mixture: 1 T cinnamon, ½ tsp nutmeg,
*   1 star anise pod, ground fresh, 1 tsp ground coriander)*
1 cup brown sugar
1 cup butter, very soft

ICING:

6 oz. cream cheese, softened
¹/₂ cup cream
¹/₂ tsp vanilla
1 tsp orange zest
2 T orange juice
1¹/₂ cups powdered sugar

For the bread:

Add ¹/₂ cup butter, cut into pieces, to the milk in a glass measuring cup and scald the milk in the microwave for about 2 minutes. Let cool to room temperature or a tiny bit warmer.

In a small bowl, mix ¹/₂ cup lukewarm water with 1 tsp sugar and sprinkle yeast on top. Let it get foamy.

In a large bowl, beat together ¹/₂ cup sugar, eggs, and vanilla. Stir in cooled milk-and-butter mixture and add the yeast mix. Stir in flour and salt until it is saturated. (Dough will be sticky.) Turn it out onto a floured surface and knead thoroughly until it is pliant and warm, like baby skin, about 15 minutes, adding flour as required. Return the dough to a large oiled bowl and turn it so the oil covers the entire ball. Cover with a thin, damp towel and set in a warm, draft-free place to rise until doubled in bulk. (At high altitudes, you will not want to use the trick of putting the bowl inside a stove. It will not be reliable, and may overproof.)

When the dough has risen, mix together brown sugar and spices and set aside. Prepare 3 13x9-inch pans with sides by cutting parchment paper to fit the bottoms.

Turn the dough out again onto a lightly floured surface

and gently fold it down, then roll it out into a large, thin rectangle. Spread butter over the entire surface and sprinkle it with the spices and sugar. Roll it neatly from the long end, and pinch the edges closed. Slice it into 2-inch pieces and put them in the pans approximately $1\frac{1}{2}$ inches apart to give them room to rise again. Let rise for an hour and then bake for 20–25 minutes in a 350 degree oven until golden brown and bubbly.

While the rolls are baking, prepare the icing by mixing all ingredients together until smooth. Drizzle over the rolls while still warm. Serve immediately, or microwave for 30 seconds before serving.

TEN

Vince had dropped the children with his mother on his way to work. She dismissed his worries about Jade and Natalie's constant fighting but promised to keep an eye on them when they were in Pueblo.

"And be sure Jade doesn't get baby teenager clothes," he said.

"Vince," she'd said in her ex-smoker's rasp. "I got it."

At work, the fire and rescue teams were doing training all week, brushing up on winter tracking, signs of hypothermia, winter survival in all its forms. It was a slower season for them once the hikers and amateur climbers and unskilled rafters headed home for the cold months, but there were always lost cross-country and backcountry skiers, and they did double time as house fires came front and center.

All day, Vince found himself thinking about the long limbs and straightforward gaze of Tessa Harlow. Her card was tucked into the back pocket of his jeans. He had the evening free. She was just passing through, so presumably she didn't have any big requirements for commitment and he wouldn't have to worry about his girls having much contact with her.

God knew he could use a little recreational relief.

As the guys wandered out of work, blinking in the bright

sunshine following an afternoon of training films, a couple of them invited Vince to come along to a local watering hole.

He shook his head. "Got other plans," he said, and headed home for a quick shower. Taking her card out of his wallet, he sat next to Pedro on the couch and dialed the number.

She answered, "Vince, hello." Her voice, smooth and low, percolated near the base of his neck. "I'm so glad you called."

"Me, too," he said, and at least it was honest. They arranged to meet in an hour.

Which was how he found himself in one of the lanes along the plaza, as the evening breezes began to sweep north across the river. She was sitting outside a little restaurant on a bench, wearing jeans and a simple tank top and gold sandals. A big fringed scarf, printed with wild red paisleys, was thrown over her shoulders. She didn't see him.

He stopped, filled with a hunger that had been missing in his life for a long, long time. Her tanned throat drew his eye, and he loved the wavy blond hair, the way she pulled it all into a kind of messy ponytail or something so that shiny little curls fell around her face and neck. Everything about her spoke of confidence and the solid sense of herself and clear-sighted directness he found refreshing.

Beside her, leaning against her leg, was a black-and-white dog, scruffy and badly in need of a bath and a good meal. She spoke to him quietly, rubbing his ears, touching his shoulder blades, firmly stroking down his back. The dog panted softly in the warm evening, smiling upward into the air.

Tessa looked up as Vince approached. In the twilight, her eyes were the color of new leaves, and she gave him a rueful smile. "I keep running into this little guy. I'm going to have to name him pretty soon."

"Lot of strays around here," he said. "Breaks your heart."

"You have room for one more dog, don't you? Look at this face."

Vince snorted. "It's a good-looking pup, but no can do. I have a houseful already."

"I'm so tempted to take him to my room for the night. Maybe tomorrow, then, I could take him to the humane society or something. Is there a no-kill shelter here?"

"Probably." The dog really did have a great face. Vince held out his hand. The dog sniffed it and gave it a gentle lick, then let Vince stroke his chest. "He's so skinny."

Tessa sighed. "I'm totally stuck on him. I can't leave him again."

"Again?"

"I've seen him every day since I've been here," she said. "My dad would tell me that means he's mine. And although I do try to avoid all that metaphysical crap he loves so much, I have to admit . . . this one is weighing on my conscience." Light edged her hair as she bent toward the dog. "Do you think the hotel will let me keep him for a night?"

"It's Los Padres, right? They do have a dog policy." He grinned. "Not sure they have *stray* dogs in mind. He's probably riddled with fleas, you know."

"I know, this is nuts."

"Tell you what," Vince said. "I've got my truck over there. We can put him in the back for now, have some dinner, and figure out what to do."

"I'd like to feed him."

"There's probably some dog food left from the other day when we went up to the lake. And I've always got water."

She smiled at him. It gave her skin a radiance, something

nearly supernatural. Her long green anime eyes again made him think of something. Someone. "My hero," she said in that hot-chocolate voice. "Thanks."

"Anytime." He bent and scooped the dog into his arms. "Come on, baby, we'll get you something to eat." The dog licked his neck, whimpering softly until Tessa came along and put her hand on his head. "It's okay, sweetie. Promise."

At the truck, Vince put the dog down and unlocked the back gate, letting it swing up so the dog could leap into the rubberized back. He poured water and kibble into dishes, and the dog went after the food like the starving creature he was.

"Poor baby," Tessa said, and Vince thought she might be blinking tears away. It made him want her in a way that felt like too much. He took a step backward.

The dog was happy enough to curl up on a blanket in the back of the truck, and they left him there and walked back through the gathering evening.

"I like your scarf," he said, mainly because he couldn't think of anything else.

"Thanks." She smiled at him. "Do I make you nervous, Vince?"

He stopped. "Maybe a little. You're not really like the women I usually meet."

She stood looking up at him, her hands caught behind her back, which afforded him a pleasant view of her not-insubstantial breasts, sloping away into darkness beneath her tank top. "What are they like? Your lovers?"

"Lovers?" He nearly coughed. "Uh. Just . . . women, I guess."

"I'm just a woman."

"No," he said. "You're kind of . . . mysterious."

She laughed. "Trust me. I'm really not at all." She took a step closer, her lips still turned up at the corners, teasing and sweet at once, and he thought of his fantasy of her lying on the shores of the lake half naked, pleasuring him. Her gaze went to his mouth. "Here is something unmysterious—I've been thinking about kissing you since the first night we met."

"Is that so?" He looked at her mouth, and, feeling way over his head, bent down to kiss her. Thinking maybe it would just be a little taste, an appetizer. Her lips were pillowy soft and yielding. Her breasts barely brushed his chest, and her arms were still locked behind her, which was weirdly arousing. He stepped slightly closer, aware that they were on the corner of a lane that was not well traveled but there could be someone passing at any moment, and yet the moment was so sweet, so engrossing, he couldn't think of a reason to stop.

Instead, he angled his head a little and she tilted the other way, and he took her head into his hands, feeling hair on the backs of his fingers, the angle of her jaw against his palm, her sweet mouth opening and inviting his tongue inside. So he dove, and she made the softest sound and followed him back when he would have retreated. Her hands came up to his sides, the backs of his arms, and he felt the brush of her body down the front of him, nudging breasts, belly, thighs. It gave him a massive hard-on—slightly embarrassing in so public a place—and he lifted his head. "We have to stop this."

She half-closed her eyes, resting her cheek on his palm. "I love your voice," she said. "It sounds like something wild. The wind or an elk."

Her lower lip glistened, and he bent as if in a trance to suck it gently into his mouth. "How hungry are you, really?"

She laughed. "Hungry enough we do need to eat."

It broke the tension, and Vince managed to pull himself together. He took her hand as they walked toward the restaurant. "Where are your girls tonight?"

"My mother took them to Pueblo to go school shopping. It's a pretty good-size town about three hours north of here."

"I would have thought Albuquerque was closer."

"It's about the same. Easier driving north, and my mom's sister lives there." He felt that ripple of worry over the fighting again. "I'm hoping a break will shake things up and they'll stop fighting so much."

"They are clever at pushing each other's buttons. And Natalie is a little intense."

He paused, his hand on the door to the restaurant. "What do you mean?"

"She's just a little prickly." She narrowed her eyes. "Protective. Doesn't like it that Pedro likes me."

"Picked up an awful lot in an hour."

She raised an eyebrow. One side of her mouth lifted. "Did I step on your toes? I didn't mean to. It's part of my job to be observant, figure things out."

"You didn't step on my toes."

"Yeah? So, were you ever going to open the door, then?"

Maybe, he thought, she was too brash for his tastes. Too plainspoken. He pulled the door open and she brushed by him. A scent of lemon and nutmeg rose from her skin, and in response, a rush of saliva filled his mouth. He didn't even like lemons. Too astringent.

And yet he discovered he was again watching her ass as she walked ahead of him, rear end shapely from all that hiking.

A young hostess seated them on the patio, brought water. "Have you eaten here?" Tessa asked, scanning the menu.

Vince shook his head. "Hasn't been here long, I don't think—a year or a little more."

"It has a pretty good reputation," Tessa said.

The menu was new American, pretty simple stuff. Local

meats and fish, trout and bass, and even some game meats—
venison and rabbit—cooked simply and straightforwardly. The
side dishes were unfussy —roasted summer squash and roasted
ears of corn. Tessa ordered venison stew, along with a salad of
fresh greens and the roasted corn. After his long day, Vince was
starving, and he ordered a steak and a beer. "You want me to
order anything else?" he asked. "We can try the beets, too."

"Sure," she said. When the server gathered their menus and
departed, Tessa inclined her head. "You've done restaurant tast-
ings or something?"

"My wife was a big fanatic for food television. She fancied
herself a gourmet."

"Ah. What kind of food did she cook?"

"Classic French style—Cordon Bleu, the whole nine yards."
He shrugged. "Let's not talk about her."

"Is that a painful wound, still?"

"No," he said, meeting her eyes. "I'd just rather talk about
you."

A slow grin spilled over her face. "Good answer." She leaned
back and the scarf slid sideways, showing the smooth line of
her collarbone. "What do you want to know?"

"Tell me where you lead your tours."

"Small talk, then." She smiled at him. "Okay. I've been in
thirty-seven countries, and lived in four. I like it. I like learning
new things, meeting new people, just the adventure of it."

"Where have you lived?"

"I've been based in Santa Monica for the past two years.
Before that, it was Tasmania, and before that, New Zealand,
and Crete." She frowned, looking at her hands.

"Which one was your favorite?"

"Tasmania," she said without hesitating. Something flickered
over her mouth. Melancholy.

"You miss it."

She nodded. "There are things about Los Ladrones that make me think of it, oddly. The mountains, the sort of hostile environment, maybe."

"Not sure I know where Tasmania is."

"I didn't know, either, until I went there. South of Australia."

"Did you see Tasmanian devils?"

"Do you know that everyone asks that question?"

"It's the only intelligent question to ask." He leaned forward, elbow on the table. "Did you?"

She twirled scarf fringes around one finger. "I did. They're kind of a cross between a rat and a squirrel. Black and white, with these weird ears that turn bright red when they're eating. And they are savage, savage little things. Absolute eating machines, that's all they live for."

"I know a dog like that."

She chuckled. "The devils are endangered, actually. There's a really nasty face cancer that spreads among them and kills them in about three months flat. Scientists aren't sure they can save them."

"That would be sad." Light began to fade behind her. It set the edges of her pale hair afire and illuminated the wistfulness in the lines around her eyes. Vince guessed, "But it wasn't Tasmanian devils you loved there, was it?"

She shook her head. "No, there was a man."

"But not a husband?"

"We lived together for four years. A scientist," she said. "Studied penguins."

Vince grinned. "Really?"

"Yes."

"That's pretty cool."

She looked down, twirled the fringes again, and he could see plainly that she missed her old lover. "Yeah." Then, as if realizing her own body language, she sat up and leaned toward Vince, her pale, beautiful eyes focused entirely on him. "But I'd rather talk about you."

For a minute he met her gaze, aware of a rustling of jealousy in his belly. Then he leaned back, signaled for another beer. It wasn't going to go anywhere. It wasn't going to be anything. He didn't have to collect her whole life story. They could go back to the hotel, have a good fuck, and be done. It was what he'd been thinking about since seeing her that first night.

He would enjoy it, but it would be a mistake to gather too much information, find out too much about her, give too much away about himself.

Keep it light, man.

The food came, elegantly arranged on square white plates garnished with orchids and nasturtiums and a green leaf Tessa didn't know. Before she even tasted the food, she knew she would be faintly disappointed, and she was. The venison was adequate, if a little tough, and she ate a bit of it. Even the corn, which should have been brilliant this time of year, was bland. Drinking water, she sat back in her chair. "How's yours?"

He lifted one shoulder. "Okay. Not the best, not the worst." He gestured with his knife to her unfinished plate. "No good?"

"It's fine." From her back pocket, she took a notebook and a pen and made a few notes, thinking as she wrote of the encounters this morning at Green Gate Farms. The eerie sense of something lost moved through her chest again, cold and hollow.

"You okay?"

Tessa looked up. "Yes, sorry. Woolgathering."

"Don't take this the wrong way, but I keep thinking you look familiar. We must have met somewhere."

Tessa nearly told him that she'd been here as a child but then just didn't want to get into the whole weird history of it. "They say everybody has a twin." She shook her head. "It's been kind of an odd day."

"Want to talk about it?"

Tessa looked at him, pulled the scarf closer around her shoulders. Hurricane lamps were burning on the white-covered tables, and waiters moved quietly and ubiquitously through the well-dressed patrons. In contrast, he sat like an elk amid Abyssinian cats, his eyes calm and dark. He looked tired. He had shaved, hastily, and cut himself. She thought of his belly, of the blue T-shirt flung over his shoulder the other day, thought of him picking up the dog and carrying him to his truck.

"Maybe I do," she said finally. "But not here."

His mouth lifted on one side. "I know a place."

"Said the spider to the fly."

He laughed, the sound as big as the rest of him, so vivid that several diners turned around to see where it came from. A spectacular brunette with three giant diamonds dripping delicately down her cleavage smiled, and Tessa realized she was an actress. A very famous actress. Who looked Vince over as if he were dessert.

He noticed, waggling his eyebrows at Tessa. "She can't help herself."

"I suppose not."

"C'mon." He stood and dropped some bills on the table. "Let's blow this pop stand, sister."

"You didn't really say that."

His grin—that sexy, sexy, small twinkle—caught her, mid-chest. In the distance, lightning flashed. She saw it and thought, *Uh-oh,* but followed him out anyway.

As they wound through the narrow old lanes, gusts of wind skipped through, sending dry leaves clattering across the cobblestones. Tessa caught her hair and twisted it close to her neck. She heard a howl in the distance, like a banshee screaming. The hairs along her nape rose. "What the hell *is* that?"

"An owl, maybe."

Tessa frowned. No owl she'd ever heard.

"You know what this is, don't you?" Vince said, stopping to lift his face to the wind, like a dog scenting something. "Summer, blowing away. Tomorrow will be fall."

Thunder ambled across the mountains, quietly. "Summer doesn't end for almost three weeks."

"You'll see."

And suddenly she did feel colder. She tucked her scarf around her shoulders. She was glad when he led her into a cantina—there was no other word for it—with a ragtag band playing bluegrass in the corner. A pool table took up the far end of the room, and most of the patrons sat around the bar. Vince and Tessa sat a table near the back. "Quiet here," he said.

Everything seemed edged with luminosity: the plants hanging around an old-fashioned skylight, girded like a Victorian conservatory; the tiny purple lights looping around the bottles behind the bar; the musicians playing their eccentric instruments. "This is great."

"It's my favorite," Vince said. "Hasn't been corrupted yet."

"Have things changed a lot here?"

Vince rested his arms on the table in front of him and pursed his lips, looking around the room as if to evaluate it. Nodded. "It's not all bad, but yeah."

A woman in her sixties, with dyed black hair and the pouches of too many late nights beneath her eyes, dropped a cardboard coaster in front of each one of them. Waited.

"You order for me," Tessa said.

"You're not a margarita kind of woman, I don't think."

She shook her head.

"Tomato beer for me," he said, and narrowed his eyes. "And . . . let's see . . . a Guinness for my friend here."

Tessa sat up straight. "They have Guinness?"

"We got everything."

"Guinness it is." She grinned at Vince. "Well done."

The dark eyes glittered, focused entirely on her face. It was both disconcerting and heady.

"So what makes all the change a good thing?"

A single lift of his shoulder. "Well, it was just a dying little mountain town before all the tourists started showing up. So that's good. People need jobs."

"But?"

"Taxes have skyrocketed, which means not everybody can keep their land. And I don't want to see the land all turn to million-dollar retreats."

"Right. Classic story." The woman brought their drinks, and the Guinness was decent. Not too cold, deep and bitter and strong. "Do you live in town, then?"

"No, just outside. I bought some land for my girls when we came back here after my wife died. It's a good house for them, the old kind of farmhouses they built in the twenties, all red-sandstone blocks. Really solid."

It was easy to imagine him in a house like that, with those little girls—a life so unlike her own. She had thought that, perhaps, her life in Tasmania would be like that.

Which she hadn't admitted to herself very often. She took a

swallow of stout, pursed her lips around the flavor, and heard that little voice say again in her head, *Here I am.*

"So what made your day weird?" Vince asked.

Tessa took in a long breath, blew it out, and made a decision. "I lived here when I was very small. At the commune."

"Wow. Maybe that's why you look familiar."

She smiled. "Yeah, maybe we were sitting at the drugstore, side by side, long, long ago."

"Could have happened," he said in that rumbling voice. His mouth tipped up at the corners in that sexy, barely there grin.

"Yeah. Anyway. I went out to Green Gate Farms today, to check out the possibilities for the tour, and"—she paused, picking her way through truth and lies—"it was weirdly familiar. It kinda freaked me out."

"You're bound to remember something, right?"

Tessa nodded. "I don't know why it bothered me. Kinda silly, I guess." She rubbed the edge of one eyebrow, squinting as if to focus it all a little better. "It's like what I think I remember is a movie, and something else is there."

"There was a lot of drama there a long time ago. Do you know the story, how everybody came there?"

"Some of it."

"It's all hearsay, of course. I don't actually remember any of it." The band started to play Crosby, Stills, Nash & Young's, "Teach Your Children." Both Tessa and Vince glanced over. "Weird," he said.

"It's me. I'm having a Crosby, Stills and Nash day. Third time I've heard one of their songs today."

"*Déjà Vu,*" he said, naming the album.

Tessa laughed. Touched his hand. "Anyway. Tell me the story."

"Fact number one: I was born at the commune."

"No kidding? How long did you live there?"

"I didn't. My mother used a midwife and the birth didn't go well. As you might imagine," he spread his hands, "I was a pretty big baby, almost ten pounds, and although my mother is six feet tall, it was too much. She ended up hemorrhaging, and they rushed her to Santa Fe and we both nearly died. That was that, for her, so she moved to town and bought the bookstore, and that's where I grew up, over the store."

Tessa feigned swooning. "That would have been my ultimate dream come true as a ten-year-old—access to all those books whenever I wanted."

"It was great. It's still great." He raised his beer. "To reading."

She toasted with her glass. "What do you like to read?" She asked, and drank deeply. It was actually very good for Guinness not in Ireland.

"Mostly fiction. Mysteries, science fiction, horror, big history sagas, you know, like kings and battles and things like that. How about you?"

"Literally everything." She laughed, a little ruefully. "I always read everything when I was a kid—and I do mean everything, from Nancy Drew to Dickens to my dad's John D. MacDonald— but then I went to regular school and the English teachers started telling me to read 'real' books, so I tried. And you know, I kinda went off reading for a while. I had already been reading literary novels and the classics mixed in with whatever else, but—" She waved a hand. "So I went back to reading whatever I wanted, whenever I wanted to—reading had been my greatest pleasure in all the world. I mean, I never really watched all that much television, because we were moving around, never really had solid digs until I was thirteen, so reading was everything."

Vince leaned in, looking happy. "Me, too. Not the moving around, but the reading. I didn't read nonfiction, and I didn't really like mysteries in those days, but I read everything else. *Everything.*"

"Are you nearsighted?"

"Lasered."

"Me, too!" She slapped the hand he raised. "What were some of your favorites?"

He leaned on the table, and the edge of his tattoos showed beneath the sleeves of his T-shirt, a pale earth color with *There's no place like roam* on the front. "Big on Stephen King. Asimov, of course, and all those big, juicy sagas that they used to have in the seventies and eighties, you know, like *The Adventurers* and—"

"Oh, yes," she cried. "And Sidney Sheldon."

He made a face. "He was okay, but maybe too romancey for me, that guy."

"Yeah, he's probably more of a writer for women. Like Tolkien is more for guys."

"You think so? I know women who like him."

"Mostly tomboys, I bet."

He grinned suddenly. "Probably." He winked. "And they say reading is dying."

"No way. So, tell me the drama about the commune."

"Okay." He put the bottle down precisely in the middle of the cardboard cocktail pad the server had put on the table. "So two brothers came out here from California. Wealthy kids, you know, looking for something. They had a vision for a commune and got it going, and from what I understand, it was pretty good for a few years. My mother lived there from the early days, '67, '68, with some of the original people, and it was pretty smooth."

"Right, I heard some of this earlier." She pulled out her notebook and flipped back a few pages. "Paula, who runs the farmers' market stand, and Cherry, her daughter, and the two brothers who started it all, Jonathan and Robert Nathan."

"Right. My mom and Paula are still good friends."

Tessa nodded. "So what ended the idyll?"

"Drugs, basically. Lot of people who came out to the commune were just there to get laid, loaf around, smoke dope."

"The usual." Tessa found herself noticing the vein running along the side of the muscle in his forearm and disappearing again into his wrist. Sexy.

"One of the people who came was a guy named Xander," Vince said, "from some big shipping family in the northeast. Really good-looking, very intelligent and charismatic, and he used it to his advantage, sort of set up a harem of women and children who were all living in a big old house out on the land."

Something thudded through her belly. "The Victorian, right? I saw it."

"Yeah. Later they made a school down there for all the commune kids, but at that time it was mostly Xander and his women, and a few other guys and their women."

Tessa shook her head. "I don't get the appeal of that life."

"No. Me, either. But we have the advantage of being post–baby boomers, right? There was a whole lot of shaking going on. They shook it loose for us."

Tessa had said much the same thing to her father, about the commune turning into the farm. "So what happened to Xander?"

"Somebody shot him right through the heart. They've never solved the crime or even tried that hard. Several women disappeared right after that, and a couple more moved to town, and the commune fell apart."

Tessa inclined her head. "This is only part of the story that I heard this morning. Cherry also said somebody made off with kilos and kilos of marijuana."

His eyebrows rose. "I've never heard that part."

"That's what she said. She also said there was a writer out there a few years ago, trying to piece it all together, and nobody talked."

"Yeah, it's all really mysterious. I guess the most we know is that something bad happened, and Xander died, and after that the commune lost most of the members."

Including Sam, Tessa thought. Including herself.

Overhead, a pattering began on the skylight, loud enough to be heard over the music. "Uh-oh!" Tessa looked up. "I'd better get back to the hotel. It's starting to rain."

He measured her. "I was thinking maybe you'd like to come to my place for a little while."

Tessa met his eyes. "Maybe for a little while."

ELEVEN

Later, she remembered the night in exaggerated cam-era shots, as if in an art-house movie. They dashed through the rain to Vince's truck. It was dark and, as they ran, water splashed over their ankles. When they got to the truck, she put a hand on his biceps and looked up at him.

"Vince," she said, just his name, and it was enough. His other arm swept around, engulfed her, and that big head blocked the rain as he kissed her. And again. Rain ran in cold tiny rivulets down her face, dripped down her cheek to fall on his chest. She felt the wet on her forehead and the part of her hair and her shoulders. His mouth was a pool of heat, succu-lent lips, thick tongue, and his arm hauled her close, over his thigh, against his belly. In ancient greeting, they pressed groins together.

She started to shiver.

"Do you want to come to my house?" His voice was so deep it was nearly inaudible.

"Yes. I'll follow you."

He paused. "It's just down the State Road, about three miles. I'll meet you there." He kissed her again. "Remember, I've got your dog."

Tessa drove her car out of the hotel parking lot and followed Vince to his house. In the car, she turned the heat on, shivering in her wet clothes. When they reached a gate, he got out, opened it, and they drove through, then he had to get out and close it again.

The house was two stories, as square as a schoolhouse, with a porch on two sides and a wide meadow rolling away down to a stand of trees. She parked and rushed up to the porch. The rain was coming down in steady, drenching sheets. Her clothes and hair were stuck to her. Her sandals slid off her feet as she walked.

Vince got the dog out of the back and coaxed him into the house, then flipped on the foyer light. It was blazing and un-pleasant, but it stayed on for only a second. They were plunged into darkness. "That's the power. There's a bad transformer somewhere along the route, and if it rains hard, we lose elec-tricity."

Tessa wrapped her arms around her body, shivering; at her feet, the dog did the same thing. "We might want some towels," she suggested gently.

"Right. I'll be back in a second." He dashed up the staircase. Tessa stayed where she was, afraid to knock something over if she started moving around. Vince came down a few minutes later and gave her a towel. He bent to rub the pup dry, talking in that way people do, in a soft voice, reassuring. "There you go, not so bad, right? Let me get your belly."

"Spooky in the dark," she said, drying her hair. At the sound of her voice, a dog made a sound in another room and came skittering around the corner to greet her, his nails skating un-certainly over the hardwood. He barreled into her legs, his usual greeting, and Tessa laughed. "Hi, honey," she said, digging her hands vigorously into the thick fur at Pedro's neck as he half-turned upside down. "I'm glad to see you, too."

The border collie pup gave her a sad look. "It's okay," she said, bending down to scratch his ears. "I still love you, too."

"You are so not giving that dog away," Vince said.

"My dad will take him." She stood. "Where's your other dog?"

"Sasha? Here somewhere. She's deaf as a post and half blind, so unless there's food involved, she's usually asleep on the landing upstairs. But open a cellophane wrapper and release one single molecule of scent, and she's right there, baby."

Tessa laughed.

Vince came close, holding up a candle. "C'mon. Let's get warm." He took her hand and pulled her upstairs to a giant bathroom with a big claw-footed tub, and although Pedro would have come in, Vince said, "No," and pointed him down the hall. "Is your cast okay?"

Tessa nodded. "Wet." She inclined her head. "I don't think it will survive a shower."

He smiled. "Steam bath."

He put the candle on the sink and pulled a shower curtain around the tub, started the water running. Steam rose over the top of the curtain as Vince turned back to her. He pulled off his shirt, but when Tessa would have followed suit, he said, "Let me."

She opened her arms, palms up, offering herself. Vince stepped forward and tugged the tank top off over her head, leaving her standing in an ordinary bra. "I didn't bring anything sexy with me," she said.

"This is plenty sexy for me." He skimmed his fingers along her shoulders, along the straps, along the edges of her breasts, and then unfastened the clasp and her breasts fell free. Not as high as when she was younger, not as perky, but Vince gave a hot little sigh and he scooped the flesh into his hands. "Wow," he said roughly. "Gorgeous. Better than I imagined."

She imagined him imagining her naked, and it made her dizzy. Suddenly his scent seemed to fill the room, bright and hot and fierce, like chiles and pine, and she reached for him, pulling his head to hers, digging her fingers into his hair. She made a noise as he captured her, lifted her into him, pushing her against the bathroom door, their chests slapping together, his hands grabbing around her bottom to haul her hard against his erection. Tessa wrapped her legs tight around him, moving in timeless sinuous curls. The kiss was violent, hard, tongues and suction and teeth. She felt her tooth cut his lower lip and tasted blood, but he only made a soft noise and hauled her closer.

He pulled her legs from his waist, and Tessa rested against the door. His skin gleamed in the steamy room, the hair on his forearms and chest gathering tiny droplets that caught the candlelight and glowed amber. She let him unfasten the jeans, but then made him halt as she pulled out a condom from her back pocket, holding it in her right hand as she let him shove the jeans from her hips.

When he would have taken his jeans off, she slapped his hands. "Fair is fair," she said. "Take this." He took the condom out of her hand and held out his arms as she unbuttoned his jeans, freeing an impressive leap of flesh. "Well, well, well," she said, and looked up at him.

Vince chuckled, shook his hips a little. "Howdy."

Tessa laughed and yanked the jeans down to his ankles, leaving him naked and crookedly, heavily aroused. She touched his member, rubbing her thumb around the top, and he grabbed her wrist and pushed her back against the wall, reaching between her legs with the other hand, spreading her open as he kissed her again.

Then, strong as an ox—an elk, she thought—he lifted her and drove into her all at once, hands gripping her buttocks to pull her tightly into him, his mouth on her neck, biting, like a cat. She leaned on the wall for purchase, exhilarated by his power, and he bent and sucked her breast into his mouth, nipping her lightly, shoving himself deeply, and Tessa cried out, overwhelmed, and then they wrapped up fiercely together, jolting and surrounded with thick steam, chests skidding wetly, her thighs slippery on his sides, and finally they had to finish on the floor, Tessa riding him to an explosive release for both of them. The steam was so thick she could see only the glistening darkness of his throat, the edges of his hair, and she collapsed against his chest. "Holy shit, Batman," she said.

His hands smoothed over her back, clutched a hank of her hair. "Yeah." Abruptly, he caught her bottom and sat up, hauling her into his lap, joined tightly. He pulled her hair away from her face, cupping her head in his hands to kiss her. Lightly this time, tenderly. "Warmed up?"

"Oh, yeah."

"Let's go crawl into bed."

"Much more comfortable," she said with a wicked little grin.

He ran his tongue along her bottom lip. "Something like that."

Vince drank of Tessa for hours. His bed was a big, soft island in the darkness of his bedroom, lit only by candles and rainlight shining through the windows. He explored her body from stem to stern, collarbone and neck and ribs, belly and shins, spine and thighs. "Don't," she whispered shyly, when he held up the candle. "I don't want you to see my cellulite."

"I want to see it," he said roughly. "I want to see everything." He opened his palm on the dimpling over her bottom, and slid his thumb between her thighs, stroking her until she wiggled a little and turned over.

And she explored him in return, tasting his thighs, his throat, the ruddy weight of his testicles, which she held loosely in her hand. "Mighty nations," she said with an earthy lift of an eyebrow.

She spread her hands on his thighs. "When I first saw you, this is what I thought of," she said, and climbed on top of him, not touching his still spent but suddenly much less weary genitals. The promise of the dark recesses between her thighs, so close by he could feel the heat, was enough to at least tweak his organ. "I wanted to climb on top of these thighs."

"Jesus," he said, "where did you come from?"

In the candlelight, she looked at him, her eyes pale and shiny, her hair a wild tousle, her mouth very sober. He read in her expression the same stunned connection he felt himself, and to keep either of them from breaking the lightness, bringing too much weight into this night that was meant to be a relief, not a beginning, he sat up and captured her, kissing her mouth lightly. "Are you hungry?"

"For food, yes?"

He laughed. "Yeah. Food."

"Starving."

"Stay here," he said. "I'll get us some food."

"I can help."

He shook his head. No way he wanted her in his disaster of a kitchen. "I'll get it."

He raided the kitchen and brought back roast beef sandwiches and baby tomatoes, cheese and beer and even some store-bought chocolate chip cookies. "Not exactly elegant," he said, "but it'll chase the wolves from my belly."

"Isn't that wolves from the door?"

"Right." They ate by the light of a pillar candle burning on his bureau, cross-legged and facing each other on top of the covers. Tessa had donned his shirt. Outside, the rain pattered down steadily.

Vince watched her looking at the room, the bare walls.

"You may not have heard that in this culture it is customary to hang a picture or . . . something on your walls."

"I've heard that." He took a big bite of his sandwich, looking around. "Even if I had time, I wouldn't know what to do."

"Put up a poster or something. A picture of a mountain or"—she glanced over at the trio begging piteously at the edge of the bed—"cute dogs."

"Yeah, one of these days." Her hair tumbled down her back, half wavy, half straight, and her thighs were smooth and muscular. He watched her mouth move as she spoke, mesmerized by the smoky depth of that voice. To keep her talking, he said, "Why'd you choose tourism as a job?"

"It kinda chose me. I like being outside, and the hiking came up, and one thing led to another, and here I am, fifteen years later."

"And it's lonely."

She met his eyes, and in darkness, the pale color seemed to practically glow. "Sometimes. But I also really love it. I mean, they pay me to hike and teach other people about hiking. Not a bad job."

He waited, taking another bite of his sandwich. Sometimes people kept talking if you didn't interrupt.

She did. "Okay, I have to admit it's been kind of a drag the last couple of years, since I came back to the States. Before that, when I was living in Tasmania, when I lived with Glenn, he would go study penguins and I would go off on hiking tours and we would come back together and be happy. It was good."

A swirl of jealousy oozed through his middle. Surprising him. To quell it, he prompted, "What happened?"

"He fell in love with someone else. Another scientist."

"Ow. Sorry."

She shrugged one shoulder. "It happens."

"Yeah, but it still sucks when it happens to you." He reached for a lock of her hair and pushed it over her ear. Tried to remember that he didn't have to find out her whole life story.

Still couldn't stop.

"What I don't get," he said, "is why you went for that vagabond kind of life when I got the impression you didn't much like it as a kid."

"You're a good listener," she said, inclining her head.

"Thanks."

She took a nibble of cookie. "I guess I was looking for freedom. That's my dad's favorite word."

"Lot of different kinds of freedom."

"True. He's all about freedom from 'the man'—freedom from capitalism, from doing things for money that you don't want to do—about living in a relaxed way and not keeping up with the Joneses."

He was grinning. "He really is a hippie, isn't he?"

"Totally." She examined the cookie. "I did think I wanted something more solid, but in the end maybe you just get stuck."

"Stuck?"

"With certain ideas. It would be pretty hard for me to go live in a suburb somewhere and . . . go grocery shopping once a week and get hooked on *CSI* or something."

He laughed. "Well, that's the dull part of life, for sure. But it doesn't have to be like that. What about having poker parties with your friends, or hiking on Sundays, or just being connected to other people, having a witness to your life?"

For a moment she looked so stricken that he reached for her, but she brushed him away softly. "No. Don't. That's the heart of it, isn't it? Having someone who knows you. Who's been there, seen the story unfold."

He nodded. "Maybe you keep wandering," he said, "because you're afraid to stop."

"I ain't a-scared o' nuthin'," she said, cocking her head like a ten-year-old and shaking it. "I tried it," she said. "Before I went to college. I settled down with my boyfriend and lived in a house and did the everyday thing, and I was completely nuts inside a year."

"How old were you?"

"Eighteen."

He cocked an eyebrow and picked up a cookie.

"I know," she said. "I was out at the commune today and—"
She stopped.

"And?"

She measured him for a long moment. "I had a conversation with a woman who grew up out there. All she wanted at fifteen was to go to the normal high school and wear the usual clothes. It made me sad for her." She winced. "Oh, I don't even know what I'm talking about. Ignore me."

"Sounds like you do know," he said. "Sounds like you're close to your dad, though, and maybe you wanted his good opinion."

"Definitely."

"I hope my girls like me as much as you like him."

"Your girls love you."

"I said 'like.'"

She smiled, and it brought softness into her face. "I love my dad, and I like him. He's just a really good person. Good father, even if he was—is—all Mr. Surfer Dude Magician Man."

Vince laughed. "I guess. But kids want stability. That's why I came back here when my wife died, so we'd all have an anchor."

"The anchor needs pictures," she said, looking at the bare walls.

"Yeah, probably. Not my gift." He pointed with the cookie. "Stability, I mean. Kids need stability. You couldn't have had that drifting around."

"But I did." She popped a tomato into her mouth. "The landscape changed, but the same people were around all the time, and we had our rituals and routines."

"Oatmeal for breakfast."

"Exactly. And I went to bed at the same time every night and we did my lessons at the same time." She frowned. "Do you remember every single thing I've said?"

"Probably. I pay attention."

"Verging on the creepy."

"I seriously wanted to get in your pants."

She lifted up the shirt and looked beneath it. "Looks like you did."

The casual gesture, the triangle of hair, the depth of invitation in the glance she sent him, snared him all over again. Deliberately, he moved the tray of food, took the tomato out of her hand, and pushed her down on the bed. "Looks like I did."

. . .

When Tessa awakened, she first heard the sound of rain pattering against the roof and windows. Somewhere, blackbirds whistled an alleluia. For a long moment before she came fully awake, that celebratory, peaceful sound wove its way into her dreams, filling her with a vast sense of well-being, a rightness that she'd not felt in a very long time. She allowed herself a space of time to simply float in it. The bed was soft, and she had made a nest of pillows, as was her habit. A weight held her legs to the bed. It snored softly. A dog.

Her eyes popped open. An uncurtained window, densely green with tree branches, let in silvery morning light. In the distance, thunder rolled into the mountains. There were no photos, no paintings, not even a postcard on the walls, papered with ancient faded roses. The window casings and baseboards were old, carved, painted a glossy white. She was naked beneath the covers.

It all rushed back—the endless kissing, the athletic sex, the lust-drunk depth of their explorations. She was in Vince's bed, with Vince.

And his dogs. One of them huffed, perhaps disturbed by her faint movements. Tessa slid her leg out from under him. By the weight, it had to be Pedro.

Very carefully, she rolled over. Vince slept deeply, face half-buried in the pillows, only his beard-darkened jaw and the top of his head showing. And even that much made her chest ache in a warning way. That round of his left arm with its winding tattoo of words she couldn't decipher, the scatter of that very, very dark hair. She wanted to lean in and kiss that angle of cheekbone, put a finger gently to his full lower lip, curl up with him. So beautiful. So real.

It made her feel breathless.

She took a mental snapshot, tucking the moment away. And

as quietly as possible, she slid out of bed, worked her way around the dogs. She found her clothes on the floor of the bathroom. It took a little longer to find her underwear, and they were soggy wet, the crotch missing. She gave Pedro a glare, but he only wagged his tail.

Moving soundlessly, she crept into the hallway, past the open doors to the girls' empty bedrooms—much tidier than his own, and warmer. The first held a set of bunk beds, with pictures of princesses and cheery pink curtains. This must be Jade and Hannah's room. Creeping noiselessly the rest of the way down the hall, she peeked into the last room and knew instantly that it was Natalie's. Her bedspread was red and gold paisley, with the same pattern on the simple curtains, which someone had obviously sewn for her. An antique chest of drawers stood against the wall, and there were pictures of dogs and horses and bears all over the room. Paperback books were stacked on her nightstand and cluttered the floor, along with her shoes and a sweater. It smelled of sunshine and cinnamon and Herbal Essence shampoo.

Tessa lingered, feeling that ache low in her ribs again. Yearning, maybe. This was a bedroom where a girl could grow up, where she could change the curtains and the poster and still look out at the same steady view of meadow and mountains.

Firmly, she turned around and eased down the stairs, soundly built so they didn't squeak.

And there in the foyer was the black-and-white pup. He raised his head, and the very tip of his tail slapped on the floor. In a surge of feeling, she knelt beside him and buried her face in his neck, rubbing his ears. Kissed the middle of his brow. "Good morning, baby," she whispered. How could she leave him?

He gazed at her in worry and worship. Tessa thought of her

father and what he would say about this whole situation. That this was her dog, that he had something to give her or teach her, and she had an obligation to him. Dogs as angels, she thought, and a quiver of tears caught at the top of her throat before she could clamp them down.

Whatever. She made a soft kissing sound and gestured toward the door as she stood. He got to his feet and trotted obediently in the direction she pointed, waiting politely as she picked up her sandals and purse and scarf.

It had been pretty dark the night before, so she had not seen the extent of the clutter in the living room. Bad. It was bad. Not like a bachelor pad, stacked with pizza boxes and beer bottles and dishes crusted with food. This was laundry folded on the table in piles that never got put away. Toys scooped up into a chair but not into bedrooms. Shoes and socks shed by the door in a towering mountain. Eddies of dust on everything, and squirrels of dog hair under the table, and a vacuum standing to one side, ready to be used and left where it was.

It was a single parent with too much on his plate and no skills to properly keep a house. Tessa turned away from so much need and slipped out into the first break of morning, into the rain falling in miraculous, life-giving, steady sheets. She and the pup stood on the broad porch for a long minute, surveying it—the mountains rounding the horizon like a fence against the gods, the bowl of grasslands studded with prickly pears and yucca and sage. Even from here, she could hear the rushing swoosh of the river that held the eastern boundary, filled to the brim by the rainy night.

The porch needed some hanging baskets of petunias and something besides a couple of kitchen chairs, though she liked the spool table. The flower beds needed some marigolds and cosmos.

She shook her head. Somewhere, there was a woman who'd want to take all of this on—the land and the man and the children, all hungry beyond reckoning—but Tessa wasn't that woman.

"Come on, baby," she said to the dog, thinking maybe her father would adopt one more dog. She knew he would if she asked.

At the hotel, the overnight desk clerk stopped her. "Ma'am, I'm sorry, but that dog can't go upstairs."

"I thought you allowed dogs."

"We are very happy to allow well-groomed dogs. If you'd like to have him groomed, we'll be glad to let him stay for ten dollars a night."

"Can I give him a bath?"

The clerk almost visibly shuddered. "Oh, I don't think so."

Tessa nodded, looked down at the dog, then up at the clock. It wasn't quite seven. "Okay," she said, frowning, trying to think what to do. Where could she get a dog cleaned up at seven in the morning?

It was karma, her father would tell her, a quick return on her sneaking out of Vince's house so early. He would be dismayed, and after the intensity of the night they shared, he had every right to be. She flashed on his big hands moving over her belly, his cheery stories as they ate, the sense of well-being when she woke up.

And the living room, stacked with clothes that had not yet been put away, the toys piled up in a chair, the vast loneliness written across that scene.

No. It made a panicky heartbeat flutter in her throat.

"Come on," she said to the dog. He needed a name, but the

first order of business was a bath. "Let's go find us some break-fast, and maybe somebody will know where to get you a bath."

"Lucky Dog is on Alameda, right next to the river," the clerk said. "They open at nine."

"Thanks." He was only doing his job, she supposed, but really—his shudder was a bit much.

Out on the plaza, which was mostly empty, she felt a sharp-ness of autumn in the air and thought of what Vince had said. At least it had stopped raining, and the steady downpour left everything washed clean and damp, the air as crisp as cookies. Summer fled the mountains early. As if to emphasize that fact, a clatter of leaves swept off the cottonwood and danced across the cobbles. The dog sat next to her, neatly waiting for instruc-tions, and something about his patience pierced Tessa right through the gut.

"Why did you pick me?" she asked.

The dog looked up, shifted paw to paw. Blinked. It was if he said, *Don't you remember?*

"I don't remember. I wish I did." She headed for a bench near the tree, gesturing for him to follow her. Sitting down, she faced him and looked deeply into his face. "What's your name, baby? What do you want me to call you? Something Irish, maybe, or are border collies Scottish? Something with sheep?"

He regarded her with the gentle expectation of a wise old teacher waiting for a student to come up with the answer. She threaded a lock of fur through her fingers, peered off into the distance.

Suddenly, the dog shivered and climbed under her legs, quivering all over. Tessa said, "What?"

Across the plaza strode the beautiful man from the restau-rant the very first night she'd been here, the one who made her think of a coyote, all lean fury and ragged intensity. His hair, loose down his back, lifted as he made his way across the plaza to a shadowy spot along the portico, where he tucked himself into the darkness beside a pillar and peered at a place across the way. Again that red fury rippled out from him, singeing the air like a careless fire.

He lit a cigarette and smoked it, watching his prey, whoever it was. Tessa looked over her shoulder, not seeing anything, but after a while she felt uncomfortable and stood up. The dog whimpered, skulking along the ground, and she murmured softly to him, "It's all right. You're safe with me." When she glanced back, the man was gone.

She walked around the block to the damp, cool grounds of the church. It was deserted so early in the morning, but the rain had rendered every leaf and blade a violent green. She settled on a bench by the tomatoes, the dog leaning against her in relief. "Did he hurt you, sweetheart?"

He blinked at her sadly.

"Bastard." No name came to her still, so she pulled her cell phone out of her pocket. "My dad will know."

He shifted, waiting expectantly with her as the phone rang. Absently, she stroked him, tugging out a burr from the fur beneath his ear, another out of his back. "You'll like being groomed, baby. I promise."

"Good morning, princess!" Sam said after the second ring. His voice was craggy. "You're up early."

"Oh, dang! I forgot it's not quite six there. So sorry, Dad. Go back to sleep."

"No, you know I like to talk to you anytime you call. What's up?"

"Well, I seem to have acquired a dog. You might need to take him when I get back to work."

"Is that so? What kind of dog? How old?"

"That border collie mix I told you about; maybe six months old. Oh, Dad, he's sitting here with me on the plaza, and he's the sweetest thing, and so, so, so smart. He found me the first night I got here and I've seen him every day since, and now I can't leave him."

"It's Brenna, you know."

"Brenna was a girl dog."

"Doesn't matter; you know that. I've been waiting for her to show up again for a long time. I bet he's got a star on his forehead, doesn't he?"

Sure enough, there was a star. "Dad, border collies just have those markings."

He laughed, low and dark.

"Well, Brenna or not, I need a name for him, and I thought I'd get some input."

"You ask him?"

She tugged his long silky ear and his eyes drifted half shut. "He says he's lucky," she said suddenly.

"Call him Felix," Sam said. "That means lucky."

"Are you Felix?" she said, and he licked her wrist. She laughed. "Okay, I guess that'll work. Thanks, Dad."

"Anytime, princess."

Breakfast #90

Huevos del Diablo: One of our top dishes. Two eggs, poached in medium red or hot green chile salsa, served over lightly toasted rounds of polenta, lightly crisp strips of corn tortilla, and topped with shredded cheese and a slice of fresh tomato. Served with hash browns and ice water. You'll need it.

Huevos Del Diablo

2 round slices of polenta, each 1 inch thick,
*   prepared and chilled*
2 cups red or green salsa
2 large eggs
Shredded cheddar or Jack cheese
1 slice of fresh tomato

Grill the polenta in a hot, buttered skillet until light brown. Meanwhile, in another skillet, heat the salsa until simmering, then gently break the eggs into the liquid, one at a time. Poach 4–6 minutes, according to your taste. Plate the polenta, and when the eggs are cooked to the desired doneness, gently remove them from the salsa and nestle each one on a slice of polenta. Spoon hot salsa over the eggs and top with cheese and tomato slice. Serves 1.

TWELVE

In the gray morning, Sam headed out to the beach to walk the dogs. Loki and Wolfenstein raced ahead on the sand, while Peaches made her slow way along the waterline. Sometimes, she paused to smell something or just stand in senile confusion. Sam gently brushed the ancient apricot-colored poodle's long curls every evening to give her some stimulation. The vet shook his head every time Sam brought her in, amazed she was still alive.

There had been storms for a couple of days and the beach was littered with debris, which the dogs explored with exuberance, bringing back joyous little finds—a stick, a fish head, a rock. Sam laughed. "A rock, Loki?" The dog barked and ran the other way with his buddy.

Sam spread a rain poncho out on the damp sand and sat down. Peaches hobbled over to sit close to him. She wore a sweater, hand-knit by a woman who would like to knit a whole lot more with Sam. He gently discouraged her whenever he could, though Peaches's sweater was so perfect he couldn't refuse. He petted her soft little head, then took out a notebook and a pen and tried to organize his thoughts.

He had to tell Tessa the things she didn't know. If she was hanging around the commune, running into his old friends, sooner or later she'd hear about all of it. He'd really hoped to spare her.

Why the hell had she gone trooping back there, anyway? All these years he'd kept her psyche and heart safe, and she was about to undo every little bit of it.

At the thought, his whole belly went hollow, and he prayed to a God he hadn't believed in since 1967. "Let her know I lied for good reasons," he said, and started to write.

Dear Princess Tessa,

You should take this letter and go sit down someplace. There are some things I have kept hidden about your life, and I reckon it's time it all came out. Just remember, it was all for you.

When he finished the letter, he folded it carefully, put it in a pretty envelope, and took it to the post office, where he mailed it before he could chicken out. On the way back down the street, he had to blink away tears, and that made him one damned old fool.

Tessa left the dog at a veterinarian's office, where he would be groomed and checked for fleas, diseases, and, just to be sure, a microchip. The vet would also let the humane society know a dog had been found. It was all just a formality, but she was happy enough to go through all the steps.

While Felix was being groomed, Tessa sampled the breakfast

at a high-end café hung with lacy curtains and offering choices like smoked salmon and caviar served on toast or with cream cheese and fresh bagels; imported English blood sausages and Ayrshire bacon with thyme-infused potato custard. It was very good food. Her boss would love it.

When she picked up Felix, he looked like a different dog. The groomer had tied a bandana around his neck, and his long fur was as shiny, silky, and elegant as a show dog's. It all made him look beloved.

"Look at you!" Tessa said. His tail swished happily as she approached, and he waited in shivering anticipation for her hug.

Tessa buried her nose in his soft, sweet-smelling neck. "Mmmmm."

"He's a terrific dog," the groomer said. "Smart as a ten-year-old."

"I found him. He's been following me around since I came to town a few days ago; he was obviously abandoned. Starving. I decided to take responsibility for him."

"There are a lot of strays around here. People abandon them and they live on the streets. Breaks my heart."

"How old do you think he is?"

"Six months or so. He's probably going to grow quite a bit more, since he hasn't had enough food, obviously."

"Border collie?"

"Yeah, but mixed with something else. Maybe husky or shepherd, something like that. My guess is, he'll probably end up about that size. Bigger than the usual border collie."

Felix looked at Tessa with calm eyes, and again she had the sense she'd found an ancient soul. "He's a wise old man in a way," she said, and kissed his nose. "Come on."

They sold her a collar and leash, along with a bag of good food. Tessa led him back to the hotel, paid the extra fees, and took him upstairs with her. Opening the French doors to the balcony, she let him explore while she shed the clothes she'd worn for a little too long and took a shower.

Only then did she let the night flood back in. Vince in all his animal power, the bathroom filled with steam, making their skin slippery. In the mirror, she saw the marks and little bruises from lovemaking, and it made her want to sit down and weep.

Too much. He was just too much, all that hungry need and his motherless children and the vast hole at the center of their lives, with no one to put away the clothes and cook a nutritious breakfast every morning before school. She thought of her father, making oatmeal, putting oranges in a bowl for after-school snacks, braiding her hair at night so it wouldn't tangle while she slept.

How had he become such a good homemaker? She sure had never learned the knack.

No, she was not the right woman for that empty place in Vince Grasso's life. Briskly, she combed out her hair, put on clean clothes, and pulled out the laptop so she could make notes for the interview with Vita at 100 Breakfasts this afternoon. After that, she typed up her notes on everything else and sent them off to her boss. Then she curled up on the bed with Felix for a little nap in the soft noontime air.

When Vince woke up and realized that Tessa wasn't just in another room, that she'd taken the dog and left him asleep without a word or a note, he couldn't believe it. He sat on the front porch in his jeans and no shirt, stung and angry, thinking about her, about the taste of her and the laughing they had done and—

"Get over it," he said aloud. She was just passing through. What had he expected?

He spent the morning trying to get the house together. Last spring, he'd had a girl from the high school come in once a week to vacuum and dust and put things in order a little, but she had graduated and moved to California for college. He hadn't found anyone to replace her, but he supposed he ought to get on it.

He washed four loads of clothes, cleaned up the kitchen and reloaded the dishwasher, scrubbed the bathrooms, and stacked folded clothes into piles on the dining-room table, where he'd be forced to move them if the family wanted to eat. When the girls got home, he would make them take their own clothes and toys and books up to their rooms. Natalie could vacuum the hallway upstairs, Jade could dust, and even Hannah could do something. She liked to sweep. He should get her a little broom that would fit her. As he straightened up the dining room, he wondered if he could make a center for homework and school things on the built-in buffet; there were drawers and doors, enough for everybody. He opened the top drawer. It held odds and ends of all kinds—old bills and a photo album and some cassette tapes that no longer had a machine to play them, a knee brace, and a pair of racing gloves. He closed the drawer again, defeated. Maybe he could buy some baskets or something.

Could he just throw it all away, maybe? He opened the drawer. If it had been in there all this time, it probably wasn't anything he needed. The papers for the ranch, for taxes, for all of that, were in his office upstairs. This was crap. From the kitchen, he fetched a big black trash bag and started throwing things away. It was liberating.

He had to start making the girls do more chores. They were

supposed to make their beds, and he did make them set the table and clear it and put dishes into the dishwasher every mealtime. The chaos was overwhelming to *him*—how could three little girls be expected to feel safe and secure in such a world?

A wave of anger at Carrie washed over him. What the hell had she been thinking, to check out like that? To just leave them?

As long as he lived, he'd never understand it. How did a person desert her children? How did she bear it, knowing she would never see them win a prize or wear a prom dress or graduate from college?

No, he would never understand, not even when the girls were cranky when his mother brought them in, hot from the long car ride, sick of having to be on their best behavior. He sent them outside to play in the back while his mother brought the packages in. "Socks and panties for each one," she said, and pulled out a piece of paper to help him keep it straight. "Jade's are pink and white, Hannah's are green and yellow, and Natalie had to have red and black."

In spite of the dark knot of despair in his throat, Vince laughed at that. "She's got her own drummer, that girl."

"I bought them each a few pairs of pants and some shirts they can mix and match. Although"—she pulled out one bag—"I didn't want to buy this one for Natalie, but she absolutely insisted."

It was a peasant-style blouse, white with embroidery on it, and some red corduroy pants. "I don't get it. Why wouldn't you want her to buy this?"

"Makes her look pretty chubby."

Flickers of heat licked the back of his skull. "Ma, you've gotta stop it with her weight."

"Vince, she's a plump child who is going to grow up and be a fat woman if you don't do something right now."

"She isn't plump! She's got a bit of a tummy. She's eight years old, for God's sake. I'm not putting her on a diet."

"You don't know," his mother said, narrowing her eyes, "what it's like."

Judy was a big sturdy woman without much softness. Hers was the handsome, hard-chiseled face of a Western woman: strong cheekbones, wide mouth, hooded eyes. She had big hands and feet and plenty of rear end.

"I get it," he said, putting his hands on her arms. "You want her to be pretty. I appreciate that." He looked out the front window to see where the girls were. Natalie had climbed to the top of the tree house, her blond hair wild around her face, her arms raised in autocratic direction of her sisters. She was spunky and opinionated and brilliantly smart. She reminded him of his mother in many ways, and maybe she'd grow up to look a lot like her. "I don't know if she'll ever be pretty, Ma. But that doesn't mean she can't be *happy*."

"Just make her eat a little bit less," Judy said.

He shook his head. "No diets. We'll go for long bike rides or something, but don't you dare start making her feel guilty about food. She's got a gift."

"She's got—"

Vince held up a hand. "Stop. I'm not listening to any more. She's my daughter. I get to make the rules."

She clamped her mouth together. "Fine."

Tessa met with Vita just after lunch. She was still humming with the pleasure of learning to make bread, something so earth-mother-ish that she almost felt she should be embarrassed, but it had been a lot of fun. She had even dreamed of the process, the smell of yeast, the yield of the dough beneath the heel of her palm.

"Hello, Tessa," Vita said in her warm voice. "Let's sit in the booth over there in the corner, be a little bit out of the way. Do you want some coffee?"

"Maybe iced tea instead, please."

"I'll bring it right over. Go ahead and sit down."

Tessa slid into the booth and faced the plaza. Quiet for a Friday, only a few pedestrians about in the still, hot afternoon. The tree made dappled patterns on the bricks, green and gold and soft charcoal. She pushed hair out of her sweaty face.

Vita set a plate down in front of Tessa. "Saved it for you."

The cinnamon roll was enormous, heavily scented, frosted with cream cheese icing, and studded with raisins. Tessa turned the plate, admiring it from all sides. "So beautiful. Thanks." She pointed to Vita's cup. "You never seem to eat a meal."

"I eat breakfast, but the rest of the day I'm eating all the time. Tasting, making sure everything is good. A piece of bacon, a sliver of ham. It all adds up."

"I suppose so." She tugged at her own waistband. "I've been eating nonstop since I got to this town. If we actually get a tour in here, I'll have to lead all the hiking myself so that I can eat."

"Is that the plan, a hiking tour?"

"Hiking is a part of it, always," Tessa said. She took a bite of the cinnamon roll. "Oh, man. That's awesome."

Vita smiled.

"Right now I'm just checking out the possibilities on this trip," Tessa said. "One of the things I wanted to ask you about is whether you'd be interested in hosting a bread-making afternoon or something. I had such a great time yesterday that it made me think it might be fun for other people, too."

"I don't know that we're really set up for that here."

Tessa nodded. "Right, I thought of that, too. What if you did it at the Green Gate Cooking School? It seems like you have a good working relationship with them."

Vita's mouth turned down in consideration. "I might be open to that. Never considered teaching cooking, honestly."

"You're really good at it, though," Tessa said. "The cooking, but also the teaching."

"Thanks."

"I have a list of things I'd like to ask about." Tessa flipped through her notes. She savored another bite of the cinnamon roll, put down her fork, and looked out the window.

And there across the plaza came Vince, trailing girls like a litter of kittens, the baby on his hip, headed right this way.

"Oh, shit," she said, forgetting herself for a minute. She looked at the door, but it was too late to get out without him seeing her, and she couldn't exactly run out on Vita.

Who glanced out the window and gave Tessa a curious lift of an eyebrow.

"It's a long story," Tessa said.

When Vince came inside the café, he saw her immediately. For a long minute she stared at him, flushing when she saw the cut on his lower lip, a cut her tooth had made. The moment of the injury washed over her, steam and bare skin, his tongue and his blood in her mouth. Tessa looked away. Her hands were shaking.

And, of course, he didn't just ignore her and go sit down. He came to the table, dark eyes burning into her face, his hip cocked to balance his daughter. "How's the dog?" he asked.

Tessa knocked the fork off her plate with a clatter. "Sorry."

She grabbed a napkin and wiped the sugar off the table. "He's fine. I had him groomed. His name is Felix."

"Felix is a cat's name." Natalie, dressed more neatly than Tessa had seen before, stepped up to the table.

"I know. But my dad says it means 'lucky.'"

"What kind of dog?"

"He seems to be mostly border collie." Relieved to be able to duck Vince's glowering, she said, "Wow, I love your outfit. Is it new?"

"Yes." She stood visibly taller at the compliment. "I got it for school, but my daddy let me wear it today and he's going to wash it for next Tuesday, which is the first day. Look at the embroidery." She offered her sleeve.

"Cool," Tessa said, and meant it. "The colors are good for you. I like the purple around your face. It makes your eyes even bluer."

"*I* got new clothes, too," Jade said, pushing up to the table. She wore a green top and was so tan and sleek and tidy that she could have been on television.

"I see that. Very pretty."

"Me, too," the baby said, sticking out her shoe.

Tessa couldn't help it, she was charmed into reaching for the tiny jeweled sandal on a chubby little foot. Hannah's minuscule toenails were painted red. "Good job."

Jade said, "My grandma didn't want Nat to buy that."

"None of your business, Jade," Vince said, clamping a hand down on her shoulder. "Let's go sit down now."

Jade rolled her eyes but flounced away behind her dad. Tessa watched him cross the room, thinking, in spite of her will to forget, of the way his long, beautiful back looked naked, his powerful arms.

Natalie paused a minute and looked at Tessa as if she would

say something else. Then she just lifted a hand and walked away.

"You're quite flushed," Vita said.

"Mistake," Tessa said firmly.

"Was it?"

"Definitely."

THIRTEEN

Natalie could tell something was going on between her dad and the lady who took pictures of her salt. Tessa. He'd been in a pretty good mood till they came in and saw her, and now he kept looking at her and it made Natalie feel scared and sick to her stomach. Everybody kept saying that sooner or later her dad would "get over it" and fall in love again, but Natalie didn't think so. He sometimes went on dates, which she knew because he shaved at night and put on after-shave before he took them to Grandma's house. Nat even knew who one of the ladies was, Andy who worked in the supermarket, but she had a lot of boyfriends, so it was okay.

This lady was different. First Pedro, who was *her* dog, and now Daddy acting all weird. Natalie didn't get it. Why would her dad even like Tessa? She was definitely not as pretty as Mommy. Not even close.

But he did. Grown-ups thought kids were so stupid. Natalie was not stupid. She knew lots of things grown-ups didn't know she knew.

Vita came over to bring their drinks, just to chat, like always. Nat liked Vita best of almost everybody in town. She didn't talk like you were a baby, and she sometimes saved special things she cut out of magazines for Natalie. She put the drinks down on the table and said, "You guys excited about school starting?"

Jade raised a hand. "I am!"

"I'm not," Natalie said. "I hate school."

"Is it third grade?"

Natalie nodded glumly, thinking of the classroom from last year, the smell of dust and pee and all those kids making so much noise and not a single one of them who wanted to be her friend. She especially, especially hated the days when they had parties, and room mothers would come in with cupcakes and cookies and drinks, the mothers all talking to each other in the corner, laughing. They did that after school, too, parking their cars and standing there talking in their shorts and sneakers, with their hair pulled back in ponytails. Everybody had a mother but her.

Plus there was the problem of friends. Back in Denver, she'd had three friends. Here, everybody lived so far apart that they all rode the bus to school and everybody had been friends since they were born, practically, so there was no room for Natalie. She didn't like them, anyway, but she could think of lots of other things to do besides sitting in a classroom at some banged-up old desk, writing out math problems. "Booooring!" she said.

"Maybe not, though," Vita said. "You learn fractions in third grade, don't you? You need to know how to work fractions to be a good cook."

"I guess."

"How 'bout you, Little Bit?" Vita asked. "You headed off to preschool?"

"I'm going to Mrs. Garcia's school."

"Good for you!" Vita touched Jade's head. "Bring me your report card when you get all your A's, kiddo."

A girl came over then to take their order. Natalie had been trying to decide and trying to decide—she had a goal of eating every single breakfast on the menu—and finally chose: "I'll have eggs Benedict, please," she said.

"Are you sure, honey? Don't you want pancakes or a waffle or something?"

"No," Natalie said, and sat up as straight as she could. "I want to try the eggs Benedict."

The girl still looked at Nat's dad to see if that was okay. He nodded and she wrote it down, her fingers like a crab over her paper. Hannah did order the pancakes, because that was the right thing for a baby. Jade always ate the exact same thing: the fruit soup with granola sprinkled on top. It tasted pretty good, Natalie had to admit, but how boring would it be to eat the same thing every single time? And especially just because it was *pink*?

After the girl left and Vita went over to sit down with Tessa, Jade started to babble about all the cool things she thought they studied in second grade (which she didn't even bother to ask Nat about, even though Nat had that very same teacher and classroom last year), and their dad started staring again at Tessa, pretending that he wasn't.

Natalie felt as if a volcano was bubbling in her chest, *bubble bubble, bubble bubble*. She played with the salt shaker, pouring a little tiny mountain out on the table, trying to ignore the bubbling. The salt shaker was a pretty one, with a pointed cap top and carved crystal sides that swooped down like a lady's skirt touching the floor. For a little while she swirled and jumped the shakers across the table, pretending they were dancers. Pepper was the man and Salt was the woman, and they swirled around, curtsying and dancing to a song Natalie hummed under her breath.

The evil thought started to nag her—she wanted to take this salt shaker home. It would go so perfect with the salt cellar! She could save up and buy some Hakata roasted sea salt, which was very very fine, and put it in here, and save the red salt for the salt cellar.

When everybody was looking at something else, talking to each other, Natalie pulled the salt shaker off the table and put it in her pants pocket. Something cool went through the lava in her throat, and she said, "Can I get out, please? I have to go to the bathroom."

Vince moved aside and Natalie scooted out, trying to act perfectly normal. Nobody looked at her at all, and she ducked into the bathroom and closed the door behind her. Feeling a dizzy happiness, she took the silver cap off the shaker and poured the salt down the sink so it wouldn't spill in her jeans, then carefully screwed the lid back on and put the whole thing in her pocket. The white shirt poofed out just right over it, so you couldn't see it at all, even if you were looking. Brushing her hair back, she arranged her face into a normal expression and yanked open the bathroom door.

And jumped about a foot. A woman from the kitchen stood there, with an apron wrapped around her body. She had tattoos around her wrists and hair that was choppy, all different kinds of lengths and two colors.

"Hi," Natalie said, and turned to head back into the dining room, touching the lump in her pocket with one finger, ever so casually.

"Hold it," the woman said.

"What?"

"Give it back to me and I won't tell anyone."

Sweat broke down Natalie's back, and her mouth suddenly had too much spit in it. "What?" she said again.

"You know what."

"I don't have anything."

The woman lifted an eyebrow and waited, palm open.

Natalie couldn't breathe. Her ears sounded like she had a dishwasher going in each one, and for a minute she thought she might actually faint. She shot a glance down the hall, where her father sat with her sisters, and she thought about how humiliating it would be to have to look at her dad.

The woman squatted down in front of her. "Let me show you something." She pulled up her pant leg, and there was a heavy black band around her ankle, with a black box attached to it. "You know what this is?"

Natalie shook her head.

"It's an electronic bracelet, and it tells the police where I am every single minute, day and night. I never get to take it off. I have to sleep in it, even."

Natalie didn't say anything.

"I have it because I went to jail, and it was not a good place. It was a really bad place." She looked right into Natalie's eyes, and her irises were a pale color like a marble. "If you promise to give me that salt shaker and never do it again, I will not tell anybody."

Trembling, Nat pulled the salt shaker out of her pocket and put it in the woman's hand. "I'm sorry," she whispered. "I don't know why I keep stealing stuff. I even prayed and everything."

The woman stayed kneeling, bouncing the salt shaker in her hand. "Stealing a lot of things, are you?"

Natalie bowed her head. Nodded. Tears filled her throat, but if she cried, she would have to tell her daddy why.

"What if, next time you feel like taking something, you don't, and come talk to me?"

Natalie looked at her.

"Right, that's weird. I have an idea. I know a charm to help you stop. Come back whenever you can and I'll leave it for you at the front."

"Okay. I don't know when we'll be back."

"Doesn't matter. I'm going to make it tonight, and it'll be here whenever you want after that." The woman stood and cocked her head toward the dining room. "Go on."

Natalie ran.

Vince tried to give his attention to his girls, since it was supposed to be a treat afternoon. They were happy, coloring in the coloring books they brought with them, choosing crayons out of a giant box of ninety-six Crayolas he had for once remembered to bring with him.

Even Natalie, dressed up in the new outfit she loved so much, was relatively cheerful. She loved the eggs Benedict and devoured it with devotion in tiny, reverent bites, taking time to look at the food, the colors, the textures. She understood more about ingredients than twenty adults combined. She noticed him watching her. "Want a bite?"

"Sure."

She carefully cut a triangle of egg, Canadian bacon, and English muffin, swirled with Vita's very good hollandaise, and offered it up to her father. He bent and took the bite from her. "Mmmmm," he said, nodding. "That really is fantastic. I love the mix of egg yolk and sauce."

"Me, too!" she said, her eyes wide.

He rubbed her back lightly. His little eccentric. He wanted to protect her from the world that would not take her passions seriously enough. He wanted to shove them all off a cliff when they judged her appearance, which was as eccentric as her approach to life. Eventually she would grow up and find her tribe and all would be well, but in the meantime she had to endure childhood. Tenderly, he smoothed a lock of curly hair from her forehead. "It's so much fun to have meals with you, Natalie."

"Thank you."

When he glanced toward Tessa, he slammed right into her steady gaze, and he saw something stricken there, which lit flutters in his throat and set something burning down his spine. His lip throbbed, and he pulled it into his mouth, licking the swollen spot. He told everyone he had bitten it by accident, but as he tasted it, he felt her skin on his as acutely as if it were happening now.

Too much. He looked away. Hannah was struggling with the syrup dispenser and he lifted it for her, pulling back the sticky spout.

Tessa materialized at his side and put a napkin down on the table next to his hand. She said nothing, only stood there for a moment, her fingers on the paper, and then left.

He waited for a long, long minute, then picked it up. She had scrawled only two words:

I'm sorry

Vince balled it up and threw it on the table.

When the girls had finished, Vince let Natalie visit the salt store and the cooking store next to it while he and the other two girls played beneath the tree in the plaza. It was so hot it didn't feel like autumn was on the way, even though the humidity from last night's rain had burned away to nothing. Heat hung in bars of sunlight and in pockets close to the ground. Jade played jacks by herself on a relatively flat square of pavement, and Hannah chased a moth, fluttering white through a stand of dandelions. "I'm glad school is starting," Jade said. "I'm getting sick of having nothing to do."

"I bet."

"Do you think I could have a cell phone this year?"

"No," he said.

"Why not?" Her tone was calm and reasonable.

He shifted his position on the ledge. It was always a mistake to underestimate Jade's fierce intelligence and ability to manipulate the world and other humans to her own agenda. He considered his reasons carefully before he spoke. "Because you're going to be talking on the phone for the rest of your life, every minute of every day, and your voice will be worn out enough."

She laughed. "Daddy!"

But it defused the request for now, and when he saw Natalie skipping across the plaza toward them, he stood. She said, "She let me taste the Murray River salt!"

"Cool." When Vince had bought the hideously expensive red salt, he had a little talk with the owner, explaining Nat's passion for food and ingredients—and her talent. "Encourage her," he'd asked.

"Okay, guys, let's go say hi to Grandma, then we can go home."

His mother's bookshop was around the corner from the main plaza, in one of the narrow archaic lanes that zigzagged away from the central square and into the more secretive landscape of the town. It was a long, deep affair, rambling through ten thousand square feet. The Quill and Page was known as one of the best independent bookstores in the country, and

Judy had built it from the ground up, pouring her love of all poetry and literature into the shop when he was a baby. To Vince's knowledge, Judy had never had a boyfriend—only Vince and her bookstore.

Like many other independents, the Quill had been slammed hard by the Internet and Amazon and other avenues through which readers could get the hard-to-find and obscure titles that had been her lifeblood. She had developed some specialties that kept her afloat—collecting first editions of classics, tracking down the very rare, and, most of all, developing a social marketing program to make the Internet work for her.

"You guys look around. I want to find some new books to read before we go home." They scattered to their favorite spots. Vince ambled down the fiction aisles, not sure what he was in the mood for. Something dark, maybe. Serial killers always made life look good.

Or not.

He pulled a book off a shelf here and there, flipping through, putting it back. This is what you missed on the Internet, he thought, turning a corner into a long set of stacks—the pleasure of discovering something you've never heard of, that was never in anybody's sights, or maybe it was a big bestseller in 1974. Harold Robbins or Irving Stone. Maybe he'd read *Exodus* or *The Carpetbaggers*. That would be fun.

When he rounded the last aisle, he saw Tessa, leaning one shoulder against the wall, her head tilted as she read so that her glittery hair spilled down one arm in waves. Vince halted. As if she sensed his shadow falling on her, she looked up and stuck one finger in the book braced on her cast. He couldn't see the title.

He wavered between turning around and walking away or

going forward. He had too much on his plate to add an irrational obsession with a woman who was leaving town in a couple of days. And yet, as if she were a magnet, he found himself moving toward her, his cells boiling the closer he came.

He stopped a few feet away. "I don't know what the sorry was for."

She lifted her shoulders. "I don't know, either. I just—I don't know."

He might have turned around then, but her eyes were on his mouth, and he touched the sore place with his tongue, and as if she were mirroring him, she touched her tongue to her own lip. Vince stepped closer, his skin blistering as he reached for her, and slid a hand around the back of her neck to pull her into his kiss. She made a soft, swallowed noise, and the air around them smelled of wood smoke and grass, and that made him think of something just out of reach, something he yearned for. He moved closer still, putting his other hand on her face, fingertips lightly against her cheekbone, her jaw against his palm. Her hair scattered over his forearms, creating a silken shock as she kissed him back. Hungry. Starving.

He gentled a little, tracing her cheekbone, her jaw, suckling her lips. It made him dizzy.

Suddenly she pushed him away. Held up a hand to stave him off. "No. I can't do this, Vince. You have your girls, all that. You don't know me. I'm not the right person for . . . all that."

"All what?" he said quietly, moving closer again, looking over his shoulder to make sure they were alone. "I thought this was just a hot little connection we could explore until you leave town or it burns out."

The long anime eyes, pale and sensual, blazed. "Is that so."

"It's pretty hot, at least from my side." He reached for her. "You seemed to enjoy yourself."

She caught his hand. Shook her head. "No," she said, and tried to duck under his arm.

He caught her easily, one arm around her waist, her back to his chest. "It was more than that, wasn't it?" he whispered against her neck.

"Yes," she said, and bowed her head. "And I just can't go there."

"Why?"

"I'm just not that person. The right person."

"Okay." Vince bent and put his face against her hair, kissed her ear. Let her go.

She fled.

Breakfast #42

Eggs Benedict: The great classic—two poached eggs and thinly sliced back bacon served open-faced on a toasted English muffin, smothered with tangy hollandaise sauce. Served with fruit.

HOLLANDAISE SAUCE

It takes a little practice to make a good hollandaise, but don't be intimidated. Keep the heat low, add butter slowly, and have some faith that you can make it great.

1/3 cup plus 2 T cold butter
2 egg yolks
2–3 tsp lemon juice

2–3 tsp water
¹/₄ tsp salt
Dash cayenne pepper

Melt the ¹/₃ cup of butter, set aside.

Get a heavy skillet ready with several inches of water on simmer.

Place the egg yolks in a small heavy saucepan and whisk until thick. Add 2 tsp of lemon juice and 2 tsp of water and the salt. Whisk for another 30 seconds or so. Add half of the cold butter. Put the pan over the simmering water and whisk until egg yolks are creamy, about 3–4 minutes, being careful not to let the yolks scramble. When the sauce is clinging to the whisk and you can see the bottom of the pan through the whisking, remove the mixture from the heat and add the remaining cold butter. Whisk until melted, then begin to add the melted butter a few drops at a time until it is fully absorbed into the yolks. Add a dash of cayenne pepper; taste for additional lemon juice and salt. If it is too thick, whisk in a few drops of water. Hold the sauce for up to a half hour in a bowl over warm water.

FOURTEEN

Rattled, Tessa knew she needed a walk to clear her head. The afternoon was stifling. Finished with her work list for the day, she gathered a bottle of clean water and snacks and took Felix out for a walk. She had a leash, but he didn't seem to need it.

It was time to face the river. With Felix as company, she would be less afraid. They walked through town at a good clip, Tessa watching from the corner of her eye in case Vince and the girls showed up again—it was just weird how often they ran into each other—and let her breath go only when she found the path to the river.

It was about a mile from the plaza, reached by a newly minted trail through pine forest and scrub oaks. Little signs along the path told the story first of the missionaries who'd arrived and built their camp along the river, then of the Indians who had ousted them, and the settlers who eventually built the town. Felix stuck close by, trotting ahead a few feet, then checking back to make sure Tessa was coming. "I'm right here, sweetie. I promise I won't abandon you."

It felt great to walk, to be in her body, smelling the air, feeling muscles move and legs lift and feet hit the earth. Her left foot was markedly better today, and she took pleasure in that, too. With an injury it always seemed there was a turning day, and it seemed that day had passed for the foot. Excellent.

She wiggled her arm inside the cast. Soon the cast would be gone, too. Thank God. It was really getting itchy the past few days.

They emerged abruptly from the trees to the banks of the river, the landscape opening to a watercolor vista of red earth and coppery water and the blues of mountains all around. Tessa paused to take it in, bathed in the colors, drinking them in as if they were nourishment.

"Amazing," she said aloud. Felix looked at her and sat down patiently.

Near the water, the advance of autumn was obvious. The cottonwoods suddenly had yellow leaves, and the grass along the path was more yellow than green. They walked on a little farther, sheltered by grand old trees, and finally came to a clearing. Tessa halted, breathing in, getting her bearings. Felix, headed at full tilt for the water, seemed to sense her hesitation and returned, tail down, to make sure everything was okay. He nosed her palm.

A quiver crossed her throat. *Just keep breathing.* She was determined to avoid a panic attack. Birds flitting through nearby trees made more noise. She could smell the water faintly, a waft of coolness brushing against her ankles in the heat of the day.

So far, so good. No speedy pulse. No roiling belly. Nothing.

"Okay, baby," she said to Felix, "let's go. Are you a water dog? Are you going to get all soaked if I let you stay off the leash?"

He woofed softly, though it was unclear whether that meant yes or no. She grinned at him. "Okay. I'll take my chances."

Tessa walked behind him, her thumbs tucked through the straps of her pack. All of her life, she had known that she nearly drowned as a child, but she had never had a memory of it until she went into the river in Montana. Going under, gasping for breath, fighting for air, she had remembered. *Seen* it. "Mommy!" her childhood self cried. "Mommy, help me!"

Overhead, in the hot New Mexico day, an enormous black-and-white magpie squawked, jolting Tessa into the present. She stood on the banks of the Ladrones River, gazing at the water, which was flowing quickly now, but it would barely cover her ankles in many spots. A person could walk on sandbars for a long way. How could she have nearly drowned in it?

She turned north, toward the bridge that led to Green Gate a few miles upriver, and started to walk. Salt cedars, ferny pink and noxious for their ability to consume water—three hundred gallons a *day*—lined the banks on this side but had been cleared, probably by the farm, on the western bank, replaced with native shrubs and trees that would help choke them out. After a while she stopped and realized that she must be directly across from Green Gate Farms.

Felix trotted ahead, stopped and waited for her, trotted ahead. Tessa followed him without expectation, admiring the hot blue sky, dark as a postcard, the mountains huddled protectively above the valley on both sides, and the river running copper over the bed of red earth. She banged her walking stick on the ground to warn snakes of her approach. There wouldn't be any water snakes here, at least not any poisonous ones, but there might be rattlers. She hoped Felix wasn't a snake chaser. So far, he didn't seem to be.

A wind blew across the salt cedars, ruffling them like hair, and carried on it was a horrific howl, a moan. Tessa halted, and Felix rushed back, quivering.

"That's a bad place. There are bad spirits there," Sam had said.

It came again, a low, long cry of anguish, as if the very air itself had become a wail. Despite herself, gooseflesh rose on her arms, and the flutter of panic beat in her throat.

No. She banged her walking stick on the ground and set her jaw. Not spirits. Not evil. It was wind and rocks and some effect of nature. She started walking again.

But as they came to a stand of boulders that marked a long, round bend, a new prickling rose on Tessa's neck. She slowed her steps, feeling the warning rush down over her shoulder blades and pool in her hips. She emerged from the salt cedars and halted.

In front of her, on the other side of the river, the land jutted upward and broke away, no doubt sheared by the river itself over time, to leave ragged, red-stained dirt cliffs.

The cliffs.

"Stay away from the cliffs, girls!"

Dizzy, Tessa took a long breath. Felix trotted back to her, nudged her hand with a wet nose, and made a soft whine. "I'm okay," she said, petting the dog's head. "I think we need to stop here for a few minutes." Her heart fluttered against her ribs, then rose like a bird flapping frantic wings against her collarbones. She forced herself to breathe in and out—a long long long inhalation, long long long exhalation—bringing oxygen back into her system. She put a hand on her diaphragm. "Steady," she said aloud to herself. Her other hand rested on Felix's head.

This was it. The spot where she'd gone in the water as a four-year-old, an incident she had not remembered at all until she tumbled into the river in Montana, desperate to keep her eye on Lisa.

Her childhood memories surfaced:

Darkness, stars overhead. A cliff and the rushing water below. She screamed, "No!" and then a long fall in the darkness, so scared she peed her pants, and then the plunge into icy-cold water. Fighting to find the surface, coming up, sucking in air, pulled under again, surfacing, and she managed to catch a branch. "Rhiannon!" she screamed, and there was a sense of excruciating loss. "Mommy! Help!"

Now, standing in the hot sun, with a dog holding vigil with her, Tessa opened the drawer of memory and took out the shredded pieces of that night. Who was Rhiannon?

What else was there?

She closed her eyes, starting at the beginning. The stars overhead, very clear, so many in the darkness. Was there anyone with her? What was she doing at the cliffs in the dark?

A sense of running away from something terrible.

A flare of memory, quite literally: a fire. *A fire on the horizon, behind her, filling the air with smoke. An animal running with her. On the other side, holding someone's hand.*

Peering at the water with narrowed eyes, Tessa tried to gather more information, but with a nearly audible *thunk,* the drawer slammed closed again. The screen of memory went black.

But a fire—that was something that would be a matter of record. With a sense of sudden purpose, she said, "C'mon, darlin'. Let's go home. I need to do some research."

Sunday afternoon, Vince met with his mother in her exceedingly tidy office for their weekly business discussion. His girls clambered through a playhouse tucked into the back of the store. It was two stories, furnished with miniature furniture and toys, and it had a complete kitchen that Natalie adored.

"We've had new offers," Judy said, "on the acreage along the river."

"Not selling."

She shrugged, tossed the papers down in front of him. "It's my job to tell you, your job to decide."

He picked up the papers. Shook his head. The offers were beginning to verge on the ridiculous—money flung by people who had more than they knew what to do with, people who earned multiple millions for a six-month gig on a movie or had inherited grocery fortunes or manufacturing fortunes or oil fortunes or whatever. Those who earned their money by trade flocked around those who earned theirs through beauty, hoping for glamour.

More evidence—as if he needed it—that Los Ladrones had become a very hip location.

"Not interested," he said.

"I respect your desire to protect the land, son, but think about the legacy you're building for your daughters."

He paid her to give him advice. He looked again at the papers. Huge sums of money.

Once, Vince's only desire had been to flee Los Ladrones, run away from the provincial little village, away from seasonal tourists who rented houses so they could ski and snowshoe and drink too much on the plaza at night. Away from locals with their Catholic or Native American superstitions, and from hippies with their rope belts and long hair. His dreams, fueled by books he took from his mother's bookstore shelves, were to make his mark, win races, use his athleticism to pave his way into a new life.

And it had worked. Cycling, then mountain biking, had taken him into the international arena. He'd raced all over the world, landed juicy endorsements—and because he didn't need much or even want to settle anywhere, he packed the money away, year after year, into various investments that had, in the end, been the single smartest thing he'd done in his life. His mother, who had studied accounting at Cornell before she ran away to the West, had taken care of his investments, and it had been a boon to both of them. By the time he had his seventh and final accident at the age of thirty-three on a mountain in France, he had amassed a staggering sum.

By then he'd married Carrie and settled in Denver near her family. His mother, noticing the slow explosion of wealth creeping north from Santa Fe, counseled him to buy land. He took her advice, little thinking he would ever come back. It had been only an investment.

After Carrie's death, he craved stability and familiarity, and he returned to a town he found much changed and to land worth millions more than he'd paid for it.

Most of it was around Los Ladrones—he'd started with a ranch that had fallen on hard times, which was where they lived now, and had begun to buy parcels around it as they came up for sale. He now had more than ten thousand acres of land, with more than six thousand acres on the river itself. Highly prized.

"No," he said. "The land is the legacy."

She filed the papers in a folder. "They have plenty, that's for sure."

On his way out of the office, he thought of Tessa, of kissing her in the stacks. Thought of the young buck who'd made all that money out of exuberance, the guy who never took things too seriously.

That man would have pursued a woman, taken his chances in the hopes of a payoff, whatever it might have been. As long as he didn't bring his girls into the equation, there was nothing wrong with pursuing Tessa. If he was rebuffed—well, it wouldn't be the first time.

He turned back. "Can the girls hang out here for a little while? I have some business to take care of."

"A little while, but I need to get to the grocery store on my way home, and I'd rather miss the five o'clock rush."

"No problem."

He jogged across the plaza to the hotel and asked the clerk to ring Tessa's room. "No answer, sir," the Mexican national said politely. "Would you care to leave a message?"

"I'll wait."

"If you'd like, we are serving hors d'oeuvres and complimentary wine in the lobby, right through those doors."

Vince glanced through the French doors and saw a shiny crowd nibbling on strawberries. He slapped a palm on the counter. "Thanks. I'll wait outside."

But then he felt like a lovesick fool, parked in front of the hotel, waiting for a woman to return. He tried her cell phone, but the signal was dropped before it went through. The mountains sometimes made cell reception unreliable.

He leaned on a heavy, ancient post and looked over the bustling plaza. It looked as if there might be a wedding this evening. Chairs were being set up beneath the tree, and someone had tied green ribbons to the low-hanging branches. A string quartet tuned their instruments, keyed into one another.

"Hello," said a low, silky voice at his elbow. "I don't know why I thought we could politely avoid each other in a town this size."

"Why would we want to?" Vince turned.

Tessa stood there with the dog, her hair pulled back again into the omnipresent scrunchie. The same enticing tendrils curled around her long neck, lifted on a breeze. "Good question."

He said, "This time, I was actually looking for you."

"I sorta figured." She pointed at the panting dog. "He needs to be in the shade." She gestured down the way, and Vince nodded and followed her to a quiet, heavily shaded alley, where she pulled a bottle of water out of the backpack on her shoulder, awkwardly because of the cast.

"Let me help," Vince said, taking the pack.

"Thanks." She unscrewed the lid and poured water into a bowl for her dog. He slurped a hefty serving, then lay down next to the wall, panting in the heat.

"He looks great. Already fattening up," Vince joked.

"He is a great dog, and he eats like a sixteen-year-old boy! But then, we've been walking a lot today, checking out all the trails around here."

"How's your foot doing?"

She lifted one shoulder. "Pretty good. How's my Pedro?"

Vince grinned. "Fine. Just fine." He pointed at the dog's feet. "Were you at the river?"

She was drinking from the bottle now and nodded, screwing the tin lid back on. "Yeah. I'm trying to desensitize myself. I almost drowned there when I was four."

"In the Ladrones River?"

"Yeah. I don't remember it. Or at least I didn't remember it until I fell in a river on a hiking trek in May. Then I remembered just enough to drive me crazy. Do you remember a forest fire?"

"Yeah, quite a few."

"Like, mid-seventies sometime?"

Vince frowned, thinking back. Late elementary school. "I remember a few small things, you know. Nothing much."

"There wasn't anything in the newspaper files. I guess I have to keep looking."

"Are you hanging around here for a while longer?"

"You sound irritated."

"No. But I'd like to know where we stand, maybe."

She slapped his belly. "You have to lighten up. Coming on a little strong."

To his amazement, Vince actually flushed. "You know what? You're right." He gave a dry, humorless laugh. "You have no way of knowing, but this is not me."

She caught his shoulder. "Doing it again."

Vince turned, and she stood over him on the step. His face was a little lower than hers, and she put her hands on his face.

"Now smile," she said.

He gave her the fakest smile he had, ear to ear, bottom teeth and all.

"Better." She tucked her hands in her back pockets and inclined her head. "Now, here's the question, Vince: Do you want to play—and I do mean *play*—while I'm here, or let it go? I'll be here another week or so, and then, if I get approval, I'll be in town to set up the tour, and we can either be . . . um . . . friends, or not."

He put his hands on her waist, taut and lean. "Friends. Now kiss me."

Tessa laughed and bent in, pressing her mouth to his.

And just like that, the lightness blew away. The taste of her, the smell, the way she clutched his shoulders and pressed into him, all of it. He was as horny as a fifteen-year-old at his first dance, his dick as hard as glass. Pulling back a little, he took a breath.

"Jesus," she whispered. "The chemistry is intense, isn't it?"

He leaned closer, met her eyes and pressed their bodies together. "I want to fuck you until you can't stand up."

"That would take some doing," she returned, and he dug his fingers into her back, laughing.

His phone rang, the sharp trill that signaled work. "Sorry," he growled, and pulled it off his belt, keeping one hand around her body so she wouldn't run away. "Grasso here."

"We've got three lost teens in Rifle Canyon."

"Missing since when?"

"Yesterday," Jason said. "They were supposed to report back by five p.m. and still haven't."

"Damn it. Five last night? Why didn't they call yesterday?"

"Who the hell knows."

"I'll be there in twenty," he said, and hung up. "Sorry, gotta go."

"You're just doing this to raise the anticipation, aren't you?" she said, slanting him a hot look. "You want me to sit up in my room fantasizing about what you're going to do to me when you get back."

His entire body reacted to that visual. He kissed her, deep. "Hold that thought. I'll call you." Straightening, bringing them both back to the real world, he added, "There's no way of knowing when I'll be finished, or even if it will be today, or what kind of shape I'll be in when I'm done."

"I get it." She lifted a shoulder. "You know where to find me."

FIFTEEN

Vita liked to run in the last light of the day, before twilight came creeping in with its ghosts. Along with cooking, running had been her salvation, and perhaps the two together were a good combination, because she'd never put on weight, which was more and more a surprise the older she got. She wasn't vain about it—considered it a lucky accident of preferences and genes.

Tonight, the oppressive heat that could sometimes fill the valley in September had finally been blown down the river by a vigorous wind, and Vita decided not to run the long trail down by the river—there was always the slight worry over West Nile, which had hit the town pretty hard a couple of years back. Vita never got it, thank heaven. Mindful of the threat, she ran the perimeter of the town on a dry dirt trail. She'd already run her one marathon of the year, the Chicago, so she wasn't in training. Just running for pleasure and stress relief and to keep her bones strong. The air smelled of dust and crushed leaves and sage, a scent that would be in her clothes when she got home.

The trail looped behind the plaza and around through open pine woods, down along a flat, open stretch lined with prickly pear and walking-stick cactus, over the trail to the lake, and back down. As she ran, she rearranged recipes and let the day flow through her feet into the ground, where she left annoyances like the dishwasher who had been a no-show for the third time and a delivery of bad bananas. She thought of skinny Annie and her bad hair, humming under her breath as she flipped a pair of eggs, and of Vince Grasso glowering at Tessa the other day in the restaurant—something going on there, that was for sure; Vince didn't bother with women much.

A lot to bother with in Tessa, Vita thought. Whenever Vita was with her, she had the sense of glimpsing an iceberg—just the edge, not enough to make sense of. A sense that there was more to her than she said, than she wanted to reveal. It made Vita careful in return, guarded, and she never was these days. Tessa was hiding something, but Vita didn't think there was anything malicious about it.

Why, then? What did she really want in Los Ladrones?

God knew there was plenty for all of them to get twitchy about. Secrets aplenty, especially at Green Gate, that terrible summer. They all kept expecting the past to dry up like dust— they were in their sixties!—but it never did.

She completed her six-mile trek and slowed to a walk, cooling down as she came back into town. A fox dashed across her path, and Vita caught her breath. Seeing something like that startled and delighted her every single time, which was one big reason to never return to the cities of her youth. Wonder was worth pursuing.

If not for the fox, she might not have seen the man skulking along the apartment block above the western block of shops. He was lean and dark, beautiful in that sensual way that could be so dangerous, and his hair was tied back in a leather string. He was clearly stalking something. Someone. Looking at the windows, along the ground. Vita pulled out her phone and shot a picture. She would show the police, because, even though they sometimes laughed at her worries, they also understood, and they loved her for her protectiveness of the young women who came through the diner.

She watched until he skulked away, then looked to see if she could make out what—or who—he was watching. There, framed clearly by a kitchen window with little clippings of plants in jars, was Annie.

Vita's blood ran cold. The woman had never said, but the evidence of an abuser was all over her face and body. Tonight, Vita would take the cell phone pic to the police. Maybe she wouldn't show Annie yet. She was just beginning to feel a sense of safety. It would be a shame to knock that out from under her.

Tessa had dinner, then collected all of the notes she had made on the town, the farm, and the restaurants and began to arrange them into an itinerary for her boss. Working with the door open to the breeze, she typed it all in and then wrote a letter giving him an idea of the overview.

To: Mick.Harrison@ramblingtours.com

From: Tessa.Harlow@ramblingtours.com

Subject: Los Ladrones Tour possibilities

Attachments included

Hi, Mick.

Please find attached a couple of possible itineraries for tours in Los Ladrones. I've included photos you might use in the brochure/catalog. It's great! The town is rich with history, riddled with celebrities (staying in my hotel this very minute are three A-list actors, one of whom appears to be scouting out land for a retreat home), and so much for foodies! The market is gorgeous, and Green Gate Farms (see attached itinerary and photos) is worth a trip all by itself, and there are gourmet shops like a salt store and a kitchen store in addition to all the restaurants. There are also plenty of trails we can use to map out day hikes for varying levels of ability. I still need to hike to the top of the mountain (pilgrims walk it barefooted to atone, which seems kind of a cool offering, though we probably need to make it an optional day, since it's such a religious thing), but in general I think this would make a great base for a new tour. I'm visualizing it as a food tour with modest hiking, maybe one day of long hiking, rather than the more vigorous hiking tours I've been doing. Just don't know that I really want to go back to that. Maybe we could add in a photography angle or something? (Just brainstorming.)

I've included two itineraries as possibilities. Look it over and let me know what you think.

Tessa

PS—As per our agreement, I'll be checking out of the hotel tomorrow, but I think I'm going to hang around for a while, rent some cottage or something for a few weeks. I'm enjoying it here, and since I'm not working yet, there's no reason to get back to CA. Will let you know when I get settled.

The last paragraph surprised her. She had not realized that was her plan until she typed it out, but as she sent the email, it felt right. More right than anything had felt in a long time.

Felix was out on the balcony, watching the plaza, and she joined him, scratching his ears. The wedding had moved to a reception, perhaps. Across the way, one of the shops had strings of white Christmas lights around the windows. Music rose into the quiet night, gliding guitar and a woman's smoky voice, swirling out into the warm air and drawing Tessa down to the plaza. She looped her camera around her neck and leashed Felix for the sake of politeness.

Felix snuffled around the base of the ancient, spreading tree, while Tessa simply let the place fill her up—the juxtaposition of a whole store devoted to gourmet salt a few doors down from a forties-style drugstore, complete with soda fountain and rubber tomahawks, across from a hotel where movie stars sipped aperitifs and made big deals right next to a plaza where Comanches had stolen seven women and an old hippie-commune-turned-major-organic-farm sold fresh produce.

What an intriguing place.

Tessa unleashed Felix and let him explore the daily dog blog around the legs of park benches and bushes while she experimented with low-light shots of the neon in the drugstore window and signs. She shot the square of light visible over the pass-out bar at Vita's café and turned toward the blaze of the movie theater sign: *CHIEF.* The letters were white, with neon blinking in tubes of pale pink and green and blue. She could hear the buzz of it clearly in the night, along with crickets and faint music. Lovers wandered by, and tourists, and people on their way to dinner. Felix explored. Tessa disappeared into the camera.

Maybe it was the meditative state or the visit to the river the other day, or finally just being here long enough, but all at once the door to her memory opened, and, instead of seeing the jumble of puzzle pieces scattered in a pile, she saw whole scenes. Again she saw the angry blond woman hurrying them across the square, and now she saw who made the other part of "them": another girl, with long hair pulled back in a braid, crying because she was in trouble. They were both in trouble, she and Rhiannon.

Rhiannon.

Feeling airless, Tessa sank down on a bench, keeping her eyes on the gently radiating blinking sign. Felix came over and sat heavily on her foot. Absently, Tessa stroked his head in thanks, letting the memories pour through her.

For years she'd remembered a pink tricycle. Now she saw it was decorated for a contest in the plaza. Tessa rode it dressed in a red and white bathing suit and red cowboy boots, her dog trotting on a leash beside her. Brenna.

Tessa looked down. Felix looked just like Brenna.

Do you remember now?

"I think I might."

Nearby was another trike, this one blue and decorated with tissue-paper roses. They had looked and looked for blue tissues and finally found some, and they wrapped them with green pipe cleaners.

Uneasily, Tessa let the blips reel out. Little things. Other children, a group of them playing jacks in a tower room with windows all around. Cold, shivering as it snowed outside and an adult lit a fire.

Whirling by like one of the snowflakes was Tessa's father, his hair very long and dark down his back. He was doing magic tricks with a circle of children around his feet, and Tessa was laughing as he pulled a coin out of her toe. It made her ribs ache somehow. Even then, he'd been the greatest dad around.

The angry woman, hurrying them. Again.

The fire and running, squeezing Rhi's hand, the whole forest burning, filling the air with smoke, running and running, holding hands, and then a blank, and water filling her mouth, a scream and a cry, and surfacing, crying: "Rhiannon!"

Enough. Tessa leapt to her feet, gasping for breath as if she were drowning right now, this very minute, in the darkness of the plaza. Her heart was racing, pounding so loudly she couldn't hear over it at all, and her vision fizzed at the edges, as if she would faint. She felt like she might throw up, fall down, die of terror.

Some reasonable part of her brain said, *Panic attack.*

Tessa felt Felix's cold nose against her palm, a focal point that helped her come back into her body, out of her head. She told herself it was only in her mind, that she could breathe, even if she didn't do it until she fell over and had the wind knocked out of her. Thinking of Felix's worry if she actually fainted made it possible for Tessa to take a slow, long breath in, let it go. Ragged at first, then more smoothly.

Good God.

Shaking in reaction, she decided maybe a margarita was in order. It was not her drink of choice, but only an idiot drank shots of tequila at her age. Bending over, she kissed Felix. "Good dog. Thank you." Felix licked her nose.

As she sat down over her margarita in the courtyard of the hotel, she realized one thing that was off-kilter: Her memories were not those of a four-year-old. The tissue-paper flowers. The trikes, the dog. Not four. More like five or six, like Vince's daughter Jade's age.

And it was beginning to seem as if she'd had a sister. Which meant that Sam had lied to her.

Why?

Natalie sometimes liked sleeping at Grandma's house, even if she didn't like to eat there. It was nice to be close to town, and there were four bedrooms with clean, shiny floors you could slide on in your socks, and pretty views of the mountains, and Grandma's big family room where they watched movies together. Natalie had a room of her own here, too, and an altar that Grandma let her set up, even though she said something like religion was the drug of the masses, which Natalie didn't get until she realized Grandma didn't mean Mass but big groups of people.

They had eaten at the diner so late today that Natalie didn't need anything else, so tonight she skipped the sodium-free organic soup Grandma opened. She took Pedro and went into her room and started to pray the rosary, just like her mother taught her:

"Hail Mary, full of face, the Lord is with thee . . ."

Pedro slid down beside her, resting his back against her. She loved him best of all the animals she had ever met. Distracted, she stretched out on the floor beside him and scratched the place on his chest that he loved so much, right below his collar. His eyes were exactly the same color as the afternoon sky, and sometimes, it seemed you could see into another world in there. His pointed ears seemed to always have something to say, twitching, leaning, or, like now, going soft so that the tips flopped over like an envelope.

He also had the softest fur in the universe, like a pillow, and she scooted closer to put her face on his side, breathing in the dusty dog smell of him. She wished there was perfume like dogs. She would put it in her bed so she could pretend pillows were dogs.

The idea made her giggle. Dog perfume! Pedro turned and delicately licked her face, right across the eye. It felt nice. She slid down flat on the floor and he gently, thoroughly washed her face.

Jade came barging into her room without knocking, but for once Natalie didn't care. "Hey, Nat, wanna come watch movies with us? Grandma said we can pick whatever we want and make some popcorn and she'll even watch with us!"

"Yay!" Natalie jumped up and generously asked her sister, "Which one do you want?"

"I don't care. What do you want?"

"You don't want *Cinderella*?" Jade liked the part about getting a dress made from flowers.

"No, you can pick."

"Even *The Sound of Music*?" Natalie loved the singing children. "Only up to the part where they sing 'So Long, Farewell.'"

"Okay."

For once it seemed like everything would be just nice. Disaster didn't strike until it was almost time for bed. In between, all four of them—Grandma, Natalie, Jade, and Hannah—piled onto Grandma's big corner couch with all its fancy places to put drinks. They made bowls of popcorn, and Grandma let them have some Sleepytime tea without any sugar. Sasha sat by the couch, all alert, and waited with happy, bright eyes for them to throw her kernels of popcorn.

"That dog lives for popcorn," Grandma said.

"She lives for food," Natalie said.

"Just like you," Hannah said. If Jade had said it, Nat would have got mad, but Hannah was only telling the truth.

"At least I like *good* food," Natalie said. "Sasha eats cat poop!"

They all cracked up at that. They sang along with the songs from the movie—even Hannah, who didn't really know the words, and Natalie was so, so glad that the lady at 100 Breakfasts had stopped her from stealing the salt shaker, because if she had it in her drawer or her pocket tonight, it would be like a great big giant noise roaring over everything until she got used to it. Instead, she got to just lie here on the couch and sing along with her sisters and eat popcorn.

Just before the song when all the children sing good night for the guests at the party, Pedro whined to get outside and do his business. Grandma got up to let him out and came back to sing the last song, then used the remote to click off the TV. "That's it, girls. Time to brush your teeth and get to bed. I'll come hear prayers in a few minutes."

Outside, Pedro yelped, really loud. Nat felt it right in her gut and ran to the door. Grandma grabbed her from behind and hauled her away. "Stay right here. You don't know what kind of animal he might be tangling with."

She flung Natalie away, practically throwing her, and flipped on the porch light so she could see. Natalie ran to the window to peer out, putting her hands to the glass to block the inside light. Her heart was pounding.

"No coyotes, no coyotes, no coyotes," she chanted. One of the boys at school last year said coyotes could sing your dog out to play, tricking them, and then they would tear out their throats.

But there was Pedro, racing for the door, making a weird, high yelping noise. He streaked up to the porch and Grandma opened the door. He barreled in, then came right over to Natalie, making a deep, sad whine that made her know he was hurting.

"Oh, no!" she cried, grabbing him by the ruff so she could look at him. "He's got long stickers all over his face! And one is right by his eye!"

Grandma swore and knelt down beside him. "Porcupine." She looked at her watch. "Get my phone, Jade. He's probably going to have to go to the vet." She sucked air over her teeth, touching the one by his eye. "That's really close."

Natalie blinked back tears. Pedro was crying, waiting for

them to do something, and it made her heart feel like somebody was holding it in a tight fist. "Why can't we just pull them out with tweezers?"

"Because there's a little hook on the other side of the quill, and we don't want to break it off." She rubbed Natalie's knee. "He's going to be fine, honey, don't worry."

Natalie leaned in and kissed him on the neck, where it wouldn't hurt him. "You hear that, Pedro baby? You are going to be okay."

Jade rushed the phone over and Grandma called the vet, who promised to meet them at the office in ten minutes. She also tried to call Daddy, but he must have been high in the mountains, because he didn't answer. Grandma left a message.

"Get your shoes, girls, and a blanket. We have to take Pedro to the doctor."

Natalie was the oldest, so she got to help, sitting by Pedro. The big dog whined all the way to the vet, which wasn't very far, but it seemed long because of the scariness. She leaned her head against him, rubbing his throat and his side, trying to make him feel better. He kept shaking his head and sneezing, making a sound like a horse, and finally Natalie started to sing the songs from *The Sound of Music.* Jade joined in, nodding, putting her hands on his other side, and he seemed to feel a little better at least.

The vet let everybody come in while she looked at Pedro, and then she took him away to get an X ray, though Grandma said she didn't really know why.

When the vet came back, she had a strange look on her face. "We've been seeing this dog since you got him, haven't we?"

"Yes. What's wrong?" Grandma asked.

She shook her head, rubbing her hands along Pedro's back, down his legs. "His pelvis was obviously shattered at some

point. But I—I don't know how he could walk after being dam-
aged that way."

"No, he's fine."

"He is," she said. "There might be something wrong with the
machine, but I'd like you to bring him back and take some
more pictures with my assistant, if you don't mind."

"Is he okay?" Natalie asked.

The vet knelt down. "Yes. He's great. He's going to be your
crazy dog for the next ten years if you take good care of him.
Keep him away from porcupines."

"And skunks," Jade said, petting his tail. "My friend's cat got
sprayed by a skunk, and it was *bad*."

"I'm sure it was." She shook Grandma's hand. "Bring him in
to me, if you will. No charge."

In her small room, Annie took a nap after work and awakened
just before full dark. She puttered around her apartment, tidy-
ing things up for the morning, making herself some supper.
Her legs were tired, not used to the long days in the kitchen yet,
but it seemed like a good thing to make some kind of food for
herself. Feeding herself the things she liked, the way she fed
other people what they liked, as Vita put it. It made her happy.

She wasn't a good cook, not yet anyway, but it was easy
enough to make peanut butter crackers and chicken noodle
soup, which was something that made her feel happy and con-
tent. As the soup heated, she made five saltine-and-peanut-
butter sandwiches, then set the table using a place mat and new
cloth napkin she'd bought on sale for four dollars at the ritzy
kitchen store on the plaza. A lot of money, but not if you had
to buy only one, and since there was only her, she didn't have to
worry about anyone else. One of the counselors at prison used

to tell the girls that: "Try to worry about just yourself. What do you want? What would make *you* happy?" Not some man, which was why most of them were in jail, anyway, for trying to please some man. Most of them were so used to doing for everybody else they didn't even know where to start. They practiced imagining how to spend ten dollars on themselves—what would they buy?

Annie never thought she'd buy a cloth *napkin*, but she liked the table in the corner with the window over it, and she liked having nice things, since she had so very rarely had anything in her life. The napkin was pale yellow, to match the flowers on the table, with a cheerful, embroidered edge in red and white, very simple and pretty.

Her other indulgence when she got paid was a set of oil pastels and a pad of decent paper from the drugstore. She had bought the small set of pastels, and the paper was really just a tablet of blank paper, but it was very white and a good weight. She couldn't wait to play with them. Maybe she would be brave enough to go out to the church and sketch the graves or even sit on the plaza and sketch the tourists on her day off.

As she sat at the table, eating, a cat jumped up on her narrow strip of second-floor porch and meowed at the screen door. It was a little white thing, not very old, and Annie had been feeding her sometimes because she looked like a cat Annie had as a child. The cat rubbed on the screen door now.

"Oh, okay," Annie whispered. "Come in for a minute."

She went to the door. Standing against a wall across the plaza was a man with long dark hair, loose on his shoulders. For a second, Annie's heart went cold, as it always did until she remembered.

Oh, yeah. She was safe now. Smiling to herself, she pushed

open the screen door and the cat trotted happily inside. "I bought you something, too." Leaving her soup on the table, she opened a can of super-cheapy cat food and put it in a little saucer. The cat crouched over it delicately, politely. When she tasted it, she started to make a growling *meow meow meow* noise that was so cute Annie sat down on the floor with her, eating her own supper while the cat ate chicken-flavored mush.

When they were both finished, Annie washed their dishes and put them away, then folded her napkin neatly for next time. She found an old comb and used it to smooth out the knots and tangles in the poor thing's white fur. The cat liked it, swirling back and forth under the comb, purring so loud you could probably hear it in Nebraska. Afterward, she climbed up on Annie's lap, and they watched television until it was time for bed. Annie was strictly not allowed to have pets, but she didn't have the heart to put the cat out. One night couldn't hurt, surely.

Breakfast #4

Our homemade raisin toast, thickly sliced, served with coffee or tea and jam of your choice.

HEARTY CINNAMON RAISIN BREAD
~ 2 loaves

1½ cups water
1 tsp vanilla
1 cup raisins
1¼ cups milk, scalded

1 stick butter
1 cup rolled oats
3 T sugar, divided
1 packet yeast (¼ oz.)
2 cups white flour
2 cups whole-wheat flour
1 T salt
1 T cinnamon
1–2 cups white flour for kneading

To prepare for the bread, begin by soaking the raisins in 1 cup of water and 1 tsp of vanilla. Set aside. Scald the milk and let the butter melt in it; let cool and pour over raw rolled oats.

When raisins and oatmeal have soaked for 30 minutes, pour ½ cup of lukewarm water into a small bowl along with 1 T sugar and stir until sugar is dissolved. Add yeast to proof, set aside.

Combine the 4 cups of flours, oats-and-milk mixture, yeast-and-water mixture, remaining sugar, salt, and cinnamon in a large bowl until the dough holds together (it may be sticky at this point). Generously dust a work surface with white flour and begin the kneading, adding flour as needed. Knead for at least five minutes, and then mix in the drained raisins until they're evenly distributed through the dough. Put in a large oiled bowl, turn the dough so it is entirely coated with oil, and cover with a thin, damp cloth. Let rise in a warm place for 1 hour.

When the dough has doubled, turn it again onto a lightly dusted work surface and punch it down. Divide the dough in two, shape into loaves, and dust off as much flour as you can. Nestle into greased bread pans to rise for another 90 minutes.

Bake at 375 degrees for approximately 40 minutes. Bread is done when it is nicely browned and you can hear a hollow sound when you thump the bottom.

SIXTEEN

Vince and his partner, Jason Martinez, found the three teenagers at the bottom of a ravine—cold and hungry, a little banged up, but otherwise fine. They delivered them home and checked out and it was still only a quarter to ten.

Ten o'clock was the cutoff with his mother. If he worked until ten, he left the girls with her. If he was finished before that, he called to see what state they were in. Tonight, he was going to let the girls stay with Judy. It made him feel a little guilty, but if Tessa was leaving in a week, he wanted to see her as much as possible.

A voice mail on his cell made him waver. It was left at 9:37 p.m., only a few minutes before. "Pedro tangled with a porcupine," Judy said. "We're going to the vet, but he should be fine."

He held the phone in his hand. A porcupine. Damned dog.

If he was a good man, Vince thought, he would go rescue his mother and his girls and his dog. But he'd buy his mother something really sweet to make up for being a heel tonight. Not that he intended for her to ever find out. No way. She'd kick his ass, and he honestly did need her help.

Before heading into town, he stopped at his place and showered away the sweat of the past few hours, put on a crisp, clean shirt, and shaved. He told himself it was just good to escape his life for a few hours, to have some relief from the heavy responsibilities he carried.

And then he felt like an ass. Tonight his mother was taking on his responsibilities. Not only his children but the care of his dogs, and all of them at the vet at once would be no fun. If it wasn't for Judy, he'd have to hire a nanny, and while he was sure there were plenty out there who were great, none of them would be Judy. Over the past few days, she'd had his daughters more hours than he had.

As he headed out again, he punched his cell to check the time—10:23. Definitely in the safe time slot, but, just to be sure, he didn't return her call until he got all the way into town. Her voice mail picked up. "Hey, Mom," he said. "Sorry to miss the excitement. I'm headed to town for a little while if you want to give me a call."

He put the phone down on the seat beside him. A CD played on the deck, System of a Down, good solid rock and roll, and he turned it up, singing along in the darkness, feeling good. Hopeful. Young.

Hungry.

At the hotel, he parked in the lot in the back and walked around to the plaza. It was quiet here. A single couple ambled along arm in arm, talking quietly. On the patio by the hotel restaurant, a few late diners lingered over coffee and dessert while a woman sang torch songs in a sultry voice. From beneath the tree somewhere came the sound of a woman weeping softly, inconsolably, but peer as he might, he couldn't see where she was.

On the second stories around the square were lights burning

in apartments and hotel rooms. Vince saw it all in excruciatingly perfect detail, as if it mattered. As if he would remember it later.

He found Tessa's number in the history of his cell phone and punched the talk button. It rang once, twice, three, four times, and Vince began to wonder if she'd gone to bed when she picked up. "Hello?"

"Hi, Tessa. Did I wake you?"

"Not at all. I'm sitting on my balcony having a glass of wine. Where are you?"

"In the plaza."

"You are?" The phone made noise as she moved around. "I'm looking at the plaza and I can't see you. Can you see me?"

Vince looked at the row of balconies bound with heavy vigas. A woman was outlined against the light of French doors. He said, "Lift your hand above your head." The woman lifted her hand, and Vince moved toward her. "I can see you."

"I still don't see you at all," she said.

"Keep watching." He walked to a spot right below her, and now he could see her leaning on the railing, her long curly hair falling over her arms. *"But, soft!"* he said quietly into the phone, *"what light through yonder window breaks?"*

She laughed. "Quoting *Romeo and Juliet* doesn't seem very auspicious."

"They had a good time while it lasted."

"True. Would you like to come up?"

"Yes," he said. "I think I would."

When Vince knocked on her door, Felix leapt up protectively and gave a serious warning bark. Pleased, Tessa bent and gave his chest a vigorous rub. "Good dog."

She peered through the peephole, to be safe. When it was indeed Vince, she changed her voice, opened the door, and said happily, "Friend!" spreading her hand to indicate Vince. Felix wagged his tail and came over to sniff Vince's knee.

To her surprise, Tessa felt shivery. Shy. His hair was freshly washed, too long, but that deep molasses shine was even more emphatic. Very good hair. And eyes, she thought, that dark-brown glitter. And his face, all broad lines and solidness.

"You make me think of an elk," she said, leaning on the door-jamb, looking up at him.

He raised his eyebrows. "I hope that's good."

Tessa nodded. She stepped back and let him in, and suddenly the room seemed minuscule, with the bed taking up most of the room and Vince filling the rest. "What can I get you?" she asked, picking up her wine from the dresser where she'd left it. "We might have some time before the bar closes. I can order something."

"Are you nervous?" he asked, that very small, very sexy smile playing over his mouth.

"No." She gestured so broadly with her wine that she spilled some on her thumb. "Yes."

"I won't bite you." His voice rumbled so deep, it seemed to come from his chest instead of his throat. "Get me a beer out of the minibar and let's go sit outside. Sound good?"

Tessa nodded and bent down to look inside the fridge. "Heineken, Coors, Budweiser."

"Whatever. Grab one." He moved around the bed and stood by the French doors. He held out his hand. "I'm here for the woman, not the refreshments."

For one long minute, Tessa felt literally dizzy, as if she would remember something, but then she realized it was just that she had been thinking about him all day. His kind, deep eyes and wide mouth and powerful thighs. Now that he was here, it seemed dangerous, something way too big to be playing with. The thought gave her a sharp feeling in her ribs.

He stood there, solid and patient, waiting for her, his eyes steady on her face. "Let's just sit outside, Tessa," he said. "No pressure."

She nodded and gave him his beer, and they stepped out into the darkness, lit only by stars and the twinkle of Christmas lights across the way. Felix trotted out with them and collapsed by the wall with a sigh. The silky sound of Carla Bruni rose to polish the hard edges of their slight awkwardness. Vince took her hand as they sat down, side by side. His thumb moved on hers, softly, and in a moment Tessa took a breath and let it go.

"That's better," he said.

"How did your rescue go? Or shouldn't I ask?"

"It turned out fine. Our big rescue was finding three teenagers who had walked into a box canyon and couldn't get back out. No harm, no foul. They're fine. Although"—he raised a finger—"I had a message from my mother that Pedro tangled with a porcupine."

"Oh, poor baby." She scowled at him. "He needs more supervision."

"He's a dog, Tessa."

"And this is a dangerous environment. Cars and porcupines and probably coyotes and mountain lions and people who don't like dogs who could be mean to him."

"Yeah, I'd like to see a mountain lion mess with Pedro."

"He could get hurt, Vince. He did tonight!"

He looked at her. "You could be right."

"I am right. Remember, I'm the one who saw him dashing across the highway after a rabbit."

"That's still bizarre, honestly—that you saw him first, before you met me."

A vision of Pedro, dashing across the highway with his tongue lolling happily, flashed through her imagination. "You need to fence him," she said firmly, "to keep him safe."

"I'll think about it, I promise," he said. He moved his fingers over the bones on the back of her hand. "What's on your mind tonight?"

"I'm thinking about the river," Tessa said, and an embarrassingly melodramatic shiver shook its way down her spine.

"I felt that. Did something happen? You were at the river this afternoon, right?"

"Nothing happened today," she said. "I told you that I nearly drowned when I was four but that I couldn't remember it until I nearly drowned on a trek in Montana last May." She held up her cast, dropped it down. "That's when I did this. But when I fell in the river, I remembered the first near-drowning."

"Trauma amnesia," he said.

"Is that what it is?"

"It happens a lot to children who have some traumatic experience; it's a protective thing."

Tessa felt the familiar creeping regret and let go of a breath.

Quietly, he asked, "That wasn't childhood, was it?"

"No."

"Tell me."

Tessa felt overwhelmed at the many layers of history. "Oh, it's a long story," she said, and waved it away.

"You don't want to talk about it?"

"It's not that, it's just one of those convoluted things that folds over itself."

"An origami story?" His eyes danced, and Tessa felt a breath of lightness move through the heaviness in her chest.

She nodded. "It's hard to even figure out how to start it."

"Pick a spot."

Tessa considered the fact, sucked in a corner of her lip. "There are always tours that don't go well. It's part of the job. The weather is bad, or you have a group that isn't as well trained as you'd hoped, or someone gets really sick or injured. I had a guy break his ankle at ten thousand feet on the Milford Track, and it was a challenge to get him out. In the end, it took helicopters. But the weather was good that time, and we were not far from a hut, so it worked out okay." She shrugged. "Lots of things can go wrong. You do your best."

"Right."

"This tour was cursed from the get-go. Bad weather, a group that was so varied in fitness it was like a junior high school gym class, some people pushing ahead, others trailing behind. It was frustrating."

He nodded. "I can imagine."

"We had rain nearly every day—not all day, but gully-washers for an hour at a stretch—making the trails soggy, muddy, sloppy. Everyone got soaking wet and cranky. We were spending nights in hostels, very basic accommodations along the way, so they'd be okay, get pumped up, and be ready to start again the next day.

"So," she reiterated, "not great weather or trail conditions. A mixed group of fitness levels. And I got the spider bite the first night. It kept getting worse and worse, ulcerating, but I honestly thought it was just the wet conditions making it harder to heal. Every night I cleaned it up, doctored it, kept it dry overnight, and it would be a little less painful in the morning."

Vince said nothing. Listened.

"Thursday, we woke up to sunshine. It lifted everybody's

spirits. We had a good breakfast and got moving. My foot was killing me by then, but that's the job—you do what you have to do. I felt so damned lucky to do this every day, and, really, I wasn't going to complain about a freaking sore foot, you know? There were people with devastating blisters and they were walking anyway. So would I.

"It was the most challenging day on this particular tour—ascents and descents of about two thousand feet and several miles at above eleven thousand feet, which makes it hard to breathe. The weather report was decent for a change, at least, and we were shedding clothes in the hot sun by ten a.m., when we had the first break. Everybody was doing okay, or maybe I only thought that because my own foot felt like it was on fire. I didn't even want to take off my boot. It was one of those things. You learn to live with it."

"Go, sister."

"Toward lunchtime, there was a descent into a heavily treed valley, and the clouds moved in. Here we go again! Everyone just groaned and pulled out their ponchos and trudged along. I was trying to be upbeat—'You can do it! We're halfway through. You can look back on this and laugh one day.'"

"I've had a few bike rides like that."

"The day got worse—heavier rain, and heavier, and then there was hail and it got slippery. We took shelter under a rock for a while, and nobody said a word. We just stood there and glared at the hail. I poured hot ginger tea out of a thermos and passed it around, we split a few cookies, and when the hail stopped, we headed out. There was muttering and complaining and I knew they felt miserable.

"Again, things I couldn't do anything about, right? But if my foot hadn't been in such pain, I might have been thinking more clearly. I might have realized that there was a bad bit of trail ahead and at least called out some caution."

She stopped, narrowing her eyes so that the lights across the square turned blurry. Through the fog of light, she peered into the past.

"Or not. I don't know." She shook her head. "What happened was that a pine tree, loosened by the rain, went down sideways. It was a steep part of the trail. Not dropping a thousand feet to a rocky death or anything like that—thank God—but a long, steep fall to the base of the ravine. The tree started rolling, and that set off a little avalanche of dirt, and the trail washed out from under us. We all went with it."

"Whoa. Nasty."

"Yeah, it was. The slope was modest, but you can imagine there was an avalanche of mud that came with that tree—"

"Oh, yeah."

"There was a river at the bottom of the slope, and two of us went in. I managed to get out on the other side and pulled Lisa out, too, and there we were, stranded on the wrong side of the river from the rest of the group. Everyone was muddy and soaked and scared, and we had lost most of our supplies. I had broken my arm." She lifted it to illustrate. "One guy had a pretty nasty broken leg, and there were some other injuries—cuts and bruises and things like that—but we were lucky: Nobody got killed."

"How many of you?"

"Eight."

He nodded.

"Lisa and I were on the right side of the river, so we headed out, walking, leaving a pretty capable guy in charge of the others. We had no cell phone reception, and the rain was horrific, and we were freezing cold—God, it was just horrible."

"And your arm was broken. And you had an infected spider bite. You had to have been in shock by then."

Tessa nodded. The darkness pressed in, the black hole. She took her hand away from Vince and put her palms over her eyes. "Ugh! Why am I telling you this story? It's stupid. All you really need to know is that she died and it was my fault."

Vince said nothing for a minute. He sipped his beer, and Tessa heard the echo of "she died" hanging in the air like a vile curse.

"What I know about search and rescue," he said finally, "is that survivors need to tell their stories over and over until they get them into narratives they can manage." He put his big hand on the place between her shoulder blades, gently rubbing in a circle. "You haven't told this story much, right?"

"No. I don't want to seem like I'm trying to get sympathy when I really was terribly irresponsible."

"I won't give you any sympathy, if you don't want it. I'll just listen." His hand kept circling, circling, on her upper back, a deeply soothing motion. "Go back to walking down the river-bank, freezing cold."

"Right." She leaned elbows on her knees, letting the images come back. "Lisa was one of the girls I loved to see come on my trips. She was quite plump, maybe sixty or seventy pounds overweight, but working on becoming more fit. Sometimes it was pretty challenging for her, but she had a lot of moxie, she worked really hard and never, ever complained." She paused, put a hand to her throat. "Only twenty-two or twenty-three, this adorable, shy blonde. We were walking through the rain, soaking wet, freezing, and she *never* whined."

His hand stalled, moved again.

"I only lasted for maybe an hour, and I just couldn't go any farther. We should have stayed put, tried to find someplace dry to get warm. Since it was so cold and wet, they would be expecting us at the hostel, so they would have sent someone out to find us. It had probably been stupid to start walking in the first place. But by then I was so out of it that I made some very bad decisions."

He nodded ruefully.

"I got panicky, thinking we were going to have to spend the night outside, and I—ugh. Honestly, it's kind of hard to remember this part. I remember having a conversation with Lisa and she volunteered to keep walking until she got to the hostel. She helped me cover up with leaves and stuff, and . . ."

"Take your time."

"It must have been a couple of hours, but I was hallucinating. I thought there was a mountain lion with me, keeping me company." She gave a little shake of her head, rolled her eyes. "And I thought I was four and they had just hauled me out of the river—Los Ladrones River—and I was calling for someone."

She paused and took a long swallow of wine. "The hostel did send out a rescue party, and they found the group who stayed put, predictably."

Vince nodded.

"And they found me, though I seriously don't remember that at all. By then I was in pretty bad shape. I didn't really come back to myself for two or three days. They did surgery on my arm, cleaned out my foot, IV antibiotics and hydration, and I was fine."

"Relatively speaking."

She shrugged. "Lisa never made it to the hostel. They didn't even find her body for three weeks. She drowned, somehow. Probably the bank gave way at some point. Not that it matters. She died."

"How about the rest of your group?"

"They were okay. The one guy had a broken leg, but it was fine. Only Lisa—"

"Who was twenty-three and blond and plucky."

The words brought tears to her eyes. "Right."

Vince said nothing, and after long minutes she looked over at him. He sat calmly, looking out at the night. As if he felt her gaze, he said, "You made some bad decisions, especially as a trained tour leader, starting with the first choice to go out with a badly infected foot."

His calm reiteration of the facts eased the darkness rather than added to it. "You should have stayed where you were once you went down the mountain, too, of course, but that's a rough situation, and not one anybody would be able to manage well. But I get it. You feel responsible, and you are."

Tessa blinked the tears back. Nodded. "I'm not sure how to live with it forever—that's the trouble, you know?"

"Right. You're not a monster, either, and I like it that you know that, too." He took her hand. "How does this story fold back to the time when you were four?"

His voice, his touch, his matter-of-factness made it easier to simply tell the truth. It was too intimate, and she would regret it, but for months she'd been lugging around all these tangled memories and sorrows, and it was a huge relief to simply lay the facts all out on a table before a witness. "When I went under, I remembered the drowning from when I was four. Or six." She frowned. "Since I've been here, I've been thinking that I wasn't four. My memories are very mixed up, but I remember things that wouldn't be from a four-year-old's point of view." The strange, building sense of worry rose into her throat. "I think my dad might have lied to me about my age."

"Did you ask him?"

"Not yet. I'm a little worried about opening a Pandora's box." She took a breath. "I'm starting to think he might have been mixed up with whatever broke the commune apart." She put both of her hands around his giant one. "Please, don't tell anyone, okay? I mean, if there's something he ran from, something that would get him in trouble, I would never forgive myself."

"See, that's what I like, how you protect him." He brushed a lock of hair away from her face. "I promise, Tessa, I will not say a single word to anyone."

"Thank you."

"So, what do you remember?"

"When I woke up in Montana, the memory that surfaced was of being hauled out of the river as a little girl. I remembered falling off the cliffs and being in the water and my dad pulling me out. But a lot of other images just don't make sense. I have a sense of other people with me."

"But not who they are?"

"My mother, of course, because she was with me." Tessa rubbed her forehead. "I'm starting to think she tried to kill me."

"Wow." He bristled slightly. "At least Carrie didn't do that." His hand moved on her back. "I'm so sorry."

"And, come to that, why don't I ever think about my mother? Ever? Why haven't I, ever? It's weird. Looking at your girls, at Natalie, I think—why don't I remember?"

"But you said you were Jade's age or younger, so . . ."

"Right. You said Jade doesn't really remember, either." She blew out a big breath of air. "Sorry. I do go on and on." She stood up, uncomfortable with herself, the space. Something. She leaned on the railing.

Vince joined her. Overhead, the stars were a deep sparkle,

the night still and quiet. He put his arm around her. "Do you mind?"

"No, I like it."

He tucked her close to him. "My wife killed herself," he said, and she heard the words coming through his chest, against her ear. "I saw it coming for almost three years, from the time Jade was born, but she just kept slipping away and slipping away, and in the end she climbed into her car and drove up to the top of a mountain and drove herself right off."

Tessa tried to pull back so she could look up at him, but he held her close to his side. "How do you know it wasn't an accident?"

"People saw her. And, as I said, it had been coming for a while."

The tears that had risen over her own guilt now rose again for Natalie, with her blue-raspberry eyes and the hostile tilt to her head. "Poor Natalie. She must miss her terribly."

"Oh, yeah." He moved his hand on her arm, up and down. "I knew Carrie was depressed, and I didn't do anything to make it really better. She went to a doctor and took some antidepressants, but she didn't like the way they felt, and then—I don't know. I didn't stay on her. It was sort of embarrassing or something that she had this mental illness." He growled to himself. "I just wanted her to get over it, pull herself together."

Tessa thought about the way he'd listened to her, and she gave him the same in return. She couldn't reach that spot on his shoulders, so she rubbed her hand over his belly, the only place on him that had any softness.

"Everyone always feels so sorry for me, this widower with three little girls, wife's a suicide, how could she do that." He shook his head. "I fucked up," he said plainly. "And there isn't a damned thing I can ever do to make that better. But I also think that we can't always save people. Sometimes, fate is lying there like a snake, and it'll take you no matter what you do to try to stop it."

"Maybe," Tessa said.

Vince shifted and put his hands on her face. "I'm going to kiss you now," he said, and Tessa nodded. And then they didn't do a lot more talking, and it felt like fate, though Tessa really tried to tell herself that was foolish and girlish and she was old enough to know better.

In her dream, Tessa was small and standing on the edge of the cliff. A woman held hard to her hand, and Tessa was screaming, *"Mommy, no, Mommy!"* and trying to pull away. On the other side was another child, also screaming, but Mommy was strong, and she dragged them with her, diving over the side, where she let go. Tessa felt the long, empty drop, tasted smoke in the air, and then came the foamy plunge into the icy water, down, down, down, bubbles coming up all around her. Her foot touched bottom, and she pushed off as hard as she could, bobbing up into the night, the darkness, the flickering orange light in the distance. She clung, coughing, to a tangle of roots, screaming, *"Help! Help! Help!* Help!"

And then there were hands hauling her up out of the water, dripping and shivering violently, crying. Crying. The person pulling her out of the water held her against his chest. Sam. *"I've got you, baby. You're okay now. Breathe."*

She fought against him, screaming, and then she kicked herself awake, falling into her own bed, pressed up against a broad, naked male back.

For a long moment she was disoriented, unable to place herself in time or location or her life. What bed was this? What room? Which dog sleeping on her feet?

Slowly, the shape of the French doors revealed themselves. Los Ladrones, then. Vince. She moved, pressing her smaller body around his, an arm snaking down around his waist. She was shivering in reaction, and his skin, so hot and smooth, warmed her. Tucking her forehead into the hollow of his spine, she found it possible to stop shivering.

Vince turned and gathered her into the solid circle of his body. "You all right?" he rumbled.

"Bad dream," she said, and tried to go back to sleep. But every time she closed her eyes, she saw the dramatic plunge into the water, and all the cold terror came with it.

After a while, Vince said, "Are you asleep?"

She said, "No, are you?"

"Do you want to go get something to eat?"

Tessa laughed. "It's the middle of the night!"

"So? I'm a big guy. I haven't had anything to eat since lunch at 100 Breakfasts, and it's been pretty busy since then." As if to underscore the plea, his stomach growled. Loudly. "See?"

"Okay. I could eat," she said.

He smoothed a hand upward, cupping her breast. "You have no idea what a relief this has been. Just being with somebody, letting everything go."

"Ditto," she said. Light from the doors edged his mussed hair, the curve of his shoulder. "Kind of a surprise for me, too."

"A surprise?" He lifted up on one elbow. "How so?"

"I don't know." She felt shy, revealed now in the pale light. "It's really easy to be around you. Like I already know you."

"Maybe it's not just dogs who come back to life. Maybe we knew each other in Mesopotamia."

"Could we make it somewhere a little more interesting? Medieval Venice or something?"

"I can go with Venice. Were you a courtesan?" He traced a circle around her breast.

"Oh, no. I was the haughtiest noblewoman in the whole of the town. And you"—she narrowed her eyes, letting the story unfold—"were a bishop in the church, sworn to uphold vows of chastity until death."

The tips of his fingers skimmed her throat, and he bent close enough to brush his lips over her lower lip. "Was I successful?"

"What do you think?"

Vince rolled her over onto her back, his hands on either side of her shoulders, and nestled in between her legs. She felt him nudging her, playfully, heatedly. He bent, slowly, slowly, slowly, and touched his mouth to hers, swirled his tongue over hers, and she met him in kind, running her hands over his chest, then his arms and buttocks, poised for a plunge. "I think you drove me mad," he growled, "and I took you when your husband was in the other room."

Tessa laughed throatily. "Show me."

He dove in, and then they were tangled again, making love with a fierceness Tessa couldn't remember feeling for a long time. A long time. His hands moved on her chest and caressed her heart. His breath moved on her lips and animated some dead fragment of her soul. His voice, ragged and rumbling and rich, set thrumming some answering sound in her own throat. Everything shivered when he touched her. Everything blazed.

Dangerous, she thought as they moved.

He braced himself over her and put his hands beside her face. "Look at me, Tessa."

Her breath was shallow as she opened her eyes.

"Promise you'll tell me before you leave town."

"I promise," she whispered. "I promise." Then they were both sliding away into their own shared world, constructed when they met, demolished when they parted. Unique in all of time.

Vince drove them out to a truck stop off the interstate, nearly thirty miles away, where no one would see them or even care. Felix came with them, riding in the back. He curled up happily on a blanket but didn't want to be left behind.

The humans settled under the green fluorescent glare in a booth next to a window, where they could see his truck. An individual jukebox and heavy white mugs ready for coffee furnished the table. A skinny, heavily eyelinered waitress in a pale-pink uniform and white shoes shuffled over to slap menus down. "Coffee?" she asked, pot poised over cups.

"I'll have tea, please," Tessa said. "Very hot water, if you can." The woman nodded. She poured coffee for Vince, gathered a handful of mini-creamers out of her pocket, and set them down gently. Tessa shot Vince a cheerful wink. Her cheeks were rosy.

He excused himself to wash his hands, and when he came back out, she was studying the menu with great intensity. She had the look of a woman who'd been having sex for hours—the slightly swollen mouth, little nick of passion on her throat, eyes sleepy. Her hair always looked slightly untidy, and in truth it was no different now, but it added to the general postcoital look. He wondered if the other men noticed and glanced around, glaring at them, as savagely protective as a bear.

Chill, he told himself, rejoining her, but then she looked up with those light-green anime eyes and he realized he was in trouble. He'd been doing fine the past year or so, getting laid now and then, taking care of the girls. He was tired. He was lonely. But he'd been doing okay.

Tessa suddenly made that world seem like a sepia photograph—a still life absent color or passion. He bent his head to study the menu. "What are you having?" he growled.

"I don't know, Mr. Bear," she said, and lowered her own voice to a growl. "What do you recommend?"

He glanced up to catch the shine in her eyes. "Not oatmeal."

She smiled. "I'm way too hungry for oatmeal." She slapped the laminated menu closed. "I'm having the works—eggs, bacon, hash browns, biscuits, and gravy."

He grinned. "Hungry, doll?"

She raised an eyebrow. "All we ever do is eat and have sex, you notice?"

"We had a picnic."

"Only by accident," she said. "And that's eating."

"True." The girl returned, and Vince ordered blueberry pancakes, eggs, sausage, and milk. Tessa ordered her massive meal, too, then turned her attention to the jukebox.

"Hmm. Do you think they'd get mad if we played things?"

He glanced around. There were three men hunched at intervals over the counter, likely all truckers stopping in for a cup of coffee so they could keep going another couple hundred miles. "Probably."

"Too bad. They have all kinds of good stuff."

"What would you play?"

"Aerosmith, and Guns N' Roses, maybe a little Led Zeppelin."

"Really?"

She grinned. "No. I thought you'd like them, though."

"Good call." He leaned in to see the selections. "Yeah. 'Dream On.' 'Welcome to the Jungle.' 'Black Dog.' All good."

"So predictable," she said with a *tsk*.

"What would you choose, Ms. Supercilious?"

She flashed him a coquettish glance. "Beach Boys. ABBA. Motown. All happy, all the time, much to my father's despair."

"Not what I would have expected." He stirred three sugars into his coffee. "Don't tell me—you have a secret passion for *The Sound of Music.*"

"Not secret. I *love* it. And *The Music Man*, and every Disney song every recorded, and all the bubble-gum-pink pop you can think of."

Vince shook his head in disbelief. "And I was worried about being cool in front of you, world traveler and Renaissance festival woman."

"You should see my iPod lists. My dad literally groaned aloud when he saw it. Not"—she rolled her eyes—"that I can get him to own an iPod."

"My mom probably knows your dad, you know."

"I suppose they probably would know each other. Or did." She shook her head. "Weird to think of them all in that world, right? All young and full of passion and vision." She inclined her head. "And look what came of it, too—the farm, which is cool."

Vince let her ramble, sleepy and overamped from too little sleep and lots of sex. Her oddly deep, musical voice washed over him in welcome waves. He watched her red mouth moving, and the float of a hand drawing a point in the air, and her thin, long eyelashes, and the tiny elliptical fold at the corner of her eye that gave her that Asian anime look. He looked at the hollow of her throat and the curve of a breast, and everything about her was exactly perfect.

It occurred to him that he had fallen, hard.

And he suddenly had a suspicion that he knew who she was. He'd have to check out some pictures at his mother's house. If he was right, her story was a lot more complicated than she thought.

For now he wouldn't say a word. He would just drift on waves of Tessa, lazily and at peace for the first time in longer than he could remember.

SEVENTEEN

It was the first very sharp morning of the year, and Vita started making biscuits and sausage for the morning special. Nothing like a solid plate of biscuits and gravy to get a person moving. She was vain about her biscuits, which she'd learned to make from a Southern girl who'd lived at the Boulder house, decades before. They always turned out light and fluffy and tender, no matter how she grew the recipe.

It wasn't yet dawn when Annie came in. Vita had taken the cell-phone picture over to the police station, but they said it was too murky to see well. She scowled and told them to keep an eye on the area anyway. She really didn't want to disturb Annie's peace.

"Hey, kid," Vita said now. "Hungry? I'm about to put the biscuits in the oven."

Annie huddled by the door, her hands behind her. "I actually came in early to get your advice about something."

"Okay." She wiped her hands on a towel. "What's up?"

"Can you come outside for a minute?"

Vita followed the girl out. Woman. It was hard to think of the skinny little thing as a full-grown woman, even if she was in her mid-thirties. The back door opened into a fenced area, then into an alleyway where the dumpster was.

Annie knelt and picked up a white cat that was nearly as skinny as Annie herself. "This is Athena. She showed up at my door and I've been feeding her. I know I shouldn't have, but . . ." Annie bent and kissed the cat's face, and Athena purred, tucking her head against Annie's jaw. "She's just so sweet."

And you've been so lonely, Vita thought. She rubbed a hand over the cat's skinny back. "She's a beauty. Does she have seven toes?"

"Yes! How did you know?"

"There's a whole community of seven-toed cats around here. A lot of them are Siamese mixes, but a lot of others are all black or all white. They've lived here since the Spanish came."

"Wow. You hear that, sweetie?"

Vita waited for Annie to get to her request. It was sure to be a request. Women in her circumstances had few resources and fewer places to turn. "I want to keep her, but I have to find a new place to live. And I might need some help with that. I mean, I don't have a lot of money, and I don't want to get in trouble with my parole officer or anything like that." She raised her pale eyes to Vita's face. "My ex-husband killed my last cat. And I just want to keep Athena, and this way she gets a good place to live, too."

The women and girls who came through Vita's kitchen all stole her heart in one way or another, even when they couldn't make it work on the outside and ended up back in jail, but something about Annie made her ache all through her middle. Vita smiled. "That is the most I've ever heard you say."

"I know, right? I'm not allowed to have cats where I am, and I want to make her a safe home."

"I'm sorry about your cat. That happened to me, too, unfortunately. It was a bird, not a cat, but it was the reason I finally left him."

Annie looked at her. "I'm sorry."

"Me, too," Vita said. She spread out her arms. "But, you see, here I am and I'm happy and productive and I have a life I love."

"Yeah, I see." Annie shifted the cat in her arms. "Can you help me find a different place to live?"

"You bet. For now let's take Athena here upstairs and let her sleep on my bed. Okay?"

"Very okay. I'll do extra work, whatever you want."

"You don't have to do anything, Annie. Sometimes a friend does another friend a favor."

Dawn came gray and cool. Vince dropped Tessa back at the hotel, and they stood outside his truck, kissing and kissing and kissing beneath the overcast skies. When he left to go fetch his girls, Tessa was both relieved and bereft. She had a shower and went out for a walk, ambling around the church and then around the perimeter of the town on a trail where she met swollen-eyed townspeople walking their dogs. They nodded at her and smiled at Felix, who was as polite as a little old man out for a weekend stroll. In a way it broke her heart—he seemed afraid to do anything that was even faintly puppylike. "I won't leave you, you know," she said.

He licked her hand. They walked for a long time, and Tessa was pleased at how quickly her foot was healing now. Maybe in the next day or two, she could try some of the longer trails. She'd hiked most of the shorter ones.

Later today she would have to find a new place to stay. Los Padres, while lovely, was too expensive for the long haul. She could stay one more day but would have to find something else by tomorrow. She paused at the desk to make sure she could keep the room for another day, then went back upstairs and slept for a few hours. When she woke up, it was sprinkling a little. She headed out into the drizzle, hungry.

There were dozens of other restaurants, but Tessa really only wanted to go to 100 Breakfasts. Felix was happy to be tied up outside where he could see her. She sat by the window and he sat on the other side, calmly observing the world, safe and dry beneath the eaves.

Tessa scanned the menu, looking for something that tickled her fancy—she could work it off by checking out some of the trails around here later if it stopped raining.

The local specialties were in the 90s. Breakfast number 92 was huevos rancheros with green chile and corn tortillas and refried—not black—beans. Number 95 was migas: chiles and eggs and tortillas and chorizo scrambled together. There was a breakfast taco and a bowl of green chile stew. She chose the migas.

Vita caught sight of her and waved through the pass-out bar. She waved back. Annie was there, too, with a lime-green bandana over her head. She looked as if she'd gained a little weight this week, and it made her much prettier. Something about the angle of her face reminded Tessa of someone, but in her fuzzy state it took a while to bring it into focus: She looked like Cherry at Green Gate Farms.

Maybe Xander, the leader, had spread his seed far and wide. Annie said she'd grown up in Albuquerque. Not so far away.

Which made Tessa think of the conversation she'd had with Vince about her mother and her singular lack of interest in the woman. When Tessa was young, Sam would say only that her mom had been pretty and kind but not really strong enough for this world.

As Tessa got older, he said only that her mother was troubled. And Tessa supposed she had accepted that Sam had her best interests at heart. If he glossed over her mother, then Tessa probably didn't really want to know. She knew her name— Winnie, which seemed the too-soft name of a weak-willed woman—and that she'd come to the commune from California. That was about all she knew.

Thinking now of Natalie, who was five when her mother died and at eight still fiercely kept the memory alive, Tessa suddenly found it rather odd that she remembered nothing at all. Even with the trauma-induced amnesia. She had never wanted to know any more until she fell into the river with Lisa.

The story her father had told her all these years—the fairy tale making light of her terrible story, the vagueness of backstory— now seemed patently rehearsed, as if she'd been brainwashed or something. The thought made her sit back in her seat, pulse racing. What if *all* of it was a lie?

Stop.

She was entirely too stirred up. By the town, by the rescue of Felix, by the waves of memory washing to shore. And by Vince. Staring out at the plaza, she thought of his mouth, his big hands, his low, thrumming voice, and knew that he was dangerous.

After breakfast, she stepped outside and called her father. "Hey, princess," he said. "Did you get my letter?"

"You wrote me an email?"

"No, I sent it through the mail."

"You wrote a letter by hand and sent it snail mail?"

"That must mean you haven't gotten it yet."

"No, but where would you have sent it? I don't have an address here."

"And you say that I'm the dumb one. Your hotel, honey. I mailed it to you in care of the hotel."

"Oh. What's in it?"

"Um . . . Just wait and see. What are you up to today? Finished with that lousy little town yet?"

"It's not lousy at all—I keep telling you that you should check it out again. It's not the place you remember."

"Still has evil spirits."

Tessa rolled her eyes. "Whatever. Listen, I'm calling because I remembered some things, and I'm kind of bothered by them."

A depth of silence on the other end of the line suggested her father was not pleased. "What did you remember?"

"I remembered going in the river, off a cliff. And a fire, and a woman with long blond hair who always seems angry with me, and—this is the weird part—somebody who seems like my sister." She paused, a pain in her ribs. "Do I have a sister?"

Again the quiet. "It's complicated," he said finally. "The letter will help."

"Why can't you just tell me?"

"When you get the letter, princess, take your dog and a big cup of tea and go somewhere outside. Like that church—don't you like that church?"

"You're scaring me."

"I told you I didn't want you to go there." His voice was ragged. Old. "But once you throw the lid off Pandora's box, there's no going back."

"Dad!"

"You'll be fine, Tessa. Call me after you read the letter, all right?"

She realized she was threading Felix's ear through her fingers, over and over, as if it were the satin on a blanket. "Okay."

"Promise?"

"Cross my heart and hope to die."

"I love you, kiddo. You know that, right?"

It made her smile. *Doubt thou the stars are fire,* she thought, but never doubt that Sam loved her completely.

"Yes, Dad. I love you, too."

When Vince got to his mother's house, she was putting out bowls for cereal. The girls were in their PJs and leapt up joyfully. "Daddy! We're having Cap'n Crunch!" Jade cried.

"With Crunch Berries!" Hannah added, waving her spoon.

Natalie swung her feet, hair crazy all around her head. He smoothed it down. "What about you, Miss Scarlett?"

"I'm having toast. I'm not eating all that junk food."

Judy snorted, hanging a frying pan onto the stove. "Her Highness wants an egg."

"I *said* I would have toast, Grandma!"

"But not with margarine," Judy said, glaring at Vince.

Natalie flung her feet back and forth. "It's not good for you."

"Oh, brother!" Jade rolled her eyes. Even so early in the morning, she was well groomed, her hair brushed and tied back, her pajamas tidy. She woke up washed and pressed, just like her mother. He kissed her head, too.

"Not everybody likes the same things," he said.

"I know."

Sasha and Pedro were on the other side of the kitchen, on an area rug where they were banished while the girls were eating. Vince bent down to look closely at Pedro. "You tangled with a porcupine, huh?" There were a few little marks but nothing serious. "I guess we need to keep him in a fence or something."

His mother slammed spoons down, yanked the door to the fridge open so hard that everything inside rattled. Vince finally realized she was furious with him. He stood up and put his hands on her arms. "Hey, hey, what's up, Mom? Sit down, let me do that."

"Don't you what's up me," she said, and lowered her voice. "I saw your truck over at the hotel when we were coming back from the vet."

Guilt slammed him. "Mom, it's not like that—"

"No, not in front of the girls." She shoved the spatula into his hand. "I'm going to take a shower. You finish their breakfasts and get them dressed."

Chastened, Vince fried an egg for Natalie, poured cereal and milk for the other two girls, and poured himself a cup of coffee.

"Grandma's mad at you," Jade said.

"No kidding."

"Do you have a girlfriend?"

"Don't be stupid, Jade! We would know," Natalie said.

Vince wiped up a spill of milk. "I don't have a girlfriend, Jade."

"Why'd you stay out all night, then?"

"Sometimes grown-ups do things they don't have to explain to kids." Time for a change in subject. "What happened to Pedro? Did he have a lot of quills in his nose?"

"Lots!" Hannah said, and put her hands around her face as if drawing quills hanging off her nose and jaw and forehead. "And he said, 'Mmm, mmm, mmm.'" She whined like a dog perfectly.

"That's a good whine, Little Bit. Poor Pedro, though, huh?"

Natalie looked darkly at him. "He *needs* a fence, Daddy. It made me so sad that he got hurt!" Her eyes filled with tears. "What if he got *killed*?"

He covered her hand. "Shhh. I promise we'll build a fence. Right away, okay? Don't worry. He's fine."

"Vince!" his mother said from the other room.

"Finish up, girls, then go get dressed and get your stuff together." He took his coffee with him and went to face the music.

Tessa went back to the hotel and took advantage of the free WiFi in the lobby to get online, hoping for a response from Mick, her boss, to the proposal for the tour. There wasn't one. She looked up a couple of motels and found one that seemed reasonable that was just around the corner. She'd check it out when the rain let up, and probably go with that. Nice and easy.

But now she was very, very curious about her father's dark hints. Flipping open her notebook, she looked up the names of the original founders of the commune, Robert and Jonathan Nathan, and Googled their names in conjunction with "Xander."

A string of links popped up, including, to her surprise, a Wikipedia article. She clicked on the link and read the short paragraphs, which mostly reiterated what she already knew—the two were the highly successful owners of Green Gate Organic Farms, which grew out of an old commune where Alexander "Xander" McKenzie was shot and killed by an unknown assailant under mysterious circumstances. The Wikipedia entry for McKenzie was thin, but it did have a grainy black-and-white photograph of a lean man in his early thirties, wearing a handlebar mustache and the long hair of the seventies. Even in a very bad photograph with very bad styling, he was extraordinarily good-looking.

She Googled his name and came up with a handful of articles. The rebellious but good-natured Xander was the oldest child of a Northeastern shipping family; he'd dropped out of Princeton and headed west on a painted bus. Tessa rolled her eyes. It was so hard to imagine living in a world where that wasn't a joke, where it still represented revolution and excitement, a chance for a new life. She clicked on a photo of Xander in a group of six or seven others—men and women, all in their dewy early twenties, with flowing hair and flowing sleeves and bare feet. Was one of them her mother? She peered closely at the women, but none of them looked familiar.

None of the men was Sam, either. Tessa didn't know exactly when her father had come to the commune. She knew he'd served in Vietnam, though he didn't talk about his experiences there; they were brutal and still sometimes gave him nightmares. You didn't wake Sam from a dead sleep, ever. He was an orphan who'd been on his own since the age of fifteen, from somewhere in the Deep South—Mississippi or Louisiana, she didn't know. He was vague about it. Magic had been his hobby from the time he was a small boy, and at the commune he had a chance to develop it into a polished show.

How had she never realized before how little information she had about all of this? Why had she never thought to ask? It was highly disorienting.

She rubbed the bridge of her nose, where a slight headache had started. The article on Xander commented on his charisma and his troupe of willing followers who eventually settled in a group "marriage" in New Mexico, where they lived for seven or eight years before Xander was killed, likely by a jealous lover, though nothing was ever proven. Several women made paternity claims against his estate, but they were all soundly dismissed.

Sketchy, Tessa thought. It was all so sketchy. Checking the time, she saw that it was only early afternoon, and the rain was finally stopping. There was time to get to the library, and, on the way back, she'd look at the motel.

The library was housed in an old Carnegie-style building with pillars and enormous double-paned windows. It was surprisingly large for a small community, though there seemed to be only two people working in the whole place: a librarian and a desultory older Latino janitor, polishing the foyer floor.

The librarian, a Pueblo woman with long beaded earrings and her salt-and-pepper hair cut in a tidy pageboy, had to unlock the reference room for Tessa. "Microfiche readers over there," she said. "The reels are filed in these drawers. Some papers are bound in books, too, so you can check those volumes over here." She paused. "Looking for a particular event?"

"Well, sort of. I want to read about the commune."

Her mouth tightened. "Just like everybody who comes through. You'd think all the rest of our history would matter." She shook her head. "It's over here."

Tessa thanked her and settled in to read. At first, she found very little that she didn't already know. It was fun to read about the reaction of the town to an invasion of hippies, who lit bonfires by the river and had wild parties. Orgies, even. The word was used in a letter to the editor from an outraged citizen of the valley.

She flipped through the pages, not really sure what she was looking for. There were few photos.

But wouldn't Green Gate have some kind of archives from that time? She would go there next. In the meantime, she found the local account of Xander McKenzie's death. A photo of a clean-shaven version of the mustachioed man showed up, and this one was much less grainy. He had a high-bridged nose and exotic, long eyes, and she recognized him instantly. In a dizzy overlay, she saw the living face in memory, colored and animated, overlaying the black-and-white shot.

"Guinnevere had green eyes," he sang, along with the album playing in the room, *"like yours, milady, like yours. . . . "*

Tessa closed her eyes and let it come. Memories rushed in as if they were birds coming through the windows.

She saw him laughing, spinning a woman around, and then Tessa held up her arms—"now me, now me!"—and he sang that lyrical, lovely song to her. To her green eyes. She could see the room clearly, too: eight windows in a circle around the tower room, with beds tucked into the angles and the stereo on a table at the back. It was cold and snow fell outside.

And more:

She sat at a long table with other children, all of them eating sandwiches. A woman with her hair falling out from beneath a scarf gave them each an apple.

"You want to trade with me?" asked a girl next to her. *Rhiannon. She had green eyes, too.*

That was it. Feeling shaky and somehow demolished, Tessa put everything away and went back to the hotel.

Breakfast #16

Biscuits and Gravy: One of the great comfort foods—Vita's fresh organic sausage, crumbled and cooked to perfection, served in

a silky cream gravy over hot, tender Southern-style biscuits.
With orange slices and cubed watermelon (in season).

BREAKFAST SAUSAGE
⌒ Makes 5 lbs.

People are often intimidated by making sausage, but it's really very simple and creative—a mixture of fresh meat, herbs, sometimes fruit or vegetables, and whatever flavorings you want to experiment with. Play! This is a traditionally flavored breakfast sausage everyone enjoys.

5 lbs. ground pork from humanely raised hogs
2 T kosher salt
1½ T sage
1½ tsp thyme
½ tsp ginger
¾ tsp nutmeg
½ tsp white pepper
¼ tsp chile powder
½ cup water

Grind the meat into a bowl that's sitting in a bowl of ice. Mix all ingredients together and stuff into sheep casings. Or simply form into patties and cook through.

EIGHTEEN

On the way back to the hotel, Tessa checked out the motel and found it well below her comfort level. Just as well that she'd kept the room at Los Padres, because, when she got up to her room, there was an envelope on the table beneath the window, and even from ten feet away she could identify her father's calligraphic hand. The envelope was decorated with a gauzy photo of a puppy, all soulful eyes and adorability, and Tessa had to grin even through the anxiety that fluttered in her throat. He still chose pictures to appeal to the twelve-year-old she once was.

Felix fell on the floor in a heap, as if completely exhausted, and Tessa carried the envelope out to the balcony. Sunlight was breaking through the clouds, glittering on wet cottonwood leaves. The tourists were just beginning to come back out.

She didn't open the letter immediately but sat with it in her hand, aware that things would shift the minute she began to read. And, really, was that what she wanted? Her life was good. Real. Satisfying.

Except, a whole adult embraced her life, warts and all. The disaster in Montana had dredged up things she had never thought about. She had to face both her childhood and Lisa's death and her own responsibility for it. Even letting that thought in trebled the sense of airlessness the letter had brought.

As if he sensed her subtle upset, Felix got up and came over, putting his foot delicately on her knee. Tessa tapped the envelope.

What could you do once the lid was flung open on Pandora's box? The memories had begun to surface.

Taking a deep breath, she slid her thumb under the flap of the envelope and broke the seal.

It began:

Dear Princess Tessa,

You should take this letter and go sit down someplace. There are some things I have kept hidden about your life, and I reckon it's time it all came out. Just remember, it was all for you.

I have never claimed to be a particularly good man. I'd venture to say there are plenty who think I'm absolutely not. Mostly, I've just squandered my time here on earth, and there are a few things I reckon God'll punish me for. But I hope He'll take into consideration how hard I've tried to give you a good life.

One bad thing I did was when I came back from Vietnam, pissed off and doing more drugs than I could probably name now. I got mixed up with a hard-drugging crowd and we ended up at the commune. That's where I met you.

That's right. Met you. *I'm not your natural dad.*

Tessa heard herself gasp. Noise buzzed around the bridge of her nose. For a long minute she looked up, feeling her throat close tighter and tighter. Not her father.

Not her father??

Damn, kiddo, you were the greatest little girl! Smart and cute as a bug and with that pretty voice. Nobody like you in the world, and I hated it that you were living like that in that fucking commune. No running water half the time, toilets a hole in the ground, practically wearing nothing but rags most of the time. It's one thing for adults to choose a life like that, but you kids all deserved better.

Children of the tribe—what bullshit!

And I don't mean to disrespect the dead, but your mama was a real piece of work. They called her Winnie, for Winnie-the-Pooh, but she was hardly a gentle little bear. My ass. She was beautiful, spoiled rotten by her hoity-toity parents back in Maine, and strung out like nobody's business. She was also completely obsessed with a dude who had a lot of other women. Xander. Probably your dad, though he didn't claim a one of y'all. His story is a good one, but I don't have time to tell it here. He had a whole harem of women, and they were all living together in that house, and there were drugs all the time and sex right in the living room in front of the kids, and it just made me crazy. It wasn't like I grew up in some fancy house like a lotta them did, but I knew better than that. When my buddies moved on, I stuck around to look out for you.

And maybe that sounds unnatural, that I loved you so much, but it was like I'd been born to be your dad. It made me sober, Tessa, that's God's own truth. Wanting to be a better person, a good example for you in all that craziness, made me better.

Anyhow, your mama went off her rocker one night and killed Xander, then tried to drown you and herself, like La

*Llorona or something. She managed to kill herself, but I got
you in time.*

*So there you were, orphaned, and I wasn't about to leave
you in that goddamned commune.*

*And you were kinda messed up by it, too. The whole
thing broke your heart in two. It was so sad when you woke
up and couldn't remember anything. In the end, it seemed
better to let you forget it all. Get a clean start. That's when I
started telling you the princess story.*

*No way to make this any better, so I'll just say it: I took
you. There was no adoption, but since you were born out
there, there wasn't any birth certificate, either. Maybe it
wasn't strictly "right" in the way the law would see it, but
there's a higher right than law.*

*You are a princess, you know. You're my princess, and
you're the best thing that ever happened to me. Don't be mad.*

*You know most of the rest, but there's a couple things
I need to be looking at your face to tell you. Give me
a call.*

Love,
Your dad

*P.S. You were six when it happened, not four. So you're
actually now thirty-nine. Sorry about that, too.*

For a long, long time, Tessa stared into the middle distance,
holding the paper loosely in her hand. Everything in her was
hushed. Astonished.

Sam was not her father.

Not her father.

Tears rose in her throat, rushed through her sinuses, welled in her eyes, and then—they didn't fall.

As if her father—not!—was linked to her by some invisible cord, the cell on the table spun in a circle, flashing Sam's number. Coldly, she watched it spin and spin until it stopped.

There's a couple things I need to be looking at your face to tell you, he'd said.

She didn't want to know any more right now. In swift and sudden decision, she rose and tugged a hat down on her head. Cramming the letter and her cell phone into her pocket, she grabbed her backpack and whistled for Felix to come with her. She had to walk.

Tessa walked and walked and walked, following trails that looped through the foothills surrounding the town, up and down hills and along low ridges.

And this was exactly why she walked: It moved her out of her head and into her body. Every time some angle of the past came up—the far distant past she still couldn't remember; the more recent past where she was responsible for the death of another person; or the past of this afternoon—she shoved it away and focused on her feet. One foot in front of the other, firmly planted on the earth.

And it worked its magic. The fresh air and the trails and the pleasure and relief of getting slightly sweaty brought her back to herself. Tessa Harlow, alive in the early twenty-first century, who seemed to now own a dog who happily walked along beside her. He was excellent company.

He was her pack now.

When she felt she had some semblance of peace, she headed back toward town. The trail she'd been following looped over the trailhead to the pilgrimage site, and Tessa wandered into the garden of the church and sat on a bench. She gave Felix some water, and he slurped up a hefty portion, then fell against the wall in the shade. His happy collapse, his happy drinking, his happy walking made her laugh. Dogs were such creatures of joy.

"Hello again."

Tessa looked up to find the young priest, dressed in jeans and a collared shirt, kneeling amid the corn. "Hello. It's Father Timothy, right?"

"Yes. And you are . . . ?"

"That is the question of the day," she said wryly, then shook her head. "I'm Tessa Harlow."

"You seem to have taken in a stray."

"Do you know Felix?"

"As well as I know any of them. He seems a good pup." The priest tugged weeds. "Would you like to help? Weeding is good for a heavy heart."

"Really."

He grinned. "And there are a lot of weeds."

"Okay." Tessa knelt on the ground and started helping. The ground was soft and the weeds came out easily. She pulled them silently, but this action sent her thoughts flying inward, into analysis. "Hmmph," she said aloud.

"You do have a heavy heart," he said. "Priests are known to be good listeners."

Tessa rocked back on her heels. "I do," she said, and to her horror, the tears she'd been fighting rose in her eyes. "I don't know who I am. I mean, I do know—I'm not one of those people who has big issues, you know? I'm not speaking metaphorically. I know who I am."

He nodded. "Keep weeding."

She obeyed, talking as she yanked out bindweed and goat-heads. "The one thing I've always been sure of is my father. He loves me. He's always done the right thing, and I am who I am—who is this grounded, clear-sighted person!" She pulled out a big hunk of soil, and dirt went flying into the air. "Sorry."

His eyes twinkled. "It's all right."

"But now I find out he's not my father. He lied to me all my life, and things are changing right under my feet, and the things I thought I understood are not true, and I wish I could get it all sorted out, so I could get on with my life and stop being *stuck* here in this place." Dirt got under her cast, and she turned her hand upside down to shake it out. She sank back on her heels again. "And that's the other thing."

He seemed to sense the shift in her and sat up, his hands on his thighs. "Yes?"

"How do you make something right when you've done something wrong? I mean, something that led to somebody else dying? Not on purpose, not murder or anything." She chewed her inner lip for a second, struggling to stay in control. "Negligence. No," she said, shaking her head. "Hubris. My sin is hubris."

He smiled gently. "Not very many people even claim that as a sin in today's world. Your father has raised you well."

Tessa nodded, bowing her head. Tears streamed out of her eyes, and she couldn't stop them. It felt good to let it go, felt right to water the earth with tears in the company of a priest.

"That's quite a lot," he said.

She nodded. Felix came up beside her and leaned his butt on her hip.

"There is no way to make up for the loss of a life," the priest said. "But the living need to move forward. They need to make reparation."

"What a great word. Make amends, right?"

He nodded, gestured toward the mountain behind her. "That's why people undertake pilgrimages and do good deeds and say the rosary a hundred times."

A possibility of stillness moved through her. She nodded. "Thank you."

He smiled. "Anytime." He whistled, and Felix leapt up happily. The priest took a dog biscuit out of his pocket and held it out. Felix politely accepted it, and Father Timothy rubbed his ears. "Take good care of her, young man," he said. Felix gave the priest a delicate, thankful kiss on the chin.

When she got back to the plaza, Tessa's cell phone beeped with messages that had come in while she was out of range. "Hi, Tessa. It's your dad. Give me a call when you get this."

She hung up and didn't call him. Every time she thought of *more,* she felt breathless. She and Felix circled back around the little church and down the road that looped in a circle around the town, turned in to one of the lanes branching out from the plaza, and there, at the end, perched at the edge of a stand of aspens, was a cute little house with a FOR RENT sign on the gate. The wooden window frames were painted turquoise.

Tessa loped up to it and peered over the waist-high wall. A small courtyard planted with roses, pink and white cosmos and tidy stands of marigolds fronted a cottage with a deep porch and a big front window. A block of quiet houses stretched up the hill on either side, and through a break in the trees, she could just spy the river.

It was obviously empty. Tessa tried the gate and found it open. She let herself and Felix into the courtyard, which was as still as a June morning—bees humming, cicadas singing, the roof shading the porch. It faced east, to capture the morning.

She looked in the windows. A very small kitchen, a bedroom, a living room. Not much more than that. She dialed the number on the sign.

"Hi," she said when an older-sounding woman with hints of a New Mexico accent answered. "I'm interested in the house you have for rent. I'm looking in the courtyard now. Can someone show it to me?"

Within the hour, she had rented it, month to month. Two hours after that, she'd found a bed and a table, a chair and a couch and a desk at the local VFW outlet, and checked out of the hotel. It was only as she sat in the courtyard in the gathering dusk, drinking a beer and eating a sandwich she'd bought at the local subway shop, that she realized she was absolutely, dead-on *furious* with her father.

The next time her phone rang, she picked it up. "Don't call me, Dad," she said. "I have to think. When I'm over it, I'll talk to you."

"There's more you should know."

"Not today there isn't."

"Tessa—"

"I don't want to talk to you," she said, and hung up. In a moment, she dialed the number again. "There is one thing I need to know. Do I have a sister?"

"That's a hard question to answer, honestly," he said. "Kind of."

"Dad. No bullshit. What does that mean?"

"We need to talk about it when you're not mad."

"That's gonna be a while." Tessa closed her eyes and hung up the phone. Since there wasn't anything else to do, she fired up the computer, using a wireless network card.

There was an email from her boss.

To: Tessa.Harlow@ramblingtours.com
From: Mick.Harrison@ramblingtours.com
Subject: Re: Los Ladrones tour possibilities
Hi, Tessa. I've gone through the material you've gathered, and I'm sorry to say it's just not doing anything for me. I can see you're excited about it, and I'd really like to get you back to work, but this doesn't seem like the right project for our demographic—a little too sedate, maybe. I'm afraid the people who would find this appealing are the explorer women in mid- to late-middle age, and while there's nothing wrong with that, we're not currently marketing our tours toward them.

If you want to think about ways to liven it up, get some more-vigorous hiking in, some kayaking or white-water rafting, that would be great, but this is too tame.

Give me a call if you want to brainstorm.
Mick

Of course. With a *tck* of enormous irritation, Tessa pressed the power button and shut the computer down.

NINETEEN

Natalie had never felt prettier than she did the first day of third grade. She wore her peasant blouse with a pair of jeans and sandals, so she felt like a person from another land—Morocco, which was a place in a book she read, or Greece, which they had a picture of in her old classroom. Grandma gave her some new stuff to put on her hair so it was all smooth for once. And maybe school stunk, but a person had to go. Maybe they would learn fractions, which she would need if she was going to become a chef someday.

All summer long, Natalie had been dreading the day they returned to school. She hated this school, because of one reason: Billy Smithers. He was a pale boy with pale eyes and pale freckles, and a mean look in his eyes, just like a ferret. He had asthma, so everyone babied him. Sometimes he had terrible fits where he couldn't breathe at all, which were scary for everyone except Natalie, who fervently and guiltily wished him dead every single day through all of June and July and August.

All weekend she had said special prayers, and on Monday afternoon she said the entire rosary to get herself ready. She felt good in her blouse. She told herself she just wasn't going to even look at Billy.

But, naturally, his was the first face she saw when she entered her classroom. His hair was shorn and he had a tan from being outside all summer, but he saw her, too, and snorted like a pig, quietly so nobody would hear except Natalie.

She sat down, ignoring him, but he changed seats so he could sit right behind her, and he leaned forward to say nasty things in her ear. She didn't even know what all the words were, but they sounded bad. And she knew some of them just fine: "penis," for example, which he had once taken out and wiggled on her hand when he trapped her by herself in the gym. She wanted to tell on him, had in fact told on him for calling her names, but she couldn't bring herself to tell anybody that he did *that*. What would they think of her?

She pretended she didn't hear him, and as soon as another seat came open between two other girls, Natalie jumped up and sat down. "Hey," one of them said. "We're saving that seat. You can't sit there."

Natalie acted as if she didn't hear. She bent her head down and pulled out her notebooks and pencils, and just about the time they would have shoved her, the teacher came in and the girls had to turn around. But not before giving Natalie the evil eye.

Still, she sat up straight in her seat. This year would be different. She just knew it would be.

The girls had a ritual for the first day of school, which included Judy picking them up from the bus stop and taking them to her house for tea and cookies, so they could tell her all about their day. She gave them dinner, and Vince came to get them when he was finished with work at six. They would then stop by the grocery store, choose some fruit and treats for their lunch boxes, go home and take baths, read a book, and get to bed by eight-thirty.

Ritual. Judy was big on ritual, and Vince had to admit he found it helped—not only the girls but his own life.

At the market, he let them take their time picking out the fruit for the week. Jade wanted red grapes. Hannah chose bananas because she always ate bananas and no other fruit, ever. Natalie carefully looked at everything—the pineapples in rows and oranges in pyramids and kiwis and grapefruits—before choosing tangelos. "I do think we should go to the farmers' market more often," she said primly, giving him the bag.

"We can try, kiddo. Sometimes I have to work Saturdays."

"Not always, though." She flipped hair out of her face, and he noticed that there were blue rings beneath her eyes.

Tenderly, Vince nudged her shoulder. "Come on, let's finish up and get you guys home. I want to hear all about the first day."

He pushed the cart through the store, remembering he needed eggs and soup. Natalie brought over some whole grain pasta she'd seen on some show or another, and he shook his head. "I don't know what to do with that."

She sighed and took it back. Jade asked for Cocoa Krispies and he rolled his eyes. "No way." Hannah sat in the carrier and sucked her thumb, looking like a zombie.

And around the corner came Tessa, carrying a red basket that had some fruit and milk and eggs in it. She wore shorts and flip-flops and a flowered athletic tank that clung to her flat belly and barely restrained breasts, and within three seconds he had her stripped naked in his imagination. She caught him looking at her, and for a moment she looked absolutely bewildered.

"Hey," he said. "Looks like you're laying in supplies."

She looked at the basket and to the shelves. "Yeah."

"You okay?"

"Um." She smoothed a hand through her hair, pulling the waves away from her face, as if she felt guilty. "Not really, but I can't go into it right now?"

"Okay." Very weird vibe coming from her. She still hadn't met his eyes. And surrounded as he was by his girls, he couldn't very well ask straight out what was going on. "I see," he said. "Well, you know my number. Give me a call if you want."

Only then did she look up, and her eyes were startlingly bright in the fluorescent light. He glimpsed her misery. Thought he saw conflict when she looked at his mouth, his throat. "Thanks," she said oddly. "Ditto. Or email if you want. It's on my card. I'm staying for a little while. Maybe a month. I rented a place."

Relief wafted through him. He nodded. "Good."

"I'm tired!" Jade said, leaning hard on his leg.

"Okay, honey," he said. "We're leaving." He lifted his chin toward Tessa and pushed the cart down the aisle away from her, willing himself to pay attention to what really mattered. His daughters. The sane, clean, simple life he could build for them. "Where's Natalie?" he growled, and she came up beside him.

"I'm here."

"Let's get out of here, girls. You need bubble baths, right?"

"Yay!"

He nosed the cart into line behind a stout old man and gently tugged Hannah's thumb out of her mouth. "Not good for your teeth." She pulled it back, her eyes glittering, and when he tugged it out again, it made a big pop that made her laugh. He laughed, too, and kissed her head. "You're so silly."

She stuck it back in her mouth, playing, and Vince was

about to pull it out again when a man came up behind him. "Sir," he said. "I need a word with you. Will you come with me?"

"What?"

The man wore brown slacks and a short-sleeved dress shirt, and his store name tag said *Tim Bok, Store Manager*. His thinning brown hair and slim brown mustache made him look like a refugee from 1982. "I need you to follow me into the back. Bring your children."

"Uh, I've got to get home and get them to bed. Can you tell me what this is about?"

"I'd rather not do it right here, sir."

Irritated, perplexed, Vince turned the cart. "Come on, guys. It won't take long."

The man marched through the baking aisle, his head up like a drum major.

Jade whined, "I want to go *home!*"

In the baby carrier, Hannah sucked her thumb and rubbed her fingers on the hem of her shirt.

"Daddy?" Natalie said.

"Not right now, honey."

The manager pushed open a pair of gray swinging doors with portholes and led them into the stockrooms beyond.

"Daddy, I think—"

"Natalie, please. It will wait."

The manager turned around. "Now," he said, hands on his hips, staring at Natalie, "young lady, would you like to tell us anything?"

Vince frowned. "What . . . ?"

Natalie bent her head and opened her backpack, which she'd been wearing slung over one shoulder. She pulled out a hexagonal jar of jam or honey or something. It had a black label. She flashed her dad one single, pointed glance, a glance that managed to be both accusatory and guilty, then she handed the jar over to the manager.

"Well, what do you have to say for yourself?" the manager asked. "You can't just steal things, young lady."

"Sorry," Natalie said, but she wasn't. She was furious, shoulders rigid, chin tilted at that arrogant angle.

"Natalie!" Jade said in a sharp whisper. She grabbed her sister's arm. "Why did you do that?"

Nat shook her off. "Because." She didn't look at any of them, only off in the distance.

Vince frowned and gripped Natalie's shoulder. Not hard, but enough to get her attention. When she looked up, he gave her his sternest look. "You don't sound sorry," he said.

And finally she looked as if she might cry, as if the situation was sinking in. "I am." She turned to the manager and said, "I'm really, really sorry, sir. I know it was wrong."

He said, "I will let you go this time, but next time you will be in serious trouble, do you understand me?"

"Yes."

Vince felt nine hundred million years old. He could hear the buzz of a fluorescent light high above and the faraway flush of a toilet. A cold breeze blew over his ankles. A clock on the wall pointed to 7:45. "Thank you," he said. "I need to get these girls home, if that's okay. They have school tomorrow."

The manager nodded, lips pressed severely together. Vince knew he was being unfair, but, really, it was an eight-year-old girl and a jar of honey, not a seventeen-year-old with a stolen car.

But one, he supposed, led to the other. As they headed back down the aisle, Vince said, "Why didn't you ask for honey?"

"Lemon curd," Natalie said. "It was lemon curd."

"Why didn't you ask for lemon curd, then?"

She shrugged.

"You know you're in trouble."

She nodded, chewing the inside of her cheek.

"Let's just get home right now."

Natalie didn't trust herself to say a single word on the way home. She didn't feel bad, actually. It was more like she'd drunk bubbles and they were rising up through her chest, into her head, making her dizzy.

In her imagination, she could see the jar. Beautiful lemon curd, which she knew was made in England. You put it on cakes or things like that, and it looked so elegant in its jar with many sides, with a black label. She *wanted* it. It was so easy, to pick it up and pretend that she was looking at it, that she was going to carry it down to her dad. Then she put it in her backpack. She didn't think anybody saw her.

When they got in the kitchen, their dad went upstairs with Hannah, who was asleep, and told Natalie and Jade to stay there and he'd get them a yogurt before bed.

Jade gave Natalie the devil look, with her eyes all narrow and slitty, like a snake, her mouth squeezed up so the edges turned white.

Natalie slammed her pack on the table and glared at her. "What?"

"You know what! You're a thief! I can't believe you did that! What if somebody from our school saw?"

"I don't care."

Jade shoved her. "Just because you're a big oinker and nobody likes you doesn't mean the rest of us don't have friends!"

"Don't call me that!" The stuff that had been building up in her belly all day suddenly exploded. She shoved Jade, hard, and felt happy when she fell on the floor. "Mind your own business."

"I *hate* you!" Jade screamed, and jumped up, grabbing Natalie's hair and yanking so hard it brought tears to Nat's eyes. "I don't even want anybody to know you're my sister!"

Natalie slammed her back, and they fell into a chair. "I hate you more!"

Natalie tried to pull away, but Jade yanked her hair again, super, super hard, and Nat stumbled and felt the top of her head go right into Jade's tooth. They both howled and let go, then Jade screeched, "You broke my tooth!" and punched Natalie right in the eye. Her glasses broke, smashing into her temple.

It *hurt.* A lot. Sparks flew across her vision, and circles of pain went around her eye and eyebrow and cheek for what seemed like a long time. She started to cry and wanted to stop fighting, but Jade was so mad, so so so mad, that she came after Natalie again.

"Quit it!" she screeched, and pulled away. But Jade held on to her sleeve and yanked, and the fabric of her brand-new shirt tore away, right along the shoulder.

Sasha started barking and barking. Pedro ran out of the kitchen, and Natalie went blind mad. She roared and dove at her sister, and they went down on the floor, scratching and biting and hitting, until there was a big deep roar—a Daddy roar. He hauled Jade into the air, holding her hard against his side. "What the *hell* is going on here?"

Natalie sat up and looked at her sleeve, which was torn but also now had blood on it from Jade's mouth. "She ruined my brand-new beautiful shirt!"

"She broke my tooth!"

"She called me an oinker!"

"*STOP* it!" Daddy yelled.

They stopped. He shifted and put Jade on the ground, then looked at her mouth. "It's broken, all right. What did you hit her with?"

Natalie bent her head to show him the bleeding place. "She pulled my hair."

"Sit at the table, both of you. Don't move." He took a couple of sandwich bags out of the cabinet and put ice into each one. Then he got a wet cloth and wiped Jade's mouth. Natalie felt sick to her stomach, looking at the big gash on Jade's lip and the broken tooth inside. It made Jade look snaggletoothed, and she would never have made her beautiful sister look ugly, not ever.

But Jade could be *so* mean!

"Your lip won't need any stitches, but I'm going to have to take you to a dentist tomorrow to get your tooth fixed up." He filled a glass with water and salt and put a bag of ice in her hand. "Go upstairs and get ready for bed, and don't brush your teeth. Swish this around in your mouth; then, when you get in bed, put the ice on your lip so it doesn't get more swollen."

"Don't you want to know what happened?" Jade said.

"I want you to go to bed, Jade," he said in his don't-mess-with-me voice. "I'll be up in a few minutes to tuck you in."

She huffed, but nobody back-talked him when he used that voice. Natalie felt him look at her, but her face hurt and her head hurt and her blouse was wrecked, and all of it came pouring out of her eyes.

He didn't say anything, just knelt down in front of her and used a cloth to wash the top of her head, then her face. "You're going to have one big shiner tomorrow," he said.

Natalie nodded, pursing her lips. Hot tears poured out of

her eyes as if somebody had turned on the bathtub. "S-or-r-y," she hiccuped.

He sat down on the floor in front of her. "What's going on with you, baby girl?"

She couldn't stop crying. Couldn't stop. It wasn't loud, but she couldn't get the tears to quit. They just kept pouring and pouring and pouring. "I . . . don't . . . know."

He put the ice on her face, and it felt so good Natalie caught her breath. She looked at him. "Am I in big trouble?"

"I don't know right now what your punishment is, baby." He pushed hair off her face, looked at the cut in her part. "I'm worried about you."

She looked down.

"Why did you steal the jam? Why didn't you ask for it?"

She shrugged.

"Was it because I didn't get the whole-wheat pasta?"

"No." The ice started to burn and she moved it to her eyelid, which hurt a lot. "It wasn't jam. It was lemon curd, and I wanted to try it."

"And you couldn't just ask?"

"You guys all think I'm too young to want this stuff. Grandma gets mad at me all the time and won't buy me anything I like; she always wants me to be somebody else and wear different stuff and eat her stupid food, which is horrible. And when I ask for an apple, she won't let me have it, and there's this boy at school who is so mean to me that it makes me scared to go to school, and now my beautiful shirt is ruined, and I . . ."

"Oh, honey," he said, and picked her up like she was a tiny girl. Natalie put her head on his shoulder and let go. She cried and cried and cried and cried, until her eyes were all swollen and she couldn't breathe because her nose was all stuffed up. But the lava flowed out of her with the tears, and she didn't feel so furious. Her daddy held her, rocking back and forth, back and forth, rubbing her back as if she was a baby, and Natalie didn't care that she wasn't a baby. It felt good.

After a long time, he took her upstairs and helped her get undressed and put her in a cool shower, which made her face feel better. "You're going to stay home from school tomorrow and we'll talk everything out."

"Can we fix my shirt?"

"I'll do my best, honey, I promise." He gave her some children's Advil, then Natalie got into bed. Pedro jumped up on her feet and looked over his shoulder at her daddy, but he didn't say anything. Natalie put her hand in Pedro's thick fur and fell asleep so fast she hardly had time to say her prayers.

TWENTY

Tessa's cell phone rang at ten p.m., which seemed late. She gave an exasperated sigh, thinking it was Sam again. She looked at the screen, and she saw it was Vince instead. "Hey," she said, and it was such a relief to talk to someone that she wanted to double over.

"Hi. Is this a bad time?" He sounded absolutely exhausted, his voice rough and craggy, "I could use a little female advice about something."

"No, it's fine. I'm sitting here in the dark, listening to the crickets sing and the river swish."

"You can hear the river?"

She took a breath. "I can. It's a little cottage I rented. Don't worry, though, I'm not the kind of girl to cramp your style. I'm not going to start ringing you twelve times a day to see what you're up to."

"Yeah, I've noticed you're the really needy type."

His voice sounded so good. So good. And yet, just this moment she had so much crap in her head it would hardly be fair to lean on a man who had as much on his own plate.

Rescue me.

"You needed advice with something?"

"Yeah, my daughters had a big fight. Natalie was wearing a brand-new shirt that she's in love with—"

"The peasant blouse?"

"Yeah, yeah. You saw it, I forgot. Well, it got torn at the arm, which I think is fixable, but she also got blood all over it."

"Must have been some fight."

He took a breath and let it go. "It was horrible. But I'm worried about the shirt. What can I do to get the blood out before it sets?"

Everything in her softened, and for a moment she closed her eyes. Thought of his big hands, the delicate blouse. "Put it in a sinkful of cold water right now," she said. "Then while it's soaking, mix some dishwashing liquid with a little peroxide and rub it into the blood spots before you wash it."

"Will that work?"

"It should. Don't put it in a dryer or let it dry until you know you've got the blood out. If the blood is on the white part of the shirt, you can bleach it, but that's pretty delicate fabric and it might not be good for it."

"Thanks," he said. His voice sounded squashed.

"You all right?" Tessa asked. "You sound kind of strung out."

"I don't know what's going on with her. She—" He stopped. "It's a long story. She got in trouble today and then this fight, and she just seems so furious all the time. I don't know how to fix it."

She thought of the way the priest had absorbed her long string of words this afternoon at the church, and said only, "That's hard."

"My mother means well, and I'd be up a creek without her help, but she's making the situation with Natalie worse."

"How so?"

"She doesn't know how to let Natalie be herself. She's always nagging her about something or other. She loves her, don't get me wrong, but it hasn't been easy for my mom to be this big strong person. She never has a man in her life, and, I don't know, maybe she doesn't want one, but she wants Natalie to be thin and pretty, like Jade." He paused. "I don't know that pretty is what Nat is supposed to be, though. Does that make any sense?"

If she'd been holding on to any illusions about how much she liked Vince Grasso—not lusted for him, which she also did, but *liked* him—that last speech would have clinched it. "It makes perfect sense. She's beautiful in her own way, but pretty is something . . . else. And I've had friends who were really pretty—it didn't always help them all that much."

"Yeah," he said. "My wife was pretty, and she was miserable her whole life. I just want my girls to be happy. Be themselves, you know, whatever that is."

"That's terrific."

"By the way, I wasn't saying that you aren't pretty. Or, I mean—" He halted. "Shit. Sorry."

Tessa laughed softly. "'Pretty' isn't a word people use to describe me. Hot, yes. Devastating, perhaps. Alluring, even." She shook her head. "Not pretty."

She had met her goal: It shook loose a chuckle. "Definitely hot," he agreed. "Devastating? Hmmm. I don't know."

"Oh, come on, give me alluring, at least."

"You're mysterious," he said. "Mostly mysterious."

"No, I'm not! I told you my secrets."

"Maybe. You're still mysterious. Unpredictable. And . . ."

"Yes?"

"Very sexy."

She thought of him, over her, kissing her, and a shiver ran down her spine. "Well, so are you."

"Yeah? What else am I, Tessa?"

"Solid," she said. "And honorable." Afraid that was too serious, she added, "And very climbable."

He laughed.

Neither of them spoke for a long moment. Tessa didn't want to let him go, and yet the whole thing could hardly continue this way, could it? "I'm going to be around for a month or so, I think. Do we see each other or not?"

The raggedness was back in his voice when he said, "If we can work it out, yes."

"Fair enough," she said.

"Sorry," he rumbled. "I'm just tired right this minute. I guess I should let you go."

"All right. Let me know if the treatment works."

"I will." There was a long pause on the other end of the line. "Good night, Tessa."

"Good night, Vince. Get a good night's sleep."

"I'll sure try."

Sam woke at dawn and walked out on the beach with Loki and Wolfenstein, leaving old Peaches asleep on a blanket that had been on Tessa's bed.

He had left at least six messages for his daughter, and she had not returned any of them. He was afraid she would not ever return them again. In the quiet of the gray morning, he walked along the shore, watching the restless waves, smelling seaweed and brine and fish. A sharp wind whistled in over the water, and for the first time in more than thirty years, he was afraid. Not of the past. He didn't believe in regrets. Life came at you like a hurricane, and you did what you could with whatever it blew into your hands, good and bad. Given the choice, he'd do it all exactly the same.

But here life had tossed out this card on the table, a big dark omen when Tessa decided to go back to Los Ladrones. Why had he ignored it? He had just kept telling himself it was all such a long time ago it wouldn't matter.

Hands deep in the pockets of his jacket, he paused to look out over the wide black rolling sea, which he loved. As a boy growing up in Alabama, he'd dreamed of the ocean, had made models of big fish and old sailing vessels, read tales of pirates, and imagined a life of adventure and possibility.

He'd not actually *seen* an ocean until he was eighteen and headed to Vietnam, drafted into the Army. In his heady foolishness, war seemed to offer as much adventure as a pirate ship. At least he would get the hell out of Nowhere, Alabama, away from the smell of cow shit and the promise of a life like his bitter father's, who had died mad when Sam was twelve. His mother had followed soon after. Sam lived with relatives, this one and that one.

Vietnam had twisted him forever. Even now he could suffer nightmares over it. But the sea had lived up to her promise. He loved her, more truly than he had loved any woman, that much was sure.

He loved only Tessa more. He sat for an hour on the sand, shivering and damp, saying his farewells, soaking the cool sweet brine into his body. Then he went back to his house, called the woman who knitted dog sweaters for Peaches, and asked for her help packing things up. She'd watch over the margarita shack until he came back and found a renter for the house. She tried to coax him into a little farewell spoon, but he gently refused.

Sam drove an old covered camper truck for this reason— you never knew when you'd need to get on the road, and with dogs, you had to be able to make their lives all right. He packed his sleeping bag, a cooler full of fresh California fruits, a few cans of tuna fish, some bread and peanut M&Ms and plenty of fresh water for himself and the dogs, just in case. The two big dogs rode in the back, on pallets made of old blankets, and each of them had access to a tiny window through which they could stick their noses for fresh air. He'd leave the vents on the roof open, too, and they'd be fine. Addled, ancient Peaches rode in front with Sam, on a bed of Tessa's clothes and blankets. The only possession he couldn't travel without was his thick notebook of CDs. Music could get you through anything.

He was on the road by ten, in a drizzle that was cooling and hardly dangerous, drinking coffee out of a plastic go-cup he'd had since the early nineties. The Grateful Dead played "Friend of the Devil" on the CD player, and Sam sang along.

Tessa made a simple breakfast of fruit and bread and tea in her little kitchen. If she was staying for a while, she'd need to get some good English tea bags before much longer; they were easy to order online, but the shipping was horrific. In town, she might get lucky and find a cheaper source.

It was a relief to be awake after a night tossed with strange fragments of dreams, minglings of Sam and the rivers and Lisa and even Vince mixed in there somewhere.

She sat at the counter in the kitchen, enjoying the moody, misty light. The house was ancient, with slightly crooked window frames, wide pine boards on the floor, and adobe benches built right into the wall next to the fireplace and beneath the window in the kitchen. Both kitchen and bathroom had been recently outfitted with modern appliances and new tiles. The furniture was battered, but what could you expect from the VFW?

She braved the mist and clipped some of the cosmos from the garden along with one long red rose and arranged them in a Ball jar she found in the cupboard. The pink and red and white flowers in the simple jar were so beautiful that she took out her camera and shot a series of photos, finding serenity again through the lens. Scatters of yellow pollen littered one ridged pink cosmos petal. The rose was velvety, like chocolate cupcakes. She even enjoyed the clear blues and greens in the stems sticking into the water in the jar. She shot it all on the table, then put it on a windowsill and experimented with the light coming through the jar, through the petals and stems.

It was startling to realize she'd been at it for more than an hour. Even then, she wasn't ready to stop. She photographed the open door leading to the courtyard filled with flowers, and the smeary blue of mountains beneath low clouds, and the kitchen window by itself, and the curve of adobe on a bench, and the rumpled bed in the low, clear, pale light.

Her heart danced.

She shot Felix gazing up at her in the wary way dogs had with cameras, captured his black ears and his long white muzzle, and she fell so in love with him that she put the camera aside, kissed his forehead and nose, and wrapped her arms around his shoulders. He made a low, grateful sound in his throat and licked her neck.

"I guess," she said to him, "we have to make a trip out to the farm. Let's get your leash."

Loading him into the rental car, she realized that was something she'd need to address, too. She didn't have a car and couldn't afford to keep driving this one. It was due back in a couple of days, and she'd have to figure out what to do. A bicycle, maybe. The area was easily navigated with a bike, at least until winter set in.

By then she'd be gone. On to whatever tour she and Mick decided upon.

In the gray day, she drove out to Green Gate Farms. Before she spoke to her father—no, not her father; Sam—she wanted a few more answers on her own.

Rather than parking in the main lot, Tessa drove farther up one of the side roads, looking around for the one that would take her to the hot springs she and Cherry had talked about. From there, she could walk down to the house and see if they'd let her in.

A green pickup truck stopped, and a man with gray hair in a long braid said, "Can I help you with something?"

Tessa smiled. "I was just driving around. It's pretty. Do you mind?"

"We have specific times for guided tours. I'm sure you can understand why we can't let the public go traipsing through the fields."

"Oh, I'm not going to get out of the car. Promise."

He smiled. "I'm sure you wouldn't, sweetheart, and I know it sounds downright paranoid, but we have to protect the integrity of our products here. Been a lot of food scares in recent years."

Tessa nodded. "Right, I get it." She put her hand on the gearshift. "Maybe you can tell me where to find Paula or Cherry, then?"

"At the greenhouse, probably. But if you go up to the visitor center, they'll find anybody you want."

"Thanks." Tessa turned the car around and headed back to the main lot. The guy followed her, so there was no way out. She thought she might elude him by waiting until he went wherever he was headed, but he simply parked and got out of the truck, pulling a cell phone out of the pocket of his jeans.

"You wanted to find Paula or Cherry, you said? Particular about which one?"

"Both; either."

The man was about sixty or a little more, with an aristocratic face sharpened by years of harsh sun and wind. He punched in a telephone number and waited for somebody to answer, and Tessa felt in her bones that she knew him, but she couldn't call it up. Frustrated, she looked away as he made his phone call.

And from this angle, she saw a stand of aspen trees and the edges of a tepee. She took an involuntary step toward it, remembering an open meadow, pale green dotted with tiny white daisies, and the inside of the tepee itself, with sleeping bags and beds and—

"You all right, sweetheart? You look like you saw a ghost."

Tessa shook her head. "I've been seeing ghosts since I landed in this place. I can't really remember anything, but I was here with my . . . father as a child."

"There were a lot of people here for a little while, off and on. What's your name?"

"Tessa Harlow," she said without thinking.

He narrowed his eyes, then shook his head. "Doesn't ring a bell." He offered a strong, hardworking hand. "My name's Jon Nathan. My brother and I founded the place."

"Oh, hey. Good to meet you. I've been reading a lot about it all, trying to get a cooking tour into the school."

Light dawned. "Ah, right, right. Cherry told me."

"You should be proud of what you've accomplished here," she said. She took off her hat, shaking out her hair, and tucked her hands in her pockets.

"What's your name again?" He had gone quite still. "Who did you say your father was?"

Even if she was furious and wanted answers, Tessa couldn't bear to tell anyone else just yet. Giving Jon Nathan her most charming smile, she sidestepped the question. "Now you look like you've seen a ghost. Do I remind you of someone?"

He frowned. "Paula is on her way down. She'll meet you in the café." His cell phone rang, and he punched a button. "Hello?" he barked, and pointed Tessa up the hill to the café.

She didn't have any choice—she lifted a hand and headed for the café. Felix trotted behind her, sitting politely at the door while she ordered a cup of the heady tea. "I'd like to buy a half pound in bulk, too," she said.

When the girl handed her cup over the counter, Tessa was snared again by the scent and bent her head down, closing her eyes so she could smell it, breathe it in deeply.

A vast sense of well-being moved through her, but no memories surfaced. She carried the cup to a table beneath the roof outside. It was chilly, but she wanted to stick with Felix, and the light was fantastic. She'd left her camera in the car but took mental photos of the squashes spilling out of whiskey barrels and the quiet mood of the fields.

A woman in jeans and a jacket and a bandana came over. "Hello," she said. "You must be Tessa, right?"

It was the eyebrowless woman from the farmers' market. "Right."

"I'm Paula, Cherry's mother." She shook hands by encasing Tessa's hand in a sandwich between her own and looking deeply into her face. "Has anyone told you that you have the eyes of the children born at the commune?"

"No," Tessa said, startled. "What kind of eyes?"

"Green eyes," Paula said. She didn't let go of Tessa's hand.

"Like Guinnevere," Tessa said, without thinking.

"Yes." She smoothed her palm over Tessa's knuckles. "Are you one of Xander's children?"

To her horror, Tessa's eyes filled with tears. "I don't know." She looked away. "Maybe."

"It's all right. Drink some tea."

"I do remember this tea," Tessa said, trying to calm herself, to think of something besides the tide of emotion that was rising so suddenly and emphatically. "I remember the smell."

"I've been making it a long, long time." She kept a hand over Tessa's. "How old are you, honey?"

"Thirty-seven—I mean, thirty-nine."

Paula chuckled. "Do you lie about your age already?"

"No, it's complicated. I thought I was thirty-seven, but my . . . birth certificate was . . . lost."

Beyond the roof, the rain began to fall more heavily, pattering on the ground and the leaves. Felix moved closer to Tessa.

"You're not really here for the tour possibilities, are you?" Paula asked.

"Actually, I am. I didn't remember all . . . of . . . this until I got here."

"I see." Paula leaned forward. "How can I help you, sweetheart?"

Tessa shook her head, then bowed it. "Dang it," she said fiercely. "This is embarrassing. I'm sorry. I didn't know I'd feel so emotional."

"It's okay. Take your time."

"One thing I keep remembering is a sister. I think I had a sister. Who looked like me."

Paula nodded. "You probably have many sisters. And brothers. You all look alike. Blond, green-eyed, lanky. My daughter,

Cherry, is one of Xander's children. He was a beautiful and charismatic man."

"How many children?"

Paula shook her head. "I don't know. A dozen, maybe more. Not many stayed after he died."

My mother killed him. "How did he die?" Tessa asked.

"That, I'm afraid, is something we don't talk about." Her smile was as beneficent as a nun's, her hands neatly folded. "It was one of the darkest days of the commune, and we nearly didn't get through it."

Tessa nodded. She took a breath. "There is something I'd like to do, if it's possible."

"I'm happy to try."

"When I was here a few days ago, Cherry told me that there was a conference going on in the house, that old Victorian. I'd really like to see the tower room. I remember playing there."

"Oh, that's easy." Paula stood. "I just came from there. We're cleaning up and getting ready to close it for the winter. It's too expensive to heat, so we use it only in the summer. We can go in my car."

"Can I bring my dog?"

"Absolutely. Dogs are people, too." From her pocket she produced a small dog biscuit. Felix accepted it delicately. "And this, I can tell, is a great dog." She cocked her head. "Right. Let's go, kiddo."

Kiddo. Tessa smiled. It was what her father called her.

A pinch moved in her lungs. Not her father. Sam.

When they got to the house, it looked somehow sinister under the eggplant sky, and Tessa suddenly felt afraid. An anxiety attack started to rise in her chest, closing her throat, pressing her lungs tight against her ribs, making her stomach burn. She managed to breathe through it as they got out of the car. Felix waited on the wraparound porch as Paula led Tessa inside.

The foyer and the rooms opening from it were all classically Victorian, with wide-sash windows, fireplaces with carved wooden mantels, and bay windows looking out over the valley. Floors gleamed with polish, and the furniture was deep, inviting, covered in fabrics that gave a nod to the period—cranberry and forest, red and deep brown—without going into a tearoom bazaar of antimacassars and crystal.

Startled, Tessa said, "This is beautiful."

"I'm sure you wouldn't recognize this part. It was a mess and we never lived in it. We all lived upstairs." Gently, she smiled and led the way. Tessa found her gaze on Paula's sturdy leather clogs and knitted woolen socks. They climbed past the second floor, which had less light than below, and to the third, where Tessa followed Paula across a passage into the tower.

"It's storage now," she said, gesturing to the boxes. "But it was once where the children slept."

"I remember," she said, and the enormous tide of emotion rose in her throat, pressed against the bridge of her nose, equal parts joy and loss.

She floated into the round room with its uncurtained windows and turned in a circle. "It's smaller than I remember. We had beds all along the windows," she said, and turned again. "We played jacks and hopscotch." She went to a window and looked out. "Here. I slept here."

Unconsciously, she turned toward the right. "My sister—" She stopped. "I can see her so clearly," she whispered, suddenly flooded with a picture of a girl with long, long, long blond hair in a white nightgown, eating a cookie.

"Seven or eight kids slept here, I think. On cots," Paula said.

In Tessa's memory, the girl with long blond hair flung out her arms, spinning, and cried, *"Come dance with me, Guinnevere!"*

Herself. "Guinnevere," she said, choking. She bent over, covering her mouth. "My name is Guinnevere and I had a sister. I had a sister, and I don't know where she is."

"Oh, dear," said Paula. "Guinnevere."

Tessa turned to look at her. "That is my name, isn't it?"

"Yes, it probably is." Paula's brow was troubled.

Tessa sank to the floor, arms limp. Her cast knocked against the floor with a little thump. "Not even my name is right. Not even my name."

Paula knelt beside her. "Now you know. You are one of Xander's children. At least you know that."

Tessa swam up through the inexplicable grief swamping her. "How can I make sense of my life if I don't even know my name?"

Paula simply stroked Tessa's hair. Quietly, gently. "We haven't had any children come back," she said. "But I'm very glad to meet you again. We all thought you died."

Somehow, that steadied her. "In the river, right?"

"Yes."

"In a way, I did," Tessa said, and wiped her eyes. "My sister's name was Rhiannon, right?"

Paula nodded. "You were twins."

Tessa bowed her head. "And she went in the water, too. My dad—the man who raised me—pulled me out."

Paula closed her eyes, and she let go of an audible sigh. "Sam Harlow."

"Yes."

"He was so protective of all the children, but especially you. I used to worry about it at first, but I think you were just his destiny. It changed him, taking care of the children, all of you. He became a better person."

"Yeah," she said. Oddly, however, there was no hint of a panic attack. "Aside from that little matter of lying to me my entire life."

"Life gets complicated sometimes."

Tessa bent her head into her hands. "A sister," she whispered.

Paula sat with her, and Tessa cried for the sister she never had and sorely missed and had wished for all of her life.

Breakfast #95

Migas: One of the simplest and most cheerful of southwestern breakfasts—2 eggs scrambled with onions, corn tortillas, chorizo, and a little cheese. Served with green or red salsa and coffee.

MIGAS

1 link chorizo sausage, thickly diced
2 T chopped onions
2 corn tortillas, shredded roughly
2 eggs, lightly beaten
2 T chopped green chiles
Shredded cheese

In a heavy skillet, fry the chorizo until done. Remove sausage and drain. Pour off all but 1 T fat, and add onions and tortilla pieces. When the onions are tender and tortillas crisp, add eggs and chiles and sausage. Scramble until done. Sprinkle generously with shredded cheese.

TWENTY-ONE

Vince sent Jade and Hannah to school, leaving Natalie asleep in her room until after he made a handful of phone calls. To the firehouse to take the day off; to the dentist, who assured him such accidents happened all the time and he would see Jade right after school today; to the eye doctor to replace Nat's broken glasses; to the school counselor, who agreed to a meeting just before school got out; to his mother, who wasn't home.

He left Judy a message, preparing her for Natalie's absence and Jade's fat lip. "The war between the girls," he said, "may be getting a little out of hand."

Natalie was still asleep at nine, so he started a load of laundry, cleaned up the living room, and made his bed. At ten, he went into her room and gently woke her. "Why don't you get up now, sweetie? We'll go have breakfast."

When she came down the stairs, she wore an old T-shirt with a unicorn in faded glitter and jeans that were frayed on the hem. Her hair was tousled, her face showing the brawl in a purple shiner and a trio of scratches down her cheek.

He held up her blouse. "I got the blood out. Now we have to

ask Grandma to fix the shoulder." He put his fingers through the hole. "It's right on the seam. Should be easy to fix."

She nodded. Her eyes were swollen above and below the shiner, and she looked absolutely exhausted. "Are you feeling okay?"

"I'm just sad."

"What are you sad about, Nat-baby?"

"I'm sorry I hurt Jade. I'm sorry I stole the lemon curd."

He rubbed her shoulders and wondered how to get to the bottom of all this. The counselor would help. "I know. We're going to talk about that, and about everything else, but how about we go get you some breakfast at Vita's café?"

"Okay," she said without enthusiasm. "But I thought I was supposed to be in trouble."

He sat across from her and took her small hands in his own. "Babe, you don't have to carry the world. I've got it, okay?"

Her dark-blue eyes met his. "I know," she said without conviction.

It was well past the rush by the time they wandered into 100 Breakfasts. The smells of brewing coffee and frying bacon and baking bread perfumed the air, and the low murmurs of conversation made the music of the café. Vince waved a hand. "Where do you want to sit?"

"At the counter." She clambered onto a stool, her legs hanging free far above the floor.

The man on the other side of her said, "Hey, little lady. Who you been brawling with?"

Natalie gave Vince a dark look. He shrugged. "Better get used to it."

She sighed and said, "My sister."

"Ooh. Hope she looks worse than you."

"Not really." She took a menu and opened it reverently, bending her head over the columns and columns of food.

Vince reached for the tidy pile of read newspapers, feeling his nerves ease a little just by being here. Vita greeted him with a cup of coffee. "Looking a little haggard there, kiddo. You okay?"

"Kid troubles," he said, and his voice was a burly rasp. "Nothing your breakfast can't cure."

"It is well known that a good breakfast can cure just about anything. How about you, Miss Natalie? What will it be this morning?"

"I have to think."

"Take your time." Vita bustled away, all lean arms and legs and purpose.

He leafed through the menu. What would heal this raw spot on his heart? Pancakes, maybe. With peaches if there were any left. Berries if she had some of those. Or maybe he'd put himself in Vita's hands. When she came back, he said, "You choose."

"I can do that." She topped off his coffee. "What about you, Natalie?"

She said, "I will try the huevos del diablo."

"*Whey-vos,*" Vita said.

"*Whey-vos,*" Natalie repeated, nodding. "I knew I probably didn't have it right."

"That's all right. You can't know if you don't give it a try. Do you want it hot or medium?"

"Medium, please."

"How many left to try, kiddo?"

Natalie said, "Sixty-eight."

"Wow. I'm impressed!"

"I haven't actually ordered every single one," she confessed. "Some of those I just tasted somebody else's."

"That's all right. It counts." Vita tapped Natalie on the head with the menu. "You're gonna come work for me one of these days, aren't you? A girl with your talent needs to be in my kitchen."

"Oh," Natalie breathed, putting her hands on her face. "*Yes.*"

Vita gave her the thumbs-up, winked at Vince, and headed for the kitchen.

This, he thought, had been exactly the right place to come.

Vince said, "You know, we're gonna have to come up with a way for you to make up for the stealing."

"Shhhh!" she said, shooting a glance over the pass-out bar, where the woman who saw Nat steal the salt shaker was bent over the grill. "Do you want the whole world to know?"

"Sorry. Let's talk about something else."

"Can I have the comics?"

Vince passed them over. "Sure."

When she left the farm, Tessa felt light-headed with information. She thought about stopping at the library again to look up anything they might have reported in the newspaper about the drowning. Or a fire. Something about a fire kept flickering at the edge of her memory.

Trees, running—

But she'd had about enough for one morning. All the peace she'd stored by shooting the still quiet of a vase of flowers was now gone. She headed for Vita's café, which had come to feel, in a very short time, like Cheers, where everyone knew her name.

Even if she didn't.

She felt winded as she walked in, carrying secrets and losses and newly discovered grief like a child.

And there, of course, was Vince. It was as if their feet ran on parallel train tracks and pulled in at the same stations at the same time, over and over. Relief flooded her. Maybe she had come here looking for him—the sight of his dark hair, his sober jaw, made her feel better.

She sat down next to him, letting her hand linger on his shoulder blade, not realizing until she said, "Hey, handsome," that Natalie was on his other side.

He glanced up as Tessa caught sight of Natalie's face. The whole side of her left eye and cheekbone were bruised, emanating from a red star at the corner. "Oh, baby, that looks like it hurt."

"It did. My sister hit me."

"Wow. Were you in a fight?"

"She called me an oinker."

Tessa frowned. "Really? You're not fat."

"Kindà." She patted her tummy.

"Not even kinda. You're just growing. You know how puppies and kittens have a round tummy when they're small, and then they grow out of it?"

Natalie nodded. The iris of her left eye had a burst blood vessel, making the color of the syrup blue even darker.

"Like that. You're a puppy."

Natalie laughed.

Vince looked at Tessa, mouthing "thank you," and put his hand on her thigh. Squeezed lightly. His big palm sent sparks through her muscles, deep into her femur. Their eyes met, a quiet greeting that lasted a good long minute. The smell of his hair hung around him like a halo, spicy and alluring, inviting her to bend her nose into his neck and inhale. She found herself looking at the spot just below his ear, wishing she could just do that, lean in and kiss him, right there.

"How did the treatment work on the blouse?" she asked.

"Great, thank you. Came right out." Vince turned toward Natalie. "It was Tessa who told me what to do to get the blood out."

"It's still torn, though." Her face was glum. "I don't know if we can fix it."

"Sure we can. C'mon," Vince said, nudging her. "Chin up."

"I think we should sit in a booth," Natalie said, and looked at Tessa. "If you want to, that is."

"Absolutely."

They moved to the window, and Vita brought out the food for the other two and took Tessa's order. Tessa pointed to the green chalkboard. "I'll have the breakfast pizza. That sounds fantastic."

"Where are your glasses?" Tessa asked Natalie, and then winced. "Oh, I bet they got broken in the fight, yeah?"

Natalie nodded.

"It was a pretty terrible day for Natalie," Vince said, cutting into his pancakes. Perfect. Exactly what he needed. The cords in his forearms moved, powerful and beribboned with vein. She glimpsed the edge of his tattoo beneath his shirtsleeve, thought about his chest.

"Do you know about *Alexander and the Terrible, Horrible, No Good, Very Bad Day*?" Tessa asked.

Natalie grinned. *"Some days are like that,"* she quoted.

Together, they said, *"Even in Australia!"*

"I love that book," Natalie said. "How do you know about it?"

"I had it when I was kid." She leaned her arms on the table. "And you know what else? I lived in Australia."

"Really? Was it cool?"

"Yes," Tessa said. "It really was." She poured sugar into her tea. "But there were bad days, even in Australia."

Natalie looked relieved, and something about her face, her awkward, blustery, forthright *personhood,* snared Tessa right then and there. A burst of fierce affection rose through her, easing all the tense darkness, letting her put her burdens down for one minute.

As they sat there, Annie came out of the kitchen. "Hi, Natalie," she said. "Can I talk to you for a second? I have a question about an ingredient, and Vita said you might know."

Tessa was watching Nat, and the funniest expression crossed her face—wariness and calm and hope, all mingled together. "Sure. Daddy, can you let me out?"

The two of them went to the back, skinny Annie and round Natalie, looking thick as thieves. "Wonder what that's all about," Vince said.

"Something," Tessa agreed.

Annie was working the grill this morning. It gave her a great vantage point over the restaurant, which she liked because she'd been having bad dreams again. It seemed like danger was creeping closer and closer—although the bread rose fine this morning, and Vita had told her if danger came in the door, the bread wouldn't rise.

But Annie also knew that Tommy was gone. He would not hurt her again.

So what was this threat, thick in the air, dark and malevolent?

Vita had helped her find a new place—a little apartment in the middle of a row of apartments, only two rooms plus the itsy-bitsy bathroom, but plenty of room for her. So much more than she'd been used to in jail, and the manager accepted cats. Vita even helped her pay the deposit, saying Annie could pay her back later, or five dollars a week if that worked—and she helped her negotiate taking the red kitchen table with her. It was a straight switch—the table from the new apartment traded for the one in the old apartment. One of the cooks at the café helped her move, putting things in his truck.

The kitchen of the new apartment opened into a walled garden, so Athena would be safe. The person who lived there before had planted marigolds and daisies in the raised beds, and Annie moved her table outside for now, until it got too, too cold.

This was the happiest she'd ever been in her life. This morning she'd put a little blush on her cheeks, and maybe she'd even take her hair to its normal color one of these days. Maybe.

Across the pass-out bar, Annie saw the little girl from the other day and her father. The girl had a nasty, nasty black eye, and it made Annie's stomach upset. It was hard not to glare at the dad, but she'd seen him in here so much with those girls it was hard to imagine he would ever hit one of them. You could never tell, though, and she felt obliged to say something to Vita.

"What happened to the little girl?"

"Who? Oh, Natalie," Vita said, plating a casserole with sprigs of fresh thyme leaves and a cross-hatching of long chives. "She and her sister had a nasty fight. I gather Jade has a broken tooth from Nat's head."

"Yeow! I bet that hurt." Carefully, Annie broke an egg on the very hot grill. She was getting pretty good at it but still broke the yolks sometimes. "She's in a little trouble, that one, isn't she?"

"Hold that thought," Vita said. She gathered two more plates and carried them out, took an order, hung it on the ring, and came back into the kitchen. "What do you mean?"

Annie weighed her promise to the little girl with the feeling that something really was wrong there. "Don't say anything, but I caught her stealing a salt shaker the other day."

Vita's expression didn't change. "That's good to know, Annie, thank you."

"I told her I wouldn't tell, and I made her a little magic charm." She shrugged and tugged it out of her pocket. It was only a braid of rosemary, with tucks of marigold in it, but Annie knew it wasn't so much what a charm was made of but what you believed. "I thought it might help her. Do you think it would be okay?"

"Very okay, Annie." She inclined her head. "Why don't you go give it to her."

After breakfast, Natalie asked Tessa if she'd ever been to the salt store, Le Fleur de Mer. "I haven't," Tessa admitted. "But I'd love to see it if your dad isn't in a big hurry."

"Can we?"

"Sure, why not?" He held the door open, lifting a hand to wave at Vita. He'd been planning to get her opinion on the problems with Natalie, but maybe he needed to wait on that, anyway. Vita didn't have children of her own, but she was good with all the parolees who came through her kitchen, giving them dignity and something useful they could do with themselves. Maybe she'd have some insight about a little girl.

But today he was just as happy to wander down the covered walkway to the salt store, watching Tessa's rear end swing back and forth in a pair of jeans. Natalie walked beside her, not bouncing but quietly dignified, brushing her hair away from her face as she looked up to say something to Tessa. "Do you like to cook?"

"Sometimes," Tessa said. "Not very good at it, though, since I have been traveling for a long time."

"Oh."

"Do you?"

"Nobody really lets me do it very much, but I think I'll be good at it when I get bigger." She stopped, gesturing almost reverently. "Here's the store."

Vince understood the appeal of the place, even if he didn't get the whole gourmet-salt angle. Shelves held jars of various grades and colors and textures of salt, with labels that gave details about where the salt came from, how to use it, and in which dishes. There were other spices, too—dried Turkish chiles and rose-colored peppercorns, organic vanilla beans and saffron. A sturdy shelf held tiny bottles and spoons and dispensers.

The proprietor came out, a pinched-looking woman with a long nose and the carriage of a dancer. "Hello," she said coolly.

"Hi," Nat said. "We're here to look at all the salt. My friend hasn't been here before."

Tessa smiled at Vince.

Natalie pointed out her favorites. "I don't know how to say that word."

Tessa bent. *"Grigio di Cervia,"* she said. "From Italy. It says you can put it on meat to make a nice crust."

Natalie pointed out the river salts and Welsh harvest and then took Tessa's hand. "And this is the red salt you took the picture of."

"It is. It's a great picture, too, Natalie. You should see it." She stood. "I wish I had my camera now. This is wonderful." To the proprietor, she said, "Can I come back and shoot the salts? I'll buy some, too, of course."

"Certainly. I'd be delighted."

"Okay. We'll come back, Nat. How's that? You can think about which one you want and we'll get it then."

"I want to show you one more." Natalie pointed to a softly lit shelf at her eye level, where large crystals of pink salt spilled out of a velvet bag. It sat on another slab of pink, ribboned with light and dark veins. "This one is my favorite," she said reverently.

"But," Vince said with a chuckle, "nobody is buying her that slab, at least for a while."

"It's beautiful," Tessa agreed. "I'd like to try it sometime."

"Me, too," Natalie said.

Vince never lied to himself if he could help it. What he knew about himself today was that he had fallen for Tessa Harlow in a big way. Maybe from the first second he'd laid eyes on her in the cantina that night, and a little deeper every moment he'd spent in her company since then.

But this morning, when she saw straight into Natalie's bruised heart and said the exact thing to make her feel good, he had gone right over the edge. She looked weary herself, full of secrets, and yet she found the kindness to offer a quiet soothing hand to a little girl she barely knew.

After they left the store, Tessa called Felix, who waited on the portico. "Thanks for showing me the salt store, Nat," she said.

"Can you send my dad the picture?"

"Actually, if you want to walk over to my house, I can show it to you now." She looked to Vince for affirmation, and he saw what he'd been missing: She was just as freaked out by her reaction to him as he was by his reaction to her. They were both a little too old to believe in love at first sight, but how long had she been here? Not quite two weeks.

"If you have time, that is? I rented a place just a block away." Vince said, "Sure. I don't see why not."

"Can we get Pedro and Sasha and go to the river?" Natalie asked.

Maybe it wasn't supposed to be a vacation day, he thought. Maybe he should be giving Natalie punishments instead of rewards for the terrible day yesterday, but he couldn't remember the last time he'd seen her so . . . normal. Like a desert plant, she was blooming under the attention Tessa was raining down on her.

And, really, what would he say, anyway? *Stop stealing. Stop fighting with your sister.* She already knew that. The stealing and fighting were not the problem. Her grief was. And he needed help to figure out what to do about that, which was what he would be seeing the counselor for this afternoon. How long did a child grieve? How could he help her get through it?

"Okay, but only for a little while," he said. "We're parked right behind the plaza."

Pedro leapt out of Vince's truck to greet Tessa as if he'd been waiting for her. Felix nervously leaned on her leg as if he might be supplanted. She laughed, her hair falling down around her face as she bent and kissed Pedro's head, gave him a good rub, and put her other hand on Felix. "This is my dog. You met him the other day, remember?"

Pedro bent in a playful bow and barked. Felix lifted a paw happily. Even Sasha, in her slightly confused way, came over to get some attention. Tessa gave her a good rub, too, and the dog smiled.

"Her hearing has been a lot better lately," Vince said.

"Poor baby, you're just old, aren't you?"

The rain earlier had left the ground damp, the plants glittering with droplets of water. The clouds overhead seemed to be threatening more. "Maybe you guys should go to the river first and circle back to my house? It looks like more rain."

"Come with us," Vince said.

Natalie reached up and took her hand. "Please?"

Tessa hesitated and met Vince's eyes. He held her gaze steadily. He was here, meeting the situation as it unfolded. He didn't have any answers, either.

"Okay," she said. "My dog will like it, too." But she had a pensive expression.

Vince let it be.

At the river, Natalie and the dogs played with a stick, while Tessa, Vince, and the elderly Sasha sat on the bank. Low clouds hung in the distance, bringing with them a scent of autumn and the promise of snow, not far away. Winter came early to the mountains, and she could feel the bite of it close to the ground, nipping at her ankles.

In this light, at this angle, the river gave her no memories. It was just another waterway she'd admired in the course of her life, and there had been dozens. Maybe hundreds. It suddenly seemed as if that life of wandering belonged to someone else.

But maybe she was only reacting to all the shocks of the day. She gave a little sigh.

"What's up?" Vince asked. "You look exhausted."

She rubbed her face. "Oh, just one thing after another."

He nodded, accepting the boundary she posted. "Thanks for being so good to Natalie. She needed it."

"Poor kid. That's one brutal black eye. How's Jade?"

"Furious that she broke her tooth on Natalie's head." He chuckled. "Jade likes things to flow according to their proper place. I don't know where she gets it. I'm not like that, and neither was her mother."

"More and more it seems to me that we're born who we are."

He inclined his head. "Think so?"

"Well, a lot of it, anyway." She looped her arms around her knees. A lock of wavy hair came loose and blew in the wind. She ignored it. "I mean, what if Jade was raised with my dad? Living on the road, going to Renaissance festivals. How would she meet that challenge?"

He laughed. "She'd put a tablecloth on a picnic table and ask the trapeze lady to iron her shirt, and the women in the group would all be vying to braid her hair."

"I can see that." Tessa chuckled. "Whereas Natalie would be ordering the mess tent and figuring out how to make a turkey leg elegant."

"She's really something. A born foodie." He cleared his throat. "She . . . uh . . . stole something at the grocery store last night. That's where the whole thing started."

"Oh, sorry. What did she steal?"

He paused. Raised his eyebrows. "Lemon curd."

Tessa laughed. And once she started, she couldn't seem to stop. She had a deep belly laugh, and Vince finally joined in, both of them laughing as much in reaction as to anything truly funny. She shook her head. "Boy, you really have your work cut out for you."

Nearby, Sasha whined softly, shifting her arthritic body. Tessa got up and sat down beside her, running hands over the wiry fur, rubbing along her spine and belly. "Poor baby," she said to the dog, "you have lots and lots of lumps and bumps, don't you, darlin'?" Sasha fell over sideways, happily stretching out so Tessa could rub her all over. "Oh, that feels good. Let's get under the arm."

Vince held up a hand and let it droop. He made a sound like a dog, and Tessa gave him a sultry glance. "Believe me," she said, and looked over her shoulder to be sure Natalie was far enough away that she couldn't hear, "I'd love to give you the once-over."

"And I would gladly return the favor."

She sat back on her heels, hands resting on her thighs. "But right there is the reason we can't really let this go anywhere." She gestured toward Nat, dancing with Pedro and Felix.

"How long are you staying?"

"Rented the house for a month."

"Plenty of time for play." He looked at her mouth. "I would like to try that trick again, the one that—"

A little shudder rushed over her shoulders and she held up a palm. "Don't make me think about it."

"Okay, I'll think about it for us." He held her gaze as he thought about her lean nakedness sinuously writhing while he lazily lapped his tongue against her flesh.

"That's evil," she said.

"Oh, I can be so much more evil," he said. "Trust me."

It started to sprinkle, and they headed back to Tessa's house so Tessa could show Natalie the photograph. They were all damp by the time they got there, humans and dogs alike. Tessa brought out a few towels. "Sorry there aren't many. We'll have to make do."

Pedro shook himself as if to say he didn't need no stinkin' towel. Felix followed suit, and when Pedro plopped down on the floor, Felix dropped down beside him, panting in happiness. Sasha paced around the room, sniffing all the corners.

"She's making sure there are no crumbs that have gone un-eaten," Vince said.

"Speaking of that, is anybody hungry?" Tessa asked.

"I am!" Natalie cried, holding up a hand. "I've been playing hard!"

"You have," Tessa agreed. "There's not a lot of choice, but let me see what I can do." The tiny blue fridge held milk and goat cheese and a couple of yogurts, some olives and green onions and peaches. She took out the goat cheese, olives, and peaches. "I know what we'll do."

She unwrapped a rustic loaf of sourdough bread and put a plate on the counter. "Do you want to help, Natalie?"

"Sure!" She dragged a chair over and stood on it.

Tessa gave her a container of grape tomatoes and the olives. "Start by arranging those on this plate. Have you ever had a salt-cured olive?"

"I don't think so."

"Try it." She glanced at Vince, who leaned on the counter, watching Natalie's face. "Pretty strong flavor."

Natalie's eyes opened wide. "Yum! These are the kind they have at the Italian store in Pueblo!"

Tessa offered one to Vince. He shook his head. "Don't like olives at all."

"His mom can't cook," Natalie said sadly. "That's why we eat out so much. He doesn't cook that much, either."

"Ah, well, I'm not the best. This is what we do on hiking trips. Goat cheese, tomatoes, olives, and fresh bread. If you have sun-dried tomatoes, they're really good on this."

She sliced the bread and put it out with the rest of the offer-ings, and put the peaches out, too. "The peaches here are amaz-ing," she said. "I can't stop eating them."

"So, do I put it all on one piece of bread, or like a sandwich, or what?" Natalie asked, a bit tense.

"You know, that's the beauty, Nat," Tessa said. "You can do whatever you think looks best. All separate? All rolled up in the bread? Whatever you want."

"Can I have a little plate?"

Tessa grinned. "Absolutely." She pulled a battered small plate from the cupboard. "Have at it."

Vince picked at the bread, nibbled a slice of goat cheese, watching the other two dig in to the food. "Not your thing, I take it?" Tessa asked, grinning.

"That's all right. I like seeing my girl eat. Do you like it, Nat?"

She had rolled the bread around everything and nodded vigorously, her mouth full. "The olives are great!"

"They are my favorites."

Sasha sat politely nearby, bright button eyes trained on the humans. She was pigeon-toed and cheerful, and Tessa asked, "Can I give her a treat?"

"Not until we're finished, or she will beg and whine forever." Vince nodded at the dogs. "I think your dog likes mine."

Felix had curled up with Pedro and put his chin on the bigger dog's back. Pedro snored, worn out from his run at the river. "Dogs are pack animals," she said. "That's why my dad always has three."

"Humans are pack animals, too," Vince said.

"Not all of them."

He nodded. "Even you."

Natalie couldn't believe what a good day it was turning out to be. Her dad had barely even yelled at her, and then she got to eat something new at 100 Breakfasts, and then Tessa was so nice to her and they got to go to the salt store. She loved the picture Tessa took of her hands and the red salt on the avocado, and her dad promised to have it printed at the drugstore so she could put it up on her wall. To make sure, Natalie stood by the computer and watched as they sent it online, not happy until the screen popped up and said, *You can pick up your prints in 1 hour, 59 minutes, and 12 seconds.*

Natalie also liked the dog, Felix, and the little house. It had a peaceful feeling inside, especially with the rain, and Natalie loved the way Tessa left the door open to the air, so the smell of rain came inside. She heard it pattering on the sidewalk outside. The flowers drooped, but even they looked pretty.

When her dad started moving around like he was going to leave, Natalie said, "Oh, I don't want to go yet!"

"I have to drop you with Grandma," he said. "I have to go to the school, and Jade has an appointment at the dentist, remember?"

Natalie drooped, just like the flowers outside. Her dad might not have yelled at her, but Grandma sure would. "Can I go with you to the dentist?"

"Sorry, but I think Jade deserves a little alone time, too. She's pretty mad, you know."

That almost made Nat cry. "I really didn't mean to hurt her so bad."

"Baby, I know." He rubbed her shoulders. "You hurt each other, you know. It takes two. It's not all your fault."

"I'm the older sister, though. Grandma tells me that all the time. I'm s'pposed to be responsible."

Daddy nodded. "But you are only eight. It takes time to learn all that."

Tessa said, "I don't know if it would be any better, but I'm just going to hang around here. Natalie can stay here if she wants. If you don't mind."

Natalie jumped up. "Please can I?"

"Are you sure?" Daddy asked.

"I would be happy to have some company," Tessa said. "We can look up good recipes online or something."

Natalie held her breath.

"Okay. I'll call Grandma and tell her not to come until later. You still have to go to the eye doctor to get some new glasses, so she'll be here at three-thirty. Be ready to go right then."

"I will. I promise." She touched her heart.

"And one other thing," he said, and looked up at Tessa. "Would you mind giving us a minute?"

"Not at all. I'll be in the other room."

He folded his hands and got his dad look on, all serious eyes and straight mouth. Natalie thought he was going to tell her what her punishment was, but he said, "You know she's here for only a few weeks, right?"

Natalie flushed. "I know, Dad."

"Good. The other thing is, Grandma will want to talk to you about stealing, and I want you to listen to her, okay? I told her I'm going to handle your punishment, but I still haven't thought of what would be a good idea, so I'll tell you tonight, okay? You tell her that. That I'm thinking about it."

"Why don't you just put me on restriction or something?" Natalie said. "That's what everybody usually does."

He pursed his lips. "That's not the answer this time. I think I might have you do some volunteering somewhere."

"The lady at 100 Breakfasts has a bracelet on her ankle that she got for being in jail."

He grinned. "That might be a bit much." He stood up and kissed her head. "You just tell Grandma what I said, all right?"

"I will."

And then he left them, Natalie and Tessa, alone with the dogs and a computer. They looked up recipes for red velvet cupcakes, which Natalie thought looked so, so beautiful. "It's too late to do it today, but I'd like to try them," Tessa said. "Maybe we could get all the stuff and do them some other day."

Afterward, they played rummy, and Tessa braided her own hair and offered to braid Natalie's. She had soft hands, and the brush felt so good on her head. "My mommy used to brush my hair," Nat said sleepily.

"Nice," Tessa said. "My mom died when I was little. I can't remember her at all. Do you remember yours?"

"Yes. She had blond hair, like Jade's, and she used to wear this pretty necklace with beads that dripped down from a chain, just like blood. I think they were rubies."

"Sounds beautiful." Tessa kept brushing Natalie's hair, slowly, deeply. "What else?"

"She sang songs to us all the time from *The Sound of Music.*"

"Oh, I love that movie! You, too?"

"It's my favorite, except for *Aladdin.*"

"Cool. Do you want me to braid your hair in one braid?"

"I don't care," Natalie said, even though she wanted that a lot.

"Let me see if I can do a French braid for you." Tessa laughed and in her deep, soft voice said, "I used to do it for Renaissance festivals when I wasn't much older than you are."

"What's that?"

"Oh, it's like a country fair, only everybody pretends it's back in the days of kings and princesses and they dress up like wizards and queens and peasants."

"That sounds fun."

"It is fun." Tessa started to hum under her breath.

Natalie heard the tune and turned suddenly. "Do you know the words to that song?"

"Wait a minute and let me hear what I was humming." She ran through a few notes and then started to sing:

> *"There are suitors at my door,*
> *o le le o bahia."*

Pedro heard it and came over to sit on their feet, but something hot was born in Natalie's heart. She stared at Tessa. "How do you know that song? That was my mommy's song."

"I'm sorry. Did I upset you?"

"No!" Natalie said, but there was the burning in the middle of her chest, right where her heart should be beating like a normal person's. "I just want to know how you know it! It was *her* song. Nobody else ever sings it!"

"Oh, honey, I'm sorry." Tessa brushed her hand over Natalie's arm, but Nat yanked it away. "To tell you the truth, I don't know how I know it. I think it might be a Girl Scout song. There are a lot of songs I sing that I don't know where they came from."

"My mommy was a Girl Scout. I have her sash." Natalie closed her eyes. "Will you sing the whole thing?"

Tessa sang.

TWENTY-TWO

Tessa was chopping celery for soup when Vince pulled up in front of the house. She watched him through the kitchen window, stepping down heavily, the weight of the world too much for even those broad shoulders. His expression when he thought himself unobserved showed his worry.

By the time he got to her door, he'd wiped that all away and said simply, "I really wanted to kiss you so much earlier that I came back just to do that," and he bent down and did it. He smelled like spice and rain and the kind of wind that blows through the mountains, and his hands were so huge they cupped her whole face. It felt so good to be so wanted that Tessa could only lift her arms and kiss him back, drawing him into the house so she could close the door.

"I only have an hour," he said.

"That's enough time," she said, and led him into the plain bedroom with its double bed and soft light. She took off her shirt and skimmed out of her jeans and he followed suit, so they were standing only in underwear as they came together, bellies and thighs, his hands moving down her back and up into her hair, over her breasts. She closed her eyes and imprinted the shape of his buttocks into her memory, the feeling of his hair falling against her neck as he kissed her breasts. He was too big to make the missionary position comfortable, so he pulled her sideways and they made love slowly, bathed in the soft blue light reflected in the room, and then lay face-to-face, stroking each other. He touched the hollow of her throat. She followed the powerful line of his thigh, his arm.

"I don't want to freak you out or anything," he said, his voice as deep and rumbling as thunder, "but I really think I'm falling in love. It's fast, and I know there's no future, but there it is."

Tessa swallowed. "I know—me, too. But it's not going to be okay. You know that, too, don't you? It's not a fairy tale. Love isn't going to change my essential nature or change what you need."

"What's your essential nature?"

"I'm a wanderer."

"Are you?" He bent in and took her lower lip in his mouth, moving his tongue lazily over the flesh. "You stayed in Tasmania. You fell in love and stayed with the scientist."

The easy emotionalism rose in her throat. Tears pooled in her eyes as she thought of Glenn, but more as she thought of her father who wasn't her father, and she ducked her head into his shoulder. "I don't believe in happy endings."

"How about happy episodes?"

"Maybe." She closed her eyes, breathing him in. She curled closer and put her hands in his hair, wishing he didn't have to go.

Under her breath, she began to hum.

"Is that 'Let It Be'?" Vince asked.

Tessa listened. "Yes," she said, and laughed. "My single most annoying habit, by the way. Humming all the bloody time."

"It's kinda cute."

"The first twelve thousand times, maybe." She wiggled a little. "Sorry, I have to attend to Mother Nature. Be right back."

For a second she dithered over whether she ought to put something on, and then she just let it go, dashing into the bathroom naked. She peed and looked at her face in the mirror, flushed and sweaty, and wished she could stay here, in this time, in this place, forever. From the counter in the kitchen, she grabbed her camera and carried it back into the bedroom.

"Do you mind?" she said, holding up the camera. "The light in here is beautiful and, really, you look great."

He propped himself up on his elbow. "I wish I could take *your* picture right now. Naked woman with camera."

"I'm not particularly shy about being naked, actually," she said, and raised the camera. "Is that a yes or a no?"

"Go ahead."

"Thank you. On your belly first, please." Tessa looked at him through the lens, the soft gray rainlight pouring over his back. "You have very beautiful skin," she said, shooting the long curve of his spine, the buttering of light along his shoulders, the biceps with the tattoo. Then buttocks and legs, those massive thighs. He turned over, winking at her, and she shot the frontal view, too, his broad chest and thick, lazy erection, and then zoomed in on his face, the dark-brown eyes and tousled hair and beautiful mouth. "Zeus," she said, and laughed. "God, you are so gorgeous."

He held out a hand. "My turn?"

"Are you going to sell them on the Internet?" she asked. "Pass them around to your friends?"

"I will if you will."

"First this." She fell down beside him, head to head on the

pillow, and held the camera up overhead. "Look up." She clicked the shutter, shifted the camera, shot again, and then again. "Okay, it's yours."

"I've never taken a picture of someone naked before," he said, standing up, and aimed the camera at her. Tessa played coy and covered bits and looked at him from under her hair and laughed until he came down beside her and put his hand around her breast and took a picture. And then he was over her, in her, and they were lost, the camera forgotten.

Before he left, he said, "Come have breakfast with us this weekend, at Vita's."

"Do you eat there every day?"

"Not usually. Usually we go only on the weekends, but it's been a little unsettled."

"It's a bad idea, Vince."

"One more time, and then you can be my secret lover until you go."

"It just seems—"

He kissed her thoroughly. "Think about it. We'll be there around ten on Saturday."

She sat up. "Oh, I forgot—I meant to tell you that I was humming a song this afternoon, and Natalie heard it and said it was her mother's song." She sighed. "It really upset her, I think." She shook her head, feeling the edge of that sucking depression creeping around her belly. "Makes me sad."

"Hey, are you okay?"

"No, not really. I found out my father lied to me about a lot of stuff, and I'm pretty upset about it."

"Lied about you? About him?"

"Lied," she said. She took a breath and said it out loud for the first time. "He's not my father. It seems I am one of Xander's 476 children."

"Ah."

"Did you know that?"

"No. But you look like them, the commune kids." He stayed where he was, one arm propped behind his head. With his other, he stroked a thumb over Tessa's wrist. "What can I do to help?"

"You can't, really. It's just weird. The dude sounds weird as he can be, like Jim Jones or something."

"No, I don't think so. It was another time, Tessa. It wasn't the same thing—it was a big social experiment, and it didn't work out, exactly. But that doesn't mean that all the children were a mistake."

"I know." She plucked at the bedspread. "The other thing is, I kept remembering a little girl with long blond hair. My sister."

"There were a lot of kids out there."

"I know, but I talked to Paula, and she remembered my actual sister. She drowned, along with my mother, at the same time I went into the river." She twisted threads into a knot. "A twin sister, actually."

He went still. "Guinnevere and Rhiannon were the twins."

She nodded.

"Which one are you?"

"Guinnevere, evidently. Not that I remember. I still don't." She looked at him, shrugged. "Not completely."

He had an odd expression on his face, both stricken and relieved. He brought her hand to his mouth and kissed the back of it. "I'm so sorry." He held her hand close to his face. "I have to go soon, but I don't want to leave you at the moment of revelation."

"I know, I'm sorry. It just came out."

"It's okay." He kept her hand close. "I have a couple more minutes."

Worried that he would remember that Tessa's mother was a murderer, Tessa asked, "Do you know who killed Xander?"

"No. The few people who might are not ever going to talk. Somebody offered a $250,000 reward a few years ago, and there were no takers."

"Thick as thieves," she said.

"Yeah." He sat up. "You okay?"

Tessa smiled, and it was genuine, if a little rueful. "Yes, I'm fine. It's all water under the bridge—ha-ha."

"Very funny."

"Thanks for listening, Vince. Seriously. It's a lot to process."

"I wish I could stay. I have to go get my girls. Call me later and we can talk about this some more."

"I understand." She stood up and started to put on her own clothes. "Did you talk to the school counselor about Nat?"

He pulled on his boxers, picked up his jeans from the floor. "She's going to work with her."

"Good. Poor baby."

Vince nodded. He finished dressing, then kissed her. "I'll call you this evening. If that's okay."

"Yes."

The weather grew more cantankerous as Sam drove into the mountains, and by the time he reached Flagstaff, it was plain he would need to stop for the night. He found a motel that allowed dogs. He fed and watered them, then got Peaches settled in a comfy spot, covered with her little blanket, and took the other two out for a good long walk to shake out the kinks.

He'd come this way back then, too, riding a Kawasaki 400—which wasn't exactly a big bike—across the desert with his hair blowing free, like in *Easy Rider*. Most of it was a blur, lost in time and the general haze of drugs and drink that marked that era of his life.

As he walked the dogs tonight, whistling them into obedience when a car drove by, he breathed in the cool, crisp mountain air. Another life. In a way, it all seemed so innocent now, despite Vietnam and the acid trips and all the runaway kids that must have broken the hearts of their parents. All those kids qualified now for AARP, the generation that wouldn't get old.

Not that they had grown old the same way. Whatever else had come from the psychedelic sixties, he knew that his generation of sixty-year-olds was not the same as that of the sixty-year-olds he'd known as a child, the bent grandmothers and snowy-haired sages in their pristine Buicks.

What would he find when he got to Los Ladrones? He was nervous about revisiting the town. Nervous about seeing the commune again, which he'd have to do, even if it was buried in rubble and yucca. It didn't sound like that would be the case, though. Nervous that Tessa would never forgive him. Ever.

The dogs, soggy with the rain that kept falling, hustled him back to the motel. He dried them off, but the smell of damp dog still filled the room for the rest of the night. Sam ordered a pizza for delivery, drank some 7Up so caffeine wouldn't keep him awake, and fell asleep before the news came on.

After work, Annie was determined to figure out how to make poached eggs. She bought a full dozen eggs at the supermarket. Vita had loaned her a heavy cast-iron skillet and a slotted spoon and walked her through the steps one more time before she left. "Practice makes perfect."

And how. She was getting the hang of a lot of things at the

café, but poached eggs defeated her every time, the threads of white scattering in the water until the eggs looked like an amoeba or a jellyfish or something. Not like an egg.

She stopped by the cards, too, and picked a funny one to send to her brother. He'd written her a lot while she was in jail. He was actually her foster brother, a member of the family that had finally let her stay, when she was thirteen and worn out from going place to place to place whenever a family got tired of her or one of the siblings got mad at her. He'd joined the Army when he was eighteen and had traveled all over the world. Right now he was in Afghanistan, a sergeant.

When she got home, she fed Athena and then put all of her utensils and supplies on the counter. She started water simmering in the skillet, about two inches deep. It boiled too much at first, and she turned the heat down until it was a mild simmer. To the water she added a tablespoon of vinegar, which Vita told her helped keep the eggs in shape. She'd cracked two eggs into single dishes and had a wooden spoon at the ready. Holding her breath, she poured the first egg into the water, and the whites instantly spread into goopy strings, which she tried to catch and spoon gently over the yolk.

"Argh!"

Athena jumped up on a chair to watch. Annie spooned out the messed-up egg and put it in a bowl. She tried again. And again. At egg number four, she started to get the rhythm. At number six, she almost nailed it. At number nine, she poached an egg perfectly and reproduced the action for eggs number ten, eleven, and twelve.

"Guess what we're eating for supper, cat?" she said, and laughed. Wiping her fingers on her apron, she kissed the kitten's white nose and sat down to write out a note to her brother.

Dear Joe,

You would never believe what I just spent an hour doing: cooking an egg in hot water, which is called poaching. You can poach eggs in salsa, too, which is awesome, but it's way hard in water. I finally got it! Whoot!

I hope you're being safe, taking care of yourself like you should. I just got your last letter, and you can't fool me— I know it's not all flowers and butterflies over there, but you're a good soldier and I know you know how to take care of yourself. Anybody who can get through the barrio can get through the desert! ☺

I'm writing from the table of my new apartment. I brought a red table over with me from the old place, my first "official" piece of furniture, which the manager let me switch for the table here. I moved on account of a cat that adopted me. Her name is Athena. I drew a pic for you. She sleeps with me and it feels so great. I love to hear her purr.

I've got the bracelet on for a year, but it ain't bad. Job is good. This old lady is teaching me to cook. Vita, who is more than sixty years old and still runs marathons! Crazy, huh? So far, I can fry eggs and make waffles and I'm learning to bake bread, which is really, really cool. Maybe sometime you can come for a visit.

Just wanted to let you know where to mail things now. I can get a cell phone maybe next month, and I can use the computer at the library, though I haven't had time for that since I got here. Same email as always, of course, but I like written letters! Don't stop writing! I like seeing your actual handwriting and stuff.

Okay, gotta go. I've had my hair dyed for ten years, and
I'm tired of it. Got some stuff to bring it back to the
normal color.
Write soon!

Love, Annie

In the quiet of her little house, Tessa uploaded the photos she'd taken earlier of Vince, realizing only as she plugged the camera into the laptop that she'd never uploaded the flower photos, either. She forgot about Sam's lies and the history of life and the mysteries clogging up her brain and fell into the pleasure of playing with line and shadow and color.

The series of flower stems through the bottom of the vase pleased her mightily, and she uploaded them to her Flickr groups, hungry for the feedback she knew she would receive.

Only then did she let herself open and admire the shots they'd taken naked. First Vince, then Tessa, and she liked the ones he'd taken of her but nowhere near as much as she liked the shots of him.

It was just that you never saw many good photos, art shots, of the male body, like you did of women. This was it. The light, hiding and revealing, washing over his beautiful skin with such softness, gave the photos an elegant mood. In one, the light caught on his jaw, the round of his shoulder, and his massive, muscular thigh. Everything else fell into shadow. In another, he looked directly at the camera, his belly and organ and thighs wide open to the viewer's gaze. It gave her a shiver. Sexy, definitely, but not sleazy.

But her favorite was one he'd shot—of his hand around her

breast. It was in perfect focus, and the light was again very quiet, making it look nearly like a black-and-white photo or even perhaps a sepia. His giant hand, fingers curling gently, pressing into the flesh of her breast, the nipple aroused and framed by his thumb. She sent it to him in email, and within a few minutes he called her.

"Jesus," he said. "That's so hot it makes me want to come over there right now."

"They're all beautiful, Vince, I'm not kidding. I could probably sell the ones of you."

He chuckled. "Don't you dare."

"I would never. Just saying." She clicked through them again. "Are the girls in bed, all safe and sound?"

"Yes. Jade and Natalie played jacks for two hours, so I think all is well."

"And the blouse?"

"Practically good as new. Thanks."

"I didn't do anything." She clicked through the photos. "I'm sending another one."

"Is it a naked one of you?"

"Wait for it." She smiled. It was the full frontal of him.

"Huh," he said. "I have to admit I like this one. Show your friends."

She laughed softly. "I don't exactly have any friends, or I would. I can post it on the Internet, if you like."

"Why don't you have any friends?"

"I mean, I do. All over. But not close friends." She flipped to the trio of their heads side by side on the pillows, looking up. The light caught their faces from the left, leaving the right in deep shadow. One eye each looked up. Hopeful. It made her feel airless. "I had a really nice time with you today, Vince."

"I always enjoy your company, Tessa. Seriously."

"Me, too." She even liked having him on the other end of the phone, hearing his voice. "Tell me a story about your life."

"What kind of story?"

"I don't care. Winning a race. A happy day. Talk me to sleep."

"I can do that," he said. "Go lie down."

Tessa carried the phone to her bedroom and did just that. "I really do mean a story story," she said. "Not a sexy something. I don't have any energy left."

"No," he said. "Me, either. This is about winning a race and landing an endorsement."

"Perfect." She closed her eyes. "I'm already getting sleepy."

Vince chuckled, the sound like a warm breath against her ear. He told her a story and she drifted into sleep. Outside, the wind began to howl.

Saturday morning, Vita awakened out of a sound sleep and bolted upright in the darkness. For a long, long moment she held her breath, listening, but only the slight, faraway drip of a faucet disturbed the silence. Her heart pounded wildly, and she pressed her palms to it protectively—had she had a bad dream?

No. Only the velvet of good sleep came to her.

Flinging off her covers, she padded over to the window in her pajamas and pushed the curtains aside, looking out to the alley behind 100 Breakfasts and the trail that led to the river. It was raining softly, steadily, and there was no one about, not even a stray dog climbing into trash cans.

And then she heard the wailing, an eerie, familiar moan that rose up from the river on nights like this. Some said it was the wind whistling through the boulders and caves along the banks. Some said it was the voices of the missionaries slain by the Indians, or the Indians slain by the soldiers, or the seven women who'd been stolen right out of the plaza by the Comanche during a wedding feast. It made the hair on her arms lift.

Tonight it sounded like a portent. Annie. It had to do with Annie and the man who skulked around town, hiding in plain sight, like an evil spirit. For the first time in decades, she remembered things that had been carefully boxed up and tucked away from view, dark things, sad things, things she regretted, things she mourned, things so far gone she could do nothing about them anyway.

Looking into the empty street, she rubbed her arms and then got dressed. It was only an hour early, and she wouldn't be going back to sleep. Cooking would make her feel better.

She went down to the kitchen and, for the first time ever, just before she turned on the overhead light, she felt afraid, looking into the darkness for some hint of what might be coming. She peered apprehensively into the gloom, seeing only the bones of the stainless steel counter and a ladle catching light from the other room.

In the air rose a scent of thyme, an herb that always made Vita think of the days when she first arrived at the commune. It had been planted along the paths and in the kitchen garden—parsley, sage, rosemary, and thyme, like a song. She saw herself, weary and too thin, rubbing a stalk of thyme between her palms and bending into it, closing her eyes to let the fragrance fill her head. She had made carnitas with it, with thyme and cinnamon sticks and local chiles. It was a dish to steal a man's soul, and whenever she made it at the café, there were always love affairs kindled, stories settled.

It was so adamantly pleasant that she found the courage to turn on the lights. Any ghosts that had been lingering scurried into the shadows, and she started the coffee and flipped through her books for something special to make for this Saturday morning. She set a pot of oil to heat for carnitas, pinched marjoram for protection into the sausages, and sprinkled rue and black pepper along the doorways, all the while feeling that creeping sense of unease, as if some miasma were floating beneath the doors with the cold wind.

When Annie finally came in, at five, Vita said, "Are you okay?"

"Great."

"It feels like there's something in the air," Vita said, shaking her shoulders, then she made a choice. With one hand on her hip, she looked right at Annie. "I didn't want to scare you, but I keep seeing a man skulking around here, and I worry it might be your ex."

The strangest smile moved on Annie's mouth. "Not *my* ex," she said. "When he killed my cat, I killed him."

Breakfast #38

Carnitas and Eggs: A traditional hearty breakfast for a body working the fields. Spiced shredded pork stewed with New Mexico chiles, cinnamon, and other secret ingredients, served with eggs cooked your way, fresh flour or corn tortillas, and a tall glass of cold milk.

SPICED CARNITAS

2 lbs. boneless pork shoulder
6 T corn oil
1 medium yellow onion, diced
4 garlic cloves, crushed and chopped

6 cinnamon sticks, broken into pieces
$1/2$ cup diced mild green chiles, roasted, skinned,
    and seeded (or use canned)
3 New Mexico red chiles, stems and seeds removed,
    broken into small pieces
1 tsp kosher salt
1 tsp freshly ground pepper
$1/2$ to 1 cup water
Flour or corn tortillas

FOR GARNISH:
2–3 limes, quartered
Diced tomatoes
Diced onion

In a large, heavy pot, heat the oil to 200 degrees and add the pork shoulder, whole. Cook over medium heat for about 1–$1^1/2$ hours, turning regularly to ensure a crispy brown surface all around the roast.

When it is finished, remove the pork, set aside, and add onions, garlic, and cinnamon sticks, and stir until onions are tender. Add the chiles and other spices. Cut pork into quarters and add it to the mix along with the water. Stew over medium heat until pork shreds into the mixture and flavors are well blended. Serve on warm tortillas with wedges of lime, tomatoes, and onion.

For breakfast, scramble eggs enough for your number and serve along with the carnitas.

TWENTY-THREE

S am was waylaid in Gallup by a broken axle that took two days to replace, but it was finally fixed late Friday night. By then he was in no mood to deal with semis rocking their way through the mountains and delayed his start until morning. It wasn't a real long drive.

About ten miles outside of Los Ladrones, he was overtaken by a fit of nerves and pulled into a rest stop to give the dogs an airing. The weather had followed him all the way across Arizona, and now the skies even in New Mexico, where the sun shone famously, were gray and dark. Rain fell in a light, steady mist. Cold. He'd forgotten how cold it could be at higher altitudes. He shrugged into a jeans jacket that was as old as Tessa and carried Peaches into the field. The trip had been kind of hard on the poor old thing. She was barely moving this morning, stiff and confused. Tonight he'd brush her good, and just seeing Tessa would make her feel better, too.

The other two dogs raced through the field, getting soaked by the low-growing stands of sage and long grasses. Along the rim of the world was a blue smudge of mountains, like pastels smeared beneath low gray clouds. It was very quiet, as if the trees were holding their breath.

It had been a long time since he'd come this way. More than thirty years. Even in the days when he and Tessa had traveled the Renaissance festival circuit, they'd never come through New Mexico, and given his choice, he would never have come this way at all, ever again. Too much drama. Too much trouble.

But he'd forgotten how beautiful it was.

As he waited for Loki and Wolfenstein to do their business, he leaned on the truck and let the air fill him. Clear, light, breathable. He thought of his old self, and "Born to Be Wild" played in his head.

Weren't they all?

What he could see from the distance of forty years was how wrecked he'd been by his tour of duty. Nowadays they'd treat his post-traumatic stress disorder with drugs—proper drugs, not street stuff—and therapy. In those days, they self-medicated with heroin and pot and vodka. Learned to sleep under bridges. A lot of them were still there. Sam counted himself lucky on that score.

He wished, oddly, for a cigarette, despite the fact that it had been a couple of decades since he'd given them up. Even at the height of his smoking, he'd never been a hard-core smoker— maybe four or five a day, but he'd really wanted each one. Over time, he came to see that he'd used cigarettes the same way he'd once used drugs or booze or faceless lays: just a way to escape his own thoughts.

So what thought did he want to escape right now? Was there some long-delayed regret rearing its ugly head?

No. He'd made a bargain with himself at the end of his tour that he'd never again do a single thing he didn't want to do. From that day to this, he never had. He had lived exactly in accordance with his beliefs. You didn't spend your life amassing stuff and pouring poisons down the drains of the world. You didn't work all day and all night to live for six seconds on a Saturday afternoon every week. You did unto others until it came to the defenseless and weak, and then you defended them as required. You took care of the creatures—human, feline, and canine—who came under your watch until death you did part.

He had done what he needed to do. And he believed that any man who established his own code and lived with integrity shouldn't have any regret. Even when other people judged you wrong.

This morning, however, he could use some courage. It was going to take all he had to walk into a town where everybody thought a little girl had drowned and smile as if he'd played a joke.

Picking up Peaches and carrying her into the truck, he whistled for the other dogs. "Time to face the music," he said, and got into the car. He didn't wear a watch on general principles, but, by the light, it was getting to be about mid-morning. He'd head for the café Tessa had been talking about, have something to eat, then chase down his daughter.

Tessa dreamed of a fire. There was a loud noise and a scream, and then a candle was knocked over, and the flames caught in the pine needles and rushed toward the forest. *"Run!"* someone said, and she grabbed her sister's hand and they rushed away.

Someone came from behind them and scooped them up, one on each side. *"Mama, put me down!"* she cried, terrified. Her mother had done something terrible. Terrible.

—a spill of blood coming out of a hole—

"Mama, no!"

But they were airborne, suspended in the dark, and then

they plunged into the icy-cold water that was rushing and rushing, sucking them under so fast that it shocked her. She broke the surface by luck and gasped, screamed, and was sucked under again. The river—the noise of it, rushing and roaring—drowned the sound of her cries. She bobbed up and was sucked under once more, and she splashed hard to get her head out of the water. And, again, blind chance lent a hand—a tree branch caught her wrist and she pulled her head out of the water and screamed, *"Help us! Help!"*

Then there were hands hauling her out, but Tessa screamed, *"Rhiannon! Rhiannon!"*

She jerked herself awake and sat up in the cool light of her bedroom. Her heart raced and she reached for a glass of water, taking a long, long swallow.

Not real. Or no *longer* real. Felix came over and nosed her shin. "I'm okay, baby."

But she couldn't shake the pall it cast over the day. She thought it might be a mistake to meet Vince and his girls at the café, but she hadn't seen him since Wednesday, when he came over and took the photos. She washed and dressed and headed out on foot, Felix happily trotting along with her.

When she entered the café, Vince and his girls were sitting in a booth by the window. For a minute Tessa hesitated, slammed by the tableau of family they presented. He had his head bent sideways, listening to something Hannah was saying. Her chubby little hands were clasped as she explained some long and involved something, and Vince nodded seriously, encouraging her story. Jade sat next to him, coloring in her Cinderella coloring book, the pale river of hair falling down her arm. Natalie had her back to the door, and she was flipping through a book, swinging her feet cheerfully. Affection pinched Tessa's ribs at the crazy tumble of her hair, her falling-down sock, the scabbed-over mosquito bites on her calf. She deserved so much more than she'd been given.

A voice in her whispered, *Here I am.*

And, in contrast, a little flutter of panic moved in her throat over Vince. His sexy, solid strength. His goodness. His gentleness. A rescuer, she thought now, like her father. Too much to want. Too much to ever lose. She couldn't bear it.

Better to never want anything.

But now that she had some background, some *truth,* she understood why she had always managed to stay aloof and apart and why—until Glenn stole her heart by so simply and clearly finding her wonderful—she had avoided becoming attached to anybody she could lose. Her mother had killed a man and then tried to kill Tessa. Her sister had died. She might not technically remember it, but she definitely remembered it on an emotional level.

And now here was this family. This man. This café and Vita and the whole bloody town capturing her.

Just as she was about to turn and bolt, Vince raised his head and caught sight of her. The barest of smiles touched his mouth, a smile filled with layers of secrets and knowledge and promises and a thousand things she had never imagined she would find. His dark eyes burned with a steady, reliable light.

Tessa thought, *Damn it.*

Seeing his smile, Natalie turned around and waved. Tessa waved back, and Natalie leapt out of the booth and headed across the room. "Come sit with us!" she said, sliding her hand into Tessa's.

"Hey," Tessa said, "you got new glasses!"

"Do you like them? The lady said square glasses are in fashion, and I do try to think of that sometimes."

"I love them," Tessa said, and it was honest. The glasses were dark-red rectangles, as bold and forward as Natalie's true inner self. "They're almost the same color as the Hawaiian salt, aren't they?"

"You're right!"

The door opened behind her, and Tessa stepped out of the way. "Sorry," she said without looking at the man coming in, "we're right in the doorway." They began to move toward the booth.

"Tessa?" the man said.

She turned, mouth opening in surprise. There was her father, looking both weary and absolutely dear, wearing a battered jeans jacket that he'd owned for decades. In the cool rainy light, his eyes were as blue as the mountains. She blinked. "Dad?"

He came forward.

"Wait." Tessa held up a hand to stave him off. "I'm so not ready to talk to you."

He inclined his head, eyes sad. "C'mon, Tessa. My intentions were honorable."

"Well, Dad, you know what they say about intentions. The road to hell and all of that."

"Is this your dad?" Natalie asked.

"Yes, but—"

From behind Tessa came a voice, airless. "Sam Harlow?"

Tessa saw her father go pale. "Holy shit! Vita?"

She came forward, looking sick to her stomach. "Yes."

"What are you doing here?" Sam asked. "Have you been here all along?"

"Yeah," she said, and her voice was stronger now. Angry. "This is my restaurant," she said. For one long, long moment, they stared at each other. "I thought you died. In the river."

Tessa narrowed her eyes, looked at her father. "What?"

"I know." Sam held one hand out to Tessa, palm up: *Wait.* The other hand cupped toward Vita, imploring. "It was—"

Another voice chimed in. "Oh, my God." Annie, too, had come out of the kitchen. "Oh, my God," she said again, her eyes shining with tears. "I'd know your voice anywhere. You're Sam—Uncle Sam with the magic tricks." She wiped her hands on her apron and held them out, folded them over her skinny chest, looking suddenly five years old. "Do you remember me? Annie? Rhiannon?"

Tessa's mouth opened. "Rhiannon?" She looked at her father. Tessa stared at Annie, seeing her badly cut, badly dyed hair, her skinniness, and her broken nose that had changed her face so much. Saw the wear and tear of years that Tessa had escaped, and she supposed, under it all, they did look alike. "*You're* Rhiannon?"

Annie gave Tessa a quizzical look. "Yeah. Do I know you?"

Sam said, "Tessa, let's talk for a minute before—"

Tessa looked from Sam to Rhiannon to Vita, and panic ripped right up her throat, into her head, and she did the only sensible thing under the circumstances.

She yanked her hand free of Natalie's and bolted.

From his booth, Vince saw the moment when Tessa ran out of the restaurant, leaving Natalie standing stiffly in the middle of the grown-ups. After a long moment, she turned and walked back to him, and he could see that she was trying very hard not to cry. "She left."

"I see. Come here, baby," Vince said, feeling his own cheekbones burn in sympathy. "It's nothing you did. She's upset about something with that man."

"It's her dad," Natalie said. She shrugged him off and sat down across the table, carefully not looking at anybody.

"Natalie," he said again, "she's mad at him, not you."

And all at once, looking at his daughter's crestfallen face, he knew why he should never have let a woman into his circle until he was sure of her. He'd been reckless and selfish, and the knowledge burned. He reached across the table and covered her hand. "Chin up, sweetheart. She'll come back."

"I don't care if she does. She's not my mother or anything."

Jade said, "Wow."

"Shut up," Natalie said, deadly quiet.

Damn it, damn it, damn it. Vince took a breath and looked at the man. Tessa's father. From Tessa's descriptions, he had imagined a ragged old hippie, but this man was tall and fit and very deeply tanned, weathered in the way of an outdoorsman, with steely-gray hair. He wore boots and jeans and a jeans jacket, just like everybody else in the room. He touched Vita with familiarity, closing his hand around her upper arm in a curiously tender gesture, then held up a finger to Annie, who stood there looking stunned.

Jade said, "Is that Tessa's sister?"

Annie. Rhiannon. *Of course,* Vince thought. "I think so." As children, they'd been identical. As adults, they had had such different lives that you had to look hard to see the resemblance. The long green eyes, the lanky limbs.

Xander's children, he thought. All of Xander's children had green eyes and those long limbs. What an asshole the man had been, littering the landscape with children who would never have a father.

Except Tessa. Tessa had had a father, and he ran after her now. Vince saw them through the window—Tessa leading Felix toward the north side of the plaza and her own street; her father sprinting after, remarkably agile for an old guy. He said something, and she turned furiously, warding him off with an upraised palm. Vince thought she might be crying. She stormed away, and the man let her go, watching her for a long time and then turning to come back inside. What the hell was going on?

Vince eyed Natalie. For today she was his first priority, but his heart went out to Tessa, too. Her life was an avalanche at the moment, everything sure crumbling away beneath her feet.

Vita tried not to show it, but her hands were shaking. She sent Annie back into the kitchen—"We'll all talk later"—and poured a cup of coffee for herself. Around her swirled the familiar Saturday morning noises, the clop and clatter of dishes, the ding of the bell as an order came in, the rising and falling hum of voices. She stood where she was, sipping the slightly burned coffee as she tried to center herself, to bring her fluttering thoughts back into some kind of order, but they wouldn't be herded. Memories, reactions, emotions all swirled together.

She watched Sam through the windows, watched as Tessa put up her guard against him, took her dog, and went into the market, disappearing. Sam stood for what seemed like a long time, staring after her, his body as lean and beautiful as it always had been. She was glad that he'd cut his hair, come into the modern era at least that much.

When he turned and headed back toward the café, Vita felt her heart pounding in surprise and reaction—fury and joy, sorrow and despair and joy again washing over her in wave after wave, soaking her body with sweat.

He came back in and crossed the room, holding her gaze unapologetically. His eyes were still the color of the lake, deep bright blue, with a laughing wickedness that nobody but a dead woman could help responding to. Even at—what?—sixty, sixty-two, he was very sexy. It made her chest hurt.

He sat down at the counter. As if he had not disappeared. As if she had not thought him dead for more than three decades. As if she had not thought of him ten thousand times over the years, always with terrible regret.

He gave her a half grin, the blue eyes twinkling, and said, "I'm so hungry I could eat an elephant. You always were a great cook. Whatcha got back there this morning?"

Vita slapped him, hard enough that he nearly fell off the stool. It shocked her. And the entire restaurant. The whole place went still; you couldn't hear a single fork or a voice.

Sam touched his cheekbone. "I reckon I earned that."

"You sure did," she said, and looked around. "Eat your breakfast, everybody. Show's over." She turned, took a cup off the stack, poured coffee into it, and put the cup down in front of Sam. "I'll get your breakfast. I guess I knew you were coming."

At least she knew why she'd made carnitas. They always had been his favorite.

Tessa walked up and down the rows of the farmers' market until her adrenaline slowed down. The rain had stopped. Felix paced with her, but he was panting by the time she finally stopped and went to sit on a bench beneath the hanging tree. There, smoking a cigarette not twenty feet away, was the Coyote Man, with his beautiful face and mean eyes. He had one hand in the pocket of his jeans and stared at the café as if he was waiting for someone.

She narrowed her eyes. Was he dangerous? He always

seemed to be skulking around, that air of red fury radiating from him like an evil fog. It touched her, made her feel sick to her stomach. Anger added to her own anger. She had half a mind to stomp over there and ask him his business.

What she wanted to do was bend over and put her head in her arms and cry like a two-year-old. She had told herself, all these years, that she was normal. Ordinary. Sensible. Despite the years wandering as a magician's daughter. Despite the strange story of her early life—who was born at a commune? Despite all of it, she had felt normal.

And now she had to admit she was not. Her father was not her father. Her life and history were all built on a lie. She had a sister, who had been lost to her all these years, who had suffered as Tessa had not, and who bore the scars.

Sitting in airless reaction, Tessa looked toward the café. Rhiannon. Annie. Her tattoos and sad eyes and broken nose and fierce survivor instinct. Tessa wanted to talk to her, but not with anyone else around. It seemed too private, too precious, to share.

Not, now that she thought about it, that Annie had seemed particularly interested in Tessa. She'd latched on to Sam. Why hadn't Sam taken Annie, too?

She buried her face in her hands. What a mess!

"You okay?"

She looked up to see Vince standing there. Jade and Hannah were with him, but Natalie was marching along the portico toward the salt store.

"Shit," she said, realizing that she'd yanked away from Nat when she grew so angry with her father. "I'm sorry. I was thoughtless, but I didn't mean to hurt her feelings."

"Yeah, well." He shrugged, but not in a good way. This morning he was wearing a long-sleeved ivory shirt that showed off the symmetry and power of his shoulders, his chest. "You did."

Tessa bowed her head. "Sorry."

Jade came over and patted her back. "It's okay. She gets mad all the time."

"It's never okay to be mean out of selfishness," Tessa said. "But thank you. Hey, by the way, how is your tooth?"

She smiled in an exaggerated way. "The dentist fixed it! Later I might have to do something different, but it's okay for now."

"Good."

Hannah crawled up on Tessa's lap and offered her a dandelion she had picked out of the grass. She smelled of little-girl sweat and syrup and that sweet, milky baby note that disappeared after the age of four or so. "Thank you, honey," she said, and looked up at Vince. "Do you want to sit down?"

"No. We're supposed to go through the farmers' market." He inclined his head. "How are you doing, sweetheart?"

She took a breath, blew it out, felt tears threaten. "I don't know. It's all craziness. That's my dad—my not-dad—back there, in case you didn't guess."

Jade said, eyes wide, "Vita slapped him!"

That startled a laugh out of Tessa. "Good. He deserved it." She frowned, wondering what Vita had to do with the whole sorry mess.

Natalie strolled out of the salt shop and came toward them, across the cobblestones of the plaza. For no reason she could have named, Tessa felt a ripple of foreboding.

A woman came out of the salt shop. "Young lady! Come back here right now!"

Natalie broke into a run.

"Shit," Vince said, and gave Tessa a look. "Watch these two, will you? I'll be right back."

TWENTY-FOUR

Natalie looped through the farmers' market in pure terror, her breath coming in ragged gasps as she navigated the fruits and corn and around a lady with a stroller. She bumped into a man who yelled, "Hey, watch out, little girl!" but she just kept going. She ran through the market and then into an alley and out onto the trail and finally behind the church, into the graveyard, where she fell, gasping for breath. She slunk down against the wall, careful not to land on a grave, and took the salt out of her pocket. It was the gigantic crystal of pink Himalayan, and she held it up to the light. She had looked up "Himalayan" on the Internet, and it turned out to be mountains near India, including Mount Everest, the tallest mountain in the world. So now she could think about people in turbans and pretty bracelets carrying this big rock out of the ground. So far away. If she was in the Himalayas, she would never get treated mean.

She started to cry and closed her eyes, leaning her head back against the wall. Why did she *do* that? She was going to get in so much trouble, and they would never let her in that store again, and she really loved it.

Hidden beneath the trees, sitting on the damp ground, she cried and cried, afraid to move, afraid to go find her dad, afraid not to. Afraid, afraid, afraid. She wished for Pedro, or even Sasha. She wished for her grandma, all pinch-mouthed. She wished for her dad, even mad.

Most of all, she wished for her mother. She wanted her mommy to come and sit and brush her hair. She wanted her mommy to give her a bath and fix her torn blouse and tell her everything was going to be okay.

On the breeze, as if someone was right close by, came the sound of a lady singing. *"There are suitors at my door, o le le o bahia,"* the voice sang. *"Six or eight or even more, o le le o bahia. And my father wants me wed, o le le o bahia. Or at least that's what he said, o le le o bahia."*

Natalie looked around, holding her breath, but she was alone by the graves. There were no windows.

> *"And I told him that I will, o le le o bahia*
> *When the rivers run uphill, o le le o bahia*
> *And the fish begin to fly, o le le o bahia*
> *And the day before I die, o le le o bahia."*

It was her mother's voice. She didn't know how. She didn't know where her mother was, but she knew that voice. It had sung her to sleep over and over, brushing her hair back from her forehead. She could feel her doing it now, brushing her hair, softly, softly, singing and then humming.

"It will be all right, Natalie," she whispered. *"Go to sleep. It will be all right. I will always love you, you know. Always, always and forever."*

Natalie fell asleep, the enormous Himalayan salt rock clutched in her hand.

· · ·

Tessa still held Hannah on her lap when the priest came into the plaza carrying a soundly sleeping Natalie. The frantic search was called off, and everyone went back to the market, murmuring among themselves. Vince took Nat into his arms and gave the salt back to the store owner.

"I want her properly charged," the woman said.

"I understand," Vince said. Tessa could see that Natalie had been crying hard, and it made her feel sick to her stomach. She wanted to apologize, wanted to make it right, but how? Broken trust was not easily repaired.

"I give you my word as a man and a father that I'll bring her back to you and we can deal with it. But not today. Please."

She narrowed her eyes. "Fine."

"Let me help you," Tessa said.

"No."

She looked up, startled. "How are you going to get everybody into the truck?"

"You have some other things to take care of, Tessa," he said, and lifted his chin toward the café. "We'll be okay. Jade, Hannah, come on."

Hannah climbed down, gave Tessa a wave, and trotted after her father and sisters, leaving a cold spot along the front of Tessa's body and her arms empty.

It was only then that she saw her father, sitting on the other side of the tree, watching her, waiting for her to be free. Loki and Wolfenstein sat tidily beside him, and he had Peaches in his arms, whom he knew she would not be able to resist. When she looked at him, he stood up with the dog in his arms and crossed the hilly terrain of the tree roots, moving with simple grace, like Christ carrying the lamb. Loki and Wolf, black and gold, trotted beside him, until they spied her, then they dashed over, whirling and dancing in happy greeting. Felix edged a little closer to her, and she used one hand to reassure him, the other to pet the wiggling dogs.

Her father stopped in front of her. "Peaches is missing you," he said.

Tessa nodded and opened her arms, accepting the old, old poodle. "Hey, Peaches," she said, and nuzzled her neck. Peaches made a soft, sharp sound of surprise, realizing that it was Tessa who held her, and Tessa nearly cried. "How's my sweet little girl," she crooned, petting the thin fur, rubbing her hips and spine, then her chest and belly when Peaches turned over. She sang the first song that came into her mind, which was "Amazing Grace," and Peaches closed her eyes and practically purred. Tessa chuckled.

Sam squatted next to Felix. "This must be Brenna, huh?" He gave the border collie the same attention Tessa gave Peaches. "What a good pup."

Holding Peaches close, Tessa said, "So, I had a sister?"

"Looks like you still do," he said, meeting her eyes.

She took a breath, feeling utterly, completely exhausted. "I don't know what to do with that. With any of this."

"I know. I should have stopped you from coming here in the first place."

"Dad!" Anger flared in her chest again. "The secrets would still be secret. I would still not have a clue who I am. My whole life is a lie."

His mouth turned down under his mustache, as if he was weighing that. "No, it isn't," he said calmly. "I'm real. Our life has been real."

She bowed her head. Peaches curled up against her breasts.

Her father straightened. "Why don't you come on back to the café later, after it closes. We can all sit down and talk."

A wave of excruciating shyness filled her at the idea of

sitting down with Annie, knowing they were once—that they were—sisters. "She's my twin."

"Yeah."

A woman approached from the farmers' market, walking quickly. Sam turned and smiled. "Hey, Paula," he said.

"I knew it was you," she said, and let go of a little happy laugh. "Damned if you aren't just as gorgeous as you ever were!"

Sam hugged her back, and Tessa saw him close his eyes, his hands in fists. Strong emotion made him twitch his mustache. "Have you met my daughter?" he said.

"I have," Paula said, smiling that beneficent smile. "She's been out to the farm—the old commune. We're Green Gate Farms now, Sam. You should come see it. You won't believe it. A lot of the animal policies you taught us are still in place." She laughed. "We sell a lot of goat cheese."

"No kiddin'?"

She touched her heart. "Oh, Sam, it's so good to have you back." She squeezed his arm. "Come see me at the end of the farmers' market over there and I'll give you a phone number. We'll catch up. You should see Cherry. I'm really proud of her."

"I'll be over in just a minute."

Tessa, feeling weak, stood. "I have to go for a while. I'll see you later." She gave her father his dog, then put a hand to her head and realized that she'd never eaten. "Whoa. Dizzy. I need to eat."

"You all right, honey?" Paula said. "Figuring things out now?"

Tessa looked at her father. "I think so. Thanks."

She went home, had a cheese sandwich, and fell asleep with Felix curled up against her back for a couple of hours. When she woke, it was time to go back to 100 Breakfasts.

Where she sank heavily onto a stool in the now-empty café. Vita brought her a cup of tea. "He's not here yet. "

It was then that Annie came out of the kitchen, dressed in street clothes. She sat down next to Tessa. "So," she said, and her voice was perfectly even. "Guinnevere?" She held out her hand, and tears were shimmering in her eyes. "I'm Rhiannon. I thought you died."

All of the emotion that had been building suddenly burst in Tessa's heart. She put her arms around her sister and wept. "I didn't even know you existed until I came here. I'm so sorry."

Annie hugged her back fiercely, her skinny arms strong. She smelled of lavender. "It's not your fault."

Vita brought out a wet cloth for each of them, and, laughing, they washed their faces with the cold towels. "Feels good," Tessa said. "It's been such an emotional day. I'm exhausted."

"Yeah. I can't believe it." Annie looked at Tessa's face, touched her own. "Weird that we could be identical and look so different, huh?" Her eyes glittered. "I would be as pretty as you if—"

"Don't," Tessa said, bowing her head. "I hate to think of the things you had to go through. I want to know them, but right now it's hurting my heart."

"I understand."

"What happened to you? How did you get lost?"

"I don't remember a lot," she said, chewing on her inner lip. "I remembered you. I remembered her throwing us in the river. I remembered Sam. I washed up downriver, and I had a broken jaw, so I couldn't talk for quite a while. And they never found a record of me, or anyone who was looking for me, so I went into the system in Albuquerque." She shrugged.

An intense sense of loss and guilt seized Tessa. In one small shrug, she saw all that Annie had lost: No one was looking for her. No one cared. Her own mother had tried to drown her. "I am so sorry that was your life."

"It wasn't all bad," she said. "I have a great brother. He's in the Army, and sometimes he sends me a plane ticket to wherever he's stationed. I lived once for a whole year in Germany with him." She swallowed. "I was trying to get away from Tommy, my husband. Almost made it that time."

"I didn't remember anything," Tessa said. "Just this big jumble. But a few months ago, I was on a hiking trip and got caught in an avalanche and we went in a river, and then I remembered the first time. I sort of remembered that somebody was with me."

Annie touched the cast on Tessa's arm. "I broke my arm in the spring. I've had the cast off for only a couple of months."

"Weird, right? Have you ever broken anything else?"

"No. Well, my face." She rolled her eyes.

Vita came back with her cell phone. "Can you see this guy?"

The door opened, ringing the bell. All three of them—Vita, Annie, and Tessa—turned to wait.

Sam came in and looked at each one of them in turn. Tessa knew him well enough to recognize his nervousness. Half of her wanted to reach out and squeeze his arm. The other half thought it did him some good to suffer.

The mean half won.

"Vita," he rasped. "Can I get a cup of coffee?"

He doctored it and then said, "All right, I guess you want the story, don't you?"

Sam kept his eyes on Tessa. She had rings under her eyes and a look of dread in them. It was eerie how Annie, sitting beside

Tessa, looked like a "before" picture in a magazine ad for a makeover. They hardly looked the same at all.

"Once upon a time," he began, "there was a man who was completely lost. He saw things nobody should have to see. Did things he should never have been asked to do."

"Cut the third person, Dad," Tessa said. "Take ownership."

He paused, stung, and then nodded. "My tour broke something in me. Soggy feet and dead soldiers and women doing things just to survive that don't bear thinking about. When I got back here, I dived right in to drugs and drinking and women." He sighed. "Not saying it was right, just that it was what I did. What a lot of us did."

She did touch his hand then, and he nodded.

"One summer in about '71, '72, me and some of my buddies landed at the commune, over across the river. I could breathe there. The land was beautiful, and for a while, it seemed like it might really be something different, you know? I had some understanding of animals and farm work, so there was plenty for me to do, and teach, and I liked it. I liked all the kids, though i didn't like the way y'all were living."

Vita made a noise of agreement. "It was pretty awful in the main house. Cottages were okay, you have to admit."

"I guess. Anyhow, you kids did a lot for me," he said, "and I did all kinda magic tricks and made you laugh and we all had a good time."

"That's what I remember," Annie said. "Origami and really good card tricks."

"I don't remember," Tessa said, and her face looked so sad, he wanted to hug her.

"Maybe you will eventually," Vita said.

"I was seeing a woman for a while," Sam said, "and she had a couple of kids and it was good. But there was one little girl who captured me." Sam licked his bottom lip and looked at Annie. "Sorry to say it this way, honey, but I've gotta tell the real truth."

"My feelings aren't hurt. I was crazy about my own dad."

Sam nodded. "So you were. Xander. I'd forgotten that. Followed him around like a little puppy, and he was good to you."

Tessa made a noise of impatience, very unlike her, and he gave her a sharp look. She had the grace to look down.

"Anyway, there was a little girl who stole my heart right out of my chest. I couldn't tell you why, exactly. She wasn't the prettiest girl or the smartest. She was just interesting. Funny, with this deep beautiful voice that wasn't like anybody else's. And her mama was one rotten, strung-out bitch. Used to make me so mad. She'd leave you two with anybody, do anything. Never fed you right. You were always living in rags. Always hungry." Sam looked at Vita. "Remember?"

Vita nodded. "That house was a wreck. Amazing it didn't fall down around their ears."

"After a while, things went south. I can't remember what started it, exactly. Xander was a piece of work, such a ladies' man—"

"Slut," Vita said.

Sam met her eyes, clear and deep and strong, and something kindled between them, flaring. He remembered her back in the day, dark hair falling down her back, eyes flashing with passion and fury. For the first time in a very, very long time, he felt a quickening in his old body.

"Slut works," he agreed. "He had a harem of women, and one of them was your crazy mama. Most everybody accepted things as they were, and when they got tired of it, they moved on. But your mama came out to the commune with Xander. If there was a pecking order, Winnie would have been the queen. At least five or six women had his children, and he slept with a heck of a lot more than that. If a woman came to the commune, he usually found a way to sleep with her."

"Not me, for the record."

Annie frowned. "Why did I remember Sam and not you?"

"I look a lot different," Vita said. "Sam cut his hair, but he's still Sam."

He grinned, then took a breath, thinking about that year Vita came to the commune. It was early summer. Morning glories were blooming in a big tangle all over the place, Sam had just talked Jonathan into trying goats for goat cheese, and down the road came Vita. Skinny, shell-shocked, scared. Sam had recognized a kindred spirit. She was so skittish that it took him a while, but he wooed her into his bed, and she started to heal under his ministrations. They found a place for her in the kitchens, and she gained some weight, even though she was running all up and down the river valley like some kind of crazy person. She was outrunning her old man.

Bastard.

It infuriated Sam that any man had so mistreated his lover, and her scars and marks were his sorrow. For the first time in his life, he let a woman in.

"It was a pretty crazy summer that year. Vita came," he said, and their eyes met. "It was real hot and dry, and forest fires were sparking all over the place. The crops weren't doing so well, the commune was broke, Xander's women were fighting, and a bunch of freaks showed up, doing way too many drugs." He shook his head, twitching his thumb against the bottom of his coffee cup. "It was all falling apart. Lot of bickering, fist-fights, that kind of thing," Sam said. "A fight over a woman, the children all restless and fighting with one another."

"Andy drowned at the hot springs, too," Vita said. "I think that freaked a lot of people out."

"Right. Drunk as a skunk, but nonetheless." He looked at Tessa. Again the shadows under her eyes went through him. "The idyll was over," he said. "I wanted to get out of there, but I didn't want to leave Guinnevere."

He cleared his throat. "Even the weather was crazy. First the forest fires, then too much rain, and we got worried about flooding. Crazy thunderstorms every stinkin' day."

Tessa simply listened, her eyes on his face, mouth impassive.

"And then Winnie found Xander in bed with a fifteen-year-old runaway, and she completely lost it."

"Winnie was our mother, right?" Annie said. She stuck her hands in her back pockets. "I remember this part."

Vita reached over and touched her arm.

"We were playing in the tower," Annie said, looking at Tessa. "My dad was singing to us, and Mama came in and had a gun, and she shot him in the chest. Blood came pouring out so fast it looked like it was fake."

"In the tower?" Tessa said, looking at her sister with bewilderment. "Wouldn't you think I'd remember something like that?"

"That's when she took us to the river," Annie said. "And threw us in."

"I heard the shot," Sam said, nodding grimly, "and went after her. I saw her jump, and I knew she'd thrown you both in ahead of her." Even thirty-something years later, the memory slayed him—seeing Tessa bobbing in the water, so far below. He'd run as hard as he could to get her and nearly lost her twice. When he finally hauled her out, she'd been sick as a dog, throwing up river water for an hour. "I got Guinnevere out, but there was no sign of Winnie or Rhiannon." His voice was raw. "No sign."

Vita picked up the story. "There was a lightning strike near the camp, and it sparked a pretty huge fire—we had all been evacuated. It was several days before we realized that Xander was dead. By then, Winnie and you two were gone, presumed drowned, and Sam was nowhere to be found, so we thought he'd drowned, too." She cleared her throat. "I don't know what happened after that night."

Sam bowed his head, wishing he could make it up to Vita, at least. She'd surely been wounded in all of that. "I really did do what I thought was the right thing," he said, looking at each of their faces in turn.

No one replied, so he took a breath and went on. "You were pretty sick for a few days," Sam said to Tessa. "I took you to a motel up in Alamosa, and when you woke up, you couldn't remember anything right, like somebody scrambled your brains. When you started talking, all you remembered was the story I told you to give anybody who asked: that you were my daughter, and your name was Tessa, and we were going to a Renaissance festival."

Her face opened, flowering with memory. "Oh, I do remember this part! We had breakfast at a place with little jukeboxes on the table."

"Right," he said. "It was a blessing that you couldn't remember your own mother trying to kill you, that you couldn't remember your sister. So I left it alone."

"Maybe," Tessa said. She closed her eyes, shaking her head. "I need to think about it all. I'm sorry, all of you. I want—I just—" She stood up. "I can't take it in." She headed for the door, then stopped and turned around. "Why Tessa?" she asked. "I don't get how you came up with Tessa."

Annie said, "I know. It was my doll's name."

Tessa came back, took Annie's hand, and said, "Let's go to the river."

Which left Sam and Vita alone. He looked at her, but she picked up the empty cups and slammed them into the tub beneath the counter. "Don't even start," she said. "I loved you."

"I loved you, too," he said, and meant it.

"You couldn't have taken me with you?"

Sam took a breath. "It never crossed my mind."

She looked at him for a long time, then shook her head. "Well, at least that's honest."

Breakfast #32

Goat cheese and apple tart: Our savory and delicate tart served with spicy vegetarian sausage patties and cinnamon tea.

GOAT CHEESE AND APPLE TART

FOR THE CRUST
$1^3/_4$ cups flour
2 T sugar
1 tsp salt
$1/_2$ tsp baking powder
$1/_2$ cup butter, chilled and cut into pieces
5 T ice water

Thoroughly mix dry ingredients, then cut in butter using a pastry blender until the dough resembles small peas. Add

5 tablespoons of water and mix quickly, then roll dough out into a round, using a cold surface and chilled rolling pin if possible, then slide into a 10-inch glass pie pan. Partially bake for 8–9 minutes in a 400-degree oven.

FOR THE FILLING
1 onion, thinly sliced
2 large tart apples, cored and thinly sliced
¼ cup butter
8 oz. crumbled goat cheese
½ cup Parmesan cheese, grated
½ tsp fresh ground pepper
2–3 green onions, sliced into ¼-inch rounds
4 eggs, beaten with ½ cup cream

Sauté the onion and apples in butter in a heavy skillet until just tender. Place a thin layer of mix on the bottom of the tart, add a layer of goat cheese, and then apples and onions, alternating layers. Sprinkle with Parmesan cheese, fresh pepper, and green onions, then pour eggs and cream mix over the top. (The pie shell should not be more than ⅔ full to allow for expansion.) Bake in a 375-degree oven for 30 minutes, or until the top is slightly brown. Let stand for ten minutes, then serve.

TWENTY-FIVE

Tessa and Annie walked through the plaza toward the river trail. "Do you remember all of this?" Tessa asked.

"No. I didn't actually know that Los Ladrones was the town I remembered from those years."

"So you didn't come here on purpose?"

"No, they sent me here through the penal system." She smiled. "Weird, huh?"

Tessa nodded, shot Annie a glance. "I feel kind of shy with you, but I want to know everything about you."

"Me, too. Exactly." She pointed at a little apartment block. "I just moved in right there."

"Really." Tessa stopped. Pointed toward the cottage she had rented. "I just moved in right there, because I adopted a dog."

Annie laughed. "I found a cat, and I couldn't leave her. Her name is Athena."

Tessa's mouth opened. "I remember Athena! A white cat, right?"

"Yeah, yeah, yeah!" She clasped Tessa's hands. "You'll end up remembering all of it eventually, I bet."

"I would like that."

They walked in silence, and Annie said, "Do you drink coffee?"

"No, I don't really like the taste. I like tea. How about you?"

"Same! Coffee smells great, but I think it tastes terrible. So bitter! Do you put sugar and milk in your tea?"

"Yes. Two sugars and milk."

Annie nodded in satisfaction, and Tessa asked a favorite color. Orange, for both. They traded preferences, back and forth. It started to be silly and fun, missing only a few things.

When they got to the river, Tessa stopped. "Have you been down here? Did you know this was the river where we nearly drowned?"

"Is it?" She looked at it dispassionately. "Pretty. I'm not getting any bad feelings about it, though. Does it bother you?"

"No, I've been down here several times now."

Annie said, "What's with you and the girls' dad? Are you involved with him?"

"Hmmm. Kind of. We're sleeping together, but I'm trying not to get too attached. I'm only here to try to set up a tour, and my boss just nixed it."

Annie stopped and faced Tessa, a sharp New Mexico *tsk* falling out of her. "You're leaving? I thought maybe with your dad coming here and all—"

"What would I do for work?"

"I don't know. What do you like doing?"

"Photography," she said, surprising herself. "I always wanted to be a photographer, but I got sidetracked."

Annie laughed. "Of course you did. I'm an artist!"

"What kind of things do you do?"

"Color," she said. "I'm not that good at it yet, but it makes me happy. You'll have to show me your photos." She inclined her head. "Please stay for a little while, so we can get to know each other again."

Tessa nodded. "I'm here for a month, anyway. We'll see after that."

"Okay."

They walked for a time, talking about nothing and every-thing, and all the shyness Tessa had been feeling dropped away. She started to feel less and less angry at her father, too, at the world in general.

And then she thought of Natalie. "I have to go back. There's something I have to do."

"I need to get a nap!" Annie said. "It's been such an emotional day!"

Tessa put an arm around her, a head on her shoulder. "In a good way."

As they came close to town again, in the shadows of the portico Tessa saw the Coyote Man. "Look," she said. "There's the man I was telling you about. I keep seeing that man everywhere. Do you know him? He's staring right at us."

Annie smiled very softly. "You can see him?"

"Can't you?"

"Yes," she said, and took Tessa's hand. "It's my husband, Tommy. I killed him when he killed my cat. That's why I went to jail."

Tessa stared at her sister. "What?"

"He always said he'd follow me into hell if that's what it took." She laughed. "I seem to be his hell."

Tessa looked back, and even from this distance she could feel the radiating anger, so fierce and terrible. "He doesn't frighten you?"

Annie shook her head. "No. He's so angry only because he can't do anything to me anymore. I think his purgatory is having to watch me being happy. When he makes reparation, he'll be able to move on."

Tessa looked back, but he was gone. "Can you still see him?"

"No. Usually no one but me ever sees him. Not so odd that you saw him, I guess, but kind of interesting that Vita did."

"She was abused, a long time ago, remember? Maybe that's it." Tessa paused. "She's not our mother, is she?"

"Now, that I'm sure of. No. She isn't." Annie turned. "Give me a hug, Guinnevere."

Tessa hugged her sister. "Rhiannon. I'm so glad to find you."

Annie's mention of reparation gave Tessa an idea. She needed to go see Natalie. That moment of yanking her hand out of Nat's replayed itself in her head over and over, and she had to try to make it right.

Just as her father, she supposed, was trying to make things right.

Reparation.

As she drove out to Vince's house—not entirely sure she remembered the way—everything Sam said replayed itself in her mind. It was very difficult to imagine the tidy, productive, and prosperous Green Gate Farms as the place Sam painted for them, but in a way she sort of remembered some of it. Peeing outside. Always scrounging for food from people in this tepee or that cottage.

She made one wrong turn, then managed to find the right dirt road that led to Vince's house. The clouds were now breaking up over the mountains, and long gold fingers of sun reached toward the land. She got out of the car with her mouth open at the extravagant beauty and grabbed her camera off the seat. It was always hard to capture light effects like this—the mountains deep, deep blue and smeary, the clouds gray and peach and sculpted like batting, and the needles of light poking through the fabric, pointing into the fields as if there were treasures buried in each spot. Pedro barked and came running toward her, and she shot him, too, beautiful dog. Felix whined to get out of the car, and she wavered, then let him.

Vince stood on the porch, thumbs caught on his pockets. "How're you doing?" he asked.

She focused on him, too, then lowered the camera and approached. "I'm okay."

He came down the steps a little way, stopped. "I've been thinking, Tessa, that maybe this thing between us is causing trouble. You have your ways and I have mine, and maybe—" He took a breath. "Maybe you were right all along."

Tessa struggled to keep her face neutral. "Kind of a bad day to tell me this."

"I know. I'm just worried about Natalie. That she'll start trying to replace her mom with you and get her heart broken all over again."

Tessa shrugged, as if she didn't care. As if it didn't matter. "It's Natalie I came to see, actually. Can I talk to her?"

"I don't think so, Tessa." He rubbed his face. "She's emotionally exhausted."

Tessa gave a short laugh. "I know the feeling," she said, and her voice was raw. She cleared her throat. "The thing is, I think I know how to help her, Vince. I have an idea."

"What kind of idea?"

"I want to walk the pilgrimage route with her. Do it right, barefoot, and carry an offering. Atone, and make peace."

He frowned. "Why would that help?"

"The priest told me that's why people do a pilgrimage, and that's why it's always some test, really long or barefoot or whatever—so you make reparation."

"I don't know," he said.

Anger made her sharp. "Stop being a coward."

"Look who's talking."

Touché. She nodded, held her camera, looked off to the horizon. "You know, Vince, a person doesn't have to be a permanent fixture to be valuable, to be important." Her heart was aching on some deep, deep level. Something about the set of his mouth, the burly way he stood in protection of his girls, pierced her. "Life is a mosaic."

"I'll think about it."

She nodded. "Okay."

As she headed back to the car, Sasha came from behind the house, moving much more fluidly than she had been. "Hey, Sasha!" Tessa said, and bent to greet the ancient dog. "You should meet my dad's dog Peaches. The two of you could tell some old lady stories."

Sasha barked, and then spied the other two dogs and ran to join them. Tessa stood, smiling.

Behind her, Vince said, "When you met Pedro, did he get hit by a car or something?"

She turned. "Why do you ask?"

"Just asking."

Tessa nodded. "Yes. That's why I stopped. But he was okay." She felt awkward, as if her hands were too big, as if she was wearing a stained blouse. The person she had always been would have shrugged and whistled for her dog, climbed back into her car, and driven away.

Well, no, because she wouldn't have had a dog, either.

Whatever. She put two fingers to the bridge of her nose,

thought of Annie and Vita and her father and everything that had happened in the past couple of weeks, and said, "Vince, I would really like a chance to make this right with Natalie." She stood her ground, hands on hips. "Please. I know a little bit about betrayal, too, you know."

He came down the steps, and all the invisible, blistered places on her skin, every single place that he'd kissed, started to burn. Around them, the sky was going orange and purple, those crazy fingers of light dancing across the fields, and she felt utterly disoriented.

"You can't just play with people," he said.

She made a noise of exasperation and briefly closed her eyes. "I am not playing. I have been absolutely honest with you from day one."

He stood five feet away, as if he didn't dare come any closer. The light flashed over his hair, touched his mouth, as if he were a saint. She raised the camera and shot a photo. It made her belly hurt. She had stored up so many things to tell him, and now she would never be able to.

She waited for him to say something, but he just stood there, his feet bare, his eyes dark and unreadable.

"I guess I'll go."

He nodded.

Back at her house, Tessa fell into a deep sleep, as if her mind needed time to sort everything to its proper place. She woke up, made a cup of tea, and thought of the crazy light this afternoon. With excitement, she fired up the laptop, plugged in the camera, and uploaded the shots.

She gave a little squeal, and Felix came over to lick her ankle. "These are amazing, baby! A-*maz*-ing." It was the perfect combination of circumstances—the right geography, the right location for the best shots, the right camera, everything—to capture that exquisite, incredible light show. She sent the shots to her Flickr account and saw there was mail in her in-box. First she tagged and labeled the shots, and then she opened the mail.

Dear Tessa,

I'm the administrator of a national photography fellowship, and I would like to invite you to submit your portfolio for consideration. The winning photographer will be asked to shoot a natural environment for a feature in National Geographic *next year. I have loved your series in Los Ladrones and highly encourage you to submit your portfolio as soon as possible. The information is below. Please contact me with any questions.*

Sincerely,
Matthew Barker

Out of sheer force of habit, Tessa picked up her phone and dialed her father. It was ringing on the other end before she realized she was still mad at him. When he answered, she was about to hang up, and then it seemed so stupid to hold a grudge that she said, "Hi, Dad."

"Hey, kiddo."

"I've been thinking . . . want to come to my house for dinner?"

"Absolutely."

"Good," she said, and couldn't help laughing. "I have the most amazing thing to show you."

"Can't wait."

Then she called Vince. He picked up and she said, "Stop being so rigid, will you? We don't have to be lovers anymore if you don't want to be, but I'd really like to walk with Natalie."

"I was going to call you," he said, and even the sound of his voice rushed through her like a song, like magic, like morning. She closed her eyes, pressing the earpiece closer to her head. "I talked to her counselor, and she seemed to think it might be a really good idea."

"Good."

"She has something to say to you."

Tessa wasn't sure if he meant the counselor until Natalie came on the line. "Hello?"

"Hi, Nat. You're going to walk with me?"

"Yes," she said firmly. "But I also want to tell you something." Her diction was clear and precise.

"I'm listening."

"You were mean this morning."

"I know, Natalie. I am so sorry. There's no excuse. I was thoughtless and I'm very sorry."

"Okay. I forgive you."

Tears sprang to Tessa's eyes, and she blinked. "I'm so glad, sweetie. Your opinion matters to me."

"Does it?"

"Yes," she said firmly.

"My grandma said you just found out you have a twin sister. Is that true?"

"It is true. Weird, right?"

"And your sister is Annie at the café?"

"Yes."

"That's good," Natalie said. "You both seem kind of lonely to me."

Tessa bit her lip. "Thanks, kiddo. Bye."

"Bye."

Tessa waited in case Vince came back on, but he didn't. She frowned, then decided to let it go. For now.

When Sam approached the little house Tessa had directed him to, he felt more than a little exhausted. It had been a day of too many revelations, and he wanted to be somewhere he could let his hair down.

Tessa and Brenna–Felix came to let him in. He was carrying Peaches. The other two dogs sat politely in the courtyard, waiting for instructions. "You want them in or out?"

"Not a lot of room in here. They can stay in the courtyard. It's safe." She gestured to Felix. "Go ahead, honey. You can visit. They'll be nice, I promise."

Loki bowed at the sight of a new friend and gave a happy bark. Felix edged out warily, but within a few minutes they were romping together. Sam put Peaches down, and she toddled over to the area rug and sat down with a sigh. "She's doing better now she's got her Tessa back," he said.

She nodded. Smiled. "Give me a hug, Dad. *You 'came a long way just to explain,'*" she said, speaking in music lyrics. He nearly broke down.

He hugged her, hard, and all the Tessas she had been came rushing through him—the little girl, the tomboy, the princess who autocratically ruled the Renaissance festival kids, the teenager dressed in pop fashion who listened to Top 40 radio and loved musicals, the wandering student who found a calling in tourism.

And now, a fully grown woman, who seemed whole here in a way she never had before. "What do you have to show me?" he asked.

She laughed and led him into the room. "This is freaking

awesome," she said, and showed him the note and the photos of the light.

"I'm proud of you, Tessa," he said.

"Thanks." She took a breath and folded her hands loosely, leaning forward. "I need you to listen to me for a minute, okay? No interrupting or protesting or anything else."

Sam nodded.

"I get it that life is not all black and white. I think you did believe you were doing the right thing to take me, and maybe you were, I don't know. But I also think you've got to make amends somehow for the messes you've made."

"Make amends how?"

"I don't know. That's up to you. I'm guessing that it will have something to do with Green Gate Farms or maybe with Vita. Whatever it is, it's yours."

He didn't say anything for a long while, then finally he nodded. "I reckon there's a lot of good sense in that. And if you're staying here, I guess I am, too."

"I don't know if I am."

Sam smiled to himself. He knew.

It was early morning, and cool, a week later, when Tessa and Natalie took off their shoes at the bottom of the hill. Tessa's foot still showed the dark scar from her spider bite, but it no longer hurt. She had no illusions about the pilgrimage route—it probably *would* hurt by the end of the day, but it was worth it.

She and Natalie each had a bottle of water and a small pack over their shoulders. "Do you have everything?" Tessa asked.

Natalie nodded soberly.

Father Timothy had pinned a pilgrim's badge to each of them, blessing them with a prayer before they began. They walked alone, without dogs, and the rule was to walk in absolute silence. Because it was a hard, long climb, they'd worked out a signal that Natalie could use if she needed to stop or if it was becoming too difficult.

"I'm ready if you are," Tessa said.

"I'm ready."

Tessa gestured for Natalie to go ahead of her, and they began to walk. At first it was not terribly unpleasant to be barefoot. The path was smooth dirt, and cold, but not unduly so. Tessa turned her mind to Lisa, to remembering and honoring her. She carried a photo of the young woman in her pocket. Natalie carried a photo of her mother and something else she wanted to leave as an offering at the shrine at the top. She didn't tell Tessa what it was.

In silence, they walked up and up. The sun came over the mountain and touched their heads, and still they walked. The silence and the steady movement put Tessa into a meditative state where things became clear. Or at least clearer. It was what she loved most about walking.

Because of her injury, she had not had many chances over the past few months. It had knocked her off balance, especially when she had so many things to think about, so many things that had shifted in her life. Things lost, things found, things given away and rearranged.

As they climbed, the trail grew rockier and more uncomfortable. They had to slow down and pick their way over sharp stones sticking out of the ground and beware of roots. Tessa stubbed her toe and it started to bleed, but it wasn't bad enough that she felt she had to stop, and they kept going. A little while later, Natalie cut her heel on something, and they looked at it silently, but it was not bad, either. Their eyes met and they kept walking.

Walking higher and higher, Tessa gave thought to what she wanted. If she was honest with herself, she had been drifting since Tasmania, shaken by the loss of a dream she really had wanted and believed in. She had believed she would settle with Glenn, leave the wandering life behind, and have a baby or two, maybe move her father into a cottage nearby.

For the past two years, she'd been leading tours only because she had no idea what else to do, how to arrange her life, what she wanted it all to look like.

As she walked a pilgrim's trail, she allowed the possibility that she had been blocking her happiness by never naming anything she wanted.

So what *did* she want? If she made no judgments and resisted all fear, what did she want, big and small?

A different job. This one had become too exhausting for her nearly forty-year-old self.

A place to belong.

Her sister close by, and her father.

She swallowed, watching brave Natalie climb the mountain on strong, sturdy legs, her hair crazy around her head.

Natalie. Tessa wanted Natalie. To be around her and watch her come into herself. She wanted to foster that fierce passion for food, find ways to encourage her and help her grow. For a moment, she imagined Natalie at twenty, wearing the green coat of the Green Gate Cooking School, looking saucy and cheerful like Julia Child, and the vision brought tears to her eyes.

Did that mean she wanted Vince, too?

Vince was a separate issue. Vince, who was so tender and powerful, with his giant heart and giant hands and delectable lips and good mind.

Yes. She wanted Vince, too.

Under her breath, she started to hum the tune:

> *"Well, the rivers ran uphill*
> *And the fish began to fly*
> *And the day before I died,*
> *I became a blushing bride."*

Natalie hummed with her, giving Tessa a wicked and complicit glance over her shoulder. They hummed the old song until they ran out of breath, until the trail became genuinely difficult, very steep and littered with sharp, nasty rocks and scree that made them walk very carefully. Both of them had bleeding small cuts and bruises, but Tessa gave Natalie the respect of not fussing. It was meant to be hard.

Toward the top of the mountain, the path looped along a steep, dramatic cliff that showed views of the entire valley and both the San Juan and Sangre de Cristo mountains. It was slightly dizzying, but the path was a good solid fifteen feet away from the edge, and Tessa felt safe.

For some reason, however, it brought Lisa to her mind vividly—the young woman's joy in discovering that she had what it took to hike to a beautiful high mountain and conquer her fears, to be an active woman. Tessa halted for a moment, tears crowding into her throat, and suddenly she realized that a part of what she'd been feeling was *grief*.

She let the tears flow unchecked, finally. Natalie came back and put her hand into Tessa's but didn't say a word, and she was simply, honorably just there. Tessa squeezed her hand in thanks, and they continued the climb.

When they reached the top, there was a statue of the Blessed Mother, a long-haired, dark-skinned version of Mary. She had curves and plump hands and Tessa loved her immediately, imagining that the sculptor had used his wife, a wife he loved, as a model.

Before they began their climb, Natalie and Tessa had agreed to give each other privacy at the top. Natalie wanted Tessa to go first, so Natalie pointed to a grove of trees, where there was a bench overlooking the river far below. Tessa nodded, and Natalie trundled over there.

Tessa watched her go. For years, she'd been herding young women up mountains, mothering them, encouraging them, especially loving the ones who were not particularly fit or had never discovered they had power in their bodies. She mothered them because she had no children of her own.

She turned back to the statue and looked up. It would be hypocritical for her to pray, since she didn't particularly believe in sainthood or Catholic ritual.

But she did believe in something. Something that had brought her back to her sister, something that lent healing. Something that had made dogs.

And she believed in forgiveness, for herself and for others, so she bent her head and spoke to Lisa. "I'm sorry that my hubris let you down," she said. "Let you die. I hope wherever you are that it's beautiful. I hope you're looking after your mother, helping her come to terms with the loss of you. I hope you know I loved you and respected you."

At the base of the statue was a covered altar, with offerings of all sorts. Tessa took out a hat that had belonged to Lisa and placed it at Mary's feet. "Look after her," she said.

Then she stepped away and gestured toward Natalie, who stood up and came over with a very sober face.

Natalie's feet were hurting. A lot. She didn't go barefoot all that much, and now she could feel bruises and cuts and things all over them. She limped a little as she approached the statue of the Blessed Mother.

"Hi," she said aloud, and knelt on the ground, realizing that her knees were going to get awfully sore, even through her jeans, but that was okay. She pulled out her mother's rosary, made of dark-blue beads, and held it in her hand. "I'm sorry for stealing, and I will not do it anymore." It had finally come to her that it was her choice to steal. That she had to decide not to do it.

She bowed her head and began to say the rosary, not all of it, but a decade and a couple of Our Fathers and Glory Be's. The wind whipped across her body as she chanted, and it felt like it was blowing away everything in the past, scrubbing her clean. Something heavy and thick in her chest seemed to get lighter and lighter and lighter, until it felt like her heart was just normal again, like it used to be before her mother died.

Her father had taken her to the salt store, where she offered to do whatever work the lady needed for two hours every week until the lady was happy again. The police and everybody said it was okay to do it that way, and the woman had a look like the Wicked Witch of the West, all pinched, but she agreed. Natalie had gone in yesterday, and the woman just had her break down boxes and make them flat for recycling. It was super easy.

And the lady—Ms. Tonkin—started talking to her, telling her all about the history of the pink salt Natalie had stolen like a crazy person. When her dad came back to get her, Natalie asked if she could buy some of the pink salt to bring with her today, and he said she could take it out of her allowance.

So now she had an offering. She took the salt out of the bag and put it in her hand. She thought of her mother's eyes, which were always sad, always. It wasn't Natalie's fault, like she sometimes thought. It was some broken thing inside her mother, her daddy said, and sometimes that just couldn't be fixed.

When she was ready, Natalie opened her eyes and opened her hands and let the wind sweep the salt away.

TWENTY-SIX

Vince was working on the fence for the dogs when he saw Tessa driving up with Natalie. The dogs sprang off the porch in glee to investigate, and Vince put his hammer down to go help Nat if she needed it.

She limped toward him, but she was smiling broadly, the pilgrim badge on her blouse, her shoes in her hands. "We did it!" she cried, and hobbled over to him. "Look at my feet!" She sat down and held up her feet so he could see the filthy, bruised, bloody bottoms.

"Jeez, Nat, that looks like it hurts! Are you okay?"

"I'm fine, Dad," she said, and there was something so clear and solid about her that he nodded.

"Good. Why don't you go take a bath, soak those feet?"

"'Kay!" She stood up. "Bye, Tessa. Thanks again!"

Tessa waved. She had something in her hands and carried it over. She, too, was hobbling a little, though not as dramatically as Natalie. "Hi," she said.

Her voice ran like a silver river down his neck, circled his chest. "Hi," he said gruffly, and picked up his hammer.

"I brought something," she said.

"Oh?"

She grinned. "You didn't happen to notice that I was carrying a stack of frames in my hands?"

He shrugged. If he didn't let her have a crack, he wouldn't crack, and it would all be okay.

"I thought you might like something to hang on your walls," she said, and held out her gift.

They were photos, five of them—all her own work, he guessed. There was Natalie's hand with the avocado, and one of Vince with Hannah, and the coy photo of Jade with chocolate on her mouth, and one the day she'd been here to talk to Natalie, when the light had been so extraordinary. It was Vince, surrounded by the dancing arrows, looking forbidding and godlike.

"Zeus," she said.

There was something in her voice that made him look up. "I'm not leaving Los Ladrones," she said. "I'm probably stuck in that crappy rental for a while, because it's too expensive to buy, but I'm staying. My boss nixed the tour, because he thought it was too mellow for our demographic, but I'm going to work with Vita and Green Gate to develop my own tours of the area. Cooking, mellow walking. Less adventure, more joy."

He looked back at the photo. He'd never seen himself like this. "You made me look like a giant," he said.

"You don't have to say anything back, Vince, but I really need to tell you that I'm in love with you. And your girls. And your dogs and your town. I know it's fast and I know it doesn't make any sense, but sometimes you have to go with your instincts. I can take as much time as you need to prove it to you."

He wanted to believe her. If he had been on his own, he wouldn't have hesitated for a minute to take a chance, but the girls deserved better than a maybe.

As if she sensed his hesitation, she tucked her hands in her pockets. "Look at the last picture."

He put the Zeus picture aside, and there were the two of them, looking up at the camera from her bed that rainy afternoon he'd come back to kiss her. They looked calmly, steadily at the camera, heads just touching, her blond hair splayed on the pillowcase and over his bare shoulder. Eyes full of love. Both of them. He remembered that he'd turned and kissed her shoulder.

"I love this." He turned and carefully put the photos down. His hands were shaking as he turned back. "My mother brought me a photo, too," he said. He pulled the snapshot out of his wallet and handed it over. "That's me, at nine."

She looked at the photo. Vince came close and looked over her shoulder. It showed a boy in jeans and a T-shirt with a little girl on a tricycle decorated with tissue-paper roses. The girl had a sash over her bathing suit, and her long blond hair swept her rear end. "I remember this."

"Nobody ever told me that they thought you drowned. You were just gone, like everybody else. And I missed you. You were funny and smart and silly, and you loved to read whatever I brought you from my mom's store."

"See?" she said, smiling. "I knew it." She raised her eyes. "I think you should trust me. I'm not going to clean your house or suddenly make great meals, because I'm not good at that, at least not now. I'll want to be on the trails, and I want to teach the girls how to be strong and listen to their inner voices. I want to sleep with you and eat breakfast with you every day."

What Vince thought, suddenly, was that she always told the truth. He knew in his bones that she would never leave, that if she gave her word she would keep it.

"Promise?" he asked.

She raised a hand, like a Girl Scout, three fingers up. "Promise."

The rigid blocks he'd been keeping up collapsed all at once, and Vince scooped her into his arms. "God, Tessa, all I've wanted to do for a week is charge over there and order you to stay here, live here, be here." He buried his face in her neck. "I am so in love with you that it scared me half to death. I used Nat as an excuse, but it's been me who was afraid."

Her arms locked hard around him. "I have so many things to tell you."

"Do you love me?" he asked, raising his head so he could see her eyes.

"Yes," she said clearly. "I just said I did."

"Say it again."

"I love you."

He kissed her. "I love you."

Holding her, it felt like everything that had been out of alignment for so many years suddenly moved into place.

Behind him was a giggle. "Daddy and Tessa, sitting in a tree, K-I-S-S-I-N-G," Jade chanted.

"Scamp," he said, but he kissed Tessa again anyway, hearing the laughter of his daughters fill him like a song.

Tessa, curled against him, began to hum under her breath.

"What's that song?"

She stopped to listen, and laughed—Crosby, Stills, Nash & Young—then sang aloud, *"Our house is a very, very, very fine house . . ."*

"Déjà Vu," he said, and Tessa laughed.

"Déjà Vu," she agreed.

NATALIE'S RECIPE FOR A
HAPPY SUNDAY BREAKFAST

One giant kitchen with a big, big table
One grandpa with a thick mustache, who knows how
*   to do magic tricks*
One daddy, cooking bacon on an electric skillet so that
*   it stays flat*
One grandma, who loves biscuits
One auntie with tattoos around her wrists
Two sisters (I guess)
One Tessa–Mom, singing
Vita, taking the day off from her restaurant
Six dogs on the porch, watching us cook
Smell of coffee
Daddy kissing Tessa–Mom
Me, all surrounded with happiness and good smells,
*   standing on a chair to make hollandaise with Vita.*

Stir. Serve every Sunday.

ABOUT THE AUTHOR

BARBARA O'NEAL fell in love with restaurants and the secret language of spoons when she was sixteen. She spent more than a decade in various restaurants, dives to cafés to high cuisine, before selling her first novel. O'Neal teaches workshops nationally and internationally, and lives with her partner, a British endurance athlete, in Colorado Springs.